Advance Praise for
AFTERTIME

"From H.G. Wells to Max Brooks to Cormac McCarthy,
the End Times have always belonged to the boys.
Littlefield's *Aftertime* gives an explosive voice
to the other half of the planet's population: this is
the apocalypse battled head-on by a heroine who not only
kicks ass, but is driven by an instinct that only a woman can know.
Cass Dollar fights like a girl—you've been warned.
And did I mention the darkly comic flesh-eating zombies and the
downright lyrical prose? *Aftertime* is a whole new kind of fierce."
—Laura Benedict, author of *Isabella Moon*

"Sexy, chilling and hypnotically readable,
Littlefield's apocalyptic dreamscape will stay with you
long after you've put this book down."
—Alexandra Sokoloff, author of *Book of Shadows*

"Wildly original, guaranteed to give you nightmares
and allow you some small measure of hope for mankind,
Sophie Littlefield's *Aftertime* is a new generation of post-apocalyptic
fiction: a unique journey into a horrifying world of zombies,
zealots and avarice that examines the strength of one woman,
the joy of acceptance and the power of love. A must read."
—J.T. Ellison, author of *So Close the Hand of Death*

AFTERTIME

SOPHIE LITTLEFIELD

LUNA™

www.LUNA-Books.com

LUNA™

Recycling programs
for this product may
not exist in your area.

AFTERTIME

ISBN-13: 978-0-373-80336-1

www.LUNA-Books.com

Printed in U.S.A.

For M, with love and regret

There you are and always will be
In your pretty coat
Skating lazy eights
on the frozen pond of my heart

THAT IT WAS SUMMER WAS NOT IN DOUBT.
The nights were much too short and the days too long.
Something about the color of the sky said August to Cass.
Maybe the blue was bluer. Hadn't autumn signaled itself
that way Before, a gradual intensifying of colors as summer
trailed into September?

Once, Cass would have been able to tell from the wildflowers growing in the foothills where she ran. In August
petals fell from the wild orange poppies, the stonecrop darkened to purplish brown, and butterweed puffs drifted in
lazy breezes. Deer grew bold, drinking from the creek that
ran along the road. The earth dried and cracked, and lizards
and beetles stared out from their hiding places among the
weeds.

But that was two lives ago, so far back that it was like a
story that had once been told to Cass, a story maybe whispered by a lover as she drifted off to sleep after one too many

Jack and Cokes, ephemeral and hazy at the edges. She might not believe it at all, except for Ruthie. Ruthie had loved the way butterweed silk floated in the air when she blew on the puffs.

Ruthie, who she couldn't see or touch or hold in her arms. Ruthie, who screamed when the social workers dragged her away, her legs kicking desperately at nothing. Mim and Byrn wouldn't even look at Cass as she collapsed to the dirty floor of the trailer and wished she was dead.

Ruthie had been two.

Cass pushed herself to go faster, her strides long and sure up over a gentle rise in the road. She was barely out of breath. This was nothing, less than nothing. She dug her hard, sharp nails into the calluses of her thumbs. Hard, harder, hardest. The skin there was built up against her abuse and refused to bleed. To break it she would need something sharper than her nail. Teeth might work, but Cass would not use her teeth. It was enough to use her nails until the pain found an opening into her mind. The pain was enough.

She had covered a lot of ground this moon-bright night. Now it was almost dawn, the light from the rising sun creeping up over the black-blue forest skeletons, a crescent aura of orange glow in the sky. When the first slice of sun was visible she'd leave the road and melt into what was left of the trees. There was cover to be found—some of the native shrubs had survived. Greasewood and creosote still grew neck high in some places.

And it was easy to spot them. You saw them before they saw you, and then you hid, and you prayed. If they saw you at all, if they came close enough to smell you, you were worse than dead.

Cass stayed to the edge of the cracked pavement of what had been Highway 161, weaving around the occasional abandoned car, forcing herself not to look inside. You never knew what you would see. Often nothing, but…it was just better not to look. Chunks of the asphalt had been pushed aside by squat kaysev plants that had managed to root in the cracks. Past the shoulder great drifts of it grew, the dark glossy leaves hiding clusters of pods. The plants were smooth-stemmed without burrs or thorns. Walking among them was not difficult. But walking on pavement allowed Cass, now and then—and never when she was trying—to let her mind go back to another time…and when she was really lucky, to pretend all the way back two lifetimes ago.

Taking Ruthie, barely walking, down the sidewalk to the 7-Eleven, buying her a blue raspberry Slurpee, because Ruthie loved to stick out her blue tongue and look at herself in the mirror. Cutting across the school parking lot on the way home, jumping over the yellow lines, lifting Ruthie's slight body and swinging her, laughing, through the air.

Yes, pavement was nice. Cass had good shoes, though she didn't remember where she got them. They seemed like they might have been men's shoes, plain brown lace-up walking shoes, but they fit her feet. A small man, then. How she'd got the shoes from him…it didn't bear thinking about. The shoes were good, they were comfortable and hadn't given her blisters or sores despite the many days of walking.

A movement caught her eye, off in the spiky remains of the woods. Cass stopped abruptly and scanned the tree skeletons and shrubs. A flash of white, was it? Or was it only the way the light was rising in the sky, reflected off… what, though? There were only the bare trunks of the dead cypress and pine trees, a stand of dead manzanita, the low thick growth of kaysev, a few of the boulder formations that dotted the Sierra Foothills.

Snap

Cass whipped her head around and saw the flash again, a fast-moving blur of fabric and oh God it *was* white, a slip of a little dark-haired girl in a dirty white shirt who was sprinting toward her at a speed that Cass could not imagine anyone moving, Cass who had run thousands of desperate blacktop miles one life ago, trying to erase everything, running until her legs ached and her lungs felt like tearing paper and her mind was almost but never quite empty.

But even Cass had never run like this girl.

She was twelve or thirteen. Maybe even fourteen, it was hard to tell now. Before, the fourteen-year-olds looked like twenty-year-olds, with their push-up bras and eyeliner. But hardly anyone dressed like that anymore.

The girl held the blade the way they taught the kids now, firmly in front of her where it would have the best chance of slicing through a Beater's flesh. Because that's what she thought Cass was, a Beater, and the thought hit Cass in the gut and nearly knocked her over with revulsion. Her hands went to her hairline where the hair was just growing back in, soft tufts, an inch at most. She knew how her arms looked, covered with scabs, almost worse now that they were healing, the patches of flesh falling away as the healthy skin pushed to the surface. But that was nothing compared to the ruin of her back.

She hadn't been able to clean herself in days, and she knew she carried the smell. The long hair on the back of her head, the hair she hadn't pulled out, was knotted and tangled. Her nails were blackened and broken. Real Beaters usually had no nails left, but how could the girl be expected to notice a detail like that?

In the second or two it took the girl to cross the last dozen yards of scrubby land, Cass considered standing firm, wrists out, chin up, giving her an easy target. They were taught well; any child over the age of five could find the jugular, the femoral, the carotid, the ulnar. They practiced on dummies rigged from dolls and clothes stuffed with straw. Sometimes, they practiced on the dead.

At the last minute Cass stepped out of the way.

She didn't know why. It would have been easier, so much easier, to welcome the blade, to let it find its path to her vital core and feel the blessed release of her blood, still hot and red despite everything, bubbling over the slice in her flesh, falling to the hardened earth. Maybe her blood would help the land heal faster. Maybe on the spot where her blood fell, one of the plants from Before would return. A delicate mountain bluebell; they had been her favorite, the tiny blossoms shading from pale sky blue to deep lilac.

But Cass stepped out of the way.

Damn her soul.

Three times now it had refused to die, when death would have been so much easier.

Cass watched almost impassively as her foot shot forward, nimbly, her stance steady and her balance near perfect. The girl's eyes went wide. She tripped, and in the last moment, when the blade flew from her hand and she lurched toward Cass, the terror in her eyes was enough to break Cass's heart, if only she still had one to break.

02

EVERYONE REMEMBERED THE FIRST TIME THEY saw a Beater. Usually, it was more than one, because even in the early days they gathered in packs, three or four or more of them prowling the edges of town.

Cass saw hers in the QikGo.

Cass worked in the QikGo until the end. Where else would she go? She couldn't leave Silva, not without Ruthie. But as the world fell apart—as famine crippled Africa and South Asia, as one G8 capital after another fell to panic and riots in the wake of random airbursts, as China went dark and Australia mined its shores—Mim and Byrn held on all the tighter to their granddaughter. Cass had no detailed plan, only to wait until there were no more police, no sheriffs, no social workers, no one willing to come when Mim and Byrn called them to block Cass from seeing her daughter or even setting foot on their property.

When that day came, she would go to their house and

she would take Ruthie back. By force if she had to. It would hurt, to see the anger and contempt on her mother's face, but no more than it had hurt her that Mim refused to acknowledge how far Cass had come, how hard she had worked to be worthy of Ruthie. The ninety-days chip she kept on her key chain. The two-year medallion she'd earned before her single relapse. The job she'd held through it all—maybe managing a convenience store wasn't the most impressive career in the world, but at least she was helping people in small ways every day rather than fleecing them out of their money, the way Byrn did with his questionable investment strategies. But she and her mother saw things through very different lenses.

It would not hurt Cass to see her stepfather, who was finally weaker than she was, his ex-linebacker frame now old and frail compared to her own body, which she had made lean and hard with her relentless running. She anticipated the look of powerlessness on Byrn's face as she took away the only thing he could hurt her with. She looked forward even more to the moment when he knew he had lost. She would never forgive him, but maybe once she got Ruthie back, she could start forgetting.

That time was almost upon them. Cell phone service had started to go in the last few days and the landlines hadn't worked for a week. Televisions had been broadcasting static since the government's last official communication deputizing power and water workers; that had been such a spectacular failure, skirmishes breaking out in the few remaining places there had been peace before, that the rumor was the government had shut down all the media on purpose. Some said it was the Russian hackers. Now they said the power was out over in Angel's Camp, and every gas station in town had been looted except for Bill's Shell, where Bill and his two sons-in-law were taking shifts with a brace of hunting rifles.

Who was going to care about the fate of one little girl now?

Two days earlier Cass had stopped taking money from customers unless it was offered. Some people seemed to find comfort in clinging to routines from what was quickly becoming "Before"—and if people reached for their wallets then Cass made change. People took strange things. There were those who had come early on for the toilet paper and aspirin and bottled water—and all the alcohol, to Cass's relief. Now people wandered the aisles aimlessly and took random items that would do them no good anymore. A prepaid calling card, a map.

Meddlin, her boss, hadn't made an appearance for a few days. The QikGo, Cass figured, was all hers. No matter. She didn't care about Meddlin. The others, the fragile web of workers who staffed the other shifts, had been gone since the media went silent.

On a brisk March morning, a day after the lights started to flicker and fail, Cass was talking to Teddy, a pale boy from the community college who lived in the apartments down the block with a handful of roommates who didn't seem to like him very much. Cass made coffee, wondering if it would be the last time, and wiped down the counter. There hadn't been a dairy delivery in weeks, so she set out a can of the powdered stuff.

When the door jangled they both turned and looked.

"Feverish," Teddy said quietly. Cass nodded. The ones who'd been eating the blueleaf—the ones who'd lived—were unmistakable. The fever made their skin glow with a thin sheen of perspiration. Their movements were clumsy. But most remarkable were their eyes: the pupils contracted to tiny black dots. In dark-eyed people the effect was merely unsettling; in pale-eyed people it was both captivating and frightening.

If everything hadn't fallen apart, there would have undoubtedly been teams of doctors and scientists gathering the sick and studying and caring for and curing them. As it was, all but those closest to the sick were just happy they kept to themselves.

"Glass over over," one of them said, a man whose plaid shirt was buttoned wrong so that one side hung farther down than the other, speaking to no one in particular. A second, a woman with lank brown hair that lay around her shoulders in uncombed masses, walked to a rack that held only a few bags of chips and pushed it with a stiff outstretched hand, and as it fell to the floor, she smiled and laughed, not bothering to jump out of the way of the bags which popped and sprayed dry crumbs.

"Gehhhh," she crowed, and Cass noticed something else strange about her, something she hadn't seen before. The woman's arms were raw and red, blood dried in patches, the skin chafed and missing in spots. It almost looked like a metal grater had been run up and down her arms, her shoulders, the tops of her hands. Cass checked the others: their flesh was also covered in scabs.

Cold alarm traveled up Cass's spine. Something was wrong—very wrong. Something even worse than the fever and the unfocused eyes and the incoherent speech. She thought she recognized one of the group, a short muscular man of about forty, whose complicated facial hair was growing out into a sloppy beard. He used to come in for cigarettes every couple of days. He was wearing filthy tan cargo shorts, and the skin above his knees was covered with the same sort of cuts and scrapes as his forearms.

"Hey," she said to him. He was standing in front of a shelf that held the few personal products left in the store—bottles of shampoo and mouthwash, boxes of Band-Aids. "Would you like…"

Her voice trailed off as he turned and stared at her with wide unblinking blue eyes. "Dome going," he said softly, then raised his wounded forearm to his face and, eyes still fixed on her, licked his lips and took a delicate nip at his red, glistening skin. His teeth closed on the damaged flesh and pulled, the raw layers of dermis pulling away from his arm, stretching and then splitting, a shred of flesh about the size of a match tearing away, leaving a bright, tiny spot of blood that glistened and pooled into a larger drop.

For a moment he stared at her, the strip quivering between his teeth, and then his tongue poked out and he drew the ruined skin into his mouth and he chewed.

"Holy *fuck,* dude," Teddy exclaimed, stepping back so fast that his foot thudded against the front of the counter. Cass's stomach turned with revulsion—the man had chewed off his *own skin* and *eaten* it. Is that what had happened to his entire arm? Were the scabs and open wounds his own doing?

"Fuck dude," the man mumbled as he burrowed his teeth along the ruined flesh of his arm, his tongue probing and searching. Looking for undamaged skin, Cass realized, horrified. The pattern of the wounds—covering the forearm and upper arm, fading at the elbow—it was exactly consistent with what he could reach with his own mouth, and, as if to confirm her suspicion, the man twisted his forearm in his mouth, seeking out any bit of flesh that was left undisturbed, finally trailing up to his hand and taking a deep bite from his scabby palm so that blood trickled between his lips and ran down his chin.

"Out," Cass managed to say. "Get *out.*" She ran to the

thin woman, the one who had toppled the chip stand, and pushed. The woman staggered backward, regarding Cass with faint interest.

"Cass," she mumbled, as she found her footing. "Cass castle hassle."

Cass stared at her. Then she made the connection: this was the girl who worked at the bank, on days when Cass took the cash down to deposit. Only Cass hadn't seen her in a few weeks, since the banks closed, their windows shattered by looters who thought cash might somehow help, cash they found they couldn't get because it was sealed in vaults no one could open.

The young woman used to wear her hair differently. She curled it every morning, and she favored bright eye shadow, green that shaded to black around her carefully rimmed lashes. She'd worn low-cut tops and dresses in colorful patterns, a far cry from what she wore now, a red knit t-shirt several sizes too big that was only partway tucked into her jeans.

"Do you know me?" Cass demanded, but the girl's eyes flickered and shifted, and she murmured something that sounded like "yam yam" before shuffling over to where the others stood.

"Something's fucked up with them," Teddy said. "Do you hear that? They're all like...delirious."

Cass nodded. "We have to get them out."

Teddy slipped past the little group and held the door open wide. "We were just getting ready to close," he stammered, and despite her unease Cass noticed the "we" and was glad. Maybe Teddy would stay. Maybe he would keep her company. And when there was nothing left in the store to give away, maybe he would be there to help her figure out what to do next. Cass had been on her own for a long time now, and she had told herself she didn't want anyone else, even on the days when she felt most alone, when the craving for a drink was almost unbearable.

But maybe, now, she did. A friend. How long since she had a friend?

Buoyed by the thought, she went up to the three fever-ish people. She put her hands to the back of the girl's shirt, trying not to look at the raw and weeping flesh of her limbs, and pushed. The girl allowed herself to be guided to the door, and the others followed. When Cass got them outside, she ducked back in and shut the door, twisting the heavy bolt into place.

The day had been warm, but a low layer of clouds made a thin shadow over the sun. The three people she had locked outside looked up at the sun without blinking. Cass wondered if they were slowly going blind.

The girl took a step toward the man with the misbuttoned shirt, and for a moment Cass thought she was kissing him, pushing her face into the back of his neck. He didn't flinch, but he didn't turn to embrace her either.

"That's—he's—" Teddy said in alarm and Cass looked closer.

The woman shook her head and only then did Cass real-ize she'd sunk her teeth into the man's flesh and was tugging at it. Tearing at it. Trying to rip off a shred.

Teddy turned away and vomited on the floor, as a bright trail of blood snaked down to the man's collar, and the woman began to chew.

3

THE GIRL WITH THE BLADE WAS NAMED SAMMI, but Cass didn't find that out until later. As dawn broke, they left the road and traveled through the woods. By the time they got to the school, maybe a mile down, the sun was high in the sky. It was the clearest sky yet since Cass had returned, flawless blue, and as they rounded a sharp bend topped by a rock outcropping and what must have once been a beautiful stand of cypress, the school stood out in stark relief against the eye-searing blue.

It had been built in the last few years Before. The architect had gone in for broad stretches of stucco, a roof molded to look like cedar, vaguely Prairie-style window placement and overhanging eaves. The sign still announced, in iron letters against hewn stone, COPPER CREEK MIDDLE SCHOOL.

Cass knew this school. They'd built it halfway between Silva and Terryville. She had driven past it a hundred times, thinking about Ruthie going there someday.

She was close to home.

The girl hadn't spoken a single word. Cass tapped the girl's blade against her own thigh, loosening her grip on the windbreaker she'd taken off and looped through the girl's sleeves as a kind of makeshift harness before remembering the dangers and grabbing it even tighter. *I'm sorry,* she mouthed, but only because the girl couldn't see. She led them across the parking lot with sure, quick steps, shoulders held high, and Cass couldn't help but admire her courage.

For all the girl knew, Cass would have followed through with her threat and sliced her ear to ear. The blade was a good one, a two-edged straight stiletto with a small guard, the blade itself perhaps six inches long. Someone loved this girl. Someone had made sure she had a good weapon, had cared if she lived another day.

She pulled the girl tight against her and bit out the words, hating herself for saying them—and knowing they were lies. "When someone comes out, tell them I'll kill you," she murmured. "Tell them that first."

The girl only nodded.

It made sense to choose a school, of course. The threats of Before seemed minor now. Everyone worried that deranged people would come into schools and steal the children away, harm them, kill them. Or that one of the students would bring a gun to school and take out his classmates. Yes, things like that had happened back then, just often enough to keep everyone vigilant, and the schools had been built with more and greater safety measures until, in the end, they were fortresses, reinforced and sealed and locked down.

In some ways it wasn't so hard to stay safe, even now. A basic wall could keep Beaters away. A fence, even one that was only ten feet tall, like those that surrounded the school's courtyard. As long as there were no citizens close by, nothing to attract the Beaters and drive them into a frenzy of flesh-lust, nearly any barrier at all would be enough to make them lose their focus and wander back to their fetid nestlike encampments.

They said—at least, near the end of Cass's second life— that the Beaters were waning. Cass wasn't so sure. It was true that they had formed larger and larger groups, nomadic little bands that took over neighborhoods and entire towns, so they weren't appearing in sporadic places as much. They seemed to have flashes of longing for Before, just as everyone else did. You could see them sometimes, doing homely little things. It was like the bits of speech that sometimes bubbled from their lips, phrases that meant nothing, fragments that tumbled from whatever was left of their minds, dislodged from memory that had given way to the fever and the disease. Cass had seen one trying to ride a bicycle, and falling off when its jerky motions caused the wheel to spin and flip. It tried again and again and then suddenly lost interest and wandered away. Another time she had seen one at a clothesline, taking the pins off one by one and holding them in its ruined hand, then reattaching them.

Cass had known a woman who had been a social worker Before. Her name was Miranda. They had not been friends, exactly, but they had sheltered together in the library before a half-dozen Beaters came through a back door that had been left open one day and dragged her off.

Miranda had once worked with violent offenders, counseling them to look deep inside themselves to find the key to who they were before abuse and anger had changed them. She had been extraordinarily successful, the pride of the Anza County Correctional System's Anger Replacement Therapy program. Miranda had believed that in those moments when the Beaters appeared to be connecting to a memory, miming some homely everyday task, there was a chance to remind them of who they had once been. That if you could reach them in that moment—if you could reconnect the splintered shards of memory—that you could reverse the process of the disease. That the afflicted would comprehend the horror of what they had become, and choose to come back.

Miranda had wanted to try it. It wouldn't be so hard to capture just one, she had argued at one of the "town hall" meetings Bobby held every few days. Bobby was the de facto leader of the ragtag group of a few dozen people sheltering in the library. Miranda tried to recruit a few of the men: one who used to be a deputy sheriff, several hard-muscle types who'd worked in construction, and, of course, Bobby. They all listened to Miranda's plan: capture a Beater, bring it back...restrain it, observe it. Wait until the right moment and then she, trained in the ways of the desperate, the out-cast, would speak to it.

Bobby listened, but he could not contain his incredulity. "You think you're, what, some kind of zombie whisperer? Because you got a few crack whores to give up their babies? Is that it, Miranda, you think a Beater's like some guy beats his wife on payday?"

Miranda had argued back, passionately. But when the Beaters came for her that day, breaking in that forgotten back door while the kitchen detail was cleaning up from a lunch of kaysev shoots and canned apple pie filling, when Miranda had taken some trash to the back hall by herself, it wasn't reasoned argument that issued from her lips. It was screaming, as raw and desperate as the screams of any of the others who were taken, screams that echoed in Cass's mind on nights when sleep wouldn't come.

The school, though... Cass guessed that they had not lost anyone that way here. In addition to the fences, brick walls surrounded the entire courtyard. The doors would be the type that shut automatically. Guards would be posted. They undoubtedly did all their harvesting and raiding at night. Maybe they even had a few flashlights, some batteries.

Why had they let this girl out on her own? It made no sense. Even though it should have still been safe—the Beaters rarely went hunting before the sun rose high in the sky—what adult, what parent, would allow a child to go out alone? Had she somehow gotten separated from others? Had some greater threat come along?

There was a sudden clang and the door to the school burst open and a woman ran out, wailing. Her flip-flops slapped against the pavement, and she stumbled at the kaysev-choked median that once kept the carpooling moms in orderly lines. A pair of men chased after her, trying to restrain her, but the woman shook them off. "Sammi!" she screamed, but Cass pulled the girl tight against her and held the blade to the soft skin under her chin.

"Stop there," Cass yelled. And then she added the one thing that might convince them to do as she said. "I am not a Beater!"

She watched them look at her, watched the terror in the woman's expression and the fury and determination in the men's slowly tinge with doubt. She felt their gazes on her ragged skin, her scalp where the hair was only now growing back. She waited, holding her breath, until she saw that they knew.

Until they saw that her pupils were like anyone else's, black and pronounced.

"I don't want to hurt this girl," she called, trying to keep her voice steady. "I don't want any trouble. I am not a Beater and I can..." She had been about to say that she could explain her appearance, but that was a lie. She couldn't explain, and no one else could either. "I can prove it, if you let me. I'm not asking to come in. I don't want anything from you except to be allowed to continue into town."

"Let the girl go," one of the men said.

The woman sank down to her knees and extended her arms beseechingly. "Please," she keened. "Please please please please please…"

And something shifted inside Cass. A memory of Ruthie being carried away, screaming, sent to live with Cass's mother and the man she'd married. The man who'd made her life hell. She remembered her own pleas, how she had gone down on her knees just like the woman before her now, how she'd collapsed on the floor after the front door shut behind Mim and Byrn and the court people carrying her Ruthie away, how she'd cried into the sour-smelling carpet until she could barely breathe.

She released the girl then and watched her go to her mother, jogging across the pavement, but not before glancing back over her shoulder. A defiant glance, sparked with victory. The girl felt she'd won. Well, Cass certainly felt like she'd lost, so maybe that was fitting.

The mother gathered the girl up in her arms as though she wanted to meld her to herself, and Cass had to turn away. The men must have thought she was trying to leave, though, because an instant later she was knocked to the ground and she felt the weight of them crushing her into the gravel-pocked asphalt. The rough pavement smelled like tar and scraped against her cheek. The blade had fallen from her hand. No matter; these men were guards. They would have their own. And it would be a quick death, better than she deserved.

She waited, but after a moment the weight lifted and a strong hand grabbed hers, pulling her up roughly.

"Inside," he said, and that was the first word she ever heard Smoke say.

THEY HAD SET UP A KITCHEN OF SORTS IN THE
school's courtyard, and a small crew was cooking over a fire
in a makeshift hearth. Ginger: the scent of sautéed kaysev
was in the air. A group of children sat at a table taken from
one of the classrooms, eating, and Cass saw that they'd made
the kaysev into a sort of pancake. She'd seen that before,
when people were figuring out different ways to prepare the
plant. After so many weeks of eating it raw, the smell of the
cakes—made with a flour ground from the dried beans—
prompted a powerful hunger she didn't know she was capable of anymore.

And there was another smell, one that made her doubt her
senses. "Is that—"

"Coffee." Her escort was a man of medium height, hard-
muscled, with broad shoulders and powerful forearms. Sun-
streaked brown hair fell into his chambray-blue eyes and
he kept pushing it impatiently aside. His mouth was on the

generous side, almost sensuous, but his expression was hard.
"Once a week, on Sunday. It's strong but you only get one
cup."

"You know what day it is?" Cass asked, surprised. Who
kept track, anymore?

The man didn't answer, but led her over to a door that
stood open, propped with a stack of books. *U.S. History*, Cass
read on the spines. Books, left out to the elements—who
would abandon a book outside to be ruined?—but thoughts
like that led straight to a spiral of despair.

Whenever something reminded her of Before, it was a
quick trip back and it hit her hard. Like now: textbooks
had been sacred, once. But books needed readers. And all
the teachers were dead from hunger or disease or riots,
or dragged off by the Beaters, or desperate, like Cass, just
to survive. There was no one left to teach children like
Ruthie.

Cass forced those thoughts from her mind as the man
guided her into the hallway, his hand at her waist gentler
now. Earlier, he'd been rough as he searched her, patting
down the ragged and stinking canvas pants and athletic
shirt that stuck to her, the same clothes she'd woken up in a
couple of weeks earlier. He'd avoided touching her scabbed
flesh, and stopped short of searching the folds and crevices
of her body, for which she was grateful. He'd lingered at her
hair, combing his fingers through its greasy, filthy length
while he held the ends bunched in his fist. The stubble at the
front had caused him to frown, but he'd said nothing.

It had hurt like hell when his hands moved along her
back, and she'd ground her teeth to avoid crying out in pain.
There, whole sections of flesh had been ripped from her
body and it was taking much longer to heal than the scabs
on her arms. An ordinary citizen would have succumbed to

infection, blood loss, exposure. But somehow in the days after the things tore into her back, she had developed a freakishly powerful immune system and was healing. How she had recovered from the disease, she had no idea.

But thin layers of skin were slowly building from the scabbed edges. Smoke had not detected anything amiss in the ruined landscape of her back, and for that Cass was grateful. She didn't want him to see.

Cass blinked as her eyes adjusted from the bright morning sun to the gloom of the interior. A single transom window lit the space; the other windows were covered by miniblinds. They were in what had been the school's administrative office. The bulletin boards had been stripped bare except up at the top where a few ragged papers were still attached with pushpins. ARTCARVED—ORDER YOUR CLASS RING NOW one read. Another advertised $$CASH$$ FOR PRINTER CARTRIDGES.

A woman came around the corner and stopped short, staring at Cass with shock, processing her appearance.

"We found her outside," the man said quickly. "She brought Sammi back."

The woman merely nodded, but Cass could see the relief written plain on her face. A child had been missing. The people sheltering here had been waiting, knowing it was likely that their beautiful young girl would never return. None of them were new to loss now—by most estimates, three-quarters of the population was dead, victims of starvation and fever and suicide and Beaters. You learned to protect yourself. But the cost of steeling yourself against grief was that you had to steel yourself against joy, as well.

"You might as well have some," the woman said, and only then did Cass notice that she carried a glass carafe of steaming black coffee. "Get her a cup, Smoke."

The man called Smoke went into the hall, leaving the woman to stare openly at Cass. She was a lean woman with poorly cut hair, pieces of it jutting unevenly at her cheekbones. But she was clean—remarkably so. Her skin looked healthy and her eyes were clear. Cass found herself wondering if she was the man's lover, and her gaze went to the woman's fine small hands, the nails trimmed neatly. Her smooth pale legs under the plain denim shorts.

"I'm Nora," the woman said.

Cass cleared her throat. Until this morning, she hadn't spoken in many days, and she was out of practice. "I'm Cassandra. Cass."

Smoke returned carrying a large blue mug. Nora poured from the carafe and Cass accepted the mug and held it near her lips, not sipping, the glazed porcelain almost too hot to bear. Her eyes fluttered closed as she inhaled as deeply as she could, and when she opened them, she saw that Smoke was staring at her with an expression that was part curiosity and part calculation, and no part fear.

She drank.

The taste brought back a sharp memory of the room in the basement where she attended a thousand A.A. meetings. The first time she accepted a cup of coffee only because everyone else was drinking it. She'd never liked it much, drank it only on the occasional morning when she needed a little extra lift to get going, but at that meeting she drank two cups and on the way home she bought a ten-cup model at Wal-Mart, along with two pounds of ground beans.

At work, she made the first pot at 5:30 a.m. when her shift started and the last—dozens of pots later—when whoever was on afternoons arrived at two o'clock.

This coffee was a little odd. It was like the kind her mother used to make before her father left, in an old tin percolator with green enamel flowers worn nearly away. For a moment Cass felt an intense ache for her mother—for who she'd been before she met Byrn, before she started insisting that Cass call her Mim. For the woman who'd once read to her at bedtime, who'd let Cass bury her face in the crook of her neck and breathe the soap and hair spray and perfume and sweat.

Slowly, not trusting her hand not to tremble, Cass lowered the mug to the table. "May I sit?"

"Yes, of course," Nora said. She exchanged a look with Smoke as he pulled out a chair for her, and Cass was certain that these two were lovers. Only, troubled ones. You could see it in the way his gaze slid warily away.

Cass leaned over the mug and let the steam warm her face. "What's today's date?" she asked.

Nora blew out a little breath before she answered. "August twenty-sixth. It's Sunday."

August 26. So it had been almost two months since the end of what she'd come to think of as her second life.

She thought about that last day. Not the last moments, which she wouldn't remember, but what came before.

She'd been sheltering in the library for a couple of months before she went to get Ruthie, determining that there was finally no one left to try to stop her. The first morning she had her baby back, they woke up together on the makeshift bed in Cass's corner of the library, away from the others, tucked in a narrow corridor behind the periodicals, beneath a water fountain that hadn't flowed in a month. Cass kept her space clean, her few possessions stacked and folded and arranged with care.

That day, she woke to the sweet scent of Ruthie's hair, her small body tucked perfectly into her embrace, her head under Cass's chin. She lay still, breathing happiness in and hope out, watching the sun cast strips of yellow light on the wall through the miniblinds. A week earlier, they'd lost Miranda, and Cass's mood had faltered. But now that she had Ruthie, life seemed like a possibility once more.

"You going to explain that?" Nora said, not unkindly, pointing at Cass's arms.

Cass folded them self-consciously. They hurt, but not as much as they had when she first regained consciousness, lying in an empty field. Then, she had been horrified at the way she looked, her wounds raw, the crusty scabs black in some places, leaking clear reddish fluid. Her back had been an agony of shredded flesh and it was still healing, but the wounds on her arms were almost completely healed, marking crisscross scars across her flesh.

"On the road," she mumbled. "Things happen, you know. I fell...I ran into things."

"No shit," Nora said.

"Go easy," Smoke murmured, a warning in his voice.

"*Look* at her," Nora hissed, her voice low and angry. "We've seen that before. You know we have."

Smoke shook his head. "It isn't the same."

"Only because you don't want to see it!"

"The same as what?" Cass demanded.

Smoke looked at the table, wouldn't meet her eyes. "There's been a few kids—"

"Not just kids," Nora interrupted.

"Mostly kids, teenagers, they cut themselves, they pull out their hair."

"Why would anyone do that?" Cass asked, horrified.

"To look like Beaters," Nora said. "To look like *you*. To mock the world. Or to come into settlements and everyone takes off screaming and then they help themselves to whatever they want—water, food, drugs, anything. That is, if they don't get themselves shot first."

"You think I— You're fucking insane." Cass'd been trying to hold on to her patience, but this—Nora's implication that she had done this to herself on purpose—it was too much. "So where's all my stuff, then? If I've been terrorizing citizens and stealing from them, where is it? I don't have anything on me, *nothing*."

"I don't mean to—"

"Just let her tell her story." Smoke glared at Nora, and after a long moment, the woman gave a faint shrug.

Cass took a breath, let it out slowly, considered how much she wanted to give away. These people could help her, or not. They could let her go, or not. Already she felt certain that they would. There was no cruelty in them, only caution, and who could blame them for that?

"The girl," she hedged. "Sammi. Why was she out alone?"

"Why don't you tell us about you first," Nora said coldly, and this time she refused to acknowledge Smoke's warning glance.

"All right." Cass gathered her thoughts. "I lived in Silva. In Tenaya Estates. You know—the trailers."

Smoke nodded. "I know the place."

"I lived…alone. I worked at the QikGo off Lone Pine. Back in the spring, during the Siege, I stayed on for a while. I thought…I didn't want to give up, I guess. But, you know, when they started coming into town more…"

She didn't add that people stopped showing up at the A.A. meetings, until one day she was the only one in the room. That day, she knew she couldn't live alone anymore.

"Anyway I went over to the library to shelter." She dug her fingernails into the callus of her thumb, under the table where they couldn't see. The next part was hard. "I was there the first time the Beaters came. When they took a friend of mine."

And the second time.

She couldn't bring herself to tell it. Not yet. "Are there still…is anyone still over there?"

"Yes, last time anyone was there, they were up to around fifty." Smoke hesitated and Cass got the impression he wasn't telling the truth—not all of it, anyway. "They got it reinforced. They haven't lost anyone…not inside, anyway, in a while. We have eighty here. There's a few dozen in the firehouse. And you know, you have your folks who are still trying to stay in their own places. More than you'd think, really."

"Fewer every day," Nora muttered.

"Not our place to judge," Smoke said in a voice so low Cass was sure it was meant only for Nora.

"Do you talk to them…the people at the library?" she asked. Now that she was so close, fear bloomed in her heart.

"We did," Smoke said. "Until…well, we had some trouble. A couple of weeks ago. Since then we've stayed local."

"Seventeen days," Nora said, with surprising bitterness.

Smoke nodded, acknowledging her point.

"What happened?"

"You don't know?" The suspicion was back.

Cass looked from one to the other, mystified. "No, I don't—I told you, I've been on my own since I woke up and—"

"Some people would just say that it's awfully convenient that you can't remember anything," Nora said. "And that you just *happen* to show up after the Rebuilders set up camp over there."

"Who are—"

"So now you want to accuse her of being a *Rebuilder?*"

Smoke said. "Really, Nora? That's a little paranoid, even for you."

Nora scowled. "Freewalkers don't threaten to kill children."

"Everyone would have thought she was a—"

"Don't say it," Cass interrupted, resisting the urge to clap her hands over her ears. She couldn't bear to hear the word, to hear the accusation, again. "Please. Look, why don't I just leave now."

"No one said anything about that," Smoke said tiredly. "You're safe here. Everyone's just on edge. It's been hard. Shit, no one needs to tell you that."

For a moment no one spoke. Cass could feel Nora's anger clogging the air still.

"All I want to know is how she's managed not to be attacked," she said, addressing Smoke alone. "Walking alone as long as she says she has—how does that happen?"

Cass glared back. "I've been lucky, I guess."

"*Lucky,*" Nora repeated, spitting out the word as though it was poison.

"Listen to me. My *daughter* was there," Cass snapped. "In the library. The second time we were attacked. We were outside. She wanted…to be outside."

What Ruthie had really wanted was to pick dandelions, one of the few plants to survive the Siege. Cass had taught her to hold the blooms under her chin, so that the yellow reflected off her pale creamy skin. *Oh, look, you must be made of butter,* she teased Ruthie, peppering her sweet face with kisses. And then Ruthie would laugh and laugh and tickle Cass's chin with bunches of dandelions wilting in her chubby little hands.

Ruthie wanted to pick dandelions, and they were hard to find at dusk, so it was barely twilight when Cass led her outside to the little patch of dead lawn in front of the library, after she looked carefully in every direction.

But not carefully enough. Because the Beaters were learning. And they had learned to hide. They hid behind a panel truck on two flat tires that had been abandoned half a block away...and they waited. And then they moved faster than Cass thought possible, awkward loping strides accompanied by their gurgling breathless moans, and Cass grabbed for Ruthie, who was tracing the path of a caterpillar with a stick and thought it was a game and danced out of the way and darted into the last glorious rays of sun as it slipped down the horizon—

The challenge drained from Nora's face. "Don't," she begged.

Smoke placed a work-roughened hand over Nora's and didn't look at Cass.

"Nora," he said heavily. "She, uh...her nephew. She was watching him."

"I was *supposed* to be watching him," Nora said hollowly. She pulled her hand away and stood, knocking over her chair. She backed out of the room, brushing against the coffeepot on the counter. It fell to the ground, shattering and splashing hot coffee, but she just turned and bolted down the hall.

"She's..." Smoke said, watching her go. Then he turned back to Cass. "I'm sorry."

"No need to apologize," Cass said, but the truth was that she did need it. Not the apology—but the way his voice softened when he spoke to her and the way his eyes narrowed with concern when he looked at her, taking in what had happened to her poor body and not turning away.

That. Most of all she needed that, the not turning away.

"Something did happen to me," she found herself saying,

the words tumbling out as though a trapdoor had been opened inside her. "Something bad."

Telling was crazy. Telling could get her thrown out of here. Or worse. But Smoke looked at her as though he saw her, saw the *real* her, and she wanted to hold on to that, wanted him to know the truth and still see her.

The kindness he'd already shown her should have been enough. *Settle for that,* she willed herself. Settle for good enough.

But Cass could never leave well enough alone. She didn't know how. She wanted someone—one other human being—to know what had happened, and not turn away.

"Your daughter," Smoke said softly. "Was she taken?"

"No," Cass said. "But I was."

SMOKE HELPED HER CUT HER HAIR.

He handed her the scissors, a pair of office shears that were too bulky and too dull to do a good job, even if she had a mirror, even if she knew what she was doing. He'd said it would give her less to explain to the others. Cass knew he was right. Still, when she made the first cut, the sight of her filthy and matted hair falling to the floor caused her to suck in her breath.

Her hair had been her best feature, once. Long and thick and shiny, dark blond burnished with gold, curving inward where it lay across her collarbones. She refused to cry as the hair fell away, but when she had cut as far as she could reach, and Smoke closed his large hand gently over hers and took the scissors away, she squeezed her eyes shut and mourned the loss of the last faint reminder of her beauty as he carefully trimmed the back.

Afterward, he gathered her hair with his hands and haphazardly piled it in a file box while Cass got control of herself. He carefully avoided looking her in the face and Cass knew that she was hard to look at, an ugly, hard-worn thing. She demanded that he take her to the library that night, and he agreed once Cass made it clear that she was going with or without him.

He tried to talk her into waiting a few days, when the full moon had waned. The Beaters had become bolder, he warned her, coming out on moonlit nights as well as mornings and early evenings. Gone were the days when they only ventured out in the middle of the day.

But Cass didn't care. She'd been out every night since she woke up; she wasn't going to stop now, not when she was so close to Ruthie.

Smoke took her to the cafeteria, which they had set up as a community room with toys and activities for the kids, and chairs and sofas arranged for conversation. Makeshift shelves held kitchen implements and plates and cups. Blankets and clothing were folded and stacked. There were rows of paperbacks, vases of the few surviving wildflowers. Board games and puzzles were set out on tables and two separate card games were in full swing.

Eight or nine kids—toddlers up to six- or seven-year-olds—played on carpet scraps arranged on the floor at one end of the cafeteria. Sammi was watching them, along with a boy about her age.

Smoke led Cass into the large open space, and the adults' conversations died. People set down their playing cards, the baskets of clothes they had been folding, the kaysev they had been separating and cleaning and preparing. They regarded Cass with open curiosity and, in some cases, suspicion and fear and hostility.

Sammi's mother was in a group of women who had been

chatting as they washed and dried dishes. There was a tub of soapy water, another of clear, no doubt creek water that had been boiled. Cass had seen the blackened fire pit in the courtyard, the hearth built of rebar and steel beams and that fireproof plastic weave.

"This is Cass," Smoke said into the silence. "She's a citizen, just like us."

"She's *not* like us," Sammi's mother said, setting down her washrag. Her voice shook. "She tried to—"

"It's okay, Mom," Sammi said. She put down the bucket of toys she'd been holding. A pretend zoo was laid out on the floor, and she and the boy had been helping the younger kids stack wooden blocks to make cages.

"It's *not* okay," her mother hissed, but she stayed where she was. One of the other women laid a hand on her arm and said something that Cass couldn't hear.

"She only did what she had to," Sammi added, glaring at her mother defiantly. "Besides, if you didn't keep me cooped up in here like I was in jail—"

"Don't, Sammi," the boy said quietly. "Not now."

"I'd rather take my chances out there," Sammi said, pointing out the window at the street that ran alongside the building, beyond the iron fence. Cass saw abandoned cars, some with graffiti painted on the side. Several had crashed into each other, by accident or on purpose, crushed metal and broken glass surrounding doors that no one had bothered to close.

Then she saw something else, something that struck white-hot fear in her heart. In the yard of a squat brick bungalow across the street, a small clump of Beaters shuffled around a kiddie pool they'd managed to drag from somewhere. One was trying to sit in it. Two others were trying to turn it over. Another stood close to the house, staring into a large picture window and absently tugging at its ears.

She wasn't the only one to spot them. A few sharp gasps, a collective wave of fear that ran through the room.

"They've started gathering here in the afternoon. Waiting…" Smoke sighed, running his hands through his hair. For a moment he looked a decade older than the thirty-five Cass had taken him for. "Sometimes a dozen of them. They wander off when the sun starts to get low. For now, anyway."

The Beaters had everyone's attention. The argument between Sammi and her mother was forgotten. Cass took the opportunity to slip out of the room, Smoke following her without a word. She could not stay there, watching the Beaters, enduring the scrutiny of all those people.

She would wait in the office, alone, until evening. After all, she'd become accustomed to her own company.

Cass added it up in her head. A hundred seventy-five, maybe two hundred people left, between the library and the school and firehouse…. Silva's population had been over four thousand before the famine and the riots and the suicides and the fever deaths. Before the Beaters began carrying the survivors away.

As the sun sank down in the sky, Cass felt restless. She had been alone in the office for hours, waiting for night to come. No one had disturbed her. No one had even walked by the door. She stood up and stretched, easing her hip and thigh muscles. They were tight all the time now, from the walking.

When she regained consciousness all those days ago, she saw the Sierra foothills in the distance, the flat dry central valley all around her. She had been lying under a stand of creosote a few yards from the edge of a farm road, one she didn't know. All those years living in Silva, ever since Mim and Byrn had moved there during Cass's senior year of high school, she had never traveled far from the long, flat, straight stretch of Highway 161 that led up into the hills from the central valley. The few times she'd made the four-hour trip to San Francisco with friends, to see a concert or spend the night on someone's friend's couch getting high and drinking cheap wine, she'd barely noticed the chicken and cattle ranches flanking the highway, the clots of houses that passed for towns, the collapsing sheds and silos left over from more prosperous times.

She had been lying in a thicket of dead brown weeds. Kaysev had taken root in patches between the dead plants, and Cass had been curled up with her face in a soft clump, its gingery scent in her nostrils along with the other smells: the metal tang of crusted blood, the rotting spoils of her own breath, her body's odor foul and acrid. Her mind had been clouded and troubled, both racing and stalled, somehow. She had no idea how she'd come to be lying, bruised and mangled, in the weeds, and she wondered if she was dead, because her last memory was praying for death when the Beaters closed their ruined fingers around her arms.

That was all she remembered, and it came to her through a dense tangle of lost and broken thoughts, so she understood that time had passed since that terrible moment. How much time, she had no idea.

The brown weeds made a stark pattern against the clear sky and Cass had wished she could just close her eyes and finish the job of dying.

But then she saw what had become of her flesh.

Stretching made the wounds on her back throb, and Cass pulled her shirt up and over her shoulders to let the room's cool air reach them. Just for a moment, just to take away the constant ache for a little while. She leaned into the stretch, and tried not to think. Only to wait, for Smoke to come and get her and take her to what was next.

A sound at the door broke her concentration. Cass pulled her shirt down hastily, but it was too late.

It was the girl. Sammi. She had approached the room so quietly.

And she had seen.

FOR A LONG MOMENT THEY STARED AT EACH other, Cass holding her breath, the girl's eyes wide with surprise and curiosity—but no fear.

"Can I come in?"

"Of course," Cass said.

The girl slipped gracefully into a chair at the same table where Cass had drunk coffee hours earlier. She had washed and changed her clothes, and her hair had been combed and plaited neatly. The braids made her look even younger, but Cass could see that she was well into adolescence, maybe fourteen. That might explain her rebellion against her mother, but Cass figured it went further than that—there was a reckless spirit to her. A spirit not so different from her own.

"So you really *were* attacked by Beaters," the girl said. "What happened?"

Cass winced. Telling Smoke had been hard enough,

especially when he asked to see her scars. The look on his face—the horror, the pity—had been almost more than she could bear, but it was worse when he turned away from her. It had taken him a few minutes to get his composure back, and he'd remained cool and distant even when he promised to keep her secret.

"I was..." Cass started to speak, found that her mouth was too dry. She licked her lips and cleared her throat, wished for water. "I was taken, yes. But, I, I woke up and I was...all right."

Sammi didn't hide her skepticism. "What about those cuts? Did one of them do that to you or did you do it to yourself?"

Cass had wondered the same thing a thousand times. The wound pattern held clues. The damage was all in places she could reach by herself, and it was safe to say she was the one who'd bitten and chewed herself.

The wounds on her back were another matter. The Beaters always started with a person's back, where the large uninterrupted stretch of flesh made their ravenous feeding easiest. Only after they chewed it away did they move to the backs of the legs, the buttocks—and eventually, when they had eaten away all they could, they turned their victim over and started on the front.

She touched her stubbled hair. "I did this."

"So, you *were* one, for a while at least," Sammi said. "It's the only thing that makes sense. Did you eat the blueleaf?"

Cass shook her head, but who could say with certainty? When the government dropped kaysev from planes all over the nation, its last act before it ceased to exist, the second strain had somehow gotten mixed in. Everyone had a theory about that: most thought the researchers made some sort of mistake, sending the wrong seed, but some people thought blueleaf had evolved on its own, that mutating cells had been heeding nothing more than the call of evolution. And some saw the hand of God in the appearance of the rogue leaves, whose edges were slightly pocked and tinged faintly blue— His punishment for the profligacy and faithlessness of the last decade.

The blueleaf took root, an occasional low-growing and stunted patch among the healthy kaysev. At first no one noticed. By the time anyone made the connection, it was too late for the first wave of the infected.

Detection wasn't the only problem. The early stage of the disease didn't hint at what the victim would ultimately become—it hid its curse in a cloak of sensual delirium.

First came the fever, of course—and that felled thirty percent of the infected, mostly the very young and the old. But if you survived that, you felt so fucking good. Word quickly spread that when the fever leveled off, you experienced a high not unlike ecstasy. Your skin pigmentation deepened, an appealing effect when coupled with the feverish sheen. The irises of your eyes intensified—green turned jade, blue shone brilliant sapphire, brown sparked gold—but your pupils stopped dilating, and without bright light you could barely see.

You ceased to care, as your mind started to take elaborate journeys on its own. The hallucinations were elaborate and often sexual. There were no terrors or suicidal impulses. You simply lay about, flushed and beautiful, sighing with pleasure.

For a week or two. Until you started to pick at your skin and pull at your hair. Until your confusion deepened and your speech grew unintelligible, and your blood burned hot and you flayed your own skin and developed a taste for uninfected flesh.

Cass had spotted a few blueleaf plants here and there as she followed the road up into the foothills. Citizens learned to kill the plant on sight, and they'd managed to drive the wretched thing nearly to extinction only a few months after they first appeared. Cass herself pulled the plants from the ground and trampled them whenever she saw them, even though her body had somehow rebuffed the disease.

"My mom says blueleaf's only here. That it's not in the rest of the country."

"What do you mean?"

"There's been freewalkers through—some guy who had this ancient radio, like from the 1960s or something? There was something about it that it could get a signal even with all the power dead. And he said he talked to people in other states and they don't have blueleaf. They have the kaysev but no one's getting sick."

"That's—that's not possible. Everyone would leave California if that was true."

Sammi shrugged. "That's what he was trying to do. He was going to walk all the way to Nevada. He just stayed one night. A couple people believed him, they went, too."

"Well." Cass spoke carefully; she knew how fine the line was between hope and fantasy. "It would be nice. Maybe, once they get the Beaters under control…"

"Yeah. I know it's a long shot and all. I'm just sayin'." She looked increasingly embarrassed, twisting her hair around nail-bitten fingers. "But I was just wondering. You know, how you got infected."

Cass took a deep breath. "I was attacked. I remember that. I don't remember what came after, but—well, I'm hoping someone at the library will know."

"You think they might still have your little girl there. Your daughter."

Cass nodded, unable to speak.

"I hope they do," Sammi said fiercely. "My mom, she worries about me like all the time? She and my dad separated back in January and he moved up to Sykes and we don't know if he, well, you know. I mean the last time we talked to him, he and this guy, this guy who had gas, you know, like a full tank or almost a full tank? My dad was going to have this guy bring him down, only the roads…"

She stopped talking and swallowed and Cass spotted the hole in her bravery.

The roads. They'd become nearly impassible in places, as gas ran out and gridlocked intensified, as wrecks piled up and people panicked and abandoned their cars and tried to make it back. A few did. Many others didn't. And a few just stayed locked inside, terrified, until they starved or someone shot them for their fuel or one of the Beaters happened to remember what it was to open a door, the memory of the mechanical motion released from the recesses of its ruined mind, a small step to feed its larger need.

A few days before she moved to the library, Cass had watched from her kitchen window as a car tried to navigate the debris-strewn street that ran along the front of the trailer park. Woodbine Avenue had once been one of the busiest streets in town, with two lanes in each direction, so it was a logical choice for someone trying to get through—or out of—town. But Cass hadn't seen a car in days. No one had gas—and no one had anywhere to go. Rumor had it that the biggest cities had fallen first, and anyone who'd set out for Sacramento or San Francisco hadn't been seen since.

But Cass didn't recognize this car, a blue Camry with a crumpled front bumper. When it slowed to a stop at the site of an accident that had blocked the road for weeks—a semi truck had overturned trying to make the tight turn, causing

a pileup that no one had bothered to clear, the drivers aban-
doning their vehicles to search for shelter—Cass waited for
the car to turn around and go back the way it had come.

For some reason, this driver hesitated.

In seconds a cluster of the diseased loped out from behind
the 7-Eleven across the street, lurching and babbling.
Most started trying to climb on top of the car, moaning
with hunger and frustration, but one held a large rock in
his scabby hand. He beat the rock against the driver side
window, persisting even when blood dripped from his arm,
cawing excitedly, until the glass finally shattered.

The Beaters screamed as they dragged the driver, a
middle-aged man dressed in a wrinkled button-down shirt
and plaid shorts, from the car.

He screamed louder.

"Maybe," Cass started. She had to steel herself for the lie
she was about to tell. "Maybe he's there still. In Sykes. There
must be shelters there. Groups of people, like this…"

Sammi shrugged, an obvious effort to be brave. "Whatever."

"I can try to find out, you know. When I get into town."

"They won't know. No one's traveling between much
anymore. I mean, besides you."

"What were you doing outside this morning?" Cass asked
gently.

Sammi looked at her hands; the nails were bitten. "I sneak
out sometimes," she said. "When the raiding parties go out
at night. I *hate* it here, it's like being in jail. And I always
come back before it gets light out."

"What about this morning?"

"I…kind of got turned around."

"You were lost," Cass clarified. "Sammi…you have to
know how dangerous it is to be out there alone."

"*You* were alone. How far have you walked, anyway?" Sammi demanded. "Since you, you know, woke up."

"Look, Sammi…you can't tell anyone what I'm telling you. About me being attacked."

Sammi nodded solemnly. "I promise."

"No, really. You can't tell *anyone*."

Sammi nodded again.

"And you have to stop going outside on your own."

This time Sammi didn't react, didn't meet her eyes.

"Say it, Sammi, please. I know you don't like being cooped up here, but just promise me you won't go out alone."

Sammi rolled her eyes. "Okay, okay, I *promise*."

Cass sighed. "I don't know how far I've walked, really. At first I didn't… It was like I was sleeping and awake at the same time. I didn't go very far for a while. I was stopping a lot…maybe that was a week. Until I felt right again. And even then…" Cass passed a hand over her eyes, rubbed the skin between her eyebrows. "Even then I didn't cover a lot of distance. Because of trying to hide when it was light out. You know, to keep watch."

And at night, when the moon went behind a cloud, or the stars failed to light the sky, she couldn't go very far at all, because she couldn't see. Back in the library, she'd hoarded matches and two good flashlights and a cache of batteries. But she had none of that when she woke up. No pack, no food, no supplies, and she was wearing clothes she'd never seen before.

How far did she travel every night: maybe a few miles? As close as she could figure it, Cass had started out about thirty-five miles down-mountain, maybe a little more since she had weaved back and forth to avoid going too close to the road. The Beaters didn't leave the roads when they could help it;

they liked to follow an easy path, and their stumbling, awkward gait did not lend itself to obstacles. On uneven terrain they stumbled and fell a lot.

Still, if they'd caught her scent, a glimpse of her in the woods, nothing would stop them from coming after her, no matter how deep she ran, so she had tried to stay out of sight of the road. And roads eventually ran into towns, which she had to avoid more and more once she noticed, like Smoke had said, that the Beaters were clustering around the population centers of Before.

One time, a few days after she woke up, she'd been dozing the afternoon away in the skeleton of a live oak tree. It was a hundred yards or so from the road, and upwind, so Cass figured it would be safe enough. Low in the foothills, the trees were sparse to begin with, and most had died; there was little in the way of cover.

A sound broke nearby and she came awake instantly, her heart racing. She almost fell as she looked around for the source of the sound. Then she spotted the man who had walked directly below the tree, his footfalls cracking on broken branches. He was walking fast, a bulky pack on his shoulders, his gait sure and strong. A loner, Cass guessed, someone who—like Sammi—would rather take his chances outside than live cooped up in a shelter.

Suddenly there was a second sound. Over on the road.

Cass had been so focused on the man that she hadn't seen them approach. Beaters—four of them, stumbling and crying out—and they'd heard him, too.

Fear turned Cass's blood cold.

For a second, the man paused, looking around wildly. His eyes went wide and he began to run, faster than Cass had ever seen a man run. After a few dozen paces he shrugged the pack off his back, and it fell to the ground as the Beaters' cries escalated into enraged screams. Unburdened, he ran even faster.

But he wasn't fast enough.

It was dumb luck that he ran forward. If he had run perpendicular to the road, the Beaters would have come close enough to Cass's tree to smell her. As it was, Cass guessed the man stayed ahead of them for a quarter mile before they caught up. She watched the whole time, willing the man forward with her entire being as the beasts knocked into each other and stumbled on the uneven ground and shoved at each other. They were so awkward, so ungainly, but their strength and speed were otherworldly.

In the end, two of them tripped each other and fell to the ground, snorting and snapping with fury as they beat at one another with clumsy fists.

But two surged ahead.

Cass pressed her face into the scratchy trunk of the tree and covered her ears with her hands, but she could hear the man's terrified screams and the Beaters' triumphant crowing as they carried their prey back down the road to wherever their nest was.

Sammi was watching her, light brown eyes wide and speculating. "Smoke's going to take you, isn't he?"

Cass nodded.

Sammi gave her a fragile shadow of a smile. "He's good. He's *brave*. You know how he got his name?"

"No."

"He was living up at Calvary Episcopal. I mean, not like because it was a church, they were just using the church for shelter."

"Yes, I remember, there were people living there when I was at the library."

"And the Beaters came and they got one of them. Or, I

don't know, maybe more than one, I'm not sure. Only, they got this one guy's wife, and he went nuts and tried to burn the place down. With everyone in it, you know, like a group suicide? They had this tank, natural gas or something. And he totally blew it up, you could see it all day, the sky was like black. You know, like...totally dark. He died, but Smoke—well, I don't know what his name used to be, it was right when we all moved in here."

"How long ago was that?"

"It was around the beginning of May. We saw the fire, we saw the sky go dark and all.... Well, Smoke got a lot of the people out."

"He rescued them?"

"Yeah, he got this whole family, Jed and—Jed's that guy who was babysitting with me. He's sixteen. His parents and his brothers and a bunch of other people, too. Smoke helped them get out. And when they came here his hair was burned but that was all. He smelled like smoke, but he wasn't burned, and people said it was a miracle. I don't know if it was really a miracle but..."

The girl seemed suddenly embarrassed.

Cass followed a stray impulse and covered the girl's hand with her own. Sammi's skin was warm and she could feel her strong pulse at her wrist.

"I don't know," she said softly. "Maybe there's still room for a miracle or two in the world."

"Maybe," Sammi said. She sounded like she thought Cass was going to need one.

LATE IN THE AFTERNOON, SMOKE RETURNED. Sammi was long gone, not wanting to worry her mother any more than she already had. Cass's heart went out to the girl; she'd once walked the same complicated tightrope of parental loyalty and teenage rebellion, the challenges of school and friends and her father's absence. Aftertime, everything was turned upside down. Kids, with their more elastic notions of what was real, rebounded and adapted while the adults struggled.

Except for the ones who lost their families. Aftertime orphans did not fare well. They were responsible for much of the looting and destruction that happened now—the ones who managed to escape predators, whose movements were no longer tracked and monitored. They found each other somehow, their senses tuned to the same frequency of grief and anger, and formed gangs who roamed the streets with breathtaking indifference to the danger, destroying everything in their path—just as everything that they had loved had been destroyed. Cass didn't doubt that the bands of fake Beaters that Nora had mistaken her for were comprised of kids like these.

Sammi had already lost one parent. Cass prayed that the girl's mother would stay safe.

Smoke brought plates piled with food and two plastic bottles filled with murky boiled water. There was a salad of kaysev greens dressed with oil and vinegar. There were also three blackened strips of jerky.

The aroma caused Cass to salivate, and she could practically taste the salty meat. Still, before accepting the plate, she asked: "Why?"

Smoke didn't meet her gaze. "They want something in return," he said. "News…there are a lot of people who won't make the trip anymore. In the last couple of weeks it's become a lot more dangerous. There's been trouble, and not just from the Beaters."

"What do you mean?"

Smoke made a dismissive gesture. "Long story. I'll tell you about it on the road. But just folks with their own ideas about who ought to be running things."

"What, you mean like who's in charge here?" Cass saw a chance to ask something that she had been wondering. "Who *is*, anyway? You?"

"*Not* me," Smoke said with finality. "We're a collective here, we make decisions as a group. But look, like I said, it's a long story. We'll have time for it later, but now you should eat."

"But…" Cass gestured at the plate. "What kind of stores do you have?"

Smoke shrugged, but his unconcern wasn't convincing. "Quite a bit, actually. We still go raiding. Me, some of the others. There are still houses within a mile or two that haven't been cleared yet. We only do one a night, take five or six of us and go."

Cass nodded. She had come across some of these houses herself, even sheltered in them.

"What about the Wal-Mart?"

Smoke shook his head. "Beaters got there first. Nested all over it. There's still a lot of canned food and other stuff in there but we can't touch it."

It was an older store, up Highway 161 outside the Silva town limits. It didn't sell produce or meat, but that would actually be an advantage, since there would be no spoilage. And there would be medicine. Diapers, clothes, toiletries, processed foods. Winter coats and gloves. Boots.

"But we're doing okay," Smoke continued. "We got to the Village Market early on."

Cass knew the place, a mom-and-pop grocery in a strip mall that stocked high-end gourmet stuff for weekenders and skiers. "Wasn't it mostly cleared out back during the Siege?"

"Yeah, but we went back and finished the job. You know—people were panicking. Grabbing stuff. We've found things in houses…. People will have a whole room full of bottled water, frozen dinners and shit they just left out when they couldn't fit it in their freezers. Not that it mattered."

Not after the power went out. Cass shook her head at the waste.

"We've got about five thousand cans. We're trying to save the bottled water we have, and just rely on the creek. There's some cereal, pasta, rice. Spices…not much meat, this is pretty much the end of it," he said, pointing at the jerky. Cass noticed that his own plate held only salad and cold kaysev cakes. "Medicine… We got into the clinic, and there's a woman here who was a doctor, a couple others, a nurse and a paramedic. So we have antibiotics, painkillers, bandages, like that."

Cass chewed, trying to savor the salty jerky. She had never liked it Before, but now it tasted better than anything she'd ever eaten. "Do you think it's true?" she asked after she took a sip from the bottle he'd brought. "Can you just live on kaysev? I mean, after...?"

After everything else is gone, she didn't say. Because no matter how many stores they had managed to lay in here or anywhere else, the survivors would go through them eventually.

Smoke shrugged. "They certainly wanted us to believe that."

Cass remembered the president's prepared remarks, distributed to all the networks after he himself had gone to an undisclosed shelter. It was one of the final broadcasts before everything shut down. Paul Palmer, of KTXT, his hair looking like he'd done it himself, the part slightly askew, his eyes hollow and his voice wavering. It was a few days before the media disappeared forever—and only a matter of hours before the planes left air bases in Brunswick and Pensacola and Fort Worth and China Lake and Everett, loaded with their secret freight, tested and developed and grown in a dozen different locations across the U.S. Paul Palmer hadn't even bothered to conceal the fact that he was reading from the teleprompter: "Full-spectrum nutritional mass," he'd intoned. Code name K734IV, later shortened to K7 and then kaysev. *Protein, calcium, vitamins, fiber.*

"They could have been lying, though," Cass said. "They obviously never tested it. I mean...if they had, they would have figured out about the blueleaf before they went and dumped seed over thousands of square miles."

"Cass...you should know. Blueleaf's only in California. At least, it was, unless it's drifted."

"Yeah, I've heard that," Cass said, remembering Sammi's story. "Only that's just one more rumor. The only people who know are the pilots who dumped it, and even they don't know what was in the seed mix."

"No," Smoke said quietly. "It's true. Travis was the only base that went for it. Even China Lake turned it down, but they were doubling back over the same flight patterns as Travis so it didn't matter."

"How could you *possibly* know that?"

Smoke was silent for a moment, not meeting her eyes. "Because I was working in Fairfield at the time. Practically right next door to Travis. I used to drink with some of those guys."

"But—wouldn't that be confidential? Why would they open up to some guy in a bar?"

Smoke's face darkened and his mouth went tight. "It was more than just a bar conversation. We were...friends. And I guess they needed to talk, when they got back from taking the kaysev up. Those guys were career pilots—that's what they knew. Who they *were*. They knew it was the last flight they were ever going to take. So yeah, they talked."

Cass thought about what he was saying. It was tantalizing to think there was part of the world—part of the country, even—that was still free of Beaters. A place where people didn't live in constant terror.

But there was something off about Smoke's story, about the way he wouldn't look at her, at the barely concealed emotion in his voice.

"How would the pilots know what they were flying?" she demanded. "I mean, the military's never been known for transparency. I would think something like that would be—what do you call it?—need-to-know. Especially if there was disagreement about what exactly they were going to distribute."

Smoke shrugged. "Look, I only told you because...well, I thought it might give you hope."

Cass didn't believe him, but she wasn't ready to let the conversation drop. "Why are you still here? If you're so sure blueleaf's only in California?"

"It's way too unstable to try to make it out of state now. That's got to be a hundred miles, most of it over-mountain."

"Sammi told me other people have done it."

Smoke laughed bitterly. "Yeah? What she told you was that other people *tried*. I met that guy. The one she's talking about. Tried to talk him out of it, but he was determined, was one of those new roaming prophet-preachers. I bet he didn't make it twenty miles up the road on foot."

I did, Cass thought darkly. She'd made it farther than that, alone, with nothing but her wits.

Although she'd had Ruthie to live for. Maybe that had bought her survival.

Smoke seemed to have lost any interest in the conversation. He reached for her plate and Cass didn't stop him; she allowed him to scrape the last of her meal onto his own plate and collect her empty bottle.

"I'll take care of the dishes," he said. "I've packed for both of us. We'll leave in an hour or so. There's wash water in the courtyard, if you want it. Women use it after dinner, then the kids. Men wait until morning. This is your chance— they're expecting you. They'll have supplies for you." He hesitated. "I told them you were shy. That you'd want to keep your undershirt on, your underwear."

He was gone before Cass could object—or thank him.

CASS FOLLOWED THE SOUND OF LAUGHTER, staying to the long shadows under the eaves. She'd already decided that if either Sammi or her mother were in the courtyard, she'd retreat without showing herself. She'd done enough damage to the fragile network of relationships in the school.

But the four women clustered around the makeshift tub were strangers. The tub was really more of a giant trough composed of sections of white plastic pipe that had been capped off and propped up on a pair of sawhorses. It had been filled with water that steamed in the rapidly cooling evening. A small fire crackled in the hearth a few yards away, a neat stack of burning madrone branches giving off a spicy, pleasant smell. Several pots of different sizes simmered on the grate above, and Cass guessed they poured the boiling water into the tub to keep the communal bath warm, and to replace what sloshed and splashed out with their movements.

Two of the four women were naked except for plastic flip-flops, and one of them held a nearly new bar of soap. The naked women washed, passing the soap back and forth. One of the other women was undressing, hopping from foot to foot as she stripped off her clothes and tossed them into a pile. The fourth woman had put her clothes back on and was toweling her hair. She was telling some sort of story that had the others cracking up, but when they noticed Cass approaching they all went silent.

"I'm sorry," Cass said. "I didn't mean to... Smoke said I might be able to wash. Except...I, um..."

"We have extra towels," the woman who was undressing said, offering a tentative smile. "I brought two. I wasn't sure if you... It's pretty casual. We keep the water hot for a couple of hours and people just show up whenever."

"*Some* people, anyway," one of the naked women said. She was a well-built girl in her early twenties who didn't seem the least bit self-conscious about dragging her soapy washcloth up and over her wide thighs, her rounded stomach. "Some folks, I don't think they've had a bath since they *got* here. They get kind of unfresh, you know what I'm sayin'?"

She gave Cass a friendly wink as her companion flicked her with her own washcloth. "Not everyone's as comfortable strutting around buck naked as you," she scolded, grinning. "Forgive Nance here. She's got no manners."

"I, um..." Cass said, swallowing. "Is it okay... Do you mind if I don't...uh, if I keep..." She hugged herself tightly, battling her warring desires to keep the evidence of her attack hidden, and to wash her filthy body.

"It's okay," the first woman said gently, handing her a small towel and a folded washcloth. They weren't terribly clean, but Cass took them gratefully. She set the towel on the ground and stripped out of her overshirt and pants before she could change her mind, keeping her eyes downcast, and then approached the trough wearing only the nylon tank and panties that she'd been wearing beneath her clothes all this time. There were only a few scars on the backs of her thighs, and they had healed to barely distinguishable discolorations, but the gouges on her back were still raw and obvious. She knew this from tracing them with her fingers—the undeniable evidence that she'd been torn at by Beaters.

But there was more to her discomfort. It had also been years since she had undressed in front of another woman, and she felt her skin burn with shame as the others watched her.

It was different with men. She'd been with so many; she'd stopped counting one weekend when, by Sunday, she couldn't remember the name of the one she brought home Friday. She hadn't been self-conscious—hadn't been conscious of anything, really, other than the driving need. Not a hunger for the coupling itself, but a need to beat her pain and confusion into a thing that could be contained again, could be put away far enough in the depths of her heart that she could keep going. Keep living. To get to that place she had to use her body, to show and undress and flaunt it, all of which was done without a second thought.

But now she felt hot shame color her face as her nipples hardened under the tight shirt, exposed to the evening chill. She had no bra—what would these women think of that? Cass didn't know what to make of it herself—on the day she woke up, when she stumbled to her feet and tried to work the kinks out of her mysteriously abused limbs—she'd gone to tug at her bra, a habit of decades, and found it wasn't there.

Cass hooked her thumbs in her socks and pulled them off,

tossing them on the pile. There was nothing more that she could take off.

"I'll—why don't I...?" the woman who had been telling a story said. She made a move toward Cass's clothes pile and hesitated. She looked Cass in the eye and spoke slowly and clearly. She was old enough to be a grandmother—old enough to be Ruthie's grandmother, anyway. She had several inches of silver roots, an expensive dye job now losing ground, what must have been a severe bob softening to a wispy cut around her chin. "I'm Sonja," she said carefully. "If you don't mind, I'll take these things, bring you back clothes that are clean, that you can wear on your... That will be good for traveling."

Cass made a sound in her throat, a rusty and ill-used sound that was meant to convey gratitude. Hot dampness pricked at her eyes and she found that her lips did not move well. But Sonja just nodded and swept up the mess of clothes, hugging them against her body as though they didn't stink, as though Cass had chosen and treasured them, rather than the truth—that she couldn't say who she'd taken them from and what she'd done to the person who wore them before.

Cass wanted to watch Sonja walk away, to watch the filthy and hated rags disappear, but she knew that if she did she wouldn't be able to concentrate on the bath, and the bath was a rare treat. She had not had or even allowed herself to dream of having such a thing in such a long time. There had been several moonlight splashes in the streams and creeks that crisscrossed the foothills, but the water never came up any farther than midankle, and no matter how Cass cupped her hands and splashed, she succeeded only in wetting her clothes and her skin, never cleansing them.

She approached the trough, the concrete cold and rough

on her bare feet, focusing on the steam that rose into the evening air.

Out of the corner of her eye she saw the woman who was undressing pause, her jeans folded in her hands. She had not yet spoken, and unlike the others, she had made no move to welcome Cass. Hostility came off her in waves. The others had somehow made their peace with Cass, with what she had done to Sammi—but this woman did not want her there.

Cass inhaled deeply of the steam. Someone had crumbled something aromatic into the water, bath beads or powder or something else that perfumed the air with lavender and created a thin layer of white bubbles. She longed to dip her fingertips into the water.

She was so filthy. She could barely abide herself, and she wanted desperately to wash even a little of her shame away.

Instead she forced herself to turn away from the water, toward the silent woman. "I'll go, if you want me to," she offered quietly.

But the woman—she was a handsome woman with a short, no-nonsense haircut and sharp cheekbones—picked up her shoes and socks and glared at Cass. "No, *I'll* go," she muttered, and stalked away.

"I'm sorry," Cass said to the others, her voice barely more than a whisper. "I should—"

"Stay," one of the women said. "I'm Gail. Trust me, you need this way worse than she does."

Cass was grateful, but she stared down at her hands, crisscrossed with cuts from running into dead shrubs and trees, and from falling in the dark. The nails were black and broken, her wrists creased with dirt. Her own odor was strong enough that she caught sour whiffs when she moved; she could only imagine how she smelled to others. "If you don't mind," she said, suddenly near tears and more humbled than she had ever felt in her life. "I'd like to stay."

"I was about done," Gail said, flipping thick brown braids over her shoulders and stepping aside to make room. "But don't worry, I'll stick around and chat."

She stepped closer, her smile slipping when her glance fell to the nearly healed wounds on Cass's arms. When she looked in Cass's eyes again, her curiosity was edged with sadness.

"Did you do that?" she asked, and for one heart-skipping moment Cass thought Gail knew, that she had guessed, about the attack, the Beaters, everything.

And then the truth hit her, bringing clarity, but no lessening of shame.

Gail thought she'd harmed herself.

And she wasn't wrong. Not about the story, only about the details.

There were days...dark days, when the end of the evening approached with no relief in sight, no one to slip into the shadows with, no strong man to bend her over double until there was no room for her own regrets, nights when every shot she downed added to her screaming headache without ever bringing the blessed numb of forgetting. And on those nights, once or twice...or three or four times...she'd found that sharp thing, the shard of broken ashtray, the coiled end of the corkscrew, the dull knife a bartender cut limes with.... She found the thing and she traced the shape of her shame until she could finally focus on the pain and forget the rest.

So, yes. Once, she'd borne the road map of shame on her skin. And was this really so different, these marks made by her own hands, in a fever she didn't remember?

She hung her head and blinked at the hot mist in her eyes. Immediately Gail put her hand, warm and comforting, on

Cass's wrist, in the small band of unmolested flesh between her hand and the first of the chewed places.

"I'm sorry," Gail murmured. "Please, just…just forget I said anything. Past is past here, if you want it to be. Everyone gets to start again."

Cass shivered, unable to speak.

"Well, look," Nance said, interrupting the moment with deliberate cheer. "Look, we're just glad you're here. You're the first new face we've had in…well, a while. I've been going nuts here with all these yokels."

"Nance isn't cut out for small-town living," Gail said, withdrawing her hand after a final squeeze. The moment had passed, nothing more than milkweed on the breeze. "She's way too upscale for the rest of us."

"I'm from Oakland," Nance said. "I just came up here to help my mother when things went bad. I never dreamed I'd get stuck here."

"Nance isn't much of a nature person," Gail said. "She keeps wishing she'd wake up and there'd be room service."

"I put in this shower last year," Nance said. "In my condo? One of those rain shower ones? There were jets along the side, steam…"

"And I bet you never had any trouble finding someone to share it with you, right?" Gail said, winking at Cass. "Nance also doesn't like the men here."

Cass dipped her washcloth into the warm water, savoring the sensation of the water closing over her fingers, her hand, her wrist. Slowly, she trailed the cloth in an underwater figure eight. "I'll ruin this water. It'll be filthy when I'm done."

Gail shrugged. "It wasn't exactly crystal clear to start with. We just drag it up from the creek. We don't bother to strain it or purify it when it's just for washing."

Nance wrinkled her nose. "Yeah, it smells a little like rotting fish. I don't know what we'll do when we run out of shower gel to hide the smell."

"We'll stink," Gail said. "Just like we do now, only by then we'll all be so used to it that it won't matter."

It was all the encouragement Cass needed. She submerged her arms up to her elbows, then lowered her face into the water and stayed under as long as her breath held out. She came up with the water dripping down her face and blinked it out of her eyes. "Ohhh," she breathed.

"Tell you what," Gail said. "I have a little shampoo left."

"Oh, I couldn't—" Cass said.

"Yeah, you can." Gail reached into a plastic tote. "Put your hand out."

Cass did as she was told and Gail squeezed out a dollop of creamy shampoo. It smelled like rosemary, and it was familiar; Cass had a bottle of it once, long ago. She held it up to her face and breathed as deeply as she could, trying to imprint the memory of the smell in her brain. Then she rubbed it onto her cropped hair and began to work it into her scalp, taking her time, making small circles.

The hair around her hairline was growing in soft and fine; Cass wondered if pulling it out had damaged the roots in some way. Before, when she was a teenager, she remembered her mother warning her that if she plucked her eyebrows too often the hair wouldn't grow back. She had believed her mother. Before Byrn. When it was just the two of them, her mother taking such care in her mirror in the morning and before dates, Cass sitting on the edge of the tub to talk to her. She thought that might have been when her mother was happiest, when she was getting ready for a new man. Before there had been time for him to disappoint her or, in the end, to leave her. When it was all possibility, when Jack or David or Hunt was still new to her. "I have a good feeling about this one," she would always say, winking at Cass as she slipped her blouse over her head, adjusting her breasts in her satiny bra, buttoning just enough buttons to give a hint of cleavage.

She always had a good feeling, before.

Even with Byrn.

Cass forced the thought from her mind. When the shampoo was exhausted, the dirt and grease in her hair overwhelming the lather, she lowered her head and let the water come up over her scalp and the back of her neck, down her shirt. She swept her hair through the water, rinsing out all the shampoo. Then she came up sputtering a second time, her hair plastered wet and warm against her shoulders.

Nance made a show of pretending to look into the trough. "Can't even tell," she said. "We'll be able to wash all the kids and a few stray dogs in here, too."

Gail made a face. "Our standards aren't very high."

"I'm… Thank you," Cass murmured. She took the soap bottle Nance offered and squeezed a little onto the cloth and started scrubbing her body. She began with her shoulders and worked down her arms. She took the suds that gathered in her hands and rubbed them into the synthetic fabric of her tank top, doing her best to clean the fabric. She wished she could take it off, that she could stand here naked and scrub until she was finally clean. But this would have to do.

"Ain't no big deal," Nance said. "What you're gonna owe us big for is taking the only good-lookin' man we got with you. Here, give me that."

She took the cloth from Cass and dabbed at the back of her neck, her shoulder blades, letting the water sluice down to soak the back of her shirt. The water stung when it came in contact with the torn flesh, and Cass worried that the fabric would cling tightly, transparently, to the canyons of her wounds, and she twisted away, pretending to soap her back as far as she could reach. Nance pulled away from her, mild hurt in her expression, and Cass wished she could explain, *No, it's not you, it's me,* that her own body was a horror she couldn't shed, that Nance's healing touch was a gift she hadn't earned and couldn't accept.

Nance squeezed the water from the cloth and folded it carefully, once, twice; then she pressed it into Cass's hands, but before she let go, she gathered Cass's smaller hands in her own large and capable ones and held them for a moment with a tenderness that brought tears to Cass's eyes. Her sense of exposure deepened; while men had touched every inch of her body, sometimes without even knowing her name, and sometimes with the kind of careless fervor that left her bruised and battered, no woman had touched her since her own mother stopped bathing her since the age at which she was old enough to turn the taps herself. The image that flashed through her mind: her mother watching her impassively, smoking, as Cass struggled to let the water out the drain—she must have been all of nine, smarting from her father's absence and shriveling from her mother's indifference.

When she finally let go, Nance picked up her own towel and began drying off. Cass finished her washing, concentrating on the sensation of the warm water as it ran down her stomach, down her thighs and calves to puddle at the ground. When the others turned politely away, she washed between her legs, lathering and scrubbing as though she could wash away a decade's shame with meager and inadequate supplies, rinsing the panties as well as she could with handfuls of murky bathwater, the synthetic fabric clinging to her skin and revealing the thick, dark patch of hair beneath.

"Smoke will come right back here after he walks with me," Cass said, wanting to turn the attention away from herself. "I just need…"

But she didn't *need* Smoke. She'd come this far on her own; surely she could manage to cross the last four miles of bare road before the outskirts of Silva, the handful of blocks to the library.

"You take him, girl," Gail said, suddenly serious. "You let that man help you. You've been out of the towns, you don't know what you're up against."

"I've seen Beaters," Cass protested. "A few, anyway, on my way here."

"It's the *people* you need to worry about just as much nowadays," Gail replied.

"You come through cities?" Nance demanded, ignoring Gail. "You seen their nests?"

Cass hesitated. The biggest town she'd passed was a half a dozen houses and a gas station clustered around a crossroads, Highway 161 intersecting a farm road that disappeared into dusty fields. But she hadn't seen Beaters there, no evidence of a nest—no alcoves or storefronts littered with filthy clothing mounded in shallow rings, no piles of household castoffs hoarded for the haphazard, long-ago memories they held. No fetid stink of unwashed, ravaged bodies mingled in restless sleep, of torn flesh and leaking, damaged bodies seized upon and devoured and, finally, abandoned.

The few Beaters she'd seen had been small and restless roving teams, and if she'd wondered where they sheltered, she cast her doubts aside, plunged them into the unknowable so that she could take another step and another, so that she could salvage sufficient hope to continue on.

The others exchanged glances. "How many at a time?"

"Two…three."

"And tell me, didn't that strike you as strange?"

It had, of course, once the cloudiness had shaken itself loose from Cass's mind and she was thinking more clearly. Since the Beaters had evolved, they had formed larger and larger packs, like a snowball rolled around a snowy field, picking up mass. They seemed to take comfort in their own kind. Occasionally, you'd even see them in a clumsy imitation of an embrace, patting each other or grooming the hard-to-reach tufts of hair at the back of their heads, even hugging. They didn't ordinarily feed on each other after the initial flush of the disease—they hungered for uninfected flesh—but occasionally you'd see them nipping and tugging gently at each other with their teeth, almost the way puppies played, biting with their tiny milk teeth.

"I don't know," Cass said. All of it was strange. All of it was horrifying.

"Well, this is new, just the last few weeks. They've started going out a couple at a time, kind of poking around together like they have a plan. We—some of us—we think they're scouting."

A thrill of fear snaked along Cass's spine, a sensation she had thought was lost to her. After the things she'd seen and suffered, she didn't think she could be terrified again. "What do you mean?" she demanded.

"They're on the lookout for opportunities. For *us*. They've started working on strategy."

Whispered: *"No."*

It was impossible. The Beaters were disorganized, stripped of their humanity, reduced to little more than animals motivated by an overwhelming need to feed. The spells of humanlike behavior were nothing but the debris left behind when the soul made a clumsy exit from the shell of a body that remained. To suggest they were evolving the ability to reason, to *plan*—that was as senseless as suggesting that a flock of ducks could orchestrate a diving attack.

"We're not saying they've succeeded yet," Nance said quickly. "I mean it's not like they get very far before they get distracted or wander off or whatever. But the fact they're coming out in small groups like that—and they hang out around the edges, across the streets all around the school—it's got to mean something."

"It might just be the evolution of the disease," Cass ventured, grasping at possibilities. "You know...like, in the whole first population, as it progresses..."

There had been a lot of discussion of the evolution of the disease, when people first realized that the sick were turning into something else, something far worse. Before anyone called them Beaters, people repeated rumors that their brains were infected with a madness similar to syphilis. But back then, much as nineteenth-century syphilitics suffered from lesions and tumors and dementia before they died, Aftertime, people had initially thought that those who ate the blueleaf would eventually die once the fever escalated.

"Maybe," Gail assented, an act of generosity. "Just, I want you to know what you're up against. Smoke knows.... He's been watching them."

"He takes notes," Nance added. "He keeps a journal. He used to be a teacher or something."

"Well, we don't *know* that," Gail corrected her. "He doesn't talk about himself much."

"He said something about it once," Nance insisted. "Teaching."

Cass toweled off her damp body and thought about the man who had offered to freewalk with her to the library. Four miles of unnecessary risk. The overwhelming impression she got from Smoke was of...depth. Layers. He would not be an easy man to know.

There was the story he told about the air force pilots. She still didn't think he was telling the whole truth. So...maybe he was a liar, or maybe he was just keeping parts of the truth to himself.

But he was brave. Or more precisely, he had a lack of concern for himself, and an abundance of concern for others. He had been the first to come at her when she and Sammi approached the school, and it had been his body crushing hers when he took her down. His arms had been hard-muscled. Despite her strength and fitness, she was smaller by several inches and thirty or forty pounds. He could have hurt her easily.

But he hadn't even bruised her.

"What about Nora?" Cass found herself asking. "His... girlfriend?"

Gail made an exhalation of air through her teeth. "Is that the impression you got? Well, they're...I don't know what you'd call it."

"They met here," Nance said. "Nora, when she showed up she was a mess. Kept to herself. Wouldn't let anyone close at first, after her nephew...once he was taken. Smoke got her talking again."

"I mean I'm pretty sure they're doing the nasty," Gail said, flashing a grin that didn't make it to her eyes. "Smoke's hot, and there's lots of women wouldn't mind a little of that."

Cass felt heat rising in her face. That wasn't what she'd meant—not sex. Just the way they had been around each other, it suggested a relationship beyond the bond of people sheltering together in close quarters, and she'd been—

What, exactly? Curious? *Envious,* the voice inside her suggested. She didn't like that answer, but it had the ring of truth. To have someone else to go through this with—what would that be like? To have someone to tell your fears to—your wishes—your regrets?

"People are funny," Nance mused. "Some people, Aftertime, it's like they're dead inside, like they were already taken even though their bodies are still here. And other people just...I don't know, it's like they light up. Not in a good way, necessarily, mind you. But more like some sort of crazy energy that they rely on just to keep them going."

"Yeah," Gail agreed. "Some people get all manic. There's been all kinds of hookups, you go looking for a flashlight or something and open a door and there's people on the floor like, well, you know. And then next time you turn around they're doing it with someone else."

"Remember Scott and Meena...?" Nance said, and then the two of them were doubled over with laughter. Cass couldn't help smiling along, their mirth was so infectious.

"What's so funny?" Sonja had returned, carrying a stack of folded clothes, which she held out to Cass. "I had to guess at sizes, but I was trying for practical. Here, I'll take your towels, I'm on wash tomorrow anyway."

Cass accepted the clothes. She hesitated, embarrassed, before handing over the sodden towel and the washcloth, dingy from scrubbing the dirt from her skin. "I don't want you to have to—"

"Don't worry about her," Nance said affectionately, tossing Sonja her own towels. "She's a shitty laundress. She needs the practice."

"Well, if I had something to work with besides creek water—"

"Yeah, yeah, cry me a river," Gail laughed. "Sonja here was a designer at Nike, Before. She had like a million-dollar budget. A staff and a fancy office, and this chore stuff has been really hard for her."

"Oh, right," Sonja said, giving her a good-natured shove. "I had my own latte machine and a Jacuzzi in my bathroom. And a dozen male interns to go down on me under my desk during lunch, too."

"Good times," Nance said as they made their way back toward the building, relaxed and laughing, the sun sinking toward the tree line in a pool of molten orange.

Cass hung back, watching. She'd never had women friends. Never known what to say, how to breach the boundaries. But now, as she prepared to go into the unknown again, she suddenly wished she'd tried harder.

CASS DRESSED IN THE CLOTHES SONJA BROUGHT. The fabric was stiff from line drying and rasped against her scabs, even through the damp tank top, but Cass was so accustomed to the dull ache that she barely noticed.

Her wounds hurt almost unbearably when she first woke, but before long she was left with a dull, constant sensation that was as much numbness as pain. The disease, which had boosted her immunity before retreating, had clearly changed her sensitivity to pain, as well. Something to be grateful for.

The clothes smelled faintly of lavender. A soft jersey shirt that had belonged to another woman. Hiking pants that were new or nearly new, maybe nabbed from one of Silva's several outdoorsman shops when the looting turned to general panic and then mass stockpiling.

The greatest luxury was a new pair of socks. Sammi had brought these to her in the small office where Cass had retreated to wait, after the bath. It was part of a warren of tiny rooms behind the old reception area, and Cass guessed it had once belonged to an administrator, a vice-principal or part-time nurse. There was no window, only a desk that had been pushed against the wall, a couple of chairs, an expanse of industrial carpeting still littered with staples and eraser dust and tiny paper circles from a hole punch. The detritus of human activity Before. The sight brought back a memory of the sound of a vacuum cleaner, and Cass realized she was moving her arm back and forth in the obsolete appliance's once-familiar arc with a sense of longing. Even when she sat in the chair with her hands pressed tightly between her knees and her eyes closed, her mind was filled with a memory of the task, and it was almost like a forbidden thrill to envision making long, slow paths on the carpet, feeling the handle vibrate in her hand, the debris disappearing into the vacuum.

After a while, Sammi came, unannounced and furtive. The socks were rolled up and hidden in her pocket, the tags still attached. Men's hiking socks, pale gray with an orange stripe knit into the band at the top. Sammi handed them over and shook her head impatiently when Cass protested that she couldn't accept them.

"They're for you. Besides, you can do something for me. If you ever get to Sykes, and if you meet my dad, tell him I'm okay," she said. "His name is Dor. Doran MacFall."

"Sammi…as soon as I get my daughter, I'm going to go to the safest place I can find. I'm sorry, but I can't promise—"

"I'm not *asking* for a promise," Sammi interrupted, impatiently. "Only, no one knows what's going to happen anymore. No one knows the future. And maybe you'll see him. I mean…you got this far, didn't you? You were attacked, you got infected, you're the only person I've ever seen who got *better*."

Fear sluiced through Cass's veins. "Sammi, I never really said—" she began, her mouth dry.

Sammi shrugged, but she held on to Cass's gaze. "Don't worry, I didn't tell anyone. But your skin…I mean, that's the way it starts. That and your eyes. They're way too bright. Most people just don't want to remember that anymore. I mean, now that they just kill anyone they *suspect* might be infected."

"Wait—what?"

"Yeah, if someone's even suspected, they're shot. There's like a special store of bullets for it and everything. They have these elections for who has to do it. Winner loses and has to kill the dude. Kids aren't supposed to know," Sammi added, shrugging, as if the absurdity of such a rule eluded her.

Back at the library, before Cass was attacked, those who were suspected of infection were rare enough—there was so little blueleaf left, and no one ate it on purpose—that Bobby ordered that they be kept in the old operations room, among the silent heating and air-conditioning equipment, until their future was clear. Other diseases brought on fever, after all, so you didn't want to kill *everyone*. In the end, only one actual infected—a silent and red-faced old man who wore canvas coveralls—had stayed there during Cass's time at the library. Even when he began pulling his hair out, tearing the skin of his scalp—even when his pupils had shrunk down so far that he couldn't see Bobby and another man coming the day they hit him on the head and dragged him to the edge of town and left him there—even then he refused to admit he was infected. The old man's speech had become a bit slurred, and that was the last of it for him.

"But…" Cass swallowed hard. "My arms…like you said." It came out in a hoarse whisper as she covered the shiny, thin scars with her hands, unable to look.

"Yeah, but you *act* normal. You're not feverish and you don't talk crazy. Once they figured out that you weren't going to kill me, you know, when you started talking and all—you know how sometimes people only see what they want to see?"

Cass nodded, thinking—*but you still see*. Maybe it was because Sammi was young. And maybe it was more than that.

Sammi gave her a little grin. "Look, you're really not so bad. You did fix your hair, kinda—and your scars are almost gone. What you really need?"

Cass smiled, moved despite herself that the girl was trying to cheer her up. "Yeah?"

"Eyeliner. Really thick, you know?" She tugged her lower lid down to show Cass where she'd apply it. Then she hesitated. "They say there's others," she finally said. "That got better. I mean it's just a rumor, this one time a raiding party went down toward Everett. But, yeah, maybe you're not the only one."

Cass felt her heart speed up, a prickling of hope radiating along her nerves. *Others.*

"Survivors?" she asked. "Who were…attacked, who started to turn? And came back?"

Sammi shrugged, didn't meet her eyes. "It was just a rumor. My mom says it's just people being confused by those fake Beaters. I mean no one here's seen it or anything, and most people think it's like, what do you call that? When people make up stories and they get passed around—"

"Urban myth," Cass said, trying to cover her disappointment.

"Yeah, that. As far as anyone here knows, no one's ever come back before. So they don't believe in it. But I do. I can tell you're different. And it's not just that…you've been on your own and they haven't gotten to you. Most people would be dead already, so that means you're lucky, too."

"But I don't—"

"I'd go with you," the girl pushed on, and Cass had the sense she'd practiced this speech in advance. "I'm not scared. Only Mom doesn't have anyone else now. I need to be here for her. But you're going to make it—I know you are. And you don't even have to go looking for my dad, just only if you happen to meet him somewhere. He's, like, six feet three and..."

And then, suddenly, just like that, she faltered. Her courage evaporated in a mist of sniffles and her smooth-skinned face collapsed in on itself. She looked like she was about to bolt, and without thinking, Cass reached for her.

Sammi didn't so much lean as fall into the hug and Cass wrapped her arms around the girl, all elbows and slender limbs, and held tight.

"I'm sorry," Sammi snuffled against the crook of Cass's neck, but she didn't let go.

"Nothing to be sorry about," Cass said softly, and then she said something else, a dangerous thing that she didn't plan and immediately wondered if she would regret. "I'll find your dad. I'll find him and I'll tell him you're all right."

"Oh, thank you...thank you," Sammi said. "Um...Cass? Could you...you know, if you *do* find my dad? I was wondering if you could tell him something for me."

"You want me to give him a message?"

"Yeah. I mean, he'll know what it means." She bit her lip and looked away. "Just tell him that I never forget, I never miss a night. And I never will."

THEY SET OUT IN THE CHARCOAL GRAY OF nightfall, the approaching darkness taking the color from the earth, leaving it a land of black forms and navy sky. Someone had given Cass a backpack, a sturdy model made for day hikers. Inside were a good blade, bottles of water, energy bars, a can of orange segments. She wished she could thank her benefactor, but no one would own up to the gift.

No one came to see them off, either. Cass understood. Despite the lighthearted moments at the bath, and the provisions, in the end they'd chosen to stand with Sammi's mother, at least publicly. No one but Smoke and Sammi knew she was attacked, and she hoped no one really blamed her for the way she'd brought Sammi back to camp, with a blade at her throat. They must have known by now that she wouldn't have killed the girl, or maybe they just trusted Smoke's judgment—and, too, she might well have saved the child, getting her back to shelter before the sun was strong in the sky and the Beaters were out in force.

But Sammi was well loved here. And everyone knew the dangers Cass and Smoke faced. Knew Smoke might not be back. Aftertime, goodbyes had become too hard when each one might be the last.

Behind them the doors closed with a solid thunk and Cass felt a shiver travel up from the base of her spine. Smoke took the lead, walking a few steps ahead. He had changed into hiking boots and a long-sleeved shirt over a t-shirt and set an easy pace.

Just a day earlier, Cass was setting out *alone* at this hour after spending the daylight hours hiding and trying to get some sleep. Her destination was the same: Silva, or as close as they could get before next sunup. Her urgency was stronger, if anything, for how close she was. But things had changed in her brief stay at the school.

After being around people again for even such a short time, she was reminded of their unpredictability, their vulnerability...their humanity. Human beings were driven by emotions and hungers and drives and there was no telling what they would do in times of stress. Her fellow shelterers had rescued Ruthie that day and Cass prayed that they had cared for her ever since. But now she allowed herself to consider what instead they might have done with her little girl. What they might have told her. Would they have cherished her, held her, read her stories and combed her fine hair? Would they wipe her tears when she cried, or would they have been too busy, too distracted, too indifferent?

Even when Cass woke up to the horror of her ruined flesh, the hair ripped from her scalp, sticky and sore in unfamiliar clothes, she hadn't been afraid for herself, only for her little girl. She had put her faith in the people who rescued

Ruthie to care for her, because she had no other choice. She would gladly have relinquished any chance to see Ruthie again, if only she knew her daughter would always be safe and loved. After all, hadn't she done so once, already? Every time she raised the bottle to her lips, she had chosen: her addiction over her baby. That was the most painful truth of her recovery, and it was hard not to believe this was her punishment, to be separated from Ruthie without even the knowledge that she was all right. If only there was something to trade, someone to trade with; Cass would rip her soul from her body and hand it to the devil himself, would walk into the gates of hell with her head held high if someone could just take care of Ruthie.

And now that the library lay ahead in the gloom, Cass could no longer prevent herself from wondering if Ruthie might have been ignored, neglected, discarded.

No, no, no—if she didn't get the thoughts under control she would lose her mind; her breath would come out in a scream that would split the air and alert any night-wandering creatures of their presence.

Cass took two jogging half steps to catch up with Smoke and wrapped her hands around his arms. He turned and held her by the shoulders, searching her face in the moonlight. "What's wrong?"

Cass could feel her heart pounding in her throat, fast and staccato. She worked her lips but no sound came out.

"Did you see something? Hear something? Cass?"

Cass shook her head and licked her dry lips and managed two syllables. "Ruthie..." And then Smoke's arms were around her in an embrace that was at once strong and cautious. It wasn't a bear hug, not as committed as that, but more like he was making of himself a support for her to lean on. She rested her face against his broad chest and squeezed her eyes shut and listened to his slow, strong heartbeat.

"I don't know if she's all right," she said after a while, keeping her eyes closed.

She could feel Smoke nod as he held her a little tighter, his arms drawing her closer against him. "I know," he whispered. "But we try anyway. Right? We try anyway."

After a while longer Cass pulled away, embarrassed, blinking away the threat of tears. She did not cry easily, not anymore, so what was happening to her? Was it the women at the bath, the illusion of friendship, was she so hungry for human contact that she had let her guard down so easily?

She didn't look at Smoke, but when they started walking again he stayed by her side. She knew that earlier he'd walked ahead to shield her from whatever they might come up against in the dark. Now she had lost that advantage. But it had been an illusory advantage at best; anything that threatened Smoke threatened her, as well.

The moon was three-quarters full and its watery light was sufficient to mark their way along the road. The smell of tar, cooling now after a day softening in the late-summer sun, mixed with the gingery kaysev and the dry dirt smell of deadwood. Far off in the distance she heard a cricket, and then another, a lonely duet. There were crackling sounds in the brush now and then. Jackrabbits and quail and snakes.

For a while, after the country's livestock had fallen to the waves of bioterror attacks, there was panic that wild animals would be hunted to extinction. At first, people worried that the pathogens killing the cattle and sheep and chickens and pigs and trout and salmon would spread to the wild— and themselves, of course—but advances made early in the second decade of the century tailored chemicals to species with astonishing specificity, allowed them to be precisely targeted, too. The agriculture industry refined their acute toxins to target specific and narrow bandwidths of pests and rodents; in the wrong hands, it was a simple enough exercise to use the same techniques on other species. Only the attacks on fowl went wide, taking out many bird species until it was a rarity to see even a common blue jay or sparrow. Terrorists killed off other food-source species with laserlike precision, and those who ate the infected meat, of course. It didn't take long until no one ate any farmed meat at all.

That's when everyone became a hunter. Traps and sling-shots were cobbled together; the many who refused to sur-render their guns in the early days of the riots put them into service. Cats and dogs disappeared first, and then rabbits and pigeons and rodents. In one surreal episode, a grassroots en-vironmental group pasted up posters of the common brown rat all over Silva, predicting its extinction and urging people to search out vegetarian proteins.

But things had worked themselves out, hadn't they? Now there weren't enough humans left to prevent the poisoned and overhunted species from coming back. Why not? Sur-viving creatures seemed more than content to graze on the kaysev. And on each other, in the case of the carnivores. Their populations burgeoned, even thrived Aftertime.

Cass herself had come upon a nest of baby rabbits a couple of nights ago. The mother stared at her with eyes wide and yellow in the moonlight, and its heartbeat had felt impossibly fast when Cass put her hands around its soft throat.

But after a moment Cass stopped squeezing and backed away, the rabbit quivering with fear, but alive. Without tools, without fire, it would have been difficult to eat the rabbit anyway.

And it wasn't necessary. A diet of kaysev truly was ad-equate. Cass never felt full; in the language of Before she might have said that she never felt satisfied—but satisfaction was an elusive and outdated concept. *Serenity—contentment—* they seemed as unlikely for citizens as the ability to fly or read minds.

But what of the women, laughing together at the baths? What of the easy banter, the sly teasing, the gentle humor? Weren't these a sign of—if not happiness—then at least ease of mind? Had the time that passed while Cass was gone been enough to heal the survivors, the denizens of this land? To make them forget, or at least accept, the worst of the horrors, and search out things worth living for?

At the library the mood had been bleak. Loss and devastation and grief pervaded every room, every corner, every conversation. There had been talk—endless talk—but it was the talk of fear and relief and guilt and desperation, a constant discussion of odds and measures and likelihoods, as though such talk could keep them safer, could keep the churning threats at bay.

Time had passed—two months—since Cass was taken. In two months the people sheltering together at the school had become a real community, built on cooperation and friendship. And love, or at least lovemaking. Cass thought about the look that had passed between Smoke and Nora.

"Did she mind?" she asked abruptly. "You coming with me. Did Nora mind?"

Smoke said nothing for a moment, and Cass wondered if it was something she had no right to ask. Smoke had offered to accompany her, nothing more.

"Yes," he finally said. "She minded very much."

"But you came anyway." A question more than a statement.

"Yes, I came anyway. And I understand that you want to know why. But I'm not sure I can tell you. I mean, I know what answers I ought to give—that it gives my life some meaning to be able to help you. Or that in Aftertime we have to think of the greater good, not the needs of individuals. Or even that we have so little of our humanity left that we need to take every opportunity we can to remind ourselves that we aren't savages."

"Those all work for me," Cass said after a moment, trying to let him know that he was off the hook, that he didn't owe her an answer.

"Well, thanks. But the truth is…I don't love her. Nora. And maybe this was a convenient way to leave. I don't know…I just don't know."

"I'm sorry. I shouldn't have pried."

"Yeah, well…some people say I think too much. They used to say it, anyway. Now…" Smoke trailed off, and they walked in silence.

He was the sort of man who went to places other people couldn't follow, and it made her want to know more. "What did you do before? If it's okay for me to ask."

"Sure. Look, Cass—" he glanced at her, eyes flashing in the moonlight "—let's get this straight, okay, seeing as neither of us knows what's coming tonight or tomorrow or next week or next month. You can ask me anything you want. If I don't want to tell you, I won't. But I don't see where some sort of notion of, of, I don't know, propriety or whatever is going to help any of us now. And talking might help."

Might help what? Cass wondered—help to pass the time, or keep her mind off the dangers and worries, or make her forget who and what she was and how she'd got that way? But she didn't ask for clarity. "Deal," she said.

"Okay, so…I was an executive coach."

"A what?"

"I helped people figure out what was holding them back

in the professional workplace." Smoke's voice carried some dark emotion. Regret, maybe. "And then I showed them how to change."

"So you basically told other people how to do their jobs? And got paid for it?"

Smoke laughed bitterly. "I guess that's one way to sum it up. On paper, my job was to guide people to be more effective in their work through an exploration of their skills and goals and challenges." He looked away, into the night-black forest. "I was good at it. Too good."

"How could you be *too* good?"

"I got a lot of my clients because they were struggling at work. They'd been put on performance review and were in danger of losing their jobs. I was like the career consultant of last resort. And looking back on it, a lot of them were probably in trouble for a reason. I should have let things play out the way they were meant to."

"You mean, and let them get fired?"

"Not everyone's suited for every job," Smoke said through gritted teeth. "Sometimes people need to fail so they don't fuck things up for others. Sometimes systems are designed so that people who should fail *do* fail."

Cass was taken aback by his barely controlled anger. She knew she should stop, should leave the subject alone—but for some reason she longed to keep him talking.

"You went around rescuing their jobs for them. Just like you did at the church, the fire. You're the rescuer. That can be your new job description."

"Don't make me better than I am, Cass," Smoke snapped, and Cass knew that she had gone too far.

She felt herself flame with embarrassment as Smoke stalked ahead of her, his body tense. But after a few moments he waited for her to catch up. "I'm sorry. I didn't mean— It's just that I didn't do anything much, no matter what they told you."

"You got people out of the fire."

"Nothing that anyone else wouldn't have done. I was already there, it wasn't any big deal to bring the others with me."

Cass knew he was downplaying the event. She understood the impulse; being talked about got you noticed, and being noticed made you public, and then people expected you to reveal more and more of yourself.

She could respect Smoke's desire for privacy. She knew well the need to keep to the shadows. So why did she want so much to know more?

11

THE ROAD INTO SILVA WOUND THROUGH MOSTLY
unbuilt land, its cracked edges sloping into a rocky outcropping
at the edge of the forest. The dead trees could not maintain their
grip on the earth where the road carved its path, and their black
roots bore clots of earth like hungry tumors. Pinecones from
forgotten seasons lay crushed by cars that had long since stopped
running.

They walked in silence.

Before, this land was shaded no matter what the season,
the evergreens thick against the sky. Then the toxins had
blanketed the land, and the trees shed their needles and
withered in defeat, their xylem choked and strangled, their
bark black and peeling. The sun bore down on the ravaged
earth during the day; at night, as now, even the moonlight
reached all the way to the earth, covering everything with a
frisson of silver.

Here and there a cabin was set back among the few

remaining trees, mostly hunting cabins built decades ago, before the Sierras were discovered by city types looking for vacation homes with easier drives than Tahoe. In some, curtains hung neatly in the windows, cheery ruffles and valences hinting at brisk, no-nonsense women with feather dusters and oil soap. In others, the panes were broken, and window boxes hung askew, spilling dirt and dead flowers to the indifferent ground.

When they rounded a bend and Cass saw the familiar glass shop that shared a parking lot with a fireplace and hot tub store, her pulse quickened. Now she knew exactly where she was. Around the next bend, small frame houses would give way to larger ones. And then the strip mall with the KFC and the Orchard Supply Hardware. Another half mile took you to the city offices, including the old town hall with the basement where Cass had attended hundreds of A.A. meetings.

A few blocks from that was the library.

Suddenly Cass wasn't sure she was ready.

"You know where you are now," Smoke said. "You all right?"

She swallowed hard, staring across the parking lot at the ruined businesses. There were cars in the lot, but their tires had been slashed, their windshields bashed in. It was shocking, the way nearly everything had ended up in ruins during the final weeks of the Siege. Some said America had been lucky: while the country struggled with outages and dwindling resources, Canberra reported they'd run out of potable water and Seoul's citizens lay sightless and bleeding from their ears in the streets, victims of a last plague attack that no one bothered to claim. And still, across the U.S., citizens raged and rampaged. Brooklyn saw twelve thousand die in the East Water Riots. The senselessness of it amazed

Cass—how a car that was of no use to anyone now that fuel was impossible to find was attacked and ravaged until it was a heap of steel and fiberglass, every part of it assaulted and broken.

But equally surprising was the care people took in other ways, the attention they gave the smallest or most unimportant details, gestures made all the more poignant because of the unlikelihood that anyone would ever appreciate them.

The glass shop's windows were gone, the interior open to the elements, and even in the near darkness Cass could see desks overturned, computers lying on the floor. But next door, Groat Fireplace and Spa was shuttered up tight, the blinds drawn in the front door, the patio table and chairs stacked and covered.

And there was the neat pyramid of smooth stones piled in front of the door.

No one knew how the stone piles started, but before long everyone knew what they meant: there were dead inside. Bodies that had been left because of panic about contamination, or because they had reached a stage of decomposition that made it hard to move them easily, or simply because there wasn't time—and now, with the threat of attack weighing heavy on every raiding party, there was *never* time— when citizens entered a house and found the dead, the piles of stones were a respectful gesture as well as giving notice to others who might come along. If the unlikely day ever came when it was possible to clear the buildings, to give the deceased a proper burial, then the stones could be returned to the fields and creeks and flower beds they came from.

Next to the pile of stones was a second form, difficult to make out in the moonlight. "What is that...?" Cass said, pointing.

"Oh, that—a pot, I think."

"What, like a cooking pot?"

"Yes…I guess you didn't— It's a new thing, a way to tell people that there's nothing left inside worth taking. No food, no provisions. The raiders started doing that as a way to show people when a house had been emptied of anything useful. It caught on fast."

"But why a pot?"

Smoke shrugged. "Why anything? Why not a shoe or a lamp or…you know how it is. Nobody knows how these things start. Maybe a pot because it symbolizes a kitchen and food, and it's mostly food that you want in a raid. Well, food and medicine I guess. Maybe just because they're sturdy and will hold up to the elements. Does it matter?"

"So that means…someone's been in there, looking for stuff. You guys?"

"I don't know. Us, or the fire station people, or even some of the squatters."

"Squatters?"

"It's what they're—what everyone's calling people who stayed in houses."

"Even if it was their own houses?"

"Yeah, I know, but that's what they call them. Not in a shelter, you're squatting."

They passed the little clump of buildings and reached another bend in the road. Around the corner the road sloped down again and widened, sidewalks lining the street where the ranchers and foursquare houses were lined up neatly.

"Are there squatters here?" Cass asked, her stomach turning with unease. "In these houses?"

"Last time I came this way, yes, there were," Smoke said. "We've mostly been going over toward Terryville when we go raiding. There's a group sheltering there in the mall, but they've had a hard time with security. Our location's good, I think—not so many Beaters since they like to stay in towns. The school's just rural enough that we don't see as many of them. At least, not until very recently."

"Do you know which houses have people in them?" Cass asked.

Smoke looked along the row. They were walking in the middle of the street, their steps echoing slightly. "I wish I could tell you. Obviously, not the ones with the stone piles. And not like *that*." He pointed at a house whose garage door had been crumpled inward by a pickup truck that was still parked there at an odd angle, back tires digging into the front lawn. A big picture window had been shattered and furniture and lamps were strewn across the front porch.

"Maybe...there," he said, pointing at a square brick house that looked relatively unscathed, drapes drawn tight in all the windows.

Cass wondered if there were people inside, sleeping with blades next to the bed, guarding against attack, waiting for the sound of scratching at the door and windows, the moaning and frantic whining when a Beater caught the scent. She wondered what kind of person would prefer living with all that fear and uncertainty rather than sharing it with others in a shelter.

But Cass knew the answer. She knew exactly what kind of person would make such a choice—*she* would. Before Ruthie, before she had something she loved enough to keep on living, she would have dealt with evil by standing firm and alone against it. Even if—*especially* if—she knew it was a losing proposition, one that was sure to get her killed.

Cass wondered where the Beaters were nesting these days. Before she was taken, they had favored places that were open to the air but sheltered, like carports and stores with the front windows broken out. They slept a lot; it had seemed that they slept as much as half the day away, not that they ever seemed to achieve a very deep sleep.

There was a group from the library who spied on them at night. Miranda, before she was taken, had gone along a few times, taking enormous risks to watch a group that took over a service bay at a Big O Tires center. Cass never went along, but she listened to their reports, fascinated, along with everyone else.

Like newborn rats, they reported. A wriggling pile, night-blinded and restless. They slept touching, their scabbed and weeping limbs draped and entwined, almost like lovers. Some people thought they felt affection for each other, but Cass doubted it. She figured it was just familiarity—or, more likely, something even more base, an attraction based on the pathology of the disease. The Beaters' senses had been sharpened drastically—they were able to sniff the scent of citizens from dozens of feet away—perhaps their sensitivity had been sharpened as well and there was some sort of comfort to be had among their own kind.

They shared their victims, too—there was that.

"Where do they nest, now?" Cass asked.

Smoke answered reluctantly. "Peace Lutheran, still, last time we were here. The Ace garden center. Those are the big ones, and there are smaller nests in other places, too. And they seem to be roving. One night here, one night there. On the move."

Cass considered the implications. "That's not good."

"No, it's pretty much fucked. No one knows why it's happening, but everyone seems to agree that the disease is changing and developing. Or maybe it's just that the first wave of infected is reaching a new stage of the disease. I mean, it makes sense. Every stage has been well-defined.

Maybe this is just the outcome of whatever's going on, you know, in their bodies."

"You mean, like maybe they'll stop eating flesh and develop a compulsion to follow each other into the sea, like lemmings?"

"Yeah. Right," Smoke said, the beginnings of a wry smile emerging. "It doesn't hurt to dream, I guess."

They walked for a while without saying anything. The pack Cass had been given was surprisingly comfortable, the weight of the water bottles and provisions well distributed. Her borrowed clothes were clean and she liked the sensation of the washed fabrics against her skin—it had been so long since she had been comfortable.

Twice they heard the eerie crowing cries of Beaters far off in the distance, a roving gang of them out on a night wander. They seemed to be heading away, rather than drawing closer, but when Smoke took her hand she held on tightly until the night was silent again. Cass knew how lucky she'd been that her journey back had been through largely unpopulated country; Beaters generally preferred towns. Now that she was back in Silva, the things were all around. Most slept, waiting for dawn, but as Smoke had explained, some were restless enough to venture out even when they couldn't see. Cass didn't know what was worse: the thought of them night-blind and stumbling a few blocks away, or knowing that tucked away in the buildings they passed were their fetid, teeming nests.

Still, she felt like she could walk for hours, just as she had every night since she woke up, as she made her steady way back up through the foothills. On those nights, she had tried hard to empty her mind of anything but her goal—Ruthie—but occasionally she couldn't help wondering how she'd gotten so far from home. Beaters took their victims straight to their nests. The idea that they had taken her thirty miles or more out of town was unimaginable. How would they have carried her all that way? When they took a victim, one of them would sling the victim over their shoulders and others would restrain the kicking feet, the grasping hands of the terrified victim. Occasionally they would knock the victim unconscious, but that was rare. The supposition was that they were afraid they'd kill the person or stun them so badly that they weren't alert for what came later.

It seemed to be important to the Beaters that people were awake for that.

"Hey," Smoke said quietly, closing a hand on her arm, interrupting her thoughts. They were on another block like the last, lined with mature trees, small houses in various states of disrepair.

"What," Cass whispered back. Immediately her senses were on high alert. She scanned the buildings quickly, trying desperately to see into the dark shadows.

"I heard something…I think. Over there, behind that house."

"*Behind?* Or in? Because—"

And then Cass heard it, too.

12

A SHRILL, WHISTLING WAIL, NOT LOUD. IT WAS coming from the direction of a wood-shingled Cape Cod on the right side of the street, where the stick-puzzle forms of dead jasmine shrubs stood sentry in front of a lawn choked with kaysev. Cass searched wildly for the source of the sound, but saw only a limp and torn cardboard box blown by the wind against a car that had been driven up to the porch, its bumper resting on the paint-flaked wood. As she squinted she saw that a form hung from the half-open car door, but it was still and unnaturally bent, and even in the moonlight Cass could see the white of its skull through skin that had rotted away. An old kill, or a heart attack, a fever death, even an accident—Cass barely gave it a thought as the wailing grew louder. Then there was another sound, from the opposite direction, and Cass whipped her head back to the left and saw something that seized her with terror.

A pair of them. One had been a woman, Cass could see,

because her shirt wasn't buttoned and her large breasts swung free as she lurched toward them. She had no hair left, and her mouth was a ruined crusted slash where she had chewed her own lips to shreds. The other one might have been a woman or a man, impossible to tell from its too-large jeans and down vest trimmed with matted fur.

Both waved their hands, wobbling almost comically as they stumbled closer. Cass felt a scream rising in her own throat and tried to swallow it back, but she couldn't help a terrified whimper.

Smoke's hand on her arm tightened until it hurt. "Quiet," he whispered. "They're tracking us by smell and sound only."

"We've got to run," Cass whispered back. They were too close. On the right, the Beater whose moaning had first caught their attention appeared around the corner of the house. It lurched into the yard, knocking into a dead Japanese maple. The branches caught on its clothes and its wailing grew louder as it flailed at the tree, trying to disentangle a branch that had gotten hooked on its jacket.

"If we run, they will, too," Smoke said. "They'll hear our footsteps, feel the vibrations in the ground. We can't—"

"Over here!" a hoarse voice bellowed from a couple of houses down the street. "I'm putting a ladder out the window, you got fifteen seconds and then I'm pulling it back up!"

Smoke grabbed her hand and they ran. Cass looked wildly for the source of the voice, and saw something glint in the moonlight. There was a clattering of metal on wood and she spotted what was indeed a ladder flipping out the second-story window of a brick two-story several houses down on the left.

Behind them the wailing grew louder and she could hear feet slapping against pavement like pounds of meat. The monsters were faster than she would have imagined; it was rare to see them go at a full run. They always seemed so unwieldy in their bodies, as though the disease had taken away their coordination, the connection between mind and muscles.

From deeper in the neighborhood Cass heard the answering wails of Beaters awakened by the hunters' frenzy. They would crawl blindly from their holes to join the chase, stepping on each other, tripping and lashing out in their fury. They'd slow each other down at first, but nothing would keep them away once blood was spilled, and their momentum would eventually be overwhelming.

"Hurry!" the voice yelled unnecessarily, and as they crossed the yard, Cass felt Smoke's hand at her back giving her a hard shove so that she nearly plowed into the ladder dangling against the side of the house.

"Go," Smoke urged, and Cass seized the ladder's frame and pulled herself up to the first rung, feeling the burn of the effort in the muscles of her arms, the adrenaline surge through her body. But the Beaters' huffing and moaning was close, so close, and as she shimmied her feet onto the bottom rung and hauled herself up, she couldn't help turning to look.

She nearly fell when she saw the half-naked womanthing with its breasts slapping against its chest as it stumble-ran blindly toward them, its mouth wide with fury, its night-blind eyes looking at nothing, its arms stretched out in front, grasping at empty air. Its companion stumbled on the curb and fell flat on the ground, facedown in the dead sod, and screamed with rage as it struggled to its feet. Coming fast from the other direction was the Beater who'd been lurking across the street; it was headed straight for a car that was parked in the house's driveway, pumping its fists in time with its steps.

Down the street came more of them, loping and staggering and waving their hands blindly in front of their sightless eyes as they followed the sounds of the others, greedily sniffing the air for the scent.

"Don't look!" Smoke yelled, shoving at her feet to urge her higher, and Cass sucked in her breath and climbed, hand over hand as fast as she could, but not before she saw that the first Beater was going to reach Smoke before he could follow her up the ladder, and the scream kept winding up in her chest. She could not watch them take him. She *would* not watch them take him. Especially because it was her fault, because he had—

She heard a grunt and a dull thud as strong hands grabbed hers and yanked, causing her to lose her footing on the ladder, but she realized after a moment it didn't matter because she was being pulled through the window, the top rung of the ladder scraping painfully against her ribs and hipbones, and she twisted desperately in her rescuer's grip because even though she couldn't bear to see Smoke taken she *had* to watch because it was her fault and it would never have happened without her and she could do very little in this life, this ruined and fucked-up life, but she *would* pay what she owed, and right now she owed Smoke witness to his last moments.

But Smoke was on the ladder.

Smoke was on the ladder and he was climbing fast, skipping rungs, big hands grabbing hard, and behind him the first Beater was sprawled on the ground below the ladder, scrabbling to right itself like a beetle on its back, as its companion tripped and fell on top of it.

Cass hit the floor and rolled and a second later Smoke

landed beside her and a large dark shadowy form of a man hauled the ladder clumsily back through the window. She had to duck out of the way as the ladder's full length was dragged into the room and dropped on the floor with a heavy clatter, and then the man put his hands to the window sash and slammed it down so hard the panes shook, and even then they could still hear the furious moaning of the Beaters below them.

"That'll fry their bacon," the man said with a ghost of a chuckle.

Cass turned frantically to Smoke, her pulse still rocketing, and put a hand to his chest, feeling the heat of his body through his cotton shirt. "You were—they almost—"

"They *didn't*," Smoke said, covering her hand with his own and pressing it against him for a brief second before he deliberately separated himself from her grasp. "That's what matters."

"I've had so many close calls I guess I don't even hardly count anymore," the big man said. There was a trace of the South in his voice, the rasp of someone who hadn't spoken in a while—but there was energy and humor, too. Whoever their savior was, he was not a beaten man. "I think I musta got some sorta guardian angel in here with me or something."

"You saved us," Smoke said.

"Ah, it was a slow night, didn't have anything better to do. Hell, they're *all* slow nights, you know what I mean? I'm Lyle. Welcome to my place."

"I'm Smoke. This is Cass."

"Why don't y'all come on down with me to the basement. Seein' as it's a special night and all, I might break out the good stuff."

He was already lumbering through the door into a hallway. Cass looked around the room; in the faint moonlight from the window, she saw the sort of simple furnishings that looked like they might have been there for several generations: a simple wood-post bed, dresser, upholstered chair. The outline of pictures on the walls. A mirror over the dresser casting a ghostly reflection.

"You'll want to hold on to the rail," Lyle called over his shoulder. "I've cleared out all the rugs and whatnot, so's I could get around better at night, but it wouldn't do to go breakin' your neck after you just escaped them critters."

"Funny guy," Smoke muttered as they followed him down the stairs. Cass held tight to the rail, placing her feet on each step with care. She'd traveled at night for weeks now, but there had usually been enough moon or starlight that she could walk with a reasonable measure of confidence. Occasionally she'd trip over some unseen root or rock, but she was fit and nimble and hadn't suffered anything worse than bruises and a cut or two.

Here, though, inside the house, the dark was absolute except for the thinnest slivers of moonlight between the boards on the windows. As they descended to the first floor, there was no stray light at all. Cass guessed Lyle had pulled the drapes tight—she'd do the same, if it was her, to avoid seeing the Beaters when they came shuffling around.

"Down the hall here," Lyle said. "And then there's the basement stairs to the right. Watch out, they ain't got risers. You don't want to go poking a foot through and breaking your ankle. Come on in and shut the door behind you and I'll spark up a light."

Cass followed behind Smoke, slipping her hand into his back pocket. The gesture felt too intimate, almost presumptuous, but she needed to hold on to something. She could feel his warmth through the denim. With her free hand she felt along the wall, brushing her fingers against wallpaper, a door frame, the entrance to the basement stairs.

She was the last onto the landing, and she closed the door tight behind them. Lyle snapped on a flashlight and Cass blinked against the sudden pool of thin light that illuminated rickety wooden stairs, an unfinished basement, and Lyle himself at the bottom, busying himself at a card table loaded with supplies. His face was obscured by a length of thick brown hair collected into a loose ponytail at his neck. As she made her way down the rest of the stairs he looked up and she saw a face with a full beard and kind eyes set in a network of wrinkles that made his smile look almost mischievous.

He set the flashlight upright on the table so it pointed up at the ceiling, filling the room with a ghostly light that cast crazy shadows on the unfinished concrete walls. He held out a hand, first to Smoke, who shook it without hesitation, and then to Cass. She was surprised at how careful his touch was, how soft his palm.

"Now this ain't exactly the Ritz," Lyle said, "but I got it set up comfy enough, I guess. Ain't any light can get out of here and these walls are twelve inches thick so those nasty fuckers won't give us any trouble tonight. When they can't smell you, they just wander off like the dumbasses they are."

He dragged an old upholstered rocker closer to the light and then went to a makeshift storage unit constructed of plywood and concrete blocks and pushed objects around, talking the whole time.

"Cass, honey, you sit yourself down in the nice chair. Us fellas can sit our asses on the fold-ups. I know they're back here somewhere…my wife used to have this place organized like the fuckin' Library of Congress or something. Probably would of alphabetized it if I let her..."

Cass considered refusing their host's chair, but it looked so comfortable and she was still shaking so badly from their narrow escape that she collapsed into it gratefully. It smelled of aftershave and tobacco, and the well-worn cushions sank under her tired body.

"Okay, here we go," Lyle said, coming back with a pair of folding metal chairs. "Sorry, Smoke, buddy, I'd go up to the kitchen for a couple of nicer chairs but I don't see no sense getting our friends out there all riled up again."

"They can hear you through the walls up there?" Cass asked.

"No, ma'am, I don't think so, but you see, they know I'm in here. Me and Travers across the street—why, ever since they figured out we were here it's just about been driving them nuts. They come around every day, whole mobs of 'em, wander back and forth between our places, moaning and carrying on like a bunch of horny teenagers going on a panty raid. Oh. Excuse me, Cass, I don't mean to be crude, it's just been a while since I've had any need of, uh, whadda you wanna call it, *social skills*." He laughed, a rich, booming sound, and reached for a Tupperware box on a nearby shelf.

"It's okay," Cass said. "I don't mind."

Smoke took the seat next to her, lowering himself with care. Cass had noticed that all his motions were deliberate. He struck her as a careful man, one who did little without forethought. She wondered if that was a result of the work he'd done Before, or if he had always been that way.

"So they've been coming around for a while?" Smoke asked. "You been here the whole time?"

"Yes, sir, I hunkered down when the shit hit the fan and I ain't moved. Got nothing against folks who want to band together, but I guess you can say I'm a natural loner. Them Rebuilders—you heard about them?—I got no need to get myself bossed around, you know?"

Smoke's expression tightened. "How do you know we're not Rebuilders?"

Lyle barked out a laugh. "No offense, boss, but Rebuilders don't go out without some serious firepower. They ain't fearless...they're just well armed. You were a Rebuilder, you woulda shot those fuckers and then held me up for good measure."

"Shooting wouldn't have done much good, not even if I was a better shot than I am—there must have been a dozen of them closing in on us."

A Beater could be felled by a bullet, but only if the shooter was using a heavy gauge and nailed the brain or the spine. Hit anywhere else, even in the heart or the gut—shots that would take down a citizen—a Beater could keep going for crucial seconds, even minutes, as it took its time bleeding out. Even a dying Beater would keep trying to claw its way toward a potential victim until its last breath left its body.

"Those Rebuilders train all day long," Lyle said. "A lot of 'em could hit my left nut from across town with one eye shut. But I take your point."

Smoke relaxed slightly. "I've had...a run-in with them myself. Don't much care for their philosophy, but I don't know that I've got what it takes to live like this, on my own, either."

"You might say I'm not much of a joiner," Lyle said as he settled his own large body onto the remaining chair and started going through the box. "I might be a stupid son of a bitch trying to tough it out here on my own. Me and Travers, he's just as stubborn as me. And them Beaters getting smarter, our odds ain't great. Only been a week or so they've started doing what you might call a regular patrol through here."

Lyle took out a folded plastic bag and carefully opened it, shaking out a half-smoked, tight-rolled joint. "I been saving this sweet little blunt for a special occasion, ain't a whole lot more where it came from, least until I figure out how to smoke me some kaysev, if you know what I mean. I'd be honored if you'd finish it up with me."

"I…not for me," Cass said quickly.

Lyle nodded and sparked up a lighter, a cheap plastic Bic he took from the box. "I got a little bit of Johnnie Black up there on the shelf, too, if you're interested."

"No, thanks. I'm, uh… I'm an alcoholic."

There was an awkward silence, while Cass kept her features as still as she could. It was not the first time she'd made such an admission, not by a long shot. But it was the first in Aftertime. There'd been drinking in the library; for some, the days were a lot easier to take through a haze of inebriation, a notion Cass understood all too well. But Bobby had put a stop to that; he designated the men's bathroom as a place people could go if they wanted to get drunk, there and nowhere else, and it was a testament to his power over all of them that everyone cooperated.

Cass had found the men's bathroom easy to resist. She'd never been much of a social drinker anyway. She had liked to numb herself in solitude.

"No worries, little sister," Lyle said softly. "I can put this away if that's easier."

"No, no—you go ahead."

He hesitated, his gaze traveling to the scars on her arm. He sighed and reached out to touch them, so gently that his callused fingertips tickled. "You've had a rough road," he said softly, and Cass realized that Lyle thought she'd made the scars herself.

Cass resisted the urge to hide them, to jam her hands under her legs. Instead she gestured to the box and forced a smile. "It's fine, really. Come on, someone around here might as well get a buzz on."

"Well, okay, if you insist. But just say the word..."

He took a deep draw on the joint, squeezing it delicately between his large, stubby finger and thumb, and held the smoke in, concentrating with his eyes shut and a look of intense pleasure on his lined face.

"That's the ticket," he finally said, and passed it along to Smoke.

Smoke took a hit before passing it back. "Not sure I know how to thank you for the hospitality."

"No problem. Mind telling me what has y'all out on the streets, anyway? Ain't any water in this block, and the raiders—no offense—but the raiders usually seem a little better organized than you two."

Cass glanced at Smoke; he returned her gaze with concern but didn't speak. He was leaving it up to her.

She considered not telling. Twenty-four hours ago, no one knew her story. The only people who knew about Ruthie were the others at the library, and even they didn't know the full story, since she'd only had her daughter back for a day before the attack. Besides, there was no way to know how many of the people who were there that day were even still alive.

But what would it hurt, now, to tell the truth? The old shame that had weighed so heavily was gone now, vanished along with everything else familiar from Before. She, like all the other citizens, had been given a fresh start. True, it came at a terrible price, and there was no way to know how long they had remaining, but Cass had wasted enough in her lifetime. Or lifetimes.

She wasn't going to waste any more opportunities. She pulled her knees up to her chest and wrapped her arms around them. The chair rocked slightly with the motion.

"I'm looking for my daughter."

13

"ARE YOU, NOW?" LYLE ENCOURAGED HER WITH a smile as he and Smoke passed the joint back and forth. "You have a little one?"

"She's almost three. Her name is Ruthie. She was at the library when I was...when I had to leave."

Lyle narrowed his eyes and waited, but Cass forced herself to take a breath and let it out slowly. Lyle probably thought she'd done something reckless while she was drunk, gotten expelled from the library. Well, let him think it. The truth would only make things worse—how likely was he to let her stay, if he knew what she was hiding under her shirt? If he knew what she had been? If he were to start imagining the things she couldn't remember doing?

"And you think your little girl's here in town?"

Cass nodded. "We were sheltering at the library. It was two months ago. Do you ever get over there?"

"Not so much inside the place. If I see raiding parties

out, I'll go along and lend a hand. Once in a while they've checked up on me and Travers over there, a few other stubborn assholes like us who insist on squatting. But I haven't heard of any kids, really. And I'm sorry, I'm not sure I would have remembered if they were talking about it—I don't know the first thing about kids."

Cass tried to cover her disappointment. "That's okay. I'll know soon enough."

Lyle nodded. "You're welcome to stay with me as long as you want. I reckon you're anxious to get moving again, especially now that you're so close, but I'm guessing the rat bastards are going to be hanging around for a while, anyway. Usually they just fuck around during the day, but now and then, like tonight, a few of 'em'll show up trying to trick me into coming out."

"You think they've evolved that much...awareness?" Smoke said, waving away the joint, which was burned almost all the way down.

Lyle took a last big puff and stubbed the spent butt out on a jar lid before he answered. "Tough to say. They don't seem any smarter than before. If anything they've lost all their, you know, whadda you want to call it, their language skills. You know how they used to say little odds and ends, almost make you think like they had something going on upstairs?"

He tapped his head for emphasis, a long coil of his brown hair springing out of the elastic.

"Yes...a few words at a time, little phrases..." Smoke said.

"Yeah, that. Well, they aren't doing much of that anymore. Now it's all this wailing and snorting and shit, like they're a bunch of rutting pigs. Only pigs are probably a damn sight smarter than they are."

"But their habits—" Smoke said carefully.

"They still look like a bunch of fucked-up retards on the

dance floor when they walk, and you still see them doing all kinds of freaky shit like they're trying to remember what it was like to be human. Like I saw this one out there with a doll, taking her dress off and putting it on again. Course then it pulled the doll's hair out. Or just the other day, here comes a couple of 'em with a wheelbarrow. I'm not shittin' you, they've got this thing loaded up with a bunch of bricks and a watering can and I don't know what else kind of crap...and they're trying to wheel it down the street, only they ain't got any balance and it's just dumpin' shit out and then they stop and try to put it back in. Best entertainment I've had for weeks, I'll tell ya, watching those two assclowns. Finally they just left the whole mess next door in my old neighbor Bess's yard, right in the flower beds. Oh, that old bitch woulda loved *that,* I'll tell you."

Lyle chuckled, a deep satisfied sound that amazed Cass. He genuinely seemed amused by what was just one more chronicle of how horrifying the world had become. Cass wondered how he did it...surely a little weed wasn't the only answer.

If it *was,* she'd happily light up.

If she thought drinking would help, she'd go right back to it.

Only she knew better. Drinking had taken away her pain, for a while. But it hadn't given her anything back but emptiness. And if she ever wanted emptiness that badly again, she'd just kill herself, hang herself from a light fixture in an abandoned house or slide a blade into the soft flesh of her wrist. It wasn't like she'd be the first.

"But you said they're stalking you, here," Smoke said. "Like they keep track of which houses have squatters. They're not just responding to catching a scent or seeing movement through the glass or..."

"Oh, for sure. Ain't any doubt about that."

"That's no good," Smoke said heavily.

"Hell, no, it ain't. It's fucked, is what it is."

"So they've got some sort of memory. And planning. I mean even if it's just rudimentary."

"Yeah, I guess you could say that. It's like they're all in on it, figuring out how they can work together. They'll do anything if there's a chance they can bring down a live citizen. They'll bang their heads into a wall until they're dead, long as the wall gives way even a little bit. And after one does it, the rest figure out if you bang on the wall long enough it'll break, and then next time it's all of 'em bangin' their heads. They're fuckin' unstoppable."

"Yeah, that's a bit newish, but still different from, you know, waiting for you to come out."

Lyle shrugged. "I figure waiting around probably feels about like head-banging to them. Sometimes I go up to the window upstairs and holler at them just to watch them get all pissed off. They'll throw themselves at the house for a while, climb on top of each other trying to get to the top windows—the lower ones are all boarded up now. One time I pushed a dresser out the window on one of 'em, broke its skull clean in half." He chuckled. "Good times… 'Course I had to drag it away later myself."

"How do you…" Cass gestured around the basement. The shelves were well stocked with supplies: cans and boxes of food, paper towels and toilet paper. "I mean, what do you, um—"

"What do I do all day?" Lyle chuckled, the sound rumbling deep in his chest. "Fair question. Well, I go out every single day. I don't aim to let the fuckers keep me cooped up. I mean, I ain't crazy, I usually go right after nightfall or right before dawn, you hardly ever see one of 'em out then. It's about four blocks to the Horseshoe, so that's a big feature of my day, 'cause I take four or five jugs with me."

The Horseshoe was a branch of the Stanislaus River that wound through town. A walking path had been laid several years back, and young mothers with strollers brought stale bread for their kids to feed the ducks, Before. Cass had taken Ruthie there when she was a baby.

"So what else," Lyle continued, ticking his activities off on his thick fingers. "Well, I go poking around in folks' sheds and garages and whatnot, see if I can find anything useful. And I been digging a new latrine…over in Bess's backyard, in fact. Dug it right next to those fuckin' roses she was so damn nuts over. If I had a nickel for every time she came over here to bitch and moan about my tree dropping plums on her rosebushes…and she had a yappy little dog, too, but luckily she took it with her when she moved on down to the library. Though I suppose someone's made dogburgers out of it by now."

Cass exchanged a glance with Smoke. When she'd been at the library, there had been a no-pets policy. Bobby had been firm on that; resources were to go to humans. Anyone who didn't like it could try their luck living on their own, outside, with their dog or cat.

Bess had undoubtedly given up her dog in exchange for safety; everyone did. Some of the most hard-core people thought that all animals brought to the library ought to be relinquished for food, but in that regard Bobby showed one of his infrequent moments of public compassion. He himself would offer to take the pet to the edge of town, where dogs could join the feral pack sometimes seen scavenging there, and cats could climb the shredded bark of dead eucalyptus.

"Were you married…? I mean, were you living alone during the Siege?" Cass asked, fascinated.

"No, luckily my last wife took on out of here a couple of years ago, back when you could still buy a bag of flour for under ten bucks. Better for her, I imagine. She hooked up with this guy from Sacramento, had a boat dealership up that way, I expect he was able to set her up pretty well, maybe take care of her during...everything. Hope so, anyway."

For the first time a troubled look crossed his face, a flicker of sadness. "I *was* fond of that one," he added softly.

Smoke shook his head, smiling. "Well, my hat's off to you, keeping yourself busy. I can think of worse ways to spend the apocalypse."

"This ain't the apocalypse, buddy, we already done *lived* through that," Lyle exclaimed, smacking Smoke on the shoulder and bellowing out a laugh. "We're the *survivors,* man. You got to remember that. Don't know how much longer we'll be around, but every day I walk outside and I give those hell-creatures a big fuck you and I figure I'm still ahead."

"You know what some people say," Smoke said, his voice oddly hollow. "Stamp out the blueleaf, we can end this in one generation. I haven't seen any sign of it since late June. It can't survive the heat."

"*I've* seen it," Cass said. "Not nearly as much as...before, and it's kind of dry and there's dead leaves on the plants, but it's out there."

Smoke stared at her, his brows knit, his expression opaque. It was almost as though he was trying to decide if she was lying.

"If it's out there, it won't be for long," he finally said. "They were invented in a lab. Kaysev's thriving, blueleaf isn't—what that says to me is the blueleaf's not going to stand up to evolution."

"Careful, friend," Lyle said gently. "You're back into theories now, and ain't any knowing when it comes to theories. You'll drive yourself crazy, you go down that path."

"All I'm saying is, you make shit in laboratories, it's probably pretty easy to get it wrong. People aren't God."

"Or else the blueleaf will develop a resistance," Cass said. She didn't like the edge in Smoke's voice. It made him seem more vulnerable. "Evolve into a new strain, a stronger one. A super-blueleaf."

"Super-blueleaf?" Smoke repeated, his voice laced with sarcasm. "That a technical term?"

Cass pressed her lips together, stung. This was a side of Smoke she hadn't seen before, an unkind side.

"I'm sorry," he said immediately. "I'm sorry, Cass, I didn't mean that. I just...I don't know, I didn't think first."

Cass waited only a second before she nodded, biting her lip. Maybe he was right, maybe the blueleaf was already dying out.

Blue Means Trouble. That was the frantic cry that went up around town, even before anyone understood the full horror of the disease. In the first weeks after the smaller, blue-tinged plants appeared among the sturdier kaysev, a quarter of the town's remaining population died, dark bile bubbling at their lips as they went into convulsions. The old and sick and very young had to be buried in trenches; the last of the fuel that hadn't already been raided went to powering the earth-moving equipment, and nearly every healthy young person helped out with the task.

Then they found out what else the blue leaves did to you.

Blue Means Trouble. The children who survived learned to run screaming for an adult when they saw the distinctive leaves with their slightly feathered edges; the adults learned to gather and burn the plants. The blueleaf strain was susceptible to the sun and heat, unlike its stronger cousin; by late May it had begun to die off on its own, unable to tolerate the Sierra summer climate.

"You're right," Lyle nodded. "Nobody's seen a one of them things since summer 'round here. But how do we know they're not thriving up north? Even if it can't root down south now, what's to prevent it from adapting, like Cass here says? The government's been up to some crazy shit—you can't tell me kaysev's not a whole new branch of botany or whatever the fuck science it is. You can make a plant like that, you can make a fucking variation for every climate."

"But nobody would—no sane person would eat the blue-leaf now," Cass protested. She was something of an expert on self-destruction, and in A.A. she'd seen just about every variety of desperation, but surely no one would choose the Beater's fate on purpose.

Lyle shrugged. "That's not the only way it's spread."

"Anyone who's attacked now ends up dead in forty-eight hours," Smoke said, almost angrily. "It's not like early days."

Early days, when the Beaters would occasionally attack their quarry in the streets, they could be overpowered—shot or cut or bludgeoned, if not to death at least into submission—and the victims brought home with a few bites, only to start to go feverish hours later. Soon the Beaters changed their tactics and started carrying their victims back to their nests.

"You're sure about that?" Lyle asked. "What if they get close, but you get away? Maybe you got a scratch or two, but you think you're okay. You going to be willing to wait and wonder?"

"It's only spread through saliva," Smoke said. "A scratch can't hurt you. And their blood can't infect you."

"You gonna stake your life on it? Only, it wouldn't be your life, now would it...it's everyone who gets left behind. Lemme show you something."

He dug into his pocket and showed them his open palm, on which they could see a small brown pill. "Potassium cyanide," he said matter-of-factly. "Got it from a buddy of mine was in the service, he picked 'em up overseas somewhere. Gave one to Travers across the street. If the Beaters get too close to me someday, I'll pop this sucker—I'll be out of my mind before those fuckers get their teeth in me, dead quick enough to spoil their party."

"That's noble, I guess," Smoke said, in a tone that clearly said otherwise.

"Hey, I never claimed to have all the answers," Lyle said, holding up his hands in surrender. "But if there's even a chance I could end up being a carrier or something, if there's Beater blood messing up my DNA, I'd rather be dead than accidentally spit on someone. I mean, I've heard the same things you have. About the spit being the only way. But let me ask you something, how exactly can anyone be sure since there hasn't been any research done since long before the first Beater took its first bite?"

No one spoke for a moment, and then Lyle dropped his hands and gave a crooked smile. "Aw, don't listen to me. I'm just a dumbass making the best of it out here in the trenches. I didn't mean to pick any fights, either. Truth is, I'm glad for the company. Don't know about you, but I believe I'll turn in for a while. I hardly ever sleep a night through anymore, but I get a few hours now, then a few hours in the afternoon... Anyway, let me show you where you can bunk up."

He was already on his feet, closing the cover on his stash and setting the Tupperware box on a shelf next to a box marked Christmas Decorations.

What he'd said... Cass reeled from the horror of the possibility that she carried within her the seeds of the disease, that she could infect others. But she would know, her body would tell her. She had become a scholar of her own body, fine-tuned to its needs, the cycle of craving and release and addiction and recovery. She knew exactly when her period was coming, when a tendril of pain would bloom into a full-blown headache, when a twinge signaled a simple muscle pull and when it was something more serious.

If the poison was within her she'd know.

Wouldn't she?

SMOKE OFFERED CASS HIS HAND, AND SHE allowed him to help her out of the old chair. They followed Lyle up the basement stairs. At the landing he turned and said regretfully, "I think we'd better leave the light here. I don't like to get 'em riled up at night. They keep thumpin' and scratchin' at the walls if they see lights on in here, makes it hard to sleep."

He set the flashlight on the landing and led them back down the first floor hall, up the steps to the second floor, where moonlight seeped through the windows.

"This is me," Lyle said, pointing to the room they'd come through earlier, when he rescued them. "Y'all take the guest room there. It's got a nice queen bed."

"Oh, we're not—" Cass said, realizing he meant for them to sleep together. Then she shut her mouth, embarrassed. There were only two rooms, separated by a small bathroom.

"I'll take the floor," Smoke said.

"I didn't mean to make assumptions, but you got a shot at a bed here, why not take it?" Lyle said. "Might as well get a good night's rest when you can."

"It's all right," Cass said. "I mean, we can share. It's just..."

Just nothing, just a man and woman, exhausted from fear and adrenaline. No doubt they'd be out the minute they hit the bed. There was nothing suggestive or sexual about it.

Aftertime was about needs. Basic necessities. Social conventions had long since disappeared. Two people could share a pail of water, or a can of peas, or a bed and it meant nothing more than survival—another day or hour or minute on a planet that had grown increasingly inhospitable.

"There's a bucket in the bathroom," Lyle said. "I wish I could offer you better. I clean it out every day, though, and I keep a stack of clean rags in there. I wash 'em down at the creek. I've never been the best housekeeper, but I guess it'll do."

"Thank you," Smoke said. "Seriously, man. I'm sorry I got a little testy with you back there—"

Lyle held up a hand to stop him. "No worries, my friend. I reckon all our nerves are shot to hell. I'm honored to have you. Y'all take first shift in the john if you want—I'll be up for a while."

Cass went first. After, she rested her hands on the sink and gazed at the mirror. She could see very little in the moonlight—but it was the first time she'd seen her reflection at all.

Her face was smooth, unmarked. Her lips were dry and chapped, but there were no signs that she'd chewed them. She felt a faint stirring of hope—maybe she'd recovered before she got really bad. Before...she'd had a chance to do anything reprehensible.

She touched her cheeks with her fingertips, tentatively. She was lucky not to have been bitten there. Whatever it was—*whoever* it was—who rescued her from the Beaters' feeding frenzy, they had been quick. There hadn't been time for the Beaters to consume anything more than the strips of flesh from her back.

Cass's hands went automatically to the small of her back, the wounds she could reach. Near her tailbone was a raw patch where, as far as she could tell, a section of skin about four inches long had been ripped away. When she first woke, her exploring fingers touched something wet and the pain was unbearable, and it had been days before she could stand to touch herself again.

The Beaters loved only flesh. Skin. They did not eat muscle or sinew or bone, and they chewed sections of flesh free and then peeled them away, their jaw strength magnified by the disease and by their furious hunger. For that reason the wounds they made tended to be elongated, shreds and strips peeled away. Of course, when they were done it didn't matter, since they feasted until little was left. Skinned, but otherwise intact, their victims were left alive and in agony, their deaths hours or days away. They died in the throes of the fever, but at least they never lived long enough to turn into monsters.

But Cass's attackers had presumably been interrupted. How, and by whom, she had no idea. Still, she was grateful that the Beaters had time to tear only a half-dozen holes in her back, from the base of her spine to her shoulder blades.

She pulled her shirt over her shoulders and slowly turned until she could see her back in the mirror, dreading her reflection, but the wounds weren't the festering and oozing things she feared they would be. They were healing, regrowing flesh where it had been taken. In the mirror they seemed to glisten, pale layers of skin filming over the red and raw underlayers.

Cass realized she had been holding her breath and turned back, pulling on her shirt as she exhaled slowly. Her hair, soft from its recent shampoo, stuck out in jagged clumps where Smoke had sheared it off, but at least it didn't look like she'd pulled it out herself. She looked a little like a punk rocker from thirty years earlier—her mother's time, when women used to cut their hair short and spike it. She thought of wetting it down to tame it and her hands went automatically to the faucet and turned the handle before she remembered the futility of the gesture. Water had not run in these pipes in months.

As the Siege worsened, it eventually became clear that not only did the government not have the ability to repel the relentless bioterrorist attacks—they were never going to be able to identify with certainty who had unleashed them. The toxins were manufactured in Japan, Russia, even Finland, outsourced across a thousand corporate shells, but terrorist groups in Greece and Sri Lanka and Colombia and Somalia took credit along with the usual suspects. As every major food crop was decimated and livestock lay rotting in stinking shallow graves, people's fears morphed into a terrible fury. Rioting, roving bands of citizens stormed every municipal and government office and the very people who were trying desperately to hold on to order were either dragged out and beaten, or ran for their lives. One by one, substations on the power grid flickered out; water stopped running through the municipal pipes; cell towers went dark. And still, everyone kept making mistakes, forgetting that the light switches no longer turned on lights, that faucets wouldn't deliver water, that phones wouldn't ring or connect anyone, that stoplights would never guide them and toilets would never flush. It took a while, but eventually everyone adapted. The things from Before—the hydrants and lamp poles and public restrooms—gradually, they became just another part of the landscape, unnoticed and untouched.

And yet here she was, hands turning the cold knobs, expecting water to fill the basin. Cass closed her eyes and focused on the sensation; she could almost feel the water rushing over her fingers. She imagined water arcing from a drinking fountain, remembered how it felt pooling in her mouth, cold against her tongue. She remembered a garden hose on a hot day, testing the water dribbling out of it and waiting until the sun-heated water ran cool before putting a thumb over the nozzle and making a rainbow-dappled spray for Ruthie to run through. Droplets sparkled like a thousand tiny crystals in the sun.

Anguish seized Cass—not just a longing for another time, but a sense that she herself was lost, that her exile from the rest of the world had left her without a place to return to. She was missing two months of her life, and during that time, the world had moved on without her. The Beaters had evolved. Citizens had evolved, too. The shelters were full of survivors who made homes inside the schools and libraries and supermarkets and churches. In the time since she was taken, they had shared meals and made friends. They'd buried their dead and given birth and made love. They'd cried and grieved and laughed and created new memories.

And she had not been there.

Cass was alone, like she had always been alone, since the day her father walked out the door and her mother hardened and changed into someone else. The bad decisions she made in high school only grew more desperate as she pushed everyone away. She piled failure onto disappointment until there was no path back. Eventually her friendships atrophied and disintegrated and the only people in her life were the people she drank with or fucked.

For a brief, shining time there was Ruthie. Ruthie brought Cass back to life, Ruthie helped her start to be a person again. Until that dark moment when she stumbled, when her darkness reached up for her and pulled her down again, and maybe Mim and Byrn were right—maybe they had to take Ruthie away from her, maybe they had no choice because Cass didn't deserve her.

Cass ground her knuckles hard against the porcelain of the sink until her bones ached. She'd finally gotten Ruthie back, only to fail her again. She'd had her daughter less than one day before she carelessly let the danger in. She'd almost let her daughter die a horrible death.

A sound came from her throat, a strangled whimper.

There was a knocking on the door, and then it swung open and Smoke was there. "Are you all right? Cass?"

His hand hovered in the air, as though he was afraid to touch her, and he said her name again.

"Cass?"

Slowly, she raised her face to the mirror and this time when she looked at herself there was a sparkle of tears in the moonlight, and Cass realized that she was crying for the first time since the day the social workers had come for Ruthie.

She stared at her ghostly reflection in disbelief, and it was only when Smoke took her by the shoulders and turned her toward him, when he reached a gentle hand toward her face to brush away her tears, that she shoved him.

"*No.*"

Immediately he put his hands in the air and backed up into the door. "I'm sorry. I didn't mean—"

"You don't understand. It's—it's what Lyle said. I could be

a…" She swallowed, hard. "A *carrier.* You know, I could have it in me, the disease. It could be in my tears."

Smoke shook his head. "No, Cass. No. I don't believe that. And even if it were possible, it wouldn't be your tears. Just your saliva."

"You don't know that. That's just a rumor."

"Not for sure, maybe, but there's a guy at the school, came out from UCSF in the early days of the Siege. One of the last ones to make it before the roads got all fucked up. He was a researcher, in infectious disease. He knew his shit, Cass. And he said it's like with rabies. You get it from being bitten, from an infected animal's saliva, and even if there's traces of the virus in other body systems it's not enough to cause infection. He said they tested one of them. One of the Beaters. Before they lost power in the lab. They didn't get very far, but the abnormalities or whatever were in the saliva, and they found traces in the spinal fluid and internal organs but at such a low level that it wasn't enough to pass on the disease."

"He could have been making it up, he could have been crazy, he—"

"Yes," Smoke interrupted. "Yes, he could have been lying. But I choose to believe him. That's all we can do anymore… is to choose what we're going to believe and what not to believe."

This time when he traced his thumb gently along her cheek, Cass stayed still. When he grazed the tender skin below her eyes, her tears spilled over and splashed hot on his skin, but he did not flinch.

"What happened to him?" Cass whispered. "The scientist."

"He moved on. He felt it was only a matter of time before the Beaters spread east, he figured within a year they'd have reached the Midwest and South. But he went north.... He thought the Beaters might not be able to handle colder climates."

"You believe that?"

Smoke said nothing, but his fingertips traced her hairline, over her ears, settled under her chin. "Yeah, maybe," he finally said. "I mean they're still human. Kind of. They'd die of exposure when the temperatures go below freezing, so I think there's a good chance they'll naturally keep moving south with the weather. Look, let's not talk about all this anymore now. Come with me, Cass. Let's lie down. I'll stay awake with you until you fall asleep. Let me help—you don't need to feel so alone."

Cass ducked her chin. The moment was broken; she was done crying for now. She followed Smoke out of the bathroom and into the guest room, and as he closed the door silently behind them she turned the bedcovers down and slid between the sheets. They were marvelously cool and silky against her skin. They smelled like fabric softener, and Cass realized that they hadn't been slept in since the last time they were washed.

Smoke unbuttoned his shirt, taking his time and watching her watching him in the moonlight. He slid it off and folded it and laid it on a chair. Then he took off his belt and boots and socks and dropped them to the floor. He got in the bed next to her, slowly, carefully, leaving an expanse of white sheet between them. He propped himself up on an elbow and gazed at her and she couldn't help it, she sucked in her breath and felt her skin grow hot.

Being watched like this...Cass felt the old stirring, the need that had always made itself known to her without subtlety. Whenever she felt her solitude too acutely, the weight of all her terrible decisions, there was only one way to block it out, and that was to smother it with something stronger.

She had started using sex to obliterate the pain when she was a senior in high school. A few years later she'd evolved it into a high art, learning to attract and control and barter, and for a while that was enough. But over time it took greater and greater risks, sheer heights and breathless drops, to satisfy her need for release.

Drinking helped. But drinking only masked the need. It never took it away. And there had been plenty of nights when she didn't manage to pass out before she had to satisfy the hunger that wouldn't be quieted. Plenty of nights when she'd done things that skated a very thin line between pleasure and pain, when she didn't recognize her own cries, couldn't tell if they were anguish or satisfaction.

Ruthie had been conceived on such a night. Only, Cass had no idea which one. There had been too many.

Now, the old swirl was hot within her, the rushing, dizzying bloom of need and fury that felt like molten iron and burning acid all at once, a killing thirst that demanded to be slaked. But something was wrong. Instead of anger, it had been stoked by fear. Fear...and loneliness. And these emotions could never be powerful enough. They could never force her to do what anger could do—because she was a creature of rage, she burned white-hot when she drank and fucked and ran miles through the foothills, when she pushed her muscles her lungs her legs so hard they screamed out for release. Without her rage she was nothing but emptiness, a shell of a person.

And yet the swirling need was there, threatening to overtake her if she didn't satisfy it. How long had it been since— Cass's mind raced as she realized she hadn't touched herself, hadn't had even that pale substitute, since she woke in her matted bed of dead weeds. How was that possible? All these long days on the road, and Cass had never once missed the touch of a man…or even the satisfaction of her own hands… until now, with Smoke next to her, Smoke whose eyes glinted even in the dark.

"I can't—I need—" she started to say, but she didn't know what came next.

"It's nothing to be ashamed of," Smoke said, his voice little more than a low vibration that traveled from his body through the soft clean sheets and blankets and mattress and pillows and into her body, spreading out from the middle, sounds and sensations that broke apart and reformed as more than just words.

"I'm not ashamed," she whispered back. But it was a lie. Her shame was so great, so powerful, it was a tiger in a cage; it was hungry; it wanted to devour her as it had devoured her on so many nights before. Its teeth were sharp. The only way to keep the tiger in its cage was to fight back with the rage inside her and she only knew one way if she couldn't drink her shame into submission, she had to let it out through her body, until the sensations overtook her, emptied her, cleansed her.

"I'm not afraid," Smoke said, and he reached out a hand and closed it over hers, but he didn't come any closer, he kept the distance between them—a gulf he wouldn't cross, a moat he would let her stay behind. "I'm not afraid of you and I don't believe you have anything evil inside of you. I could kiss you now and I wouldn't be afraid. I want to kiss you—I'm not afraid."

"No," Cass protested. She couldn't stand to look at him. She turned her face to the pillow, trembling. "No, no, no…"

But she held on to his hand, and it was her—it was *all* her—who pulled hard, who took his hand and pressed it to her body, over her shirt, ground his palm against her nipple as she found the corner of the pillowcase and bit down hard.

Smoke waited, his body tense and still next to her and only when she whispered *please,* eyes squeezed tight against everything she couldn't bear to admit to herself, only then did he trace the softest path across her collarbone with his lips while he pushed her scrabbling fingers away and locked them tight in his own.

"Don't kiss me," Cass whispered fiercely.

If she could, she'd seal her mouth, cover it over with skin so the disease, if it was harboring inside her, insidious and undetected, could only boil its toxins within her. She would not risk Smoke—she'd swallow the disease whole if she had to. She would be its host; she would give it her body, but she would not let it claim him, too. "Don't you *ever* kiss me."

Cass let him pin her in place because she wanted to be pinned and somehow he knew. She did not want to be able to fight against this. She knew herself too well, knew how savagely her body would fight if it had a chance, so she lay with one arm trapped under her hip, her other pressed to the mattress in Smoke's fist, as he unbuttoned her shirt one excruciatingly slow button at a time. He slid his fingers along the edge of the bra the women had brought her. It was a serviceable thing, nothing like the black and lacy ones she used to wear, a stretch of beige with businesslike stitching and sturdy straps, but it was a simple matter for him to unhook the front and ease it out of the way while her treacherous body slid closer to him, as close as it could while he held her in place.

She was strong but she was compact, legs and arms whittled down to muscle and sinew and not much else. Smoke was broad and dense and unstoppable, and she shivered with anticipation as he covered her body with his own and held her motionless and watched her. The window was open; Cass had not thought to worry about it, and there was no time to be afraid now—any Beaters wandering around outside could fuck themselves because she had to be here for this moment, had to be *all* here, body and mind and whatever shreds were left of her soul. Sheer curtains fluttered in the window, gossamer panels of white that waved and floated on the breeze. *A woman chose those curtains.* The breeze was cool and delicious and it blew gently across her body, across her nipples, exposed and hard and aching. The breeze was indifferent to the Siege. It was the breeze of Before, and as Smoke lowered his mouth to her, slow and unstoppable, it occurred to her that the breeze had defied the Beaters, the famine, the routed, cracked and poisoned earth. It waited for night and then it came as it ever had and Cass welcomed it and drank it in.

Smoke's mouth: it was hot. It was soft but then...oh, God, then it wasn't. He closed his lips around her and stroked with his tongue and even then he was strong, he was insistent, had she known he would be like this the moment she saw him in the little room that was once a school office? As he looked her up and down, Cass with her wrecked flesh and stinking body and misshapen clothes, her hair in knots, no better than a rabid dog...there had been something even then, hadn't there? But Cass had steeled herself against it, she had thought her body no longer carried that taint.

The things she'd suffered, in some way she'd thought they had sucked *all* the life from her. Not just hope and faith but *this,* this most elemental longing of the body for recognition. For slaking. For surfeit. This was, somehow, different from the desperate coupling she'd done a thousand times in the back room of her trailer, in backseats in roadhouse parking lots, in cheap motel rooms and alleys and up against cars. This was a bid for life.

Smoke grazed her nipple with his teeth and she cried out and bucked against him. She wrapped her strong thighs around his waist and forced him harder against her. He slid his hand into what was left of her hair. He tugged and she arched her back, and then he released her hair so that he could undo her pants, could jam the zipper down and slide the rough fabric over her hips, taking the plain white cotton panties with them. She made the sounds that meant *no,* that meant *this is not a good idea,* but the sounds somehow didn't turn into words, were just sounds, just wailing needful sounds.

He kissed her neck, traced a path around her jaw, down across her throat as his hand found its way between her legs, her legs that fell open for him in greedy betrayal. He pressed his palm gently against her and hesitated, as though he might stop there. His touch was not tentative, she knew he meant to be reassuring, and that was not enough, no, that would not be enough, it would never be enough.

Cass lifted her hips off the bed and ground against his hand and he entered her with his fingers. He was not gentle. He did not take his time. He did not coax out her moisture to ease his way. He jammed them hard inside her and she broke her own rule, she had kept her mouth clamped shut but now she cried out, a hungry desperate sound that was nearly mad with need.

Smoke plunged into her as far as he was able, but then his thumb slid against her in the mere suggestion of a caress. He barely touched her—*there*—and Cass threw herself into the rocketing sensation and kicked him, hard, on the backs of his calves. He answered with a growl that was deep and dangerous, and pushed her back against the bed with a hand splayed at her throat. She was pinned again, helpless against him and that may have been the only thing that allowed her to open her eyes and look at him. A lock of her hair had fallen into her mouth and she seized it with her tongue, chewed it.

Their eyes met and it was some trick of the moonlight or of her own fevered need that she could see into him, through what was real into what was before, into his Before self, into his days of rote striving, his complacency, his *success,* and Cass knew in that instant that Smoke had never been a man she could want, Before, and it was only the Siege that had forged and molded him into this.

Smoke lowered his face close to hers and she saw the look in his eyes. He *wanted* her to see it. He wanted it to be unmistakable as he spread her wetness all over her, found it with his insistent fingers and sluiced it into her folds and crevices, stroking her all the while, making her watch, and when her breathing grew hard and loud and ragged he plunged into her again but this time it was all of his fingers and he took his other hand and slid his thumb into her mouth and she clamped her lips around it and sucked it hard and writhed and bucked against him like she could take his entire being inside her and when she shattered she was sure she was dying because every part of her splintered and went flying into the sky in different directions and she didn't even care.

And then time passed and the breeze kept up its gentle journey and the tears—because yes, she'd sobbed when she came, probably she had been crying the entire time—the tears dried to salty tracks on her cheeks. Smoke held her, and when his hands found the wounds on her back he explored them with his fingers, so gently that it only tickled a little, and he murmured that he was sorry, so sorry, and she let him touch the entire expanse of what was ravaged and hurt.

When she shivered from the night chill, he pulled the covers up over her body.

Then he stroked her cheek and she could smell her own scent on his fingers and she turned her face away and the shame was back, just like that.

"You shouldn't...you put your fingers in my mouth."

"You wanted them there," Smoke answered, without any trace of regret.

"But I could be—"

"We could both be dead tomorrow," Smoke said sharply. And then, relenting: "Besides, I didn't kiss you."

Cass considered that. Technically, it was true. He hadn't kissed her on the mouth. But all it would take was the tiniest cut or scratch—oh, God, had she bitten him? She couldn't remember; it wouldn't surprise her—

But she had needed him in her mouth, only it wasn't his fingers she longed for, and as images flashed across her mind she felt herself blush and then she pushed his hand off her hip and wrapped the bed linens more tightly around herself.

"What," Smoke said, allowing himself to be pushed away.

"You didn't...you know. I was...that was all about me."

Smoke shrugged and settled himself on his back, making do with the short end of the blankets that Cass had left him. "You're keeping score?"

Confusion and uncertainty roiled and surged. "You say that like you think there will be a next time."

"I have no expectations," Smoke said wearily. "For what it's worth...I enjoyed every minute of that. You're an exceptional woman, Cass."

I'm not, Cass screamed, but without words and without sound. *I'm not, I'm not, I'm not.* Long after Smoke's breathing went steady and even, long after her own body went leaden with fatigue and only her racing mind prevented it from fall-ing into a deep sleep, the voice inside her raged against its walls.

You aren't exceptional. You aren't anything. You were nothing. Now you're diseased. You are the disease. You are the vessel and you are wrecked and poisoned and evil.

Calmed by the voice that was vile but at least familiar, Cass finally let go of the sheet she had bunched tight in her hand. She stopped scraping her nails savagely at the skin of her thumb as the voice lulled her to sleep with its familiar lullaby of self-hatred. This was a landscape she knew well. This was home.

But as she finally drifted off to sleep, the stretch of white sheet between them so inviolable it might as well have been a brick wall, Cass was unsettled to realize that there was a tiny tendril of hope twining up the walls around her heart.

RUTHIE WAS REACHING UP FOR HER, STAMPING her foot, stamping in frustration, her sweet little rosebud lips wobbling toward a wail. She was dressed, improbably, in the pink terry cloth onesie Cass had brought her home from the hospital in, a gift from Meddlin, who had been beside himself trying to keep the QikGo staffed while she was on her brief maternity leave.

Ruthie was a big girl now and the pink onesie had morphed into a bell-sleeved dress with a full skirt that swung around her chubby knees as she stamped and pouted. She was trying to tell Cass something but Cass couldn't hear—it was as though there were a thousand layers of sound in her ears and she could hear none of them. Tears welled in Cass's eyes and she tried with all her might to bend down and pick up her baby, or at least kiss her frown away, but she couldn't move. And then the outlines of Ruthie's dress started to break up and scatter and Ruthie began to fade, her cries turning to frantic screaming.

"Cass—Cass!" Cass felt a strong hand close on her shoulder and she fought her way awake, the horror of the dream falling away in shards. She blinked hard a few times and sat up, looking frantically around the unfamiliar room until she remembered where she was.

In daylight, the room was smaller than it had seemed last night, with a beadboard ceiling sloping toward the window, and rose-patterned wallpaper. The curtains that had drifted on last night's breeze lay limp in the window, barely stirring. There was a white-painted dresser with a porcelain lamp and a basket of pinecones. A faint scent of dried eucalyptus tinged the air.

Cass rubbed her eyes and forced herself to look at Smoke. The stubble on his face gave him a raffish air, and his eyebrows knit in concern only underscored the effect of a pirate. His t-shirt had twisted during the night, and she caught a glimpse of his stomach, flat and hard with a line of black hair below his navel, trailing down. She felt the stirring inside her, a response that last night had sealed indelibly in her mind, and she fought it hard.

"You all right?" Smoke asked, voice sleep-rough but gentle.

Instead of answering Cass rolled away from him and untangled herself from the blankets. She stood, hastily pulling up her pants, and slipped out of the room.

She retreated to the bathroom and pulled the door tight behind her. Inside, on the closed toilet seat, lay a bowl of water and an unopened toothbrush and a fresh tube of toothpaste. On the floor was a second bucket; the waste bucket had been emptied. Lyle had been up before them, and the extent of his hospitality stopped Cass in her tracks and halted the panic that was threatening to career out of control, dragging her behind it.

It wasn't that other people hadn't offered help. Some of the shelterers at the library made an effort when she first arrived, but she was so accustomed to keeping to herself that accepting an extra serving of food, a much-thumbed magazine from six months earlier, an invitation to walk around the courtyard in the evening...these were foreign notions, and it was so much easier to turn away than to risk letting a stranger get close to her.

What did it mean that she was allowing Lyle to help her now? Was she changing—had the brief contact with Smoke, with Sammi, with the women at the bath already turned her into someone different, a self that she didn't recognize? Was she growing softer, weaker in her longing for human contact?

She picked up the toothbrush and peeled back the packaging, running her tongue over her cracked lips, her teeth. Yesterday the women had loaned her supplies and she'd brushed for what seemed like hours, trying to remove the weeks' accumulation of matter from them. Among all its other properties, the kaysev stems' woody fibers did a serviceable job of cleaning teeth, but the taste of toothpaste and the cool clean sensation afterward were a welcome relief.

She brushed slowly, savoring the taste. Then she used one of the folded cloths that Lyle had left to wash her face, her hands, between her legs, trying to get rid of every trace of the night before. She did not think of Smoke, and she did not think about the dream Ruthie, though not thinking about them took all her concentration.

She thought of the real Ruthie, the way she'd looked when Cass went to Mim and Byrn's place to take her back. She'd been worried that the months of separation might have erased her from her daughter's mind, but the minute Ruthie saw her in the doorway, she jumped up from the sofa where she had been playing with a thin gray cat and ran to her, blond curls flying, eyes wide with relief and joy.

Cass took a deep breath and looked into the mirror.

The first thing she noticed was how green her eyes were and for a moment she was electrified with terror until she figured out that it was only the pure strong light of morning that had shrunk her pupils. She cupped her hands around her face and leaned toward the mirror and her pupils expanded in the tunnel of dark she had created, and she exhaled with relief. Before the turn, her eyes had been a muddy hazel green; now they were the vibrant green of lemon leaves.

Bright irises were an early symptom of the disease, one of the things that gave the infected such ethereal beauty shortly after the blueleaf appeared, before any of them had turned all the way. But the shrunken irises that followed turned Beaters' eyes into bright, soulless tunnels, passages that seemed to lead to their poisoned cores. By contrast, Cass's eyes sparkled with life, making her look alert and intelligent and…pretty.

Cass felt her face flush. She touched her cheeks, her chin. The skin was clear and almost luminous. Her eyelashes stood out against the delicately veined eyelids, long-fringed and black. Her hair looked badly cut, but not terrible; it was glossy and the same rich golden brown it had always been, the new growth at her crown nearly indistinguishable from the rest.

After taking a thorough survey of her face, she couldn't put it off any longer—it was time to look at her back. She skimmed off her shirt and turned and oh God it was worse than she'd thought, worse than she'd imagined, worse than she'd seen on anyone who wasn't already dead or dying. The pocked areas where chunks of flesh had been chewed off were red and angry and raw. Shreds of blackened, dead tissue were stuck to the crusty, shiny layers underneath. In some areas it looked like muscle was still exposed, though concentric layers of healing skin, as thin as tissue paper, skimmed over the wounds from the edges inward.

Thank God she'd hid herself from the women at the bath. What would they have done, if they knew? They had been so kind, especially the one who had washed her so tenderly, never knowing what lay under her shirt. If they saw, were forced to look at the evidence of the attack on her—especially after what she'd done to Sammi—even the most compassionate among them would be unlikely to show her any mercy.

Cass tried to force a memory from her mind, a night when she had gone on the raiding party from the library. She'd been at the library for a couple of weeks and was going stir-crazy, her only outdoor time in the courtyard where she stared at the same treetops, the same stretch of sky, day after day. So when the raiding party assembled after dark with their empty packs and bags, she put on her own knapsack and held her blade at the ready and went out with them into the night.

There was an air of forced joviality, whispered joking and brittle laughter. They went south, down past the high school, to a cul-de-sac of run-down seventies-era trilevels. One of the curious truths of Aftertime was that the most opulent homes didn't yield the best spoils: it was the solidly middle class who were most likely to have Costco-sized stores of granola bars, Midol, hand sanitizer.

They found enough to fill their packs in the first few houses. They'd come back another night and make their way around the rest of the block. There was no rush; they were like summer-fat squirrels, hoarding for a winter that still seemed far-off. The others seemed to relax, now that they were headed home—until they passed the old ARCO and heard garbled pleas for help coming through the mini-mart's shattered double doors.

It was not the voice of a Beater. "Help...please...help." Cass couldn't tell if it was a man or a woman. It was like a scream that was leaking air, agony enunciated with excruciating care.

"Walk on, Cass," Bobby said softly, drawing her away from the others, his hand gentle but insistent at her back. Bobby was always so kind to her. He wanted to be with her. He said he was willing to wait until she was ready, but how could she ever be ready? Half a dozen times she had turned him down, and still he was trying to protect her. Didn't he understand that she didn't deserve him?

"Don't tell me what to do," she whispered, backing away from him, from the concern in his eyes. She had to show him that she was not his, and though her heart hammered with fear, she walked straight over to the mini-mart, shining her flashlight in front of her.

There were none of the things inside, she knew, or they would have come loping and gnashing in pursuit the minute she and the others came close. But what she saw in the flashlight's illumination was clearly a nest, befouled clothing and blankets mounded into a pile a dozen feet wide, the space made by pushing all the store's racks and shelves to the side. The Beaters usually only left their nests during the day, when their tiny-pupiled eyes could absorb enough light to see, but for some reason these ones had gone hunting that night. The nest stink was powerful, and Cass knew any number of the things could be nearby, and she would have turned and run—except that on the nest lay one of their victims.

It was a man. She thought it was, anyway, but only because he still had his hair, which was buzzed short. He was naked, but the rest of his body held no clues to his gender, all of the skin having been eaten away. Under a basting of blood the flesh was flayed and ribboned and chewed, bone showing through in a few places, but mostly red muscles and sinew and nerves and tendons remained. The tough soles of his feet had been left whole, and his toes were undamaged, but even the flesh on top of his feet had been ripped away, the network of delicate bones showing through the gore.

His face had been left mostly intact, other than the cheeks, which had been chewed through. Facial skin was thin; maybe the Beaters found it tedious and had gone looking for another victim instead. At any rate the man's eyes were wide with shock and his lips convulsed as he tried to speak. It took several attempts for him to put the syllables together:

"Kill...me..."

"No," Cass whispered, her hand flying to her mouth. "No no no—"

A hand yanked at her elbow, and she stumbled as she tried to resist.

"Outside." It was Bobby, and his expression, magnified in the tilting flashlight glow, was grim.

Cass nodded dumbly and backed out of the building, shoes crunching on the broken glass that littered the entrance, into the night where the others waited. One, a man in his fifties who had been a highway patrolman before, had his hands over his ears to shut out the tortured moans. Cass allowed herself to be led down the street, away from the ARCO, away from the Beater nest, away from the pulped matter that had once been human.

No one said anything. Bobby caught up with them a couple of blocks later. He fell into step next to Cass and stayed by her side until they were back at the library. Cass knew Bobby had killed the hopeless victim, but they never talked about it.

She had been a coward. Now, given the chance to do it again, she would have sliced the man's throat without hesitation and held what remained of his hand while he bled out.

Was it courage, she wondered as she slowly put her shirt back on and buttoned it, or only loss that had numbed her? Or was it the effects of succumbing to and then beating the disease? Whatever the reason, she had changed. Her whole body had seemed warm since she first awoke. A matter of degrees, maybe—perhaps even fractions of a degree—but she would swear there was a difference. Her body was rebuilding itself relentlessly, her immune system hypervigilant against infection. The scabs on her arms had mostly healed. Now that she was clean and groomed she looked human enough that most people would think she was completely normal.

Cass ran her fingers through her hair, combing it as well as she could. She had been called beautiful by a lot of people, mostly men. Never Mim, who had reminded her often that she had inherited her father's coloring, which she called coarse. He had Mediterranean blood, and like him, Cass's skin darkened to olive, her hair in between brown and blond. Mim herself was pale as parchment and jealously guarded her skin, wearing big hats and sunscreen even for trips across town. There had been nothing Mim enjoyed more than reporting that she had run into some acquaintance whose crow's feet and sunspots and blemishes had worsened. "Bet they wish they'd done what I did," she'd smirk.

Mim was dead, of course. She died with her skin as flawless and unlined as ever at the age of sixty-one—but Cass supposed her storied beauty must have been marred by the red flush and frothing spittle that marked a blueleaf fever death.

At least she'd been spared the other. Dying from the initial fever meant you never had to worry about becoming a Beater.

Cass folded the used cloth and laid it on the edge of the tub and returned to the bedroom. Smoke had made the bed, but he was gone. A flicker of panic flashed through Cass before she heard talk coming from downstairs, and she picked up her backpack and followed the voices.

The men were sitting in a tidy kitchen splashed with sun streaming in the upper third of the windows. The bottom had been boarded up, and there was a flap of fabric-covered plywood on hinges at the top that could be lowered to block the sun completely. Raised, it let in sun but did not give a view to the outside.

Cass paused in the hall, listening.

"She has enough to worry about," Smoke was saying.

"She needs to know before y'all just show up at the library," Lyle said softly. "Them Rebuilders—they don't take kindly to bein' told no, as I guess you know as well as anyone."

Smoke muttered something that Cass couldn't hear.

"It don't matter," Lyle said. "You got to hear what I'm sayin' here. That story's made it all the way here, hell, it's probably got around half the state. Rebuilders gaining ground every day—they aim to take over. Hell, they want the valley, the whole fuckin' state…who knows. Folks are afraid. They want someone to believe in. And that's you. Which is all good, but you got the girl with you now, and maybe you're not the worst thing to happen to her, see? But she needs to know it ain't gonna be easy."

Cass stepped into the kitchen. "Don't you think I know that? When's the last time anything was ever easy?"

"Mornin', princess," Lyle said, raising his glass of water in a mock toast. Cass saw that a glass had been poured for her as well, and she sat in the chair closest to Lyle, not looking at Smoke. She wasn't ready to look at him yet. The sensations of the night before still lingered on her skin, but she could not afford to be distracted, not with the hardest part of the trip still ahead.

"Good morning," she said, taking a drink from the glass. The water was cloudy, with tiny specks floating in it.

"I boiled it," Lyle said, gesturing at the kitchen counter, on which plastic jugs full of water were lined up. "I get a fire going every few nights, haul up water from the creek and set in a big batch. I strain it, get it as clean as I can."

"It's delicious," Cass lied. Really, it tasted like nothing. It *was* nothing, nothing but sustenance. Even if it was swimming in bacteria her body would take from it what it needed and leave the rest. She just had to maintain, survive.

The nontaste of the liquid triggered a memory of a meeting one weeknight after she'd done a double shift at the QikGo.

Cass sat in the back of the meetings at first and participated as little as possible—until the day she couldn't leave the church basement because she knew that if she did she would get so drunk she might never recover, that she would drink until the bottle fell from her fingers and she passed out. She wanted to drink until she was dead. She wanted to drink until *everything* was dead, so instead she sat silent but trembling through the lunchtime meeting, and then stayed in the room crying and sweating until the first person came back for the five o'clock meeting. By then she was lying on the carpet next to the wall, her face pressed against the dirty rubber baseboards, and it took two people to help her into a chair.

But she stayed.

The night Cass was thinking about, she had gone to the meeting after her double shift, too tired to do anything but go through the motions. She passed when it was her turn to speak. She moved her lips when everyone else did, but didn't listen to anyone's stories.

Until the end. They stood, they held hands, they said the words. "...take what you need and leave the rest."

Take what you need and leave the rest.

Just one sentence from the stupid thing they always repeated at the end of every meeting. She'd heard it dozens of times before; it meant nothing. Only it kept going through her head as the other people in the room talked and smiled and sniffled and hugged.

What do I need? she had asked herself. It wasn't the stories. Not the burnt coffee or supermarket cookies or the company of these other people, not the chanting or the hand-holding or the hugs, which she had trained herself not to feel, not the manuals and books and pamphlets and tokens.

There was nothing in the room she needed. But when she left, she had what she needed. It was a puzzle like the ones she'd once liked to do, the riddles in her childhood. "I have no feet but I can run"..."I am as big as an elephant but as light as a feather"...

There is nothing here that I need...

What do I need?

"Thank you," she told Lyle. Then she forced herself to turn and look at Smoke, who was watching her warily, his expression guarded.

"Thank you," she forced herself to repeat, though the words were like broken glass in her mouth.

They passed the day helping Lyle move furniture around. Lyle had left thin strips of windows exposed along the top, which let in enough light to see what they were doing. His back was hurting from the effort of hauling them into the window the night before, and he needed their help to set up the downstairs rooms in anticipation of the Beaters' next escalation in cunning. They created barriers at all the points of entry into the house, putting china cupboards in front of the boarded windows, dismantling a dresser and nailing the pieces over the doors.

That left only the back door, which had no glass panes that could be broken. It had two sets of dead bolts, installed since the start of the Siege.

Twice as they worked, stumbling groups of afflicted came down the street. Their snorting and moaning could be heard even though the downstairs windows were shut tight. The second time, seven Beaters milled across the street at the house where Lyle's friend Travers was presumably still living. When Cass went to the upstairs bathroom, she could see the Beaters shuffling around the front lawn, bumping into each other. A pair lay down in a bed of kaysev growing in front of an ornamental stone bench, one nibbling gently at the other's arm. It took a moment for Cass to realize that the one being gnawed was lying still, only a twitch of its leg now and then convincing her it wasn't dead.

"Do you have binoculars, Lyle?" Cass asked. Lyle looked up from the coffee table whose legs he was sawing off. He and Smoke were planning to brace it along the bottom of a large window in the dining room.

"That I do, missy, but are you sure there's anything out there you want a closer look at?" he asked.

"I just—just for a quick look," Cass said. She couldn't bring herself to say that their moans had been traveling straight through her skin and making her thrum with anxiety; not knowing what they were up to was worse than the alternative.

Lyle merely nodded and went to the kitchen. He returned, polishing a compact pair on his t-shirt.

"Got these for hunting," he said. "Damn shame my wife made me keep my guns locked up at the cabin or we could take a few potshots and scare those suckers off."

Magnified, the Beaters looked even worse than the few Cass had seen on her journey. On those occasions she had watched from hiding spots behind shrubs or rocks. From a distance, they looked merely unkempt and wounded, their skin split and ragged, in various states of injury and flensing.

But up close, Cass could see the large patches of skin that had been chewed down to tendon and muscle and bone. One of the Beaters no longer seemed to have the use of one of its arms, which appeared to be missing several fingers and was gnawed nearly through at the elbow. It had also apparently chewed away most of its lips and its ears were crusted black knobs where it or something else had torn the flesh away.

"Oh, God…" Cass breathed. She moved the binoculars, her hands shaking, until she found the two of them on the ground and focused. The one who was being chewed on was, she saw now, twitching spasmodically, the remains of its chewed fingers jerking almost rhythmically. She moved the binoculars up its thin, t-shirt clad body until its head came into view. It, too, had suffered mutilation—its own work or that of others, impossible to know. Gouges in its neck and cheek were crusted with blood and its mouth was a gaping black hole. It was nearly bald and its head was covered with scabs.

But it wasn't until Cass moved the binoculars to take in the one crouched next to it that she understood what was happening. The other Beater had chewed through a vein, or an artery—something big, anyway. It was bleeding out, nearly dead, so far gone as to be indifferent to its fate. Both their faces and shirtfronts were covered in blood.

The others had noticed what was going on in the flower bed and were lurching over and crouching down next to their dying companion, shoving each other out of the way.

"What's going on?" Lyle demanded, and held out a hand for the binoculars. He looked only for a few seconds before lowering them.

"Oh," he said heavily. "They'll do that sometimes, nowadays, when they haven't had any fresh...you know. When they haven't caught anyone for a while."

"The blood," Cass said weakly.

"Yeah, well, they don't prefer it, but in a pinch I guess they get desperate."

Cass remembered the times, during the Siege, when she'd seen one of the Beaters who'd been cut with a blade when someone managed to get close enough during an attack.

Their own blood fascinated them. It stopped them in their tracks even if they were seconds away from snagging a victim, and they would let go of a person's arm or t-shirt to stare at the blood as it ran from their bodies. They would pat at it like a child with finger paints, seemingly oblivious to pain, spreading it around on their clothing and skin. They would taste it and suck it off their fingers, but tentatively, not thirstily.

It was that fascination that sometimes saved people. It was the reason the children had been taught to use the blades. Cut a Beater deeply enough and it would bleed out like a citizen. But even if the wound didn't kill it, spilling its blood would distract it enough so you could get away.

It worked for a while. It probably wouldn't work anymore.

But Cass closed her fingers on the handle of the blade in her pocket anyway.

IN THE EVENING LYLE LIT CANDLES. THERE WAS
canned soup and snack packs of Oreo cookies, the kind kids
used to have in their school lunches. The soup was cold,
but it tasted delicious. Afterward, Cass helped Lyle with the
dishes. They were chipped stoneware with an ugly design
of brown owls winking against an orange sun. These dishes
had no doubt been purchased by one of the wives who'd
come and gone.

Strange, to think about what people held on to. What
brought them comfort.

That thought was still in Cass's mind when she and Smoke
set out again after nightfall. Lyle shook Smoke's hand and
gave her a hug, a crushing, lengthy one, and told them they
were always welcome, and stood in his doorway watching
them make their way down the street.

In Cass's pocket was a crystal suncatcher that she'd stolen
from Lyle's house. It had been hanging in the window in

what had once been the dining room. She was sure that if she'd asked, he would have given it to her with his blessing.

But Cass couldn't ask. She had to steal. She didn't know why, and wondering wouldn't help.

It wasn't all that hard to keep the image of the Beaters—swarming across the street, feasting on their dying comrade's blood—out of her mind, Cass discovered.

Because now all she could think about was Ruthie.

Cass held her blade in her hand as Smoke held his. They walked side by side, down the center of the street. It was a cool night and a few leaves had fallen from the sycamores lining the asphalt. The sycamores had survived the bioattacks that had decimated so many of the trees of Before. Cass had never cared for them because despite their vigorous spring leafing, by late summer they grew dispirited and started to shed yellowed and drying leaves. They seemed, to Cass, to lack resolve.

Now, though, she felt a kinship for them. They, too, were survivors, and that meant something.

Cass traced their route in her mind. Three blocks down Arroyo and then a right and a straight shot down Second for a quarter mile or so before it dead-ended in the wide lawn in front of the library. A few years ago there had been a fund-raising campaign to remodel the place, for new carpet and shelves and furniture, new computers and an updated catalog and checkout system. To pay for it all, personalized bricks were sold and laid in a meandering walkway to the front door. Mim and Byrn had bought bricks. Two of them: one said "Gina and Byrn Orr," the other "Ruthie Haverford." It hurt Cass that her own name didn't appear on the bricks, even though she wanted nothing from Byrn and she herself was responsible for the chasm between her and her mother.

And it also hurt that they insisted on using Haverford for Ruthie's last name, because Cass had changed her own last name to Dollar legally the day she turned eighteen, and so Ruthie's real name was Ruthie Dollar.

Despite these hurts she knew exactly where the bricks were. Ruthie was only a baby when the walkway was put down, but Cass had brought her there in a stroller and showed her where hers was, near an oleander hedge. Later, Cass held her little fingers and traced the shapes of the letters in her name. She had been glad Ruthie had a brick, so that someday she could bring her friends and show them that she was someone.

Cass thought about telling Smoke about the brick. But she wasn't sure what words would make him understand, and she just wanted to get to Ruthie. Her hands were hungry to touch her, her arms longed to hold her. Her entire body felt infused with the frantic energy of longing for her baby.

She was alert to the sounds of the night, listening for the wailing and snuffling that would signal that they had not been lucky enough. She stayed close by Smoke's side, her fingers in her pocket brushing against Lyle's crystal teardrop, and her thoughts chased each other in circles as she tried to focus on her breathing, the way that flight attendant in her meetings had constantly been harping about. The woman carried with her an air of wounded resentment that made it hard to pay attention as she described how you were supposed to inhale hope and possibility and exhale expectations and disappointment and fear.

But now Cass breathed with everything she had, and after they had walked in silence for what felt like a hundred miles, the library finally appeared ahead in the gloom.

"We need to go around to the side," Cass said, trying to

cover up the dizzy combination of relief and anticipation that flooded through her. "At least that's where—"

"Okay," Smoke said.

He matched her pace as she sped up, barely able to keep herself from breaking into a run. But then she stopped short, several yards from the door, apprehensive.

"You have to knock," she whispered. "When they see me, they might think I'm...you know."

Smoke put a gentle hand to her back. "Cass, you're cleaned up. You look fine. And in the dark, your skin..."

Cass knew what he meant. The wounds along her arm were faded even in the daylight, but in the dark they would go unnoticed.

Smoke ran his hand gently down the side of her face, tilting her chin up so that she would have to look at him. "Are you all right?"

Cass nodded, but she didn't trust her voice to speak. She led the way to the door, but as she was about to knock it opened.

The woman standing inside held a flashlight.

"Hurry," she whispered. She stepped out of the way, holding the door open just wide enough for them to pass.

Cass and Smoke slipped inside and the door shut with a heavy thud.

Someone slid a heavy bolt into place. As her eyes adjusted to the flashlight's glow, Cass saw that four people were gathered in the small vestibule.

One of the men held a gun loosely at his side.

But as she scanned the others she realized that she knew one of them, and her alarm lessened slightly.

"Elaine—it's me, Cass."

There was a moment of shocked silence and then a flash

of recognition, Elaine's eyes widening and her lips parting as though she was about to say Cass's name.

And then she didn't. Instead, her expression shuttered, but not before Cass thought she saw her shake her head, very slightly, as she raised her arms to cross them in front of her chest.

"Do I know you?" she said.

"Elaine? Don't you…" Cass's bewilderment grew into something more, confusion edged with cold fear. She took another look at the other people in the room, their tense posture, their hard expressions.

"My name *is* Elaine," she said. "Elaine White. Maybe you took one of my yoga classes?"

Her gaze was hard and intent, and Cass hesitated. "Uh… maybe."

"I used to teach at the Third Street Gym. And I had one over in Terryville on Thursdays and Saturdays. Saturday was such a big class, I never knew everyone's name. But you look kind of familiar."

"Yeah," Cass said, trying to gauge where Elaine was trying to lead her…and why. Elaine *had* been a yoga teacher, a fact that Cass learned during one of a dozen after-dinner conversations when the two of them had worked together washing and drying dishes and ordering the stores, tasks reserved for those without children. Parents told bedtime stories and tucked their little ones in, even Aftertime, leaving the others to fill the hours before sleep with stories of their past, never talk of the future. She knew that Elaine had recently broken up with her boyfriend, a man who'd left his wife for her, that she'd had to take out a restraining order against him, though he'd disappeared early on in the troubles. That she had to leave a room-sized loom behind when she came to the library, that she missed weaving her blankets and shawls and table runners more than anything from Before. "Saturdays. I took the...uh..."

"Sacred Thread. At ten-thirty."

"Yes. That one."

For a moment they regarded each other, Elaine's mouth compressed in a thin line, Smoke standing close behind Cass—and then the man with the gun stepped forward, gesturing with his free hand at the two of them.

"All of this is very heartwarming," he said, in the flat voice of a transplanted Midwesterner. "But your little reunion can wait. Arms out, legs apart."

Cass realized they were going to be searched, and drew in a sharp breath. She'd made it this far, and she couldn't risk being turned back now, not before she got Ruthie.

"Elaine, I just need—"

"Do what he says," Elaine snapped, any trace of warmth drained from her voice. "Maybe you were in my class, maybe not. We weren't *friends*. So don't expect me to treat you like we were."

"But I only wanted—"

"Shut up," Elaine growled, and in the flickering glow of the bulb in the fixture tacked to the ceiling with builder's staples, Cass saw her reach for her belt and knew what was coming even before the woman who had once been her friend produced a gun of her own and pointed it at her heart.

17

FOR A SECOND CASS FELT LIKE THE BREATH HAD been knocked loose from her, like she was plummeting into a black hole.

Smoke took her arm and she tried to jerk it away. She couldn't let this happen, couldn't let Elaine force her to reveal herself. From the corner of her eye she saw a man, one of the strangers, draw a blade from his pocket and hold it at the ready. The man with the gun raised it with a steady hand.

"You don't understand," she pleaded, even as the others spread out warily in front of her and Smoke. Elaine, with whom she had made blackout curtains from heavy sheets of vinyl and a staple gun, with whom she had shared the last of her imported tea, exchanged a look with the armed man. And Cass realized that any advantage she had from knowing Elaine before was gone. Trust was precious, and easily lost Aftertime.

Then Smoke did something that surprised her. Without letting go of her arm he stepped in front of her, twisting so she had to double over to prevent him from breaking her wrist.

"I'll vouch for her," he said, voice steady and strong. "I'm known here. My name is Smoke. I'll wait if you like—go ask the others."

"I know you," the man with the gun said, surprised. "We raided together a couple of times. I'm Miles."

"I remember," Smoke said. "You cut your hair."

"Yeah," Miles said, and he lowered the gun, but not all the way. "Look….things are different now. It's not the same. It's…"

Cass sensed the change in Smoke. Already tense, his body stiffened, and he shifted so she was practically hidden behind him, at the same time relaxing the grip he had on her wrist. But he held on, and she let him.

"Rebuilders," he said heavily. It was not a question. "They're here."

Elaine looked at the floor, and Miles's expression changed. It contained a warning. "There was a vote," he said meaningfully, and Cass saw how he locked on Smoke, how he emphasized each word.

The other man, the one who held a blade loosely in his fingers, stepped forward and Cass understood that he was the leader. She'd missed it because of the way he'd blended into the shadows, but now she realized he'd been ready all along, had been waiting and watching.

"You're the one from the rock slide."

Smoke drew himself up tall, and Cass slipped her arm from his grip. He was protecting her, but she saw now that the threat encompassed him, too. Something was happening that she didn't understand, but she pressed close to Smoke's side. If there was aligning to be done, she was committed.

"I was at the rock slide that day," Smoke said, his voice steel. "If you mean the day two innocent citizens died. Two innocents, and a few assholes with too much power and not enough guts."

"These are deadly times."

"They didn't have to be, not that day. There were no Beaters nearby."

"Beaters aren't the only threat around."

Cass glanced at Elaine, but she wouldn't meet her eyes. She stood with her hands clasped in front of her and stared at the floor.

"I'm not sure how you can say that, friend," Smoke said. "Seems to me that people are just trying to get by, live to see tomorrow."

"So you say. But the way things are going, those days are numbered. Rebuilders have a plan. Somebody's got to step up. Somebody's got to be in charge. Otherwise what you got, you got anarchy. And then your couple of dead's gonna look like a bargain." He turned his chin and spat on the floor, looked back up with eyes blazing. "People die every day, Smoke—or whatever your name really is. Some of us aren't so scared we're just gonna let it happen. You ought to be thanking me and everyone else who's turning this sorry little camp into a place where you might just live another day."

"Yeah, but at what cost?" Smoke stared him down, hard. "I'll be dead before I'll be your errand boy—yours or anyone else's. And next time you can be sure I won't stand by and let you take what's not yours."

"Only you might just not have a choice. You're here on our hospitality. You might want to remember that."

Elaine looked up, clearly uncomfortable with the direction things were going. "Ease up, Calder. You're not—"

"You're a guest of the Rebuilders," the man said, his face coloring. So he wasn't in charge of the whole place—there was someone else he reported to. Cass tried unsuccessfully to catch Elaine's eye. The man pointed at Smoke with his blade, already turning to leave the room. "Miles—check him. Elaine, you check the girl. Then put them in the guest rooms."

"Put up your hands," Miles said uncomfortably. "I'm sorry, I don't bear you no grudge, Smoke, but I'll do what I have to."

"I'll go you one better," Smoke said, and set his pack on the floor. Then he slid his shirt off and tossed it to Miles, who nearly dropped it. Smoke could have taken his gun— they all knew it. Instead, he turned the pockets of his pants inside out, setting his blade carefully on the floor, and turned slowly, arms in the air.

"There's another blade in the pack. Provisions. That's it."

"Can't take your word for it."

Smoke shrugged and took a stance, legs shoulder-width apart, arms out. "Then do what you need to do, boy."

"I'll take her in the bathroom and check her there," Elaine said. "She can leave her pack here."

Nobody contradicted her. Miles approached Smoke cautiously and began to pat him down.

Elaine tilted her head toward a door still marked with the symbol of the women's restroom. "Come on."

Cass felt a sudden frantic reluctance to be separated from Smoke. Which was stupid, seeing as just days ago she'd been completely alone and preferred it that way.

Smoke seemed to read her thoughts. "I'll be fine. I'll see

you inside, once our friends figure out we're no kind of threat." He made it sound like a promise.

Cass swallowed down her panic. She nodded and followed Elaine, forcing herself not to look back.

Inside the bathroom, the only light came from Elaine's lantern, so when she stopped abruptly Cass ran into her, stumbling. And then Elaine clapped a hand over her mouth and shook her head, hard. Mouthed words: *don't say anything.* Only when Cass nodded did Elaine let her go. "Sorry about this," she said, her tone giving away only a trace of anxiety. "Things got a little tense in there, but it's for everyone's safety. Let's just get the search over with and we can start over. Can you take off those clothes, please?"

When Cass started to answer, Elaine put a finger to her lips and pulled a stub of pencil and a scrap of paper from her pocket. She set the lantern down and smoothed the paper on the counter. Cass reluctantly started undressing while she watched Elaine write:

PLAY ALONG. THEY LISTEN.

Cass mouthed the word *who,* but Elaine only shook her head and stabbed her finger on the paper until Cass nodded again.

When she reached for the pencil, Elaine didn't stop her. Cass wrote with a trembling hand, her fingers slick on the pencil.

RUTHIE??

Elaine looked at the paper, and then at Cass for a long moment—too long.

And Cass knew, even before Elaine shook her head.

Cass felt her knees start to go weak, her heart constricting with a sharp ache. A cry escaped her lips, a truncated sound of grief, and Elaine reached for her before she could fall. Cass didn't resist, couldn't resist, her vision fluttering, and when Elaine pressed her face close and whispered in her ear she almost didn't hear.

"*She's alive. Get your shit together or you won't be able to help her.*"

Cass staggered back, adrenaline surging through her body. She clawed at her shorn hair, ground the heels of her hands into her eye sockets, took a breath. *Where,* she mouthed, but Elaine looked away.

"Your shirt, please. Turn out the pockets."

Cass started unbuttoning the shirt, a dozen thoughts racing through her head. Ruthie alive—but not here. The library taken over by Rebuilders. People taking up arms, not against the Beaters, but against one another. Smoke, involved in things she didn't understand.

She took off the shirt, turning out the pockets as Elaine had asked. There had to be a way to find out more. She handed over the shirt and reached for the pencil again, but Elaine stopped her.

"Come on," she said briskly. "Quit wasting time. Get the rest of your clothes off."

But she started to write again, and Cass stripped off her pants as she worked.

"Okay, socks, too, and hand me your shoes."

Cass did as she was told, then hesitated. "Can I keep my…" She pointed at her underwear; she already felt almost unbearably exposed.

Elaine nodded. "Yes, but take your undershirt off. You can keep your bra on."

So she was going to have to reveal herself, her wounds.

Well, they wouldn't be any surprise to Elaine: she had been there on the last day, she'd seen it all, even the part Cass couldn't remember. Elaine and a woman named Barbara had been chatting inside the open door that day when Cass and Ruthie went down the path—only a little way down the path!—to enjoy the spring sunshine. Elaine and Barbara had screamed when the Beaters appeared out of nowhere....

Maybe Elaine could tell her what happened, after Cass's memories went blank. Slowly, she lifted the shirt over her head. And then she turned, letting Elaine see.

She heard Elaine gasp, and then silence. After a moment she turned back around. Elaine stared at her with wide eyes, her face gone pale. She picked up the piece of paper and handed it over, then turned her attention to the rest of Cass's clothes, busied herself going through them, searching the seams and pockets.

RUTHIE WAS SAVED BUT WE SENT HER TO THE CONVENT WHEN THE REBUILDERS CAME WITH THE REST OF THE GIRLS
I WILL TRY TO KEEP YOU SAFE BUT YOU HAVE TO TRUST ME

Cass read the words twice, a third time. Ruthie was saved. *Ruthie was saved.*

But there were more questions, so many more questions. She held out her hand for the pencil, but Elaine shook her head and handed her clothes back, taking the piece of paper from Cass.

"Okay, get dressed," she said.

"What's going to happen to me now?" Cass asked, as Elaine tore the paper in half, then in half again and again.

"Same as every other newcomer," Elaine says. "You'll be processed."

In moments she had a pile of tiny shreds. She scooped them carefully into her hands, and dropped them into a toilet that was clogged with debris floating in murky water.

As Elaine led her from the bathroom, Cass remembered the sound of a toilet's flush, a homely sound that she had heard a million times in her life, but would never hear again.

18

THEY LET THEM STAY, BUT ONLY AFTER THE tribunal.

Cass followed Elaine through empty halls past the conference room, and Cass glimpsed lists and maps and machine diagrams tacked on the walls where there had once been children's drawings. She saw Smoke sitting at the large conference table next to a heavyset man in a camo-printed shirt; Elaine saw where Cass was looking and nodded briskly. "That's Skiv," she said. "He'll make your case. He'll advocate for you."

Cass wanted to ask what the hell they needed an advocate for, and how a total stranger could possibly do the job, but she was caught off guard by the transformation of the conference room. When she lived here, they had pushed the table against a wall, moved the chairs to the edges, and used the center of the room as a play area for the children, a place where parents could relax and share child care. Now the windows had been partially covered, only the top third exposed to let light in the room, and the furniture had been centered in the room once again. One end of the table had been set up with pads of paper and pens and a coffee cup arranged with military precision. Smoke and the man named Skiv sat at the other end. Smoke's hands were out of sight, under the table, and Cass wondered if they were bound.

Elaine led her to one of the small windowless offices down the hall from the conference room. "Take a good look around," she said, "because when I lock the door you won't have any light."

"You're locking me in?"

"It's the procedure," Elaine said. "Don't worry. It's standard. Everyone who comes here from outside, even if they're known to someone here, they have to stay in these rooms until they figure out what to do with them."

"What to *do* with them?"

"Whether they can stay...whether they support the Rebuilders." She shook her head, a very small motion that held a warning.

"What exactly are the Rebuilders?" she demanded in a fierce whisper.

"Hasn't Smoke told you? He's, like..." The look that passed over Elaine's face was part incredulity and part admiration, but she frowned and glared into the sparsely furnished room. "His actions against the Rebuilders are well-known."

She wasn't going to give Cass any information. It seemed unlikely, but maybe others were listening, even here. Cass entered the small room and did as Elaine told her, looking around and trying to memorize the room's features. A mattress on the carpeted floor, made up with relatively clean linens and a pillow. A bucket. A plastic jug of water pushed into a far corner, where she wouldn't trip over it and spill it. The walls were bare, but there were holes in the drywall where pictures or bulletin boards had once hung, and Cass had a flash-memory of a cheerful space decorated with pictures of a laughing family, a dog with a Frisbee, a plaque decorated with flowers and the words *Blessed Are the Poor In Spirit.*

"It's like I never lived here at all," she said softly, touching a gash in the drywall where something had been ripped free.

Elaine handed back her pack. "I kept the can opener, and your blades," she said. "But you'll get them back when you leave, assuming…well, you know."

She left the room, and while Cass waited for the click of the lock and the light to disappear, she wondered what her alternatives were. It sounded like being released, sent out to fend for themselves, was the best she and Smoke could hope for. But first, she had to find out what, and where, this Convent was.

She turned it over in her mind, trying to remember if there was anything in the mountains that could be called a convent. There were churches, a Catholic elementary school…and why would they have sent the girls away? What threat did the Rebuilders pose for children?

There were too many questions. Cass needed to talk to Smoke. Maybe he knew what Elaine was talking about. Clearly, there were things he'd been holding back, whatever happened at the rock slide, for instance. She had to have faith in him, a prospect that felt far more tenuous than mere hope, but there was no one else to trust, no one to depend on. Maybe Elaine would return…maybe she would bring more information. With any luck, Elaine would tell her where to go, and they would be allowed to leave while it was still dark. It couldn't be much past midnight; they could make shelter by morning if they could manage to get out of town and use the darkness for cover.

Assuming their next shelter hadn't already fallen to the Rebuilders. Assuming they could leave behind the things Smoke had done.

Cass shivered. If she believed the others, it meant Smoke had *killed*. What did she know about him, really? They'd shared a night she wasn't sure she wanted to remember. He'd come with her—all right, he didn't have to do that, but on the other hand maybe he was already on the run, maybe he knew it was only a matter of time until he would be held accountable for what he'd done.

And what about you? the voice inside her nagged. Cass knew there was no point in trying to ignore it: she had been on the run most of her life. Smoke had accepted her, trusted her, even without knowing all of her story—even with the way she looked, her filth, her wounds, even after what she'd done to Sammi.

In the back of her mind she'd been considering trying to sneak out alone, if she could find out where the Convent was. Unlike Smoke, she had never challenged the Rebuilders. With Elaine's help, maybe she could gain their trust, convince them to help her find Ruthie. They had weapons, power and information.

But she knew that she would be killed if the Rebuilders found out she'd been attacked. And if there were still others here from before, people who recognized her, who remembered her, it would be impossible to keep that a secret. Besides, she wouldn't get far without Smoke—she needed help if she was going to stand a chance at survival, given how much more organized the Beaters had become. Alone in the unpopulated areas was one thing, but up here in the mountains, the roads were dotted with clusters of houses, and that meant Beaters.

And there was something else: she also owed Smoke. For giving her a chance, if nothing else—it was more than anyone had done for her in a very long time.

Cass sank down onto the mattress. She sat with her legs crossed and listened hard, but the only sound was her own breathing. After what seemed like a very long time, she tapped gently on the walls on either side of her, in case Smoke had been brought to the next room, but there was no response.

A little later she lay down, thinking she might as well get some rest, in case she and Smoke were going to be made to leave, but a few minutes later the door opened.

It was Miles, the man who'd held the gun on them. "Come with me," he said impassively.

She followed him down the hall to the conference room. She was ready to duck her head and cover her face if they encountered anyone, hoping her haircut would disguise her, but the halls were empty. If there were people here, they were in the main rooms of the library, the stacks and the classrooms, the kitchen and the courtyard; the administrative area seemed to be reserved for those in charge.

In the conference room, there was no sign of Skiv. Smoke sat alone opposite two men and a woman dressed in basic khaki short-sleeved shirts and fatigue pants.

"Sit here," Miles said, pointing at the seat next to Smoke, and then he took up a position at the door, watching the room with his hand resting lightly on his gun belt. Smoke gave her a penetrating look, not smiling, but his hand brushed her leg under the table.

"I'm Evangeline," the lone woman said. She sat between the others, a commanding presence. Cass figured her for the leader. Her light brown hair, tinged with silver, was pulled into a severe ponytail. She wore no jewelry, but she had a blue-black tattoo above one wrist bone, a fat, tight spiral. She saw Cass looking at her wrist and held it up for her to examine.

"The koru. Symbol of renewal. From the Maori. I understand you've been...away."

That was putting it mildly, and Cass was tempted to roll her eyes, but there was something dangerous about the woman, and she merely nodded.

"Yes. Well. The koru is the symbol of the Rebuilders."

Smoke made a sound of barely suppressed anger.

"I'm lost," Cass said. "I'm sorry, it's like you all think I know things that I don't. Who exactly are the Rebuilders?"

"Just what it sounds like," the man on Evangeline's left said. His facial hair had been carefully shaved to a very thin line along his jaw, something that would be difficult under any circumstances but far harder in Aftertime with its scarcity of grooming aids. "We're rebuilding. We're taking what's left after the rest of the world tried to bring our country to its knees—the raw materials, the resources, the people—and we're building it back into a civilization."

"'We' who?" Smoke demanded. "All I see is half a dozen folks with guns and a few dozen more without any."

"We're armed because we have to be," Evangeline said. "As long as there are people like you around—murderers and insurrectionists. But there are many more of us, as you well know. For every nut who wants to be Davy Crockett, there's fifty who know that community's built on strong leadership."

"I'm no murderer," Smoke said. "I was acting to prevent more violence. Which, I should point out, we had very little of until you people showed up."

"We know a lot about you," the other man, the one who hadn't yet spoken, said. He was an unremarkable man of average height and small eyes. The most interesting thing about him, in fact, was how entirely without expression his face was, as though nothing that had happened in his life had made a lasting impression. "*Smoke*. Or should I call you Edward? Eddy? Ted? Am I close?"

"If you know so much about me," Smoke said tightly, "then I should think you know the answer."

He chuckled, a dry, scratchy sound. "Okay. Got me there, big guy. Edward Schaffer. While we're at it, I'm Cole and that's Nyland. Pleased to make your acquaintance. You're a man of many accomplishments."

"I was a coach. A counselor. Nothing more."

More rough amusement. "You're far too modest, Ed. I mean *Smoke*. Got to admit, I'm torn here. I don't really get this renaming shit, like after the Siege suddenly everyone's hatching out of eggs all over again. Way I see it, we're all the same as when we went in. Just the dice got rolled a little different this time around for some of us."

He picked up a pencil and tapped it on the table. "I know who you used to work for, buddy," he said softly. "And we all know what *they* did. A lot of people suffered, but there's a chance to make things right for the ones who are still here. A time for justice, maybe."

Cass looked back and forth between the men, trying to understand. Who had Smoke worked for? What had he done?

"Cole's an idealist," Evangeline said. "I'm more of a practical person. An opportunist, you might say. And I'll be honest with you—when you two showed up tonight, I saw an opportunity. To take a strong and public stand against insurrection."

Smoke made a sound in his throat—disgust, contempt—and his hand tightened on Cass's leg. She sensed that many of his emotions battled for prominence—but fear was not among them.

"You were of no interest to me," Evangeline continued, staring directly at Cass. "But in the last half hour, that has changed. And now you are far, far, more interesting than anything else that has happened in a long while."

Cass blinked, trying to maintain eye contact with the woman, but Evangeline's words chilled her.

"Can you guess why?" Evangeline asked her, very softly.

Cass *could* guess. Dread collected like dew in her mind, the words echoing and reverberating. *Interesting. Far more interesting.* She ran her fingers through what was left of her hair, tugging at the ends, wanting to wrap them around her face, hide herself from scrutiny.

Had Elaine sold her out?

Had her old friend been tortured into it? Or rewarded?

"You think I'm..." Cass whispered, hating her voice for shaking.

"I *know* what you are. I've seen it before, and I know what to look for. I can tell from your eyes...and the way your hair is growing in, and there's only one way you get marks like you have on your arms. Let me see."

Before Cass could stop her, Evangeline seized her arm and ran her strong, cold hands up and down the surface, fingertips tracing the faded scars. The touch was intimate, far too familiar, and Cass reacted with revulsion. She wanted to yank back her hand. She wanted to run. She wanted to wipe the traces of Evangeline's touch from her skin.

"Have you ever met another one like you?" Evangeline asked, unable to contain a jittering hint of excitement.

Cass hesitated. Others, like her? Those who had been attacked, bitten, infected...and lived? Was it possible?

How long had it been that she felt alone, since she carried her shame with her like a skin? "What do you mean?"

"Outliers," Evangeline said, her lips curving into a perfect, chilly smile. "People like you, who survived an attack. Who got better. Who fought off the infection."

So it was true. Disbelief mixed with wild hope as Cass allowed herself to consider the possibility. Just knowing there were others...they could all be like her, weakened, damaged...but still, she would not be alone. The idea was intoxicating.

"I'm not saying I believe you but...how could anyone do that?" she asked, trying to keep her enthusiasm hidden.

Evangeline's smile grew broader. She knew she had won.

"Nobody knows," she said. "Not yet anyway. But our people are working on it. They're studying people like you. Working on developing a vaccine."

"That isn't possible," Smoke said flatly. "Don't listen to this, Cass."

"Who are you to say what's possible?" Evangeline demanded, raising her voice, fury twisting her mouth. "How far have you traveled? Do you even know what's happening outside this town? This *county?*"

"I thought you people didn't use the word *county* anymore," Smoke said, meeting Evangeline's anger with his own. He had gone very still next to Cass, his energy coiled and tense. "I thought you believed those designations were meaningless Aftertime."

Evangeline's fine skin flushed a faint pink and she glared at Smoke. The others in the room waited, eyes on their leader. At last she gave a small nod.

"You're right, of course, Smoke. Land divisions from

Before, they don't make much sense anymore…but that'll change. Do you have the faintest idea what's going on at the borders?"

"The *borders?* The borders are a myth," Smoke snapped. "Blueleaf crossed the state line the first time a strong wind came up. And you get one Beater with a bad sense of direction, he'll be up to Oregon or down to Mexico and never know the difference."

"You have no idea," Evangeline said softly, drawing out the words, enjoying them.

"We're less than sixty miles from the Nevada border, as the crow flies. If they'd armed it, we'd know."

Evangeline laughed, a rich, throaty laugh full of pleasure.

"What's so funny," Cass demanded.

"It's…it's not funny. It's sad, really," Evangeline said, wiping a mirthful tear from the corner of her eye. "Sad in so many ways…sad that even intelligent people like the two of you can be so naive."

Smoke tightened his hands to fists and laid them on the table. His jaw worked with fury as he leaned forward, closing the distance between him and Evangeline.

"Say what you mean," he muttered.

"Oh, all right, fine," Evangeline said, almost pouting—as though he had knocked down a game of checkers. "The border isn't California. It's the Rockies, all the way down to the Colorado River. They've cut off half the fucking country."

19

CASS HELD HER BREATH.

It wasn't possible. The Rockies…in her mind she called up the map from her high school Geography textbook, the West laid out in shades of sienna and gold and peach and russet. California stretching all the way down to the Baja Peninsula, up to Washington and Oregon. Idaho, Nevada, Utah, Arizona…thousands and thousands of miles stretching out to the Pacific Ocean to the west, and the mountains to the east.

No one could contain that, no matter how many fences they built, no matter how many volunteers they armed, how many mines they laid…could they? And not with the American government effectively *gone*.

"I don't believe you," Smoke said, but there was the faintest trace of doubt in his voice.

"Believe, or don't believe." Evangeline shrugged. "Now

that, right there, that's the *true* enemy of the future. Ignorance. Indifference. Failure to adapt."

"As opposed to wild theories and fearmongering? Trading on people's loss and grief to justify..." Smoke gestured around him, including the others in the room—the guns, the library, the hidden citizens. "All of this?"

Evangeline folded her arms across her chest and narrowed her eyes. "You're starting to bore me. I thought we could engage in a little intelligent discourse, but you're nothing more than an—an agitator. You didn't fool Skiv, you know."

"Fool him? What are you talking about?"

"With your whole 'they fired first' defense—"

"That wasn't a defense, that's the *truth,*" Smoke cut her off. "There are people who survived that day who can tell you the real story—some living here. At least, they were, unless you've thrown them out. For *agitating,* as you call it."

"You'll be taken down to Colima tomorrow," Evangeline continued on, as though he hadn't spoken. "To the detention camp until they can schedule your trial. Although it might be a while, seeing as there are a few other more pressing issues on folks' minds. You ought to like it, though—from what I hear, it's full of people like you." She gave him a smile, flicking out her tongue to lick her lips. "Enemies of progress."

"Smoke, what is she talking about?" Cass demanded in a whisper. Everyone could hear, but she didn't care; the panic that had lodged in her gut was escalating.

Smoke shook his head slowly, not taking his eyes off Evangeline. "Sounds like they've built themselves a jail," he said softly. "What does that say about your new society—you've built jails and an army first..."

"We've built a *community,*" Evangeline snapped. "And a

research center. In the university hospital. We've got the best
of the best working down there. We're the only hope for the
future, and people know it. You think we're *forcing* people to
stay here?"

She waited, but no one said anything.

"Anyone can leave, anytime they want. We held a *vote*.
The people here had the option to choose to go it alone.
Of course, we offered protection, resources...better facilities,
cleaner water. And when we do develop the vaccine, our
people will get it first." She focused her gaze on Cass with
distaste. "It will be quite a while before we have enough for
anyone living outside our control."

"You aren't developing a vaccine," Smoke muttered.
"There's no way—the equipment, the intellectual capital, the
infrastructure, none of that survived. They took it out—all
of it. Berkeley's a fucking smoking hole in the ground. Stan-
ford got leveled. They knew where the research was going
on and bombed the shit out of it."

"I think you've said enough," Evangeline said. "You speak
from ignorance. And I want to talk to your girlfriend now,
not you. Nyland, keep him in line."

The man with the thin beard stepped forward, gripping
a handheld wand with prongs at the end. Cass realized with
dismay that it was a Taser.

"Don't believe them," Smoke said, not bothering to lower
his voice. "No matter what happens. Promise me that, Cass."

Cass gave him a small nod, wondering how she was supposed to know who to trust. Evangeline watched her with
cold interest. "Let me lay out the future for you, sister."

"I'm not your sister," Cass snapped. There was something
not right about Evangeline, some realignment of emotions
that crackled under the surface, a tightly controlled mania.

Evangeline smiled, and suddenly Cass realized that she

was actually very beautiful. If she were capable of a genuine smile, she'd be stunning.

"Of course. You are an only child. An orphan now. Your father left the family long ago and your mother... I extend my condolences, of course. The fact that so many have been lost doesn't lessen anyone's individual pain. We recognize that."

Fear shivered its way down Cass's spine. How did Evangeline know so much about her? And what about Ruthie—the one detail she *hadn't* mentioned? Elaine, of course; it had to be. She tried to remember what she and Elaine had talked about, during the long hours they'd spent together in those early days in the library. Of course they must have exchanged life stories. Elaine... Cass searched her memory, trying to dredge up what the woman had told her. She'd been a gym teacher at an elementary school...she'd been dating another teacher, but she'd broken off the engagement earlier in the year, and that's when she opened her yoga studio. She had cats. Two cats, a white one and a striped one—there had been a photo. Yes...she remembered Elaine showing her the photo, her voice trembling when she described her cats, which had gone missing shortly after the attack on domesticated fowl, when suddenly everyone became a hunter. Oh, and she had a younger brother with problems, some sort of problems that had landed him in a group home in Oakland.

So it was possible. Even Cass, who'd lost several weeks of her life, had been able to dredge up those details. It was well within the bounds of possibility that Elaine had been able to tell Evangeline the things she knew. The question was—why? How had they gotten the information out of her? Here, in this room, with the three strangers staring at her and Smoke, Cass had no trouble believing they would do whatever it took to get what they wanted.

But Elaine hadn't told them about Ruthie. Why?

"You can't stay here," Evangeline continued. "If people know you returned, after the attack—there's a lot of ignorance, a lot of fear. You wouldn't be...tolerated well. We wouldn't be able to guarantee your safety. Down in Colima, we have scientists, we have a way to explain things in terms people can understand. And we have the others. Like you."

"If there are others, how come I've never seen them before?" Cass demanded. "How come no one has?"

Evangeline shrugged. "Simple, unfortunate circumstances. Our people think that as many as one or two in every hundred citizens is immune, an outlier. It's nothing new, there's a similar phenomenon with other infectious diseases—HIV, malaria, even Parkinson's. Only, to recover, you actually have to survive an attack or live through blueleaf fever. And as you know, it's become a lot harder to do that."

Cass knew. Once people realized where the fever led, they stopped caring for the infected. Those who didn't take their own lives were turned out on the streets or even killed, if their loved ones could stomach the job.

"We're getting close to a blood test," Evangeline continued. "Soon we'll be able to tell who's an outlier and who isn't. But we need people like you for that, people for the studies. And that's why we're going to give you safe passage to Colima."

She studied Cass, one eyebrow raised. "You'll never make it on your own. There's very little cover in the central valley, and the towns...well, I don't need to tell you. But we've got a team headed down there day after tomorrow, and you can go with them. We'll outfit you, get you a better blade. Food, water, first aid supplies—and you'll go by truck. By *truck,* Cass, do you understand me? Just like in the old days. You understand that we cannot give you a gun, but your escort will be armed. *Well* armed."

At this, the man called Nyland smiled. Guns were about as easy to come by as fresh meat. They'd been the first thing people hoarded, along with water and batteries. But it had been amazing how quickly they changed hands when people were stupid enough to use them. The outcome of any armed situation was generally that one person ended up dead, and the other added a weapon to his stash. Which didn't much matter, until people started hiding their weapons stores.

The government had issued a call for an arms surrender when street violence exceeded the capacity of the forces left to contain it, but no one knew what they'd done with the few weapons people were willing to part with. There was no doubt that there was plenty of firepower to be had, only most of it was securely hidden away, its owners dead or infected, most houses raided early on.

It had been Cass's vague hope, as she walked all those recent days, to find a hidden stash. She wouldn't be greedy. A small handgun, ample ammunition—that's what she hoped to find. She knew how to shoot; she'd shot cans and paper targets nailed to trees in the fields at the edge of town with her father for a few years before he left. But she would use the gun only for self-defense or to get Ruthie.

She'd do whatever it took to get Ruthie…and beyond that, she had no plan at all.

But she was no closer to Ruthie now than she'd been before. Unless the Convent was also in Colima—which seemed unlikely—she needed to find a way to escape the plans Evangeline was making for her. And she needed Smoke's help.

"Mr. Schaffer's fate is of no concern to you," Evangeline

said, as if reading her thoughts. "He has things to answer for."

"He's a good man," Cass protested, surprising herself, knowing that arguing with them was pointless. Besides, Smoke was nothing to her, her companion for less than forty-eight hours, a quick hand job and a little relief in the dark, a man she'd used and whom, if she remembered him at all in the future, would be only a footnote in her journey. "Whatever you think he did—"

"Fucker knows what he's done," Nyland said, a flush creeping over his face, and Cass realized that it was personal for this one. He had lost something or someone by Smoke.

"Nothing that didn't need doing." Smoke bit off the words hard.

The guy stood so fast that Cass didn't have a chance to react, knocking over the glass of water on the table in front of him, and his fist connecting with Smoke's face made a sound that was louder than Cass would have thought it ought to be.

But Smoke said nothing. Even when blood dripped from the cut under his eye and onto the table, he barely reacted at all.

20

THEY WERE LED TO SEPARATE OFFICES, AND Cass spent the night in the room with the bed on the floor. She slept fitfully until the door opened and a woman she hadn't seen before filled the doorway. She was thin and muscular in a hooded jersey and shorts and hiking sandals, and she said very little, her face partially obscured by the hood which she had pulled over her curly brown hair.

"I'm here to take you to the bathroom. Then I will take you to the courtyard, where you will be served a meal. Then you'll come back here."

They walked through empty halls toward the back of the library, steps echoing on the tiled floors. Sheer drapes covered the tall windows looking out onto the parking lot. The fabric was not substantial enough to block light, but it prevented Cass from seeing much. Pinned to the fabric were hand-lettered posters with slogans like VIGILANCE:

REPORT EVERY SIGHTING and EQUAL SHARES
FOR EQUAL WORK and CURFEW MEANS *YOU*.

The outdoor "bathroom," located in the shed enclosure
where the trash Dumpster had been kept Before, wasn't
very different from when Cass had lived in the library. The
makeshift panels separating the men's and women's sides had
been replaced by sheets of plywood joined by sturdy steel
braces, the roof now corrugated metal. A curtain hung from
a shower rod lent privacy. The pots they had used before had
been replaced by a toilet with a removable insert that could
be hauled away to be emptied and cleaned.

Cass's escort handed her a bowl of water, basic toiletries.
"Take ten minutes, I'll wait."

Inside was a makeshift shower with a water reservoir oper-
ated by a rope pull. Cass undressed, turning her back toward
the plywood wall before she took off her shirt, even though
she was alone. Then she released the water and shivered as it
trickled down onto her body in a cold, uneven trickle. She
took as long as she dared, scrubbing her hair and skin with
the sliver of soap she'd been given before rinsing with the
frigid water from the tank. She dried herself with the stiff,
scratchy towel the woman had given her and pulled on her
clothes.

She brushed her teeth and spat on the drainage hole, and
combed her hair with her fingers. She folded the toiletries
up into the damp towel and left them in a plastic basket on
a teak bench, and when she emerged from the shower the
woman was leaning against the enclosure's cinder block wall,
arms folded across her chest.

But when she stood straight and pushed back her hood,
Cass stopped abruptly in her tracks.

It was Elaine. She was wearing the same clothes as the

other woman, but her face was unmistakable in the bright light of the new day.

"What—"

"Hush," Elaine whispered and pulled the hood forward, covering her face. "Walk with me and keep your voice down."

Cass stared straight ahead and concentrated on keeping her expression neutral as they walked back through the still-quiet building. Elaine pushed open the door to the courtyard and they walked into the sunlight, the smell of kaysev and wild onion drifting on the morning breeze. A paper cup skittered and rolled across the concrete, but otherwise nothing moved.

On an ordinary day, when Cass lived here, there were people in the courtyard all the time. Children chasing each other, adults drying clothes washed in the earliest light of dawn in the creek, or preparing kaysev, or scrubbing dishes in the tubs of water they carried back. Or simply sitting in chairs dragged into the sun, talking. But now the residents rose and slept and bathed and ate on a schedule set by the Rebuilders.

The courtyard's layout was different, too, arranged for greatest efficiency. Tables had been organized in neat rows with plastic chairs. Plates and bowls and cutlery were stacked on shelves; a tarp had been rigged to cover them, but today, in the good weather, the tarps were rolled up and tied. The fire pit had undergone the biggest transformation of all: it was now a sturdy brick-and-mortar structure that rose a man's height off the ground, with a chimney twice that tall, and a series of racks and hooks to hold food and pots above the flames.

"We have five minutes," Elaine said in a low voice, biting off the words. "Exercise time. Walk with me, but don't look at me. Look at the ground. Keep a steady pace and keep your voice down."

She led the way along the edge of the courtyard, striding ahead with her hands clenched into fists at her sides, nothing like the easygoing yoga teacher Cass had known before.

"Tell me everything you can about Ruthie. Please, Elaine," Cass pleaded as she caught up. "I have to know. I have to go get her."

Elaine glanced at her; Cass saw only the shadow of her features concealed under the hood. "They're sending you to Colima tomorrow, Cass," she sighed. "Don't you understand? And you need to count yourself lucky. Where they're sending Smoke is way worse."

"I'll find a way," Cass said. "I'll get away from them—I'll run—I'll—"

"That's suicide," Elaine interrupted. "Don't even talk that way."

"I've been on my own for weeks out there. I can do it again. Besides, if I don't have Ruthie, I don't have anything." Cass swallowed down the lump forming in her throat. "I might as well be dead."

"I *said* don't talk that way," Elaine said angrily. "I'm putting my ass on the line for you here. Because we were friends. Because—because I thought you were strong. Strong enough. If you're going to give up there's no reason for me to be here."

"Okay, okay," Cass said hastily. "I'm sorry. Look, just tell me where Ruthie is and I'll—I'll be careful. I won't do anything to get you in trouble. Or any of the others. I promise."

Elaine walked silently for a few moments before speaking. When she did, her voice was softer, almost tentative. "All right. I'll tell you what I know. But you have to understand, there's no guarantee that—there's just no guarantees."

Cass thought *Ruthie*—small hand in hers, dimpled knees and cheek so soft she could kiss it a hundred times, a thousand—and pushed the panic away. Pushed it with all her might. "Fine."

"When we found out the Rebuilders were coming—a scout came first, so we knew—we sent all the girls—every female under sixteen—to the Convent."

The Convent... Cass remembered the words in Elaine's hasty scrawl in the bathroom. "What is it—like a church?"

Elaine laughed without humor. "Not like any church you've ever seen. Like a cult, I guess. I don't really know. No one's been in it. Once you go in, you don't come out. No one I know about, anyway."

"Where is it?"

"It's up in San Pedro," Elaine said.

San Pedro: not too far from Sykes, where Sammi's dad was. Maybe fifteen miles to the south. The girl's heart-shaped face, her wide gold eyes, flashed through Cass's mind—a promise she should never have made—but she didn't have time to dwell on the girl now.

"That's forty miles from here."

Elaine nodded. "It's in the old Miners stadium. They've taken over the whole damn thing, apparently."

"Who?"

"These...women. They're like, I don't know, fundamentalists, I guess. Sort of Christian...but they have a lot of their own beliefs. Kind of whacked-out is what I hear, into some strange rituals and shit like that."

"And you sent the *children* there?" Cass tried and failed to keep the accusation from her voice. "You sent Ruthie?"

"Yes, we did," Elaine said, turning to face Cass head-on,

and in a trick of the light, a bright beam from the sun that had just crested the roof of the library, her face was fully illuminated, and Cass saw the network of fine lines around her eyes, the deep groove between her eyebrows. The evidence of the toll the weeks had taken on this woman who had once been her friend. "And you would have, too. Because no matter what they're doing with the girls at the Convent, what the Rebuilders do is far worse."

21

"WHAT DO YOU MEAN—" CASS ASKED, THE WORLD falling away from her, the air sucked from her throat. "What were they going to do?"

—to my baby, my darling, the person I'd die for—

"No one knows, Cass. Don't lose your shit here, no one really knows." Elaine stared straight ahead, sped up her pace, swung her arms as though she was racing against herself. "But there were rumors."

"What rumors?"

"*Quiet,*" Elaine snapped, reaching for Cass's arm. She dug her sharp fingernails into the soft flesh of her wrist, kept digging until tears sprang to Cass's eyes and she finally, reluctantly, nodded. "Look, you can't put too much stock in this. We don't really know what's going down in Colima. They keep us in the dark. You know, they have their propaganda…."

"Just tell me."

"All right. The vaccine they were talking about? You know, against the fever? No one really thinks they can do that. But what they are trying to do is develop a test. To see if you're immune or not. And people say they're close."

"But what does that have to do with the children?"

"They say they're taking the kids and testing them first. The outliers are going to be raised together down there. Kind of a superresistant colony, get it? They're going to get the best of everything—food, medicine, whatever it takes. They're being raised drinking the Rebuilder Kool-Aid."

"But what happens to the ones who aren't?"

"No one knows. But it can't be good, right?"

Cass felt her blood go cold. "What do you mean..."

"Look, Cass, they're zealots. They use everything, twist everything for their purpose. I think some of them are even glad Before is gone, gives them a chance to reshape the world in their image. I mean, they're not going to waste an opportunity just because it goes against what regular people think of as unacceptable."

"What, Elaine? Just say it—"

"The rumor is they're putting the rest of the kids to work. The ones who are old enough. They're sending them out on raiding parties, into the buildings first, places an adult can't or won't go. They probably have them washing dishes and emptying latrines and carrying water, the things no one else wants to do. The slave labor jobs."

Cass felt faint with dismay. "But the babies—"

"Who knows, Cass? Infirmary or cradle camp or something. Come on, they're not going to let them starve. But you can bet they aren't getting much attention. Probably just enough so they grow up to join the labor pool."

Cass slowed, her body going numb with the horror of it, but Elaine did not slow down. After a moment Cass had to jog a little to catch up. "You could be wrong.... About all of it. I mean, you yourself said you don't know."

"You're right," Elaine said. "I could be wrong. You want to take that chance? You think any mother here wanted to take that chance? That's why we sent the ones away that we could."

"Their own children..."

"Look, Cass, you haven't seen the others. You wouldn't recognize them. You want to know why I got this job? Why I'm a *trusted member* of the team around here?" The sarcasm in her voice was painful to hear. "Because I didn't fall apart like some of the others. The *parents*. Do you want to know how many suicides we've had since then? No...you don't. Trust me, you don't. The Convent would only take the girls. The families with boys? They..."

She shook her head, went silent. Cass walked beside her, making almost an entire lap, both of them lost to their thoughts.

"The boys went with the Rebuilders," Cass finally said. "The girls went to the Convent."

"Yes. That's what I've been telling you. And you need to be grateful. Maybe they have to listen to Jesus talk morning, noon and night. Maybe they practice witchcraft or worship phases of the moon. Does it really matter? They're safe. They're *safe enough for now,* Cass, and that's enough. That's all we have anymore."

"But why didn't the parents go with them? The mothers, at least—if they allow women—"

"The Convent refused," Elaine said. "Only the children. The Convent takes new acolytes sometimes but only the ones they feel are called. They wouldn't take the mothers because they said they weren't called to join, but the girls were still innocents, so they could. Their leader, this woman they have, she makes all these decisions. I don't know, maybe she reads tea leaves or whatever, but she sent the word down. They took eleven girls. Ruthie was the youngest. The oldest was fifteen."

Ruthie, given away again…how many times in her short life had she been passed along to strangers? Cass felt the guilt and grief encroaching and gritted her teeth so hard her head pounded. "When did they take them?"

"Almost three weeks ago. After the scout came…they took them the next morning."

"Who? Can I talk to them?" Maybe she could find out more about the Convent, maybe they could tell her how to get in, who to talk to, how Ruthie had done on the journey, if she was frightened or sad, if someone had been there to take care of her—anything, anything at all.

"*No, Cass,*" Elaine snapped. "Don't you get what a risk I'm taking just talking to you? I just wanted you to know. The best thing for everyone is for you to go tomorrow. Go down to Colima, be grateful—let them do their experiments and feed you and take care of you, and forget all about Ruthie."

Her voice broke at the end in a little choked sob, and Cass put a hand on her arm, forcing her to stop. Elaine shrugged it off, yanking her wrist back and rubbing furiously at her eyes.

"What?" Cass demanded. "What is it?"

"Nothing," Elaine mumbled. "Nothing, okay? Only don't you think—don't you know—can you really—"

Elaine looked wildly around and then Cass realized that her old friend longed to bolt, to leave Cass standing there, that only a sense of duty and fears about being watched kept her rooted to the spot. She was acting as though…a thought occurred to Cass.

She had been gone two months. Two months was a long

time, especially Aftertime. Time enough to grow attached to someone. "You took care of her, didn't you," she said softly. "You took care of Ruthie."

Elaine wouldn't meet her eyes. "Someone had to. You weren't here."

"Oh…Elaine." Cass said. "I didn't know. I'm sorry. I'm—thank you. How can I ever thank you—all that time, and I—if you hadn't been here for her—I got here as fast as I could. You have to know that."

"But you weren't here after it happened."

"After I was attacked? I *know,* Elaine, and I—"

"No!" Elaine spat. "No! Not you. You weren't here for her after *she* was."

Dread bloomed in Cass's gut. Oh, God…no. Not that—

"When she was attacked! God damn it, Cass, don't pretend you don't remember!" Elaine spoke in a furious whisper. "I saw you watching! I saw you screaming when it happened. The whole time, when they were dragging you off—you were screaming her name and—"

"I don't remember!" Cass said, half pleading, half begging. "I don't!"

Elaine made a sound in her throat, a gasp of choked fury. "How many people are going to suffer for you? How many, Cass?"

"What do you mean?"

Elaine looked at her for a long moment, the anger slowly draining from her face, leaving her pale and tired looking.

"What do you mean?" Cass repeated, whispering. Trembling, she let go of Elaine's arm.

"I'm sorry," Elaine said after a moment. She had resumed the same stoic look that had apparently gotten her through the turbulent weeks past. "I shouldn't have—I know you've suffered, too. I was out of line."

She started walking again, trudging more slowly than before. Cass kept pace, as they made a second pass around the courtyard.

"Please, just tell me," she begged. "I swear to you I don't remember anything after—after I saw them coming, after the first one got to me. I remember throwing myself on top of Ruthie—"

Because the Beaters had been loping and lurching, colliding with each other, tripping over each other in their mad rush to reach her. And she had covered Ruthie as well as she could, pushing her down, wishing she could send Ruthie into the ground where she could be cradled and protected by the earth itself.

Elaine sighed, her shoulders slumping. "Well, you...they got to you and...took you. Four of them."

Cass nodded. By then, the Beaters had worked out a system. They didn't fall upon their victims in the street anymore; they took them back to their nests, where they could devour them in peace. Four Beaters: each took a person's arm or leg and then they hauled their victim away, taking care to keep their quarry from dragging on the ground, oblivious to their screams.

"And then?"

"There were two left. And then Bobby came running out."

Bobby? Cass racked her brain, trying to remember. Elaine at the door with a group of women, talking in the sunshine. But Bobby? Had he been there?

"He heard you screaming. He ran out of the library," Elaine went on. "You wouldn't stop screaming Ruthie's name and he ran to you. Everyone was yelling at him...but it was like he didn't hear them, like he didn't care. He was almost all the way to where you were when you..."

"I what? I *what?*"

"You were being dragged, but you were holding on to Ruthie and you screamed at him to take her."

Cass widened her eyes, incredulous. "But that means…"

"He did. He got her," Elaine said quietly. "He fought hard. He got between them and Ruthie, even though they were…they bit him. He held them off long enough for us to come and get her. Barbara and me. We waited until they were focused on him and then we ran and got her."

"And they *took* him? Away?"

"No, Cass. He was able to run, when the Beaters saw us. They let go of him for a second and he got away. Everyone ran. We carried Ruthie back inside and…and Bobby ran to the creek."

"To the creek? Why would he go to the *creek?*"

"He didn't stop there, Cass. He followed it down to the cliffs."

A sick understanding dawned in Cass's mind, the full horror of what had happened.

"The cliffs…"

A mile down, as it wound past the edge of town, the creek widened and formed a deep pool rimmed with packed-dirt banks and cattails on one side and limestone cliffs on the other. They rose hundreds of feet into the air, pitted and carved by the elements. In the water below lay broken, rock-strewn shelves of shale.

On sunny days, Cass used to take a beach towel and a pail full of toys and lie on the banks, swatting at mosquitoes and watching Ruthie try to catch the frogs sunning themselves on the rocks.

"He jumped." Elaine's voice had gone flat. "They found his body the next day, on the rocks."

22

"HE DIED," CASS WHISPERED. BOBBY DIED, SAVING Ruthie.

How many people are going to suffer for you?

Was that why she couldn't remember? Was it guilt? She hadn't been able to save Ruthie. She hadn't been able to save anyone.

"You said she was attacked," she said. "Ruthie. Did they… I mean…"

"Bobby got there so fast," Elaine said. "She had scratches, but they could have come from when you threw her down, or from the ground. That's what we told ourselves, anyway. After we lost both you and Bobby in one day…well, no one wanted to believe we were going to lose her, too. And then…"

She took a deep breath and looked off into the distance, where the sun was starting to climb higher above the tops of the dead trees. "We're out of time," she said. "I need to get you back before group one comes out."

"No," Cass said. "Tell me the rest. You have to tell me the rest."

"Fine. But I'm making it quick so don't interrupt—seriously." She started cutting across the center of the courtyard, toward the doors back inside the building. "Ruthie was fine for almost a day, and then she got the fever, and her eyes… well, you know. Some people wanted to…you know. Put her out. But she was just a baby. We couldn't do it. So…I said I would take her. I said I'd stay with her, in the mail room, because there was a slot in the door. A quarantine…until we could be sure."

"Oh, Elaine…" Cass said.

Elaine held up a palm to stop her. "Don't. Just let me finish. By the next day she was crying around the clock. Picking…well. The way they do. I was careful…I wrapped her in a blanket before I held her, and I didn't let—you know, her mouth, her saliva. I was careful. But the thing was, I knew I was probably dead. That it would only take one bite. If I fell asleep or looked away at the wrong moment… But I didn't care."

Cass waited, her heart barely beating, imagining Elaine in that little dim room, as Ruthie's tiny body grew hot and damp with sweat, as her wails escalated to screams of pain and anger, as she started to attack herself, her tiny fingers scraping at her own flesh. As the others steeled themselves against yet another loss, as they took the long route to avoid hearing the sounds coming from the mail room.

"That went on for two days. And then…well, I guess you know what happened. She started to get better. I wasn't sure at first—I thought maybe I was going feverish myself, that I was delusional. But I woke up, I was sleeping in fits and starts, an hour here and there—I woke up and the fever was gone. Her eyes were glassy and she was, like, not there? I mean, she didn't respond when I touched her, almost like she was in a coma or something. I yelled and yelled to try and yank her out of it, and finally a couple of people came and talked to me through the door. They had a meeting. They wouldn't let us out, they brought us food and I tried to get Ruthie to eat and sometimes I could get her to drink, but she was…she wasn't right. That lasted a few more days. Some people thought she had died. That I had…" Elaine shook her head. "Finally someone got the courage up to come in. They saw that the fever was gone, her pupils were normal. Her eyes were so bright, like yours, and I knew when I saw you, you were the same…. And you know how kids are…they heal so fast her scratches were next to nothing. They let us out, then."

"She's…like me," Cass said. An outlier.

"I stayed with her around the clock, in the conference room. And when she woke up, I was there." They reached the doors, and Elaine didn't look at her as she pulled the hood tighter around her face and held the door for Cass. "I'm taking you back to the room. Remember what I said. You need to *go*. To Colima. And you need to forget."

Cass followed wordlessly, watching the rigid set of Elaine's back. At the door of her cell, Elaine put a hand on her shoulder. Cass looked into her careworn face.

"Cass. When she woke up…" Elaine bit her lip, looked at the floor. "Her first word was *Mama*."

Then the door shut and Cass was alone in the dark.

Time took forever to pass. Without even a sliver of light under the door, the dark was absolute, and it started to play tricks on Cass's mind. In her thoughts she saw faces:

Evangeline's and the other Rebuilders, their expressions hard and suspicious. She remembered Elaine before, the way she used to hiccup if she laughed too hard, her sadness when she talked about her cats, her brother in Oakland. She remembered other faces from the library. Some she could put names to, others she couldn't. She wondered which of them still lived here, and what had happened to the rest.

She thought of Ruthie, the way she'd laughed and laughed when she saw the dandelions in the library's untended, dead lawn, tucked here and there among the kaysev.

She thought of Smoke, the way he'd looked at her in Lyle's guest bed the night before, the way his eyes glinted when she pressed his hand hard against her.

After what seemed like an entire day had passed, someone brought her lunch. The door opened and she squinted in the sun, bright enough to let her know it was afternoon. A tray was set on the floor and the person left before Cass's eyes had a chance to adjust enough to see who had been there, whether it was a man or a woman, someone she recognized or a stranger.

She ate by feel, a hard biscuit made from kaysev flour and flavored with rosemary, a surprise. Where had the spice come from? Was it dried and stored from before—or had it managed to return, scratching out a foothold to renew itself Aftertime?

Cass drank the tall bottle of water—gritty, bitter, no doubt boiled stream water—and did several sets of push-ups and sit-ups. A while later she did more. And then more. Maybe, if she did enough, if she pushed her body hard enough, she would grow tired enough to sleep.

Tomorrow she would be forced to go to Colima. Somehow, she had to find a way to escape. And far better to escape near the outset than later in the journey, since every mile would take her farther and farther away from San Pedro and the Convent.

Maybe forgetting would be better. Maybe if she could fill her days with other things, with chores and routines and conversations, until finally there was no room for all the memories of Ruthie—maybe then she could find some peace. But Cass knew there would never be such a thing for her, and though she pushed her body until she was drenched with sweat and collapsed on the thin mattress, the desperate need to find Ruthie was undimmed, and she lay in the dark listening to the pounding of her own heart, feeling the ache of what was missing.

When the tapping started, Cass thought it was in her imagination. It was a soft scratching sound, but then there was a snick of a dead bolt turning that was definitely real. Cass scrambled to her feet as the door opened. For a moment Cass blinked, adjusting to the light, and then an unfamiliar man came into the room and quickly closed the door behind them, plunging them back into darkness.

It was not a large room and Cass backed up into the corner opposite the mattress, feeling for the walls with her hands, panic blooming inside her. The man was bigger than her by far; her brief glimpse gave the impression of a solid build, thick arms, doughy hands. There was nowhere to go, and nothing she could use to defend herself.

But she coiled herself anyway, ready to throw everything she had into one fierce jab at the eyes or stomp on the instep, whatever it took to hurt him before he hurt her.

During the Siege there came a day when it became clear that the law was a concept that no longer had any meaning. Coalitions from Before were revealed to be more fragile than anyone guessed: prisons were opened and sheriff's departments disbanded after the National Guard admitted it could no longer call up sufficient numbers to quell riots. Restraining orders went unenforced; predators prowled and bullies sought out the weak. Plaintiffs awaiting justice ran out of hope; defendants quit pleading innocence; old animosities based on skin color and native tongue reared their ugly heads once again. There were no more good guys in charge, no upholders of reason, no reason at all. The only rule in place was the rule of might, and crimes went unpunished as long as the perpetrators were bigger or stronger or more willing to take risks than their victims.

Most people behaved according to the same moral strictures they always had, but unexpected acts of violence and heroism stretched the ends of the spectrum. Some ordinary people discovered a taste for justice, and threw themselves into protecting the innocent, even when it cost them their lives. But at the same time, rapes and beatings and murders skyrocketed. Grudges were consummated in fits of spectacular rage, and those who had harbored violent fantasies against neighbors and rivals and even strangers acted on them with impunity.

So when instead of a body pressing her into the wall, Cass heard a low voice say, "Don't be afraid," she was seized by confusion rather than relief. The scream that was on her lips died in a whimper. Her hands, clenched into fists, trembled.

"Who are you?" Cass managed to whisper.

"A friend. My name's not important, but I'm on your side. I'm here to help you get out of here."

"Elaine said—"

"There's been a change of plans. We need to get Smoke out, and the feeling is that you won't be safe here once he goes missing. Look, he's going to take you to the Convent.

And for what it's worth, we advised him against it. Do you understand what I'm saying?"

"What would they do to Smoke?"

"Considering that he killed three of the top guys in the Rebuilder command, I'm guessing the maximum sentence in what passes for a justice system down there," the man said stonily.

"Smoke killed them? Are you sure?"

"Look, no disrespect, but we don't have time for this. Getting you out just compounds the risk for all of us, and frankly we probably would let you take your chances with Evangeline, except Smoke wouldn't leave without you." He didn't bother to hide his irritation. "Now, can you pay attention? We don't have time for me to tell you twice."

"Okay," Cass muttered, chastened.

"Nearly everyone's at dinner right now and I have to get back. When I open this door I'll go create a distraction in the courtyard. You'll only have a moment. Run to the east entrance—you know the one? You remember?"

"Yes…"

"Smoke will meet you there. He'll have your packs. He'll know where to go. *Do not talk,* just follow him."

Cass nodded, and only when the man opened the door and let a swath of light in did she notice that he was wearing the khaki shirt of the Rebuilders.

23

THE STRANGER SLIPPED OUT AS QUIETLY AS HE'D entered. Cass waited, listening hard. She heard his footsteps retreating down the hall, then nothing. She tested the door and found it unlocked.

But the thought that she would need to run away from the place that had meant safety to her just a short time ago seemed ludicrous. How was it possible to find enough to disagree about Aftertime that you could fight and kill over it?

The priorities were so stark. Live another day. Protect others, if you can. Eat and drink and sleep. Care for the children. Everything else—washing, learning, creating, loving—were luxuries rarely indulged...but they haunted people's minds still. The dream of starting over ran deep.

At first, the rumors flew that the End Times had arrived. That the planet itself was dying. Defoliation would kill everyone on the planet in a matter of weeks—that was a popular theory for a while, until people figured out that not all of the plants were threatened. Then the kaysev seeds sprouted and the new panic was that it would choke out all other species and leach all the nutrients from the earth, but soon it became obvious that where kaysev grew, other plants that had survived the Siege returned and flourished.

Over and over the apocalypse theories were proved wrong. Earth did what She would; She chose life. If She was indifferent to the fate of humanity, She seemed unstoppable in her determination to restore health to Her forests and mountains and waters, as every new day seemed to bring a sprig or seedling of some species that was thought to be lost, or a flash of a silvery fish tail in the stream, or the sound of birdsong in the morning. And that's when people started talking about a future, one in which the planet found a way to host the survivors.

Not everyone looked ahead, of course. There were those who gave up. Who believed it was only a matter of time before the Beaters prevailed or the blueleaf redoubled or the kaysev fell to winter frosts.

But the numbers of the hopeful were greater. Had been, anyway. People were hungry for leadership—that was why Bobby had risen so quickly and easily. No one opposed him; everyone was happy to defer to his natural ability to organize and encourage and parcel out tasks and resources and decide disputes.

But Bobby was dead.

They found his body on the rocks.

Cass's heart contracted at the thought, and she leaned against the door frame, struggling under the weight of her guilt and the pain of yet another loss, when she heard the clatter.

It was muffled, but there was definitely the sound of crockery breaking on the floor, followed by cursing.

She didn't wait. Her feet moved on their own; she flew down the hall past the conference room before her thoughts caught up, and by then it was too late to do anything but keep running. She took the corner fast. This was the worst of it, the place where she could be spotted by anyone looking in her direction. She heard the voices much more clearly now, as she flattened herself against the wall and slunk toward the door to the outside. When her fingers touched the metal bar of the door's push mechanism, she took a chance and looked backward. Silhouetted against the light pouring into the hall from the door to the courtyard was her rescuer, holding a large plastic tub while several people knelt at his feet picking up broken dishes.

Cass took a deep breath and pushed against the door.

Before, it would have been electronically armed, but without electricity the security system was useless. Now the door had a bulky padlock, but it swung free, the arm looped through only one half of the device, and the door opened and Cass found herself in a pool of late-day sun that made her blink.

"I'm here. Come on, *now.*" Smoke's voice, and then Smoke's hand seized hers and pulled hard and she was running next to him, straining to keep up. Her eyes adjusted to the light and she saw that they were headed for the alley running behind the library and city hall, across the staff parking spaces and the bike rack, skirting a row of dead shrubs and abandoned cars.

Halfway down the alley was a low brick building with a flat roof, a restaurant of some kind. There was still a smell of rotting garbage that lingered even after all these months, and Cass—who had seen and smelled things a thousand times worse—found herself gagging on the smell as Smoke pulled her beneath an overhang of wood slats.

"Take this," he said, handing her the pack that Elaine had taken from her. It was heavier than it had been the night before in the library.

"What's in it?"

"Supplies. Rations. Weapons. You can look later. For now, we need to put as much distance between us and them as we can before they find out we're gone. And that's going to be just a few minutes, I can pretty much guarantee it."

Cass pulled the pack onto her shoulders and shrugged it into place.

"Can you handle the weight?"

"Yes—" Cass broke off when she saw that Smoke was holding a compact handgun. "Where the hell did you get *that?*"

"Our...benefactors," Smoke muttered. "I wasn't expecting it. Wish I could say I was confident I could use it."

"You don't know how to shoot?"

"I've shot some. When I was a kid. Rifles, mostly, duck hunting with my uncles. I know enough not to shoot myself or you by accident, let's put it that way."

Cass thought about what the stranger had told her, that Smoke had killed three men. Tried to imagine him staring down the barrel. Pulling the trigger. Found that it wasn't that much of a stretch. There was something about him, some dormant powerful fury, that she could sense lurking under the surface. To her surprise, it didn't frighten her. It almost seemed...familiar, a bitter mix of regret and deadly determination.

Cass herself could handle a gun. She had learned to shoot her dad's .22 on a series of clear, cold January mornings when she was ten. She'd shot magazine pages nailed to trees, her father clapping her on the back and laughing whenever she hit one.

"I don't suppose you have another, do you?"

"Sorry," Smoke said. "But would you rather be the one to carry it?"

Cass raised her eyebrows, surprised that he was willing to put his safety in her hands. "Um, no, that's okay."

"Okay, well." Smoke faltered. "Anyway, I'm hoping we won't need it. We're only going about three-quarters of a mile."

"To another shelter?"

"No. Look, Cass, the resistance has gotten pretty organized. They've got resources hidden all over the place up here. And they must be pretty keen on getting us out, because they're giving us a motorcycle."

"What?"

"I know, I know, I'll believe it when we see it, but Herkim—the guy who came for you—he told me where to find it and says it's gassed up and ready."

"And all we have to do is get there before the Beaters get us. In daylight, in the middle of town."

Smoke touched his hand to the small of her back. "It's sunset," he said gently. "That's not nearly as bad."

If it was a lie, it was a lie told to protect her. Cass thought about what the stranger had told her in the cell: *Smoke wouldn't leave without you.* She watched him out of the corner of her eye as they hurried along the alley, dodging clumps of garbage and the desiccated remains of cats and rodents flattened by fleeing traffic and left to rot.

Why did he care about her?

Why would he risk his own safety to protect her?

They turned left, toward a water tower in the distance that rose up in the sky over a residential neighborhood. "We're headed for a house near the edge of town. The bike's in a shed in the back. I've got an address."

"And you know how to get there?"

"I memorized it. This way a quarter mile, right on Jackson, left on Tendrick Springs. Number 249. White house, green shutters."

"Wow," Cass said. "I don't think I could remember my own birthday with everything...you know. Just, everything."

They moved in silence. Cass stayed close to Smoke, bumping against him from time to time. She wasn't used to looking to anyone else for reassurance. She wasn't sure how she felt about it, but she also wasn't about to question it, not now.

"When is it?" Smoke asked as they turned onto Jackson Road.

"When is what?"

"Your birthday."

Cass didn't say anything for a moment. It was January first; she had been the first baby born in Contra Costa County that year. But she hadn't celebrated her birthday in years. Her mother always sent a card, signed—in her mother's hand—"Mim and Byrn." No "love," nothing but their names.

She'd spent more than a few of her birthdays hung over. Or drunk by noon.

On her best days she told herself she would start celebrating again when she got Ruthie back. She would make a cake. They would wear hats made from sheets of newspaper.

"Is it a big secret or something?" Smoke asked. "Come on, why won't you tell me?"

"January."

"January what?"

"Does it really matter? I mean, do you think people are

still going to be keeping track by then? Tell you what, if—if
we're still alive I'll tell you the date then."

What she meant was, if they were still together...not *together* together, because it was crazy to imagine such a thing,
to give their brief acquaintance significance that it didn't
have; but if after Cass got Ruthie they ended up sheltering
in the same place. Something like that.

"Deal," Smoke said and slipped his hand around Cass's
and squeezed, letting go before she could react.

And the last of her mistrust of him slipped away.

Smoke had proved himself over and over. He'd believed in
her innocence when she arrived at the school with her blade
pressed to a child's neck. He'd come with her, voluntarily,
to the library. Now, his best course was to run in a different
direction, to go where the Rebuilders wouldn't pursue him,
but he'd come with her anyway.

And there was the other night. In the cool, clean sheets at
Lyle's place. In the breeze that reminded her of Before.

But that didn't count. That *couldn't* count, and Cass pushed
it from her mind, pushed the memory hard into a small
corner where it would be protected and preserved. Still, that
left last night when he'd faced down the Rebuilders without
hesitation, and today when he'd waited for her to join him at
the back door.

"Thank you," she said softly.

"For what?"

"For coming with me. For being here."

Smoke shrugged. "I can't go back to the school now—I
don't want to lead the Rebuilders there. No matter where I
go, they'll come after me, but if they think I'm with you, at
least they'll leave the school alone."

Cass thought she understood. The people at the school

had been strangers not long ago. But now, Aftertime, they were all he had.

"I hope they're fine," she said softly, thinking of Sammi and her mother, of the women at the bath trough, of the children playing with the plastic animals. Of Nora, with her intense dark eyes and choppy haircut.

Wondered if Smoke was thinking about her. Missing her. Wishing he could be with her.

She almost asked him, but then she didn't. She wasn't sure she wanted to hear the answer. "So what do you know about the Convent?" she asked instead.

"I'd heard rumors about it, but Herkim filled me in," Smoke said. "They started the Convent a few months ago. All women, no men allowed. Set it up in Foothill Stadium, of all places. Home of the Miners—you ever been there?"

Cass had. With her father, in fact, when she was eight years old. It was a ridiculously balmy Tuesday in May, when it seemed like it would never rain again, and every day would bring some new and splendid surprise, because her daddy was home from touring with his band and he wasn't working at the construction sites like he usually did, and he wrote a note saying she was sick and she didn't have to go to school. They didn't tell her mother, who had gone off to work as usual, because it was sort of a surprise. And her daddy bought her a souvenir pennant and a second bag of peanuts just because she asked and the next week he was gone and she never saw him again.

"No." Cass mumbled the lie. "Don't think I have."

"Well, it's not the worst place in the world for a bunch of bat-shit crazy women to hole up, I guess. They've sealed off the entrances, got some system for figuring out who they let in and out, not that they're coming out much, that's for sure."

"And they have Ruthie there?"

"That's just what someone *said*. You got to be careful here, Cass. You can't go believing everything you hear. Everyone who talks to you, you got to wonder what angle they're working, what you could provide them with that they can't get some other way."

"But it was Elaine who said it. We were *friends*."

"Okay," Smoke said. "Sorry. I'm just trying—"

Something clattered behind them, metal on pavement, and Cass whirled around. Smoke turned, too, his hand tight around hers.

A block away, half a dozen clumsy forms stumbled around a cluster of trash cans, tripping and trying to disentangle themselves from each other. It was almost impossible to make out any details at this distance, now that the sun had slipped behind the horizon and evening had laid down its hazy blue gloom.

But the moans that started up when they found their footing and sniffed the air and scented Cass and Smoke—those were unmistakable.

The Beaters had found them.

24

CASS WATCHED THE THINGS SHOVE AND KICK at each other with frustration as they got in each other's way. One was knocked to the ground, where it howled in fury, rubbing a crabbed hand at its face, as the others stumbled toward Cass and Smoke.

Smoke raised the gun and fired. But the Beaters were too far away, and the gun kicked in his hand. He fired a second time, and a third, hitting nothing.

"Stop," Cass yelled. "You only have a few more rounds."

"In the pack—" Smoke seized her hand. He knew what she did: even if he made every shot, he couldn't hit them all, and the odds of killing even one were pretty low. Besides, there wasn't time to reload.

They ran, but Cass knew they could never outrun the Beaters. For a while, sure. Cass and Smoke were strong and fit, and adrenaline would give them a boost. But within a quarter mile their pace would drop and the Beaters' speed would surge.

The maniacal frenzy of their hunger could not be tempered by any obstacle. They'd run across glass, across hot coals, across this terrible scorched earth that was the end of the world if it meant fresh, uninfected flesh. They were body eaters, after all, and that was all they lived for. They would close the gap, their voices raised in a horrifying chorus of grunts and moans, and Smoke—of course it would be Smoke, because he would put himself between her and them, there was no question in her mind now—Smoke would feel their grasping bone-hands on his clothes, his back, his arms as they took him down.

Long ago, before Ruthie, Cass had contemplated dying, wondering if it was true what they said, that in the final seconds you achieve a kind of peace. Like that guy in the Jack London story, slowly freezing to death, there would be a numbing, a lulling, a sense of complacency, rightness. Acceptance would be followed, she imagined, by something resembling an urge to have done with it. A drowning person would accept the water into their lungs. A person falling from a great height would reach out for the earth.

But there was nothing like that for victims of the Beaters. Because they knew what was coming and death was stretched out over a series of manic flashes, strips of flesh, bites into the skin. Cass knew.

So when Smoke seized her hand she ran hard. She flew like a stone rocketed over a great chasm. She pushed off with her feet and willed herself through the air, begging fate for another breath, another step, another second before hell burst upon them.

"White house," Smoke yelled, urging her faster, harder than she thought she could go. Fear did that, working miracles on the laws of physics and gravity, driving people to do the impossible.

When they were abreast of the house she understood that it was the one, the one with the shed, the shed with the motorcycle and when they rounded the corner and Smoke plunged toward a dead shrub it took only a split second for her to realize that the shrub was a screen, a fake, and she tore into the branches with her hands, pulling, yanking, the dead twigs cutting and scraping her skin. The deadwood fell away and there it was, a sagging barn-shaped box of a shed—it was badly kept, paint peeling off the cheap wood in cracked strips, the lock hanging rusted and useless.

Smoke pulled her inside and slammed the door. Yellow light filtered through a stained and spiderwebbed window, illuminating shelves of buckets and jars and garden tools— and a motorcycle. It was there—it was really and truly there, an incongruously clean and shined-up thing, front wheel tilted sportily on the slab floor.

But behind her the door swung open on creaking hinges and she could hear, not far away at all, the screaming and grunting. "It won't—they'll be—" she protested, but Smoke was pushing at a long, low oblong box, trying to block the door with it, and Cass shut up and helped.

It was an old freezer, a heavy thing, but she and Smoke threw themselves into the task and bumped and scraped it along the floor, a hideous smell rising from it as the lid jostled and fell away. Meat roasts and chops packed in plastic, now moldering and rotten—the stench reaching into her nostrils. Spoils, the scraps that no raiders found, ruined when the electricity failed. Nausea rolled through Cass's gut as the first of the Beaters threw itself against the door.

They were inches away, screaming out their rage and their hunger, and Cass leaped back. Smoke caught and held her, hard, his arms wrapped tight around her from the back. "Calm down now," he ordered, his lips brushing her ear, and there was something in his voice that made her body follow his instructions even as her mind went nearly mad with fear. She *felt* her heart slow, her hands unclench.

Only then did Smoke release her and take the handlebars of the bike, kicking up the kickstand. The light glinted off keys that had been left in the ignition. He slid onto the seat with an ease that let Cass know it was far from the first time he'd been on a motorcycle. Turning the key he revved the engine hard.

"Behind me," Smoke ordered and Cass threw a leg over the seat, slid her hands around his waist, buried her face in the soft cotton of his shirt.

And closed her eyes.

Because she was too frightened to see what he would do next. Whatever it was, they had one chance. Only one. She felt the reverberation of the bike's powerful motor through Smoke's body, through the warmth of his skin beneath his shirt, and she squeezed her eyes shut tighter and she whispered a prayer to whomever that was immediately stolen by the roar of the motor and the screaming and her own heart—

Ruthie—

And then her entire body was jarred so hard that her teeth clashed in her head and the wind was knocked out of her lungs. The bike leaped ahead like an enraged animal loosed from its cage and slammed against the back wall of the shed, splintering it, Sheetrock bursting all around her. Something struck her ankle, knocking her foot loose, and she slid sideways on the seat and nearly fell off, scrambling to hang on to Smoke.

"Cass!" he yelled, as the motorcycle chewed through vines

and fallen tree limbs toward the alley, spinning up gravel and dead leaves and dirt. "Hold *on!*"

And she did. His words again made her hold on for everything she was worth. Her hands clutched his waist hard enough to bruise, and she pulled herself back upright, her ankle banging painfully against metal, the heat of the engine blowing hard through the fabric of her pants. Her cheek stung and something warm slid slowly down her chin and she realized she was cut and bleeding.

She forced her eyes open and saw squat garages racing by. They followed the gravel alley to the end of the block where it opened onto a street, and Smoke took the corner expertly, angling so sharply that she had to clutch him tight to avoid spilling even as he accelerated into the turn and the motorcycle leaped onto smoother pavement.

A flash of movement caught her eye and Cass turned to look. A horde of them, more than she'd ever seen in one place before—there had to be over two dozen, jogging unsteadily down the street a block away. The ones in front paddled the air with their clutching fingers, eyes rolling in the ecstasy of the hunt. They followed the sound of the engine, turning and stumbling as the motorcycle powered on, and Cass pressed her face into Smoke's shirt, into the plane between his shoulder blades, and breathed shallowly of his scent, his warmth.

For several blocks neither of them said anything. They passed cars abandoned at odd angles, crumpled into street signs and fire hydrants. There was junk in the streets—an overturned armchair, sodden clumps of clothes matted to the curbs. Squashed rats. A Barbie notebook, its shiny pink cover faded by the elements. A Little Tikes Cozy Coupe in a patch of kaysev, overturned, its wheels turned toward the sky.

Smoke navigated the obstacles with ease, and Cass knew

that she had underestimated him. She'd thought him a deliberate man, because of the care he took for her safety, the way his large hands enveloped hers. She had not thought him capable of such quick reflexes, but as she slowly uncoiled from her terrified clutch, she noticed how he turned his wrist just so to make the motorcycle dip around a downed tree or an abandoned shoe, finding smooth stretches of pavement where he pushed the bike as hard as it would go, making it scream with exertion.

After the alley turned to neighborhood and the neighborhood thinned to a house here and there, Smoke finally pulled back on the gas and they hit a steady clip in the dying sun. *It's nearly night,* Cass noted with surprise, because she had been too busy with her terror and her will to survive to notice the setting of the sun or the sweetening of the thick autumnal air.

It wasn't just the gingery kaysev, either. There were other undercurrents that she couldn't quite place. Evergreen, of course; she'd seen the seedlings, everyone had—but something else, too; something thick and waxy like a camellia or a New Guinea impatiens, extravagant even Before, unthinkable now.

But who was to say?

Who got to dictate, really, what died and what fought for a foothold and what thrived? Cass took the measure of the passing scenery. A kitschy cabin decor shop, the chain-saw-rendered black bears that once decorated the entrance now cracked and toppled. A sporting goods store where she'd once shopped the after-season sale, hoping to find a snowsuit that she could pack away for Ruthie's next winter, coming out instead with a pair of fuzzy pink girls' boots that would have been inexcusable if they hadn't been so cheap.

After that, there was nothing but the twisting ribbon of

the road, a pearly shimmer in the darkening evening. Eventually Smoke slowed the bike and eased over onto the shoulder. When they came to a stop he took care in settling the kickstand before he dismounted and offered Cass his hand. Her ears were still ringing from the steady roar of the road, but she allowed him to help her from the bike.

They were heading down, out of the mountains on the far side, the side that Cass rarely traveled. She did not know this road. Eventually it led to Yosemite, she was pretty sure, though she couldn't picture the route in her mind.

Night brought its customary chill. The kaysev smell here was muted; there was clay dust in her nostrils, a not unpleasant smell she associated with endless hot afternoons running along sunbaked roads. Cass smoothed her shirt where the wind had whipped it around her waist. And as she looked around the road, she saw something astonishing, something that made her catch her breath.

"What," Smoke said sharply. "What's wrong?"

"No, no—it's just—look," she said, pointing to the tiny seedlings, a trio of them, that had caught her eye.

"Redwoods?" Smoke asked after a moment.

"I'm pretty sure those are sequoias. You know...the big ones."

"Those are the first evergreens I've seen since...Before."

Cass nodded, not trusting her voice to speak without catching. She'd thought they were gone forever.

Then she noticed something else.

"There was fire here." Sure enough, the trees here were not just dead but charred black; it had been difficult to see in the twilight, and she hadn't noticed. "It must have happened...well, if it happened right before, or during, the attacks..."

"What difference would that make?"

"When fire destroys a living tree, the cones fall and release their seeds. So if the timing was just right, it could have seeded right before the Siege, and then the seeds somehow survived, and..." *This.* She toed the road next to the seedlings for emphasis.

"That's..." Smoke seemed at a loss for words, but he caught her hand in his and squeezed. "How do you know so much about plants?"

Cass shrugged, embarrassed. "I, um...I used to think I would, that I could study it. You know, botany...landscape design." Before she realized that escaping Byrn's late-night "accidental" encounters in the hallway, his hands on her thighs under the dinner table, meant getting out with no diploma and no college and no real plan other than flight.

For a long time, she thought she'd save up some money and go back, enroll at Anza State. Then one day she looked around her tiny, dirty apartment, high-heeled shoes abandoned by the door, empty cans stacked on the table, a stranger snoring in her bed, and realized she never would.

Cass tugged her hand back and changed the subject. "That was lucky. In...in the shed."

"Luck? How about skill?" Smoke demanded, the corners of his mouth curving in a wry smile. "So says my shelf of dirt bike trophies from junior high."

"I don't think that's a dirt bike," Cass said, pointing to the shiny machine whose engine ticked and popped in the cool night.

"Little boys who ride dirt bikes grow up to ride big bikes. I had one at my place in Tahoe. Rode a lot on roads like this one."

"Along with your waverunner and your snowmobile and your powerboat and all your other toys," Cass said, trying for a light tone.

"Yeah, I had it all, didn't I?" Smoke said. There it was again, the sadness, as he slipped an arm around her shoulders, and after hesitating for a moment she laid her cheek against his chest. He pulled her closer and rested his chin on the top of her head.

This is where he tells me it will all be okay, Cass thought. But he didn't.

And Cass, who had never let any man stay much longer than the time it took him to put his pants back on, suddenly found herself wishing he would. She would take that lie.

Finally Smoke sighed, a deep intake of breath that Cass felt against her skin, and then pulled gently away from her. "We can be at the Convent before it's completely dark, as long as we don't run into anything…unexpected."

"The roads have been clear," Cass said, brushing imaginary specks from her sleeves, not meeting his eyes. It was true; there had been fewer junked cars, less debris, up this far.

"Not too populated this far in," Smoke said. "Most of the log-jamming happened nearer the city. Works for me. Once we get close to San Pedro, we might hit a few more, though."

"Well, we don't really have much choice, right?" Cass asked. She waited until Smoke slung his long leg over the bike and then slid on behind him.

Already, she found that she had memorized the way they fit together. As they roared through the murky evening, the bike's headlight tracing a golden path along the road, she imagined that they blended together into one dim shape in the descending dark.

25

THE REST OF THE TRIP TOOK LESS TIME THAN
they expected. Someone had come along before them and
cleared the way.

The fire had burned its way down-mountain, and the
road wound through acres of forest studded with the blackened skeletons of trees. Everywhere, there were soft-fringed
little evergreen seedlings, even occasionally in the cracks in
the road where ordinarily only kaysev grew.

On a straight, gentle incline, Smoke slowed, coming to a
stop with the bike balanced against his foot on the ground,
and gestured toward the bank at the side of the road.
Downed tree limbs and sections of trunk had been pushed
out of the way. The trunk was massive, at least three feet
across, a tree that had been uprooted during the fire and
fallen across the road.

"Power saw," Smoke said, pointing at a cylindrical section eight or ten feet long. "See the marks. And look at the road—they used a front loader or something."

Cass squinted in the last of the evening light. Sure enough, there were broad, arcing scrapes in the pavement, sawdust and dirt and chipped asphalt dragged in broad swaths.

"But that could have been from ages ago." Back when all the gas stations were shutting down and people were killing each other to siphon fuel from abandoned cars. As the Siege dragged on there were fewer and fewer cars on the road each day, as though the automobiles themselves were falling to a plague, until the very few people who still had gas were too afraid to drive because of the desperate gangs that swarmed cars and dragged drivers out to be beaten and left for dead in the streets.

Smoke shook his head. "Look at that. You can smell it. That's a fresh cut."

He was right, of course. The air carried a pleasant scent of pine, a smell that reminded Cass of Christmas, a holiday that she imagined no longer existed. For a moment she felt a surge of excitement.

"Maybe they're close by," she said. "Maybe we'll catch up to them. If they have gas, cars, a tractor or whatever—"

"Cass, I'd lay odds it's the Rebuilders. They're the only ones capable of something like this, anymore. At least on this side of the border."

Cass was silent a moment, absorbing his words. "You believe that? What Evangeline said…about the Rockies? You really think they've cut us off?"

"I don't know. That's where I'd do it, though. I mean, if I was trying to keep them out—quarantine—yeah, it's the only place that makes sense. Start up north, Canadian border ought to be plenty far enough, no way Beaters have spread up through Oregon into Washington or Idaho yet, and besides, it'll be getting cold up there in a month or so. I'd build a blockade down all the way to where the Colorado River empties into the Gulf."

"With *what?*" Cass demanded.

"I don't know, but people are resourceful. I mean, the Chinese were able to build a wall seven hundred years BC, and all they had was what they could dig up out of the ground, mostly rocks and dirt and existing mountain ridges. And I don't need to tell you that there's probably a hell of a lot of unemployed and very motivated guys ready to work out East, especially if they understand what's going on over here."

"What you said, back at Lyle's...about that guy from UCSF? The scientist? How he didn't think the Beaters could live up north?"

"Yeah. I don't know, Cass. I mean, it made sense to me, but look how they're evolving. If they can figure out complex strategies, learn from their mistakes, refine their attacks, what are the odds that they can't figure out how to put on a fucking coat?"

Cass wondered. It was true that the Beaters were evolving, that their hunger was driving them to adapt to their circumstances—but they were still so primitive in their responses. They couldn't walk ten feet without tripping and stumbling over each other, but they hadn't learned to put any distance between them when they went out roving. They were like children in their frustration, raging and screaming in impotent fury when they were denied. When they were hurt they were hypnotized by the sight of their own blood, so deeply fascinated that you could come close enough to fire at them point-blank before they remembered you were a threat.

One thing was sure: if a border had been built, retreating east was no longer a possibility once she found Ruthie. And to the south were the Rebuilders. Cass thought of Evangeline, of her cruel beauty, of the effortless power she wielded over the people in the conference room. She had no trouble believing that Evangeline was capable of using her for research—and other things she couldn't even imagine.

"What's to stop them from coming after us?" she asked. "If they have the means to do something like this."

"They didn't know about the motorcycle. They don't know about the resistance—well, I'm sure they're aware that not everyone welcomes their presence at the library, but from what Herkim told me, they don't know who's acting and who's just grumbling. They won't know who helped us escape, and they'll be forced to assume we're out wandering around town. My guess is they'll send out a party, check with squatters, sweep town and when they don't find us, figure we were either taken, or…or I guess, maybe that we got incredibly lucky and made it out of town on foot."

Smoke eased the motorcycle forward, weaving carefully between the bark and twigs and dirt clods left by whoever had cleared the road. When they'd passed the last of it, he increased their speed, but kept it slower than they'd been going before, about twenty-five miles an hour. Night had nearly descended, and the motorcycle's headlight lit up an eerie landscape of the black nightmare outlines of stripped and downed trees against a purple-gray sky. The occasional abandoned or wrecked car loomed like a hunkering ogre, the beam glinting off metal and glass. Maybe it was Cass's imagination, but it seemed to her that Smoke sped past these cars as though he couldn't get away from them fast enough, before easing back in the long uninterrupted stretches of empty pavement. Cass held tight to his waist, unable to relax her grip, afraid they'd hit something, afraid she'd fall, afraid of everything she couldn't see in the shadows of the forest.

The roar of the bike's motor was the loudest sound Cass had heard in a long while—if you didn't count screaming. She had grown accustomed to silence Aftertime. Once you took out the sound of traffic and the buzz of streetlights and televisions blaring through open windows and fire engines and police sirens cutting through the night, and even the soft hum of everyday electronics, it was possible to hear what lay beneath—the sigh of the wind, the murmur of water flowing in a creek, the calls of the birds that survived and the rustling of species starting their return to the underbrush. In her days of walking, Cass had retuned her ears to these subtle sounds, and now the whine of the motor cutting through the night stillness was nearly unbearable, winding her nerves tight and keeping her fear simmering.

The odds of encountering Beaters along this unpopulated stretch of road were slim. Cass held on to that thought and let it calm her as she watched the ribbon of road flashing silver in front of them, Smoke following the center line. The air rushing past was cold, and she snuggled into Smoke's shirt, pressing her cheek against the warm fabric. After a while she allowed her eyelids to drift slowly closed, and breathed deeply of the night. Kaysev and mountain sage and cool earth. Cass thought she could ride like this for a long, long time, clinging to the illusion of safety, grateful for someone else taking responsibility for the future.

Smoke's soft exclamation put her on instant alert. She sat up straight and blinked at lights in the distance, a glow highlighting a massive dark structure. They had arrived at the edge of San Pedro, and the black shadows of houses and mailboxes and cars lined the side of the silent road. Gravel skittering under their tires, they narrowly avoided the corpse of a large dog lying stiff and mangled in the middle of the road, and Smoke corrected by swerving onto the shoulder, cursing under his breath. When the bike was righted, Cass was left with adrenaline surging through her body, and she had to force herself not to dig her fingers into Smoke's waist.

The stadium was lit from behind by a hazy glow. The effect was that of a ghost ship on a night ocean, as though it had been conjured by her desperation. It was even bigger than she remembered, and the memory of walking up the curving ramps with her father all those years ago danced at the edge of her heart, trying to get in, but she pushed it back.

That long-ago day, it had been bright with banners and advertisements and the big digital scoreboard, the bright red and silver—Miners' team colors—worn by the players and fans. Now, the once-colorful edifice, like her memories of that day, was washed out and dull.

When they drew closer, Cass saw that someone was moving around the edges of the stadium, and she felt a combination of excitement and dread in her gut. They weren't moving like Beaters. Whoever it was—friend or foe—it was a citizen.

Smoke slowed again, and they came to a stop several blocks away from the stadium. A warehouse of some sort hugged a sprawling, fenced lot to their right; on the left were apartment buildings, low-slung brick six-flats with their first-floor windows broken out. The abandoned buildings could easily house Beater nests, especially the warehouse, which probably had loading bays on the back side of the building.

Cass pressed closer to Smoke. "Shouldn't we keep moving?"

She could sense the tension in Smoke's body.

"I know," he muttered. "Only...I just wish I knew what was ahead. I don't like that they've got people outside like that. Makes me think they're armed, and I'd kind of like to know what their agenda is ahead of time. Here, let me have the pack, okay?"

Cass slid it off her shoulders, feeling the pain in her shoulders where the straps had cut into her flesh. The pack was too large for her—a man's pack.

Smoke dug inside and handed her a water bottle. "Thirsty?"

Suddenly, she was. She twisted off the cap and drank deep, barely even minding the silty, earthy taste. Creek water: you could never boil the taste out of it. She let a little dribble down her chin, down her throat, wetting the collar of her shirt, before holding the bottle out to Smoke.

And saw that he was holding the gun, weighing it loosely in his hand. He ejected the spent magazine and rooted in the pack for a fresh one. "Sometimes I guess it pays to be famous. Infamous," he corrected himself.

"So where do you think they got them?"

"There's stashes," he said evasively. "I know of a few that the resistance set up. Not all by any means. I don't know how strong they are in the library, how many people…but it's got to be pretty organized. Our friend Herkim back there kept this one under wraps. Bet he's got a few more, too. Probably off-site…a house, a hole, doesn't take much, and for now at least the Rebuilders can't keep track of everyone's comings and goings during the day. Though I'm sure that's next."

He laughed, a sound so utterly without humor that Cass flinched.

"Were you with them from the start?" she asked. "The… resistance?"

"Wasn't really anything to be 'with,' just those of us who thought it was fucked up that a few assholes wanted to tell everyone else what to do. I mean, a power grab seemed like an especially bad idea when everything else was still going to hell. Way I saw it, maybe everyone ought to just pitch in and work together until the dust settled, know what I mean?"

Cass thought about Bobby, his easy leadership, the way everyone had turned to him, almost hungry for direction, for someone to tell them what to do. "Sometimes someone needs to take charge," she said softly, hoping her voice didn't betray the ache in her heart left by Bobby's death. "Someone just has to pick a direction and go, or it's chaos."

"I used to think that," Smoke said grimly. "Until I saw firsthand what happens when the guy with the power heads off in the wrong direction. And everyone follows along, like a bunch of lemmings throwing themselves over the cliff. I won't be a part of that. Not *ever* again."

There was a hardness in Smoke's voice that surprised Cass, and under her hands his muscles tensed. He revved the engine, and she could feel the vibrations traveling up through her body, and the combination of the reverberations and being so close to Smoke stirred her emotions in another direction entirely. There were so many things she didn't know about him—not just what he had done, who he had battled and even killed, but who he had been Before. There was a current of darkness running through him, a dangerous determination that she didn't understand. It made her afraid. She didn't know how far he would go when he was committed, but she sensed it was all the way, that he would go hell-bent in whatever direction he chose.

Right now, he had chosen to go with her. To protect her. And Cass felt herself pulled, almost irresistibly, toward the safety he offered. It was so tempting to ignore the questions nagging at the edges of her mind. The fact that the things she didn't know about him far outweighed the things she did.

"So..." she said, watching him turn the gun over in his hands. "You're sure you know how to use that?"

"Yeah...I'm not saying I'm a crack shot, and I panicked back there. But I can probably take care of anything that gets in our way between here and the Convent. Trick's going to be shooting before we get shot, if it comes down to it..."

"You think there's...? What are you worried about, free-walkers, Rebuilders, the Convent—who?"

Smoke shook his head. "I don't know. Nobody was real clear back there. Herkim says he doesn't think the Rebuilders have had much luck getting into the Convent, so he thinks they've sort of written it off, for now. They're picking off the easy targets at this point, and maybe later they'll come back when they've taken over all the little shelters and the squatters. But he also said the Convent hasn't exactly been very friendly to the resistance, either. They keep to themselves, no allegiance except their own, that kind of shit."

Which was why they had sent the children there, Cass hoped. Maybe they were neutral. Like Switzerland. The little bud of hope that she kept safe and hidden inside threatened to unfurl, and it was too soon, too dangerous for that. "The women in there...are *they* armed? Are they dangerous?"

But Smoke was moving again, keeping to the center of the street, following a path straight toward the entrance. "We didn't exactly have a lot of time to chat back there but I got the impression these ones here are a bunch of zealots, you know, like a cult. They think the Siege was the start of the End Times or whatever. You know, the same people who blame every bioattack on Islamic extremists. Probably crazy but harmless, at least to us."

As they came closer the stadium loomed larger until it towered above them, stretching out several city blocks in either direction. They passed a parking lot with cars still parked in a semblance of order, the guard shack splintered and toppled.

Smoke eased off on the gas when they were a few hundred feet away. "Look there," he said, pointing to an alcove to the left. "That doesn't look good."

Cass had to search for a moment to see what he was pointing at.

A figure, dressed in loose pants and shirt, holding an all-business gun, a semiautomatic, the kind that said "gang" and "mercenary" and "drug runner" to Cass, images from a hundred stupid late-night movies. Her heart lurched and she instinctively clutched Smoke tighter.

He reached very slowly and deliberately for the keys and turned off the engine. "I don't believe I'll be wanting to challenge *that*," he said softly. "You get off first. Put your hands out so he can see you don't have anything. I'll follow."

Cass did as Smoke suggested, taking her time, holding her arms out like she was trying to balance on a narrow path. She sensed Smoke behind her and then he was at her side, protecting her as always.

"We're unarmed," Smoke called out.

"Rebuilder?" the voice answered, and Cass was startled to hear that it was a woman. The figure stepped closer and Cass could see that she was tall and broadly built and that she moved with confidence.

"No," Smoke snapped. "No fucking way."

"You won't mind if I don't take your word for it. Lie on the ground, facedown, arms out. Just so you know, if I shoot, I won't bother worrying whether you make it through or not. I'm going to search your girlfriend first and unless you want to clean her off the ground I advise you stay very, very still."

I'm not his girlfriend, Cass thought as she lay down on cold pavement for the second time in a few days. Unlike the park-

ing lot in front of the school, the concrete here smelled of
stale beer and rot. But also unlike that day, the hands that
searched her worked quickly and efficiently, a pressure not
ungentle, moving so fast along her body that there wasn't
time for Cass to register much more than surprise.

When the woman finished with her she showed Cass the
blade she had taken from her pocket—and Lyle's crystal suncatcher, glinting in the moonlight.

26

CASS HAD FORGOTTEN, AND SHE CAUGHT HER breath in dismay. "That's nothing," she said, hoping Smoke couldn't identify the little trinket. "Good luck charm."

The woman didn't reply, but slipped it into a pocket of her vest. "Fine," she muttered before moving on to Smoke. Cass wasn't sure if she meant it was all right to get up, so she just turned her head to watch, in time to see the guard take the gun from Smoke's pocket.

"Unarmed?" she said incredulously. "What the fuck is this, then?" She slipped the gun into another vest pocket and finished the search, coming up with the spare magazine and another blade, which disappeared into the pocket, as well.

"Okay, time to go see the wizard," she said, leaning over the bike and taking out the keys. "What's your name, asshole?"

"Smoke. This is Cass."

"Okay, you walk the bike. Go in front of me. You—" she

gestured at Cass with the gun "—behind him. I'll be right here, don't worry about that, just keep going."

She slid the unopened backpack onto her shoulders and Smoke touched her arm briefly before starting to push the bike by the handlebars.

The guard walked behind them. Their footsteps made an echo on the quiet, dark streets. In the shadows of the sta-dium, the souvenir stands and bathrooms were mere ruins, leaning on their frames. Ahead were streets, restaurants, bars, a fire station. More parking. Beyond that, apartment build-ings and houses.

Cass flashed again on the day she had been here with her dad, the shouts of the scalpers and men spilling out of a tavern, another haggard man selling t-shirts and ball caps and pennants. Her dad bought her a little red teddy bear with a white shirt with "Miners" printed in sparkling silver script, and she clutched it close, aware that she was too old for a teddy bear, but loving it anyway.

When they rounded the side of the stadium, a vast fenced lot appeared ahead, lit up with strings of lights and the oc-casional bright spotlight. Cass drew in her breath at the sight. How were they powering all those lights? What *was* this place?

"Clear," the woman behind her yelled and from the dark-ness under the stadium a man called back.

"Who you got?"

"Couple of sheep. When are you off?"

"Two," the man replied. Cass saw him then, standing with his legs slightly apart, a gun like the other guard's slung across his torso. "Rockets?"

"Yeah, I guess. I'm covering for Baldy, pulled a double."

The man grunted and they passed by. So there were guards ringing the entire stadium, Cass guessed. But a man?

Did this mean that they had been wrong? Were men in the Convent, and if so, what if it wasn't a cult at all? Not that men couldn't be in cults, but the tone of these two—joking, irreverent, undeniably tough—didn't strike Cass as steeped in religious zealotry.

And what were they guarding against, anyway? She'd seen no signs of Beaters, no evidence of nests or recent kills. The Convent itself was quiet.

They approached the fenced lot, Cass blinking in the lights. Chain link stretched ten, a dozen feet high, razor wire twisted along the top, an entire block lit up. And tents— tents! People milling about, sitting around a fire, clustered near a makeshift bar, drinking.

"Don't slow down," the guard said behind them. "Plenty of time to look around when you get in."

"What is that?" Cass asked.

"That's civilization, sweetheart."

"Are the people in there prisoners?" Smoke demanded.

The guard laughed shortly. "Ain't anyone a prisoner," she said. "It's just the little place we call home. No charge to come on in, and you can buy just about anything you want, for a price. There's people who have more or less than others, that's about it. Dor's got the most, so it's his thing. You'll meet him soon enough."

Cass wasn't sure she had heard right. "Did you say *Dor?*" she demanded.

"Yeah, Dor MacFall. Sounds made-up, right? Maybe it is, maybe it isn't."

Dor MacFall. Cass's mind was suddenly full of the image of Sammi, that day before she left, hope and longing etched on her pretty young features. *Find my dad*, she'd said. *All I want is for him to know I'm okay.*

"What is he, a—a—" Mayor of this little squatters' town?

But the guard was done talking. When they approached an opening in the fence, a complicated gate was opened by a heavy, broad-faced woman with hair so short Cass thought it must have been buzzed with a razor. The guard ignored them and made small talk with the large woman and a second guard, a lanky man with long sandy hair. She emptied the items she'd confiscated from her pockets and handed them over along with the backpack and the gun. The man set them on a long bare table then sat down and started sorting through the contents of the pack. "See you at Rockets," she said as she turned to go, not bothering with goodbyes for Cass and Smoke.

"I'm Faye. Park that over here," the new guard said as she motioned them in. Smoke pushed the bike into a corner of the encampment where a small rider tractor was parked next to a half-dozen bicycles. "Y'all set here a minute while we inventory all this."

"I'm going to need some assurance I'll be getting that back," Smoke said as he and Cass took seats on a long low picnic bench.

Faye didn't even look up from her task.

"Did you know him?" Cass asked Smoke. "Dor MacFall? Sammi's dad?"

Smoke shook his head. "They split up before it got really bad. He moved out back before they cut off the power. But that little girl never stopped talking about him. She made me promise if I ever saw him I'd tell him she was all right."

"She made me promise the same thing."

"Yeah, well…guess now we'll have the chance."

"What are the odds? I mean, she said he was in Sykes—"

"Sykes probably doesn't exist anymore," Smoke said. "Not in any meaningful way. Anyone with any brains would have got the hell out. Town that small, you're not going to be able to get enough folks together to set up much of a defense."

"Yes, but why here?"

"Why not here?" Smoke shrugged. "Once he heard about the Convent…he's a sharp guy, he saw an opportunity, he jumped on it. Knew there'd be a lot of traffic through here, so he built himself a combination general store and strip club and KOA campground, is what it looks like. With a hell of a security detail."

"Sammi said he was a businessman—"

"That what she said?" Smoke laughed without humor. "You know what his business was? Internet marketing. But not the kind the FTC approved of—you know what I'm saying? The Siege was probably the best thing to happen to MacFall—from what his ex told me, they were closing in on him. He was looking at a few years in prison."

"And now he's like the kingpin around here," Cass said bitterly, even though she knew her disgust was only partly for the man who Sammi idolized. It had taken her two decades to realize that Silver Dollar Haverford was really never going to come back and be the father she'd needed him to be. "Still, seems like a coincidence that we'd run into him."

"I don't know…. It's a small world now, Cass."

Faye had lined up their items: water bottles, kaysev cakes, a pair of blades. She whistled when she saw the packets of Tylenol and two Balance Bars, and separated them out. "You know how it works, right?"

"Uh, no," Smoke said. "We're new around here. Which you might have gathered when we drove up on that thing."

If Faye caught the irony in his voice, she didn't let on. Instead she wrote something on a legal pad.

"Seriously," Cass tried. "All we know is that the Convent—well, we don't know anything, except that I'm looking for—"

She stopped herself. She had been about to say that she was looking for her daughter, for Ruthie. But caution seemed like a good idea, and instead she said, "Someone," and left it at that.

"Someone in the Convent or out here?" the man said in a pleasant enough voice. He offered his hand, and it was warm and strong. "I'm George, by the way."

"Inside, I think."

He frowned. "Well, good luck with that. For now, the first thing I got to tell you is that you're safe here. From Beaters, anyway."

Cass looked at the chain-link fence doubtfully. George followed her line of vision and shook his head. "No, I mean, there's no Beaters in town anymore."

"You killed them *all?*"

"Killed or captured." He pointed to the Convent. "They contract with MacFall to have it done."

"Why the hell would anyone want to capture one of those things?" Smoke demanded.

"You'd have to talk to him," George shrugged. "He keeps his business pretty close to the vest, though."

"You're saying he trades with the women in the Convent?" Cass asked.

"Yeah. There's a few hundred of 'em in there, and they got power, gas, stores, weapons. And crazy-ass determination. That's something you can't buy."

"A few *hundred,*" Smoke repeated. "In there?"

"Once they started the Convent, women just started showing up from all over. I thought that's why you were here," he said, pointing to Cass. "To join up."

"To join the Convent?"

"To join the *Order*."

"Okay, how about you save that for later, Georgie," Faye said, drawing a decisive line down the center of the page. "We got business to do."

"What do you mean?"

She gave Cass a shrewd, clear-eyed gaze. "Trading. That is, if you want to trade. If you want to turn around and walk back out, minus that Ruger, you're free to do so. 'Course, we wouldn't guarantee your safety."

"You're taking my gun," Smoke said.

"Not taking it. Trading for it. Or, for a small fee, holding it for you. Until such time as you come and get it back. There's no arms allowed in here, except guards. Of course, you'd be compensated."

"With what?" Cass asked.

"Changes all the time. Today, we got kerosene…we got baby formula, Ritalin, Vicodin."

Cass looked around more carefully. A cluster of teenagers stood in a corner passing a bottle, a few of them kicking a hackysack back and forth. One of them had an arm wrapped in bandages and held in a sling. The job looked surprisingly professional. When the boy dived for the beanbag, Cass saw that he also had a scabbed bruise on his leg, probably just the result of some ordinary misadventure. But where had they found a doctor, much less supplies, to patch him up?

In a stand of pepper trees—still thriving, from the looks of it, though inexpertly pruned—a man was lying in a hammock suspended from the branches, reading out loud from a book by the light of a headlamp mounted on a baseball cap. Below him on the ground, several people sat cross-legged or leaning into each other, listening.

The smell of kaysev being fried with onions drifted past on the air, and Cass spotted the source—a grill set up over coals, an aproned man flipping patties in the air and expertly catching them. People clustered around chatting, waiting for the food to be ready.

It was like a carnival and a camping trip all rolled up in one, and Cass realized it had been a long time since she had seen people having fun like this. Something was out of place, something besides the shouts and laughter, and Cass struggled to place it, and then suddenly she got it. Music—not loud, far-off on the opposite corner, past a row of tents: an old Red Hot Chili Peppers song that her parents used to like.

"That's— You use batteries to play *music?*" she demanded, incredulous. It seemed so indulgent, so incredibly wasteful. When batteries began to run low in the library, Bobby had made a list of acceptable uses: lights for emergencies at night; to run the humidifier in the playroom when one of the little boys started having asthma attacks; for a pair of walkie-talkies the raiders used, before they quit working.

"Generator, actually," George said, and Cass identified the other sound, the steady low rumble.

"You can give 'em a tour in a minute," Faye said to George, suppressing a yawn, "if they decide to stay. But first lemme tell y'all what kind of deal I can do for you today."

27

THE PACKET OF TYLENOL BOUGHT THEM A
night in a two-man tent near the far side of the encampment,
which everyone simply referred to as *the Box*.

Cass made one other trade with George after Smoke left
to collect their supplies and find an unoccupied tent—a
Balance Bar for an introduction to a woman named Gloria,
who Faye assured her knew more about the Convent than
anyone else in camp, having lived there until a week earlier.
The only catch was that Gloria had passed out drunk a while
before their arrival, and Faye advised Cass to wait until she
woke up in the morning before trying to talk to her.

"Now she lives here? In…the Box?" Cass asked, drinking gratefully from the Nalgene water bottle Faye offered to
share. Faye had loosened up once their business was done,
and seemed glad for the company, producing a folding chair
for Cass and inviting her to wait there for Smoke to return.
Her shift was over, and they took their chairs out of the

harsh glare of the spotlight wired to the gate to illuminate the entrance. Faye's job had to be dull, sitting here at the gate, waiting for people to show up. After all, how many freewalkers could possibly arrive each day?

Faye laughed. "Honey, nobody lives here except us employees. And there ain't none of us lookin' to get rid of our jobs. For most folks it's too expensive to spend more than a night or two here, so they just come around when they have something to trade."

"But where do they go from here?"

Faye shrugged. "Where they came from, I guess."

"But if there's really no Beaters in San Pedro, then why—"

"Look around, Cass," Faye said. She had offered Cass a camp chair and they were sitting behind her makeshift counter. The gates had been secured for the night, but Cass spotted guards patrolling both the perimeter of the Box and the stadium, moving quietly through the darkness. "What do you see?"

Cass looked. It was like a giant church camp—that was the thought that came to her mind. For a while, when her father was touring with his band in the summer and her mother was working long shifts over at County, they had sent her to one run by Saint Anne's Episcopal. Kids were bused in from all over, and it didn't take Cass long to figure out it was a camp for kids who didn't want to be there but couldn't afford anywhere else, run by people who talked a good game but didn't really seem all that interested in whether or not the kids were having a good time. Cass remembered sitting at wood picnic tables in ninety-degree heat making crafts involving leaves and glue sticks, trying not to cry while the counselors taught them a song about Abraham and Sarah.

Here, people wandered aimlessly from the bonfire set up

in the middle of the encampment to the barter tables, the little stands where they could trade for deodorant and salted peanuts and baby powder and rubbing alcohol. Open-air bars were set up under pop-up tents; a few were sturdier affairs behind plywood screens. The music never stopped, though it covered a dizzying range, from a haunting piano étude to a remarkably bad cover of "Sweet Child of Mine" by a tuneless girl band. Now some endless country song whose chorus rhymes relentlessly droned on. A few of the people around the fire seemed to be nodding off to sleep.

"I see a lot of people with nothing better to do," she said.

Faye gave her a withering look. "Then you're not looking very hard."

"Save the damn riddles," Cass said, exasperated. "I've been through a lot the last few days and I don't feel like playing games."

"Everyone here is wasted," Faye said, drawing out the final word. "Out of their fucking minds."

"Well, yeah, you sell hooch in paper cups," Cass said. She'd been surprised and relieved earlier when, smelling the cheap wine on the women waiting to use the bathroom, she found that it hadn't called out to her with the strength it once had, hadn't made her insensible with yearning.

Faye snorted. "That's nothing. They give that shit away for *free,* for the big spenders. The pill poppers, meth junkies— guarantee they're lined up back behind Rockets right now, trading their last can of SpaghettiOs for 20mg of Ritalin or a couple of rocks."

Oh.

Ohhh. *Idiot,* Cass chastised herself. Earlier the thought had danced through her mind, quickly enough that she hadn't bothered to examine it carefully, namely that the Box didn't make much sense. A few months into Aftertime, it was true that all the easy stuff was taken; grocery stores and hardware stores and sporting good stores had long ago been looted of all the valuable items, homes had been broken into and all the weapons and canned goods and medicine cleaned out. But for the brave—and at this point, almost every citizen who had managed to stay alive this long fell backward into that category to some extent—there was still more than enough to be found.

So it stood to reason that the Box's allure would be something even more special.

As the Siege followed its tortuous path, each day bringing some new abomination, some crippling terror, alcohol and drugs were at an astonishing premium. More than a few people locked themselves in their houses and proceeded to get as drunk or stoned as they possibly could. Sometimes they were in search of the courage to shoot or hang themselves. Sometimes they were trying to drink themselves to death or overdose. Some were trying to tap into fantasies they'd held secret for a long time, from a time when society had a tighter grip on the psyche. Before long there was nothing left to get numb with.

Except clearly, the people running the Box had a hell of a stash.

Cass gripped the cheap metal frame of her chair, the plastic web cutting into her shoulder blades, overwhelmed by the thought of all these people who had survived so much, only to try to drown their pain with a temporary high. She hadn't been around active users in a long time; the thought was a little overwhelming.

"You're an addict," Faye added, offhandedly.

Cass felt her face flush, but she forced herself to keep her expression neutral. "Was," she corrected Faye. "*Was.*"

"Was, like, for how long?"

"Long enough."

"Yeah," Faye said, clearly skeptical. "So it's some kind of accident you showed up here? There's nowhere else in the central valley to score, and yet here you are—"

"Because I have to get in the Convent. I *have* to get in there. I have to find...someone."

Faye's expression didn't change. "You want to find someone in *there*."

"Yes."

"Sister? Mother? Spinster aunt maybe? Your people Jesus folks?"

"Why, is that what the Convent is? Like, fundamentalists?"

"I don't know the details. I guess you can ask Gloria. She's happy to talk, talks everyone's fuckin' ears off, when she's not wasted. But, no, it's not just a Jesus thing. It's like, they worship the disease or something."

"What?"

"Or like, it's the antichrist and they vanquish it through prayer, something fucked up like that. I don't know." Faye shrugged. "For all I know they're in there dancing naked under the moon."

How could the woman not be more curious? The Convent was the closest thing to a real community that Cass had seen since the Siege. Other than the little groups in libraries and schools, no one had been able to band together in sufficient numbers to move beyond the demands of subsistence living.

"You two look cozy." Smoke's deep voice rumbled behind Cass. She twisted in her chair to see him holding a plastic bucket in one hand, white towels in the other.

"Okay, I think that's my cue to shove off," Faye said. "I'm sure I'll see you around. Nice meeting you."

Smoke waited until Faye disappeared down the main path through the tents, then offered Cass a hand. "How does a shower sound?"

"Like heaven."

She let Smoke pull her out of her chair, and peeked into the bucket. There were washcloths along with the rest of the toiletries. "What did that cost?"

Smoke gave her a sly grin. "They've got a thriving skin trade going here," he said, pointing to the end of the Box farthest from the stadium. It was lit only by a sparkling string of Christmas lights that wound from tent to tent. "In case you haven't figured it out, that's what the blue tents are for. I just, you know, stopped by and gave the ladies a taste of what they wanted, and they showered me with earthly goods."

"Ha. Ha." Cass smiled at his joke, despite herself. "God, I'm stupid. I thought those were first aid tents."

"Not stupid, only naive. Or maybe it's wishful thinking, that you can start a civilization on free trade and have it grow toward an ideal, only I doubt that ever works. I mean, look at the history of any major civilization..."

"I don't think I'm up for a history lesson right now," Cass said softly, though it occurred to her that history was bound to be lost in a generation or two, with no one to preserve and teach it. If any humans even survived that long. "Besides, it's not just the, you know, blue tent thing. I didn't get that the whole currency here is based on drugs. I just feel like an idiot."

"Well, not the *entire* trade, maybe. I got this stuff, and a couple decent single-malts and a bowl of pretzels that weren't completely stale."

Cass whistled. "Not to nag, but how are we affording this? You didn't trade away our blades, did you?"

"Nah. I, uh, put the bike up to secure a loan."

"The *bike?*"

"Yeah. I mean, it's not like we could make much use of it without fuel. Besides, I can get it back. They've got every angle covered. It's like a pawn shop—they just charge you a holding fee."

Cass shook her head. It wasn't for her to say, really. She knew that the bike, the supplies, the gun—these had all been given to Smoke because of his record with the Rebuilders. She had no claim on them.

"You coming?" he said softly. "I paid for two. Can't really use the second one myself."

Cass slipped her hand into the crook of his arm and they walked down a path lit by yellow light from a dozen Coleman lanterns hung on poles. They passed people talking softly in the entrances of tents, or bent over bongs and pipes and bottles.

A man lurched into the path from between two tents with a cut-off grunt. He had almost recovered his footing when a second man tackled him and took him down, yelling. The smell of alcohol and sweat came off the pair as they tumbled and rolled. One was trying to stab the other with a butter knife, but he was too drunk to do any real damage and the knife fell to the ground.

Cass was about to grab it to prevent further trouble when a third man shoved her out of the way. He was dressed in a black t-shirt and cargo shorts and a small receiver on his belt broadcast static and voices. His belt also held a sap, a gun and handcuffs, but he ended the scuffle instantly without using any of them by pulling the closer man off the other, yanking his arms behind his back and up, then pinning him to the ground with a knee. The other man whimpered and curled up into a ball, but another guard arrived and dragged him roughly to his feet. The would-be fighters were hustled off, the guards mumbling apologies to Cass and Smoke, and the incident was over moments after it started.

"Wow," Cass said. "That's...impressive."

"Protecting their investment, more like," Smoke said. "Part of what people pay for here is a sense of security. They've got a drunk tank, over at the back corner. Just a big locked pen with a few guys passed out in it."

"This kind of feels like the Wild West. Like you could get away with a lot, as long as you don't disturb the peace."

Smoke shrugged. "Maybe that's not such a bad thing, as long as you don't hurt other people...I mean, who really cares? It's not like a thousand little rules are really going to turn this into some sort of model society."

Cass didn't answer. At first, as the rule of law gave way to the rules of self-preservation, there had been an unfamiliar sense of freedom, an untethering from the obligations and habits of Before. But that freedom was only an illusion, at least here, where a man who might or might not be Sammi's father ruled with one hand while he offered temptation with the other. Maybe it was inevitable this sort of order would impose itself, even Aftertime.

Cass remembered the helpless anger everyone felt at the government as the Siege wore on, as one by one the threads connecting communities were broken and people were catapulted into chaos. At the time, everyone had wished for someone or something new to take charge, to make things right and tell them what to do.

Now, a few months later, someone had. Several someones. Only the choices didn't look good. There were the Rebuilders. The Box, with its promises of numbness and pleasure. Hundreds of smaller communities with God-knows-what going on behind closed walls. And then whatever the Convent offered.

Cass wasn't optimistic about finding anything more than a different brand of crazy inside the stadium, but if Ruthie was there, that's where she was going.

Later, in the tent, Cass busied herself with unrolling the flaps that served as a door and snapping them shut. Only a slim band of lantern light entered at the bottom, though not enough to cast any light on the interior of the tent, so Cass undressed in the dark. Her skin was soft and warm from the showers—an outdoor affair that ran from a heated reservoir and felt better than almost anything she'd experienced in recent memory.

Anything, that is, except for the night in Lyle's guest room. Only Cass wasn't sure if that was even in the same realm. The sensations of that night were enmeshed so completely with emotion that it was impossible to know how much of what she felt came from Smoke's touch and how much was the momentum of her own needs and fears, tumbled together in a firestorm of ecstasy.

And now she was about to lie down with him for the second time. Cass knelt on the air mattress, felt it shift beneath her weight. She ran her hands along the blankets and sheets, which were not nearly as finely made or as clean as Lyle's, and when her hands found Smoke's he took them and wrapped them firmly in his own and pulled her toward him without hesitation.

"Get under," he commanded and she wriggled into the warmth under the covers and pressed against him. For a moment it felt sweet and right, a relief, a balm, an exhalation of a breath caught in anxiety. Smoke's chest was bare. He was wearing only boxers. And even through the cotton she could feel his heat and, undeniably, his desire.

"You traded away everything we had today," Cass chided,

trying to keep her tone light. "Now we've got no aces up our sleeves. Nothing to get us out of the next jam we get into."

"Didn't give away anything we can't get more of," Smoke murmured as he put his arms around her, his hands careful and tender on her back as they sought to touch only the unhurt places. For a moment Cass let herself luxuriate in his arms, in the promise of safety there. But there was whiskey on his breath, and the smell worked away at the thin wall she'd put up over her promises to herself.

Cass had once loved to kiss a man who'd been drinking whiskey, the way it tasted like a clue to something hard to find, like earth after a rain and like a fire still burning. She never drank it herself, but there had been a dozen nights that had started with its promise.

Not a promise actually, but a trick.

It was Cass's best trick and also her only trick. The way it worked:

She would have two shots, back to back, when she got to the bar. Vodka was easiest. Sometimes tequila. It helped hone her instincts, her senses, and when she found the right one—bent over a pool table, laughing with his friends, alone at the bar, it didn't matter, she always knew—the trick was that for a moment right before one of them spoke, everything was possible. Because he could be the one who turned out to be different. He could be the one to see her for who she was, to understand that all her toughness wasn't anything but pain, to know that she threw herself on the fire over and over again not to satisfy herself but to punish herself—who would see and know all that and still want her *and* be strong enough to keep her from hurting herself long enough that she wouldn't have to hurt him just to make herself forget, to make herself believe that it meant nothing.

Because that was her dirtiest little secret of all—it never really meant nothing. She could walk away and walk away and walk away and walk away, fuck a thousand men and forget all their names and pretend she didn't remember what they looked like or how their hands felt on her, and get up the next day and do it again and again, and yet it meant something every single time, it meant another failure and another time she wasn't good enough and she wasn't wanted enough.

But that moment. That moment when he first spoke, when she caught the whiskey on his breath, when he looked her up and down and really took his time, when he touched her hand or brushed against her thigh, when he told her that her eyes reminded him of someone or that she was the prettiest thing to ever walk into that particular bar, she played her one trick and played it well. She never lost her taste for the con, she worked it every time, because *this* might be the man who would truly know her—and want her anyway.

And she felt it now, felt it as she never had before, when Smoke settled his hand into the curve of her waist and drew her closer against him, so she could feel him pressing against her, making her hot and liquid and confused. He was here with her again, just like he was two nights ago. He had taken great risks with her, brought her gifts, lain down with her... and she longed to wonder if maybe, just maybe, this might be the time things would be different.

But tomorrow she would be going to find Gloria, and Gloria would tell her what she needed to get inside the Convent, to get to Ruthie. And whatever she had to do, Cass would do, and she would find Ruthie and she would take Ruthie back. And she needed to save all her energy, all her determination, for that. She could not afford to give up even one bit of her concentration for a man, for the game she always played, for the way she always punished herself. She could not afford to hurt herself or revile herself. Not now. She had to be strong.

So Cass put her hand on Smoke's chest and with tears stinging her eyes, she pushed him away, and if she thought his hesitation and his longing might be for who she really was this time, she also knew it was only a trick of her damned and fevered mind.

28

CASS WAS IN THE FAR CORNER OF THE DIRT lot behind the High Timer.

This was familiar ground, and if she wasn't proud, exactly, to be there, backed up against the side of a pickup parked under a sycamore next to the dried-up creek, she wasn't sorry, either. No one could make her sorry, because she owned this corner of the lot, had driven dozens of men to begging and pleading and even crying hot salty tears here, the first when she was barely seventeen years old.

Only this one was different.

She wasn't sure how she got here. Couldn't conjure up a memory of the drinks he bought her or the songs he picked on the jukebox. Had he challenged her to pool? So many of them did that, thinking she'd be impressed with their hard-crack breaks or their wily double-bank shots, when Cass had learned pool from the master himself, Silver Dollar Haverford, her own daddy who could beat any man from Portland down to Tijuana. Or maybe he had danced with her, the sly dip and glide of a farm boy with town manners.

Why couldn't she remember?

She was pressed up against the cold hard door of the pickup and maybe they'd be better off inside, the truck's bench seat would be good enough on a night turning cold fast like this one was, when chilly air found its way up her skirt and inside her denim jacket. She ran her fingers through his hair as he nuzzled her neck, found it greasy and lank, wondered what she'd seen in him.

But his mouth on the sensitive dip between her collarbones: insistent and hungry, his beard scraping against her soft flesh. Only tonight the man's touch wasn't doing what it usually did. It wasn't lighting tinder up and down her body, setting the scene for a brush fire that would burn out of control until it pushed her into forgetting territory.

It felt wrong, all wrong.

Cass slid her hands between her body and his and shoved, and he left off his sucking and biting with a growl of irritation, and then she was staring into his face in the sickly light of the streetlamps mounted on galvanized steel poles.

And what stared back wasn't human. Its flesh was pocked and torn. Its lips were chewed to crusts. Its eyes were unfocused and confused and when it saw the look of fear on her face it crowed with excitement, a sound that paralyzed her with unspeakable terror, and as it lowered its face to her neck again she knew that this time it meant to tear her skin from the bone, to rip it and chew it and swallow it even while she screamed.

And screamed.

And screamed, except that it clapped a hand over her mouth and she was left gasping for breath and flailing and struggling to get away but the next second the thing became

Smoke and she realized she was in a tent, in a tent in the Box on a leaking air mattress with crazy thoughts crowding the dreams from her mind and replacing them with a nightmare made of every fear born in Aftertime.

She stopped screaming and whimpered instead and Smoke lifted his hand from her mouth slowly, tentatively, ready to clamp it back down if she didn't stay quiet.

She stayed quiet.

"You had another nightmare," he murmured.

She nodded, testing the inside of her mouth with her tongue, finding it metallic.

"Was it a bad one?" he asked, and Cass opened her eyes and found that she could see nothing at all in the dark tent and she suddenly wished she could. Wished she could see Smoke's face, his eyes, his mouth. A mouth that was a bit too generous, but without it his face might have been hard, unapproachable. Instead she realized she had memorized the shape of that mouth, and in the dark she reached for him and found his chin, rough with stubble; his eyelashes against her fingertips; and finally, his lips. She brushed against them gently, and he was very still, so still she couldn't even feel him breathe.

"They're all bad," she said softly.

"Cass." If she had expected sympathy she was mistaken: his voice was steel. He clamped his hand over hers, squeezed her fingers together until they hurt. "I can't—I don't—"

He didn't want her. Cass had only been looking for comfort but the knowledge cleaved her anyway. He held her hand away from his face as though it was a blade poised to slice through him, and Cass felt shame flood her like poison rushing through her veins.

She had wanted comfort. But he didn't want her.

She knew that if she explained, if she could find the words

to describe the emptiness that could never be filled, the chasm edged with cliffs of fear and longing, that he would provide comfort after a fashion. Because he was a good man. And only a good man would have come this far with her, taken the risks they had taken.

A good man. A prince, in fact. A damn Boy Scout. In the killing emptiness her last, best defense stirred. A wrecked and battle-hardened thing, it had been born long ago when she first discovered what her need demanded, when she first recognized her body for what it was.

That innocent, frightened girl had become a temptress, a serpentine thing, all enticing, all willing, all temptation and can't-say-no. Years ago she had been clumsy, uncertain of her power, but realizing she had nothing to lose gave her strength, and she learned to twist and beckon and lure and ride until the men she found were all used up, until she had sapped them of everything they had to give her. Which wasn't much, after you discounted the terrible convulsions of their bodies and the momentary vulnerability in their glazed eyes: other than that small gift they didn't even realize they gave, there was nothing but release.

But she'd have it now. The angry girl had pushed off the bottom of her heart, hurtled through the wavery place where Cass had consigned her, and crested the surface with a momentous burst of need. And Cass let her take over.

Smoke had offered her kindness when kindness could kill her.

He deserved this.

Cass didn't really believe that last conscious thought, but she pushed the phrase through her mind nonetheless, pushed it through and bit down on it and held it as the need took over. He deserved this because he didn't want her after he'd let her want him.

She yanked her hand back and she heard him take in his breath. She crawled across the makeshift bed, the hard ground through the limp air mattress hurting her knees, and shoved the cheap blanket and sheets aside as she straddled his body.

"Cass..." His voice was alarmed. But she had set this in motion now, and it would not be stopped.

She bent over him and let the t-shirt slide up over her thighs, her hips, leaving almost nothing between them. She pressed herself against him and found him hard, fiercely hard, and he shuddered involuntarily and seized her wrists.

"Cass." He said it again, through gritted teeth. He held her wrists so hard she felt her bones pressed together, and sucked in her breath in pain, but she didn't fight him. He was stronger. But she had other ways.

She let him hold her wrists. She gave control of her arms over to him, his for the moment. But she had the rest of her body and she used it.

She rubbed herself slowly, lightly—to Smoke her touch must have felt tentative, but it was the farthest thing from tentative—over him, feeling the outline of his hard cock through the layers of cotton that might as well have not been there at all. She closed her eyes and concentrated on letting everything else fall away, because the more she gave herself over to the rush the less of her that was left behind. It was a battle for control, and the only way for her to control herself, to control the chasm with its jagged cliff edges, was to control him. The man below her, the man who she was trying to make into not-Smoke, to make into a stranger, to make into no one, because the old equation required a man who was nothing to her.

But he kept saying her name and that would wreck it.

"God, Cass," he choked out, as though she was strangling him with the languid caress of her body against his.

"Shut up," she commanded, and pressed into him harder. The shock of the contact between them, hard meeting soft, sent sensation through her, a riveting jolt that emanated through her body but burned itself out long before it could reach her mind, her legs, her arms. "Shut up, please just shut up shut up shut up shut up shut up..."

She ground out the words in time to her movement against him. Through her anger she felt her need grow and bloom. He found her rhythm and moved with her, this man beneath her, this man who in the dark could be a stranger; if she just tried hard enough he could be a stranger. She felt his grip on her wrists weaken and she twisted her hands savagely and he let go, his reflexes were slow, too late he realized she'd freed herself and tried to catch her again but she was quicker.

Cass grabbed his hands before he could find her first. She held his strong fingers in her hands and pressed them up under her shirt, against her, and when his fingers spasmed against her she knew it was instinct that guided him and that he would still work against it and so she leaned into his touch, arching her back and moving so that her breasts fit themselves to his cupped hands and he had no choice. That's what it felt like to her and she knew it must be the same for him, that he had no choice as his fingers found her nipples and circled and seized.

From there, there was no thought. She plunged her fingers into his hair and lifted him to her so that his face was pressed against her and his mouth and lips and tongue were eager now. He didn't fight. He was hungry and he gave up any attempts to restrain her and held her to him, his hands under her arms. She felt his fingers splayed against the bones of her rib cage, imagined it expanding with the breaths she sucked in, noisy ragged breaths that were not graceful.

The things he did with his mouth made her writhe harder against him and the ride was no longer orchestrated by her, it was a course they both followed because there was no other. Their hands went to their clothes in the same instant and twined together as they pulled and yanked and tossed aside. He let go of her to pull his boxers down over his legs and the loss of his attention—even for a second—enraged the need in her and she took him in her hand and rubbed him against her hottest, wettest folds so that when he gasped and returned his hands to her sides he rocked into her just as she drove herself down on him and there was no hesitation, no halfway, nothing but trying to make him more inside and him trying to plunge farther.

She bucked extravagantly, knowing it was coming, the thunderous crest that could not be stopped now, it was as sure as the sun blazing in the morning or thunder after lightning rips the sky. She leaned back and put her hands on his legs so that her body tilted away from him. If there was any light at all in the tent she knew that he would see her body, long and strong and bent back as she rode him hard, and that seeing her that way would send him past the point where he had any control at all, and knowing that—even in the dark, even where they saw nothing, where the loss of one sense only heightened the others so it was their sharp breaths on the silent night, the slap of sweat-slicked flesh, the grunting and syllables that were only parts of words—all of this spiraled tighter and tighter and she squeezed her eyes shut and ground her teeth together and threw herself into the chasm, past the treacherous cliffs and over the pain-dusted edges and into the nothing.

It was a long and spectacular fall and partway down he

met her there and it was like they seized each other midair so that when the final crest splintered into blinding sensation, she was aware of him there with her and it was new.

It was new, it was like nothing she'd ever felt before, a feeling of being out of herself and part of him just for those seconds, her energy stretching and flickering and it seemed incredibly dangerous, like she might snap and not return to herself, but she let it happen anyway, and afterward she lay on top of him and waited for the part that had left her to come back, and the part that was him to leave her, and when it didn't happen right away she began to panic but even her panic wasn't enough to make her lift her body away from his, because she lay in a state of such exhaustion and spent and total dissipation that moving was impossible.

Much, much later she felt his hands in her hair, fingers gentle against her scalp, working the strands into tangles, and he said, "They're applauding," and while she tried to make sense of his words she marveled at the feel of his voice, the way it formed in his chest and rumbled against her cheek.

And then she realized that he meant the sounds outside the tent, which only now entered her conscious mind: a smattering of clapping and laughter and one distinct voice saying, "That's how it's done, brother," and another saying, "Could everyone shut the fuck up and let the rest of us sleep."

Cass burned with mortification. She didn't remember making any sound—in those final seconds her hearing seemed to have gone the way of her vision, as though the darkness had stolen it, too—but she must have cried out. She didn't do that, ordinarily, but she remembered the cry building in her throat right before everything splintered and it must have been loud enough to wake up the people sleeping nearby.

Her greater worry—the fact that the man beneath her was

slowly turning back into Smoke—was too much to think about now. She pushed her face into the hollow of his shoulder and willed herself not to think about it.

When he said, very softly, "Sweet dreams, Cass," she said over and over in her mind, "I do not hear you. I do not hear you."

I do not hear you, because you aren't really there.

29

IN THE MORNING SHE WAS ALONE IN THE TENT
and she thought: Smoke is a man who comes and goes
quietly.

And then she thought—*Ruthie*. Today was the day she
would find out how to get inside the Convent, and she
would search for her Ruthie.

Do the next right thing, Pat's voice—*Hello, my name is Pat
and I'm an alcoholic*—said in her head, all reasonable insis-
tence, the voice of a hundred meetings in the church basement. Pat listened; Pat never judged. Pat was bald except
for a silver fringe on the back of his head and looked like he
ought to be a grandfather, and Pat just kept listening. *What
if I don't know the next right thing,* Cass had demanded—had
whined really, if she were to be honest—and Pat had said,
It's only one *little next right thing, Cass, don't think so hard,* and
the guy with the red hair—she couldn't remember his name
now because he didn't last more than a few months—had

muttered, *Man plans and God laughs,* which had struck Cass as funny and kind of clever, in context, a lot more clever than any of the stupid A.A. phrases…but by summer that guy was gone and Cass was still there so who was right, in the end?

So she would do the next right thing, and that thing was: Find Gloria.

She took the little bucket of personal supplies to the bathroom and was relieved to find that there was no further charge to use it, because Smoke had done all their trading and she didn't know how it was done and she didn't feel like letting her ignorance show. There was no sign of Smoke and Cass only saw a few other people trudging between the tents, shivering in hoodies and flannel shirts, and she realized that it was earlier than she'd first thought, maybe six or six-thirty on a late-summer morning.

When she returned to their tent she saw that Faye was standing in front of it, holding a steaming mug.

"There you are," she said with a sly smile.

"Sorry, I was just at the, uh, ladies' room."

"Word is you two put on a bit of a show last night," Faye said conversationally, and Cass felt her face redden. "Hey, you provided everyone some entertainment around here. And you got something that did you good. So chill. You ready to go meet Gloria?"

"Yeah, just let me get—something," she said, and poked her head into the tent. Really, she only wanted to see if Smoke had returned, but nothing looked disturbed. The covers were still tangled. Her pack was where she left it.

"Okay, I'm ready."

Faye led her through the camp. They passed the merchant stands, where people were stacking and arranging their wares—their toothbrushes and playing cards and packets of aspirin and Theraflu, their paper plates and toilet paper and candles and cans of beans and condensed milk and Chef Boyardee—and righting overturned camp chairs and cleaning up litter from the night before. A fire burned in a grate near where the remains of the bonfire smoldered, and coffee boiled in a pot on top, and Cass felt her stomach growl. Well, maybe later she could ask Smoke to buy her a meal. And coffee—a cup of hot, thick coffee. But for now she would concentrate on Gloria.

"Here," Faye said abruptly, veering off to the left, past the fenced-off area where the bike Smoke had traded was parked next to other motorcycles and a few bicycles and skateboards. "The cheap seats."

Cass hadn't noticed them the night before—a row of canvas cots lined up next to the fence. In nearly all of them, motionless forms slept under drab, rough blankets, a few possessions piled under the ends of the beds.

Cass followed Faye to the end of the row, trying not to stare. At the very end a woman with long gray hair escaping its braid sat with her back to them at the edge of her cot, bent over her knees; too late Cass realized she was throwing up.

"Aw, shit, Gloria," Faye exclaimed. "Here?"

"I'll clean it up, I'll clean it up," the woman said hastily, her voice reedy and frail, a girl's voice in a middle-aged woman's body. "I'm sorry, I think I must have eaten something—"

"You mean, like a fifth of cheap gin," Faye growled. "I'll send someone. You didn't get it on the bed, did you?"

"No, no, I didn't. I wouldn't do that."

"Okay, well, I brought you someone who wants to talk to you. Take a walk with her. We'll have this taken care of when you get back."

"Yes. Yes, thank you," Gloria said. She stood and started to walk down the path along the fence, not even looking at Cass, who hurried to catch up.

"You're the girl wants to get in the Convent," she said when Cass fell into step with her, stealing a sideways glance as though she was afraid of being found out. "They told me you'd come."

Cass saw pale green eyes in a weathered face, lashes bleached by the sun, cheekbones that were still regal. Gloria had once been a beauty, but Cass saw something else, something that was as familiar to her as the chipped, heavy mugs at the meetings: more regrets than a human being could keep hidden, so that they found their way to the surface, traced in the faint lines and creases of her skin.

"I do want to get in," she said carefully. "I need your help."

The corner of Gloria's mouth twitched, a tic that only underscored her anxiety, and darted a glance at Cass. "How do I know?"

"Know what?"

"That you're who you say you are. That you're not one of theirs."

"One of...whose?"

Gloria's tic intensified and she pressed a fist against her mouth, pushing hard enough to turn her knuckles white. "They could have sent you. Mother Cora and the rest. To spy on me."

"Gloria...I don't know who that is," Cass said, trying to contain her impatience. "I just got here. I've never been in there. I need your help...please."

"They're not supposed to/come in here," Gloria whispered, walking with her shoulders hunched. "It's Dor's rule. It's his *rule*."

"The people...from the Convent, they aren't allowed in here? In the Box?"

"They can't come in here."

"But I'm here. They let me in here. So, I can't be from *there,* right?"

Cass felt a little silly trying to reason with Gloria, but she could tell that the woman's fear was real. Very gently, Cass touched her thin shoulder. Gloria startled at the touch, but after a moment she sighed and gave Cass another sidelong glance, pushing at the long gray hair that had come loose and tumbled around her shoulders.

"I wish I had an elastic," she said. "For my hair. Do you have an elastic?"

"No, I'm sorry," Cass said.

"Okay. That's how it is—anytime you think of something that would actually be useful, you can never find it."

"You mean..."

"In my house, I lived on the first floor of a nice old house. You should have seen it...I had a collection of tea tins. The ones with the pretty designs on them. Some of them were my mother's. Oh, some of them were very old. And I don't know, they may have been valuable, to someone, but I didn't even care about them. They were just...always there, you know?"

She sketched a shelf in the air with her fingers, and Cass knew she was seeing the tins in her mind, the way they looked in her kitchen. Cass had done the same thing a thousand times; nearly everyone had—remembering the things that were lost.

But then Gloria chopped the air with the hand that had been tracing a memory, a harsh gesture followed by a sharper exhalation. "I never used them. They were empty, all of them, and they sat there and I looked at them all the time and I never took them off the shelf and put anything in them. And then—one day, in the Convent, I was on washing. Me and a woman named...something. Maybe it was Alice. We were pinning the clothes on the line. We had the cheap clothespins, a pack of a thousand someone got from the Wal-Mart, but, you know, Before. And they were in this plastic bag and they kept spilling out and we tried to twist the top closed but it just kept opening, all those clothespins lying on the ground, and I thought, my tins—it would have been perfect. The clothespins in the tins, and I wished right then that I had one of them, even one, just one. I would put the clothespins in the tin and there would be that one perfect thing. The one thing that was the way it ought to be. You know?"

And the thing was, not only did Cass know but Gloria's explanation was dead-on. She'd had the same complicated regret herself, over and over, the mourning for some small thing not because she missed the object itself but because in that moment everything seemed off. All solutions were imperfect solutions. And that wasn't a bad thing, necessarily, because you learned to improvise, you learned to make do. Except for once in a while when it hit you like this.

"I know," she said, and touched Gloria, gently.

Gloria looked at her, then looked at the arm where Cass had touched her, and her eyes clouded and she picked at her crusty chapped lip. "Why do you want to go in there? It's not nice there."

"Oh, I don't. That's not why I'm here. I don't want to join. I'm looking for my daughter. Ruthie."

As she said the name the feeling was there again, the fear that Ruthie was not in the great looming stadium, that she was nowhere near here. Maybe she was nowhere at all anymore.

Gloria put a hand to her cheek and frowned. "How old is your daughter?"

"Almost three." Three in September, if anyone was still keeping track by then.

Gloria shook her head. "There's little ones there. But they change all their names when they're baptized."

"Baptized?"

"Yes. Into the Order. In the ceremony, where they take their first communion and get their new names." There was a note of sympathy in her voice, and she fixed her troubled gaze on Cass, her confusion momentarily lessened. "Tell me about your little girl. What does she look like?"

So Cass told: the hair so pale in the sun that it looked like flashing dimes. The rosebud mouth that could crumple into a wobbly frown one moment and lift into a blazing smile the next. The fold in her chubby arms where the baby fat was still smooth and soft.

As she talked Cass found herself speeding up, panicking, with the knowledge that her baby was months older now, that the rounded elbows and dimpled knees might have disappeared, that her hair would be longer and she would have a dozen new freckles and have learned to do things Cass couldn't even imagine. Cass couldn't know all the ways Ruthie would have grown and changed, and it felt like a betrayal.

"I don't know," Gloria said, interrupting Cass midsentence, shaking her head. "It's too hard to know. And they change them. They mix them up like they mix me up. I heard talk."

"What do you mean? What kind of talk?"

Gloria twisted her mouth into an expression of fury. "*Hypocritical* talk," she spat. "The kind I can't stand. The kind that drove me right back out here."

Right back to the bottle—she didn't say it, but it was clear to Cass, and Cass didn't judge. She knew how it was—the filament that wasn't strong enough, the way it stretched and stretched before it snapped, leaving you hurtling through the air toward devastation.

Still, there was hope. There were girls in the Convent, and one of them could be Ruthie, and she would find out, but she needed Gloria to focus. They approached an old picnic bench set on uneven ground under a dead pepper tree. "Let's sit," she suggested, sweeping dirt and twigs off the splintered wood, and Gloria sat, her expression troubled and confused.

"What kind of talk did you hear?" Cass pleaded, hoping the woman could keep it together a little longer.

"Talk talk," Gloria muttered. She found a groove in the weathered wood with her forefinger. Her hands were surprisingly elegant, unlined and narrow with long fingers and neat nails. She rubbed at the groove gently, seemingly oblivious to the splintered edges. "They said I didn't have enough faith. I said *they* didn't have enough faith. I know what I know. I watched…the sun painted the rocks and I saw God, I told them that but they said I didn't have the faith. I wouldn't drink the essence so they said I didn't have the faith."

"Saw God…Gloria, when did you see God?"

Gloria's skittering gaze landed on her and stayed, like a butterfly on a coneflower, skittish. "Matthew. Before Matthew…before he was gone."

"Who was Matthew?"

"Matthew?" Gloria glared at her, affronted, and Cass watched her awareness fade in the eddies and whorls of memory. "I married him…we went to Yosemite. I watched God, in the mornings, the way he painted the rocks with the sun. Matthew was there. We were happy." She startled out of her reverie and seemed surprised to find Cass there. "I *married* him," she repeated, sternly. "We were happy. They can't tell me I don't have faith."

Her twitching fingers went to her mouth again, covering, pinching, worrying, and Cass could sense Gloria turning inward again. Who knew what happened to Matthew... maybe he was Gloria's childhood sweetheart, dead twenty years in an accident. Or maybe he'd been taken, or died of fever only months ago. Either way, Gloria wore the loss like an amulet, a token against the weight of Aftertime.

"I'm sorry about Matthew," Cass said gently.

Gloria made a sound in her throat and nodded, dropping her hands to her lap. She only wanted to be heard, Cass thought—only that. And for things to be different. What anyone wanted.

But Cass needed more from her. "I'm so sorry to ask. But is there anything else you can tell me about what goes on in there? With the babies, the little girls? How they're cared for, where they end up?"

Gloria was shaking her head before Cass finished speaking.

"Not little girls, not," she mumbled. "Not little girls anymore."

"What do you mean?"

"When they're done, when they're baptized. They're only vessels. There's nothing left inside."

"WHAT," CASS MANAGED TO WHISPER, HER throat twisting closed.

"'Be thou a vessel of innocence,'" Gloria chanted softly. The skin twitched near her left eye. "'Scoured clean of this world.' They baptized them."

"What else did they do?"

"The hair and the dress," Gloria mumbled. "All the little dresses. White for purity. Purity for innocence. And no talking. No, no, no talking."

"They put them in baptism dresses?" Cass repeated, scrambling to make sense of Gloria's tormented muttering. "And there's no talking during the ceremony. And what happens next?"

"Scoured clean."

The phrase raised the hairs along her arm. "What does that mean, Gloria? They...wash or scrub them somehow?"

Gloria peeked at Cass, her darting eyes bright with her

fevered thoughts. "You won't know her," she said sadly.
"Don't go. She's not yours anymore. She's innocent now.
And they hide them."

Ruthie was always innocent, Cass wanted to scream, wanted
to make Gloria see her the way she had been, in her denim
overalls and tiny little flowered t-shirt, falling asleep in
Cass's lap. But Gloria pushed herself off the bench and started
walking again, her footsteps unsteady and lurching.

Cass went after her, put a hand on her arm. Gloria yanked
away from her touch, crossing her arms tightly in front of
her, shaking her head.

"Please," Cass said. "Just—just tell me what you can. Anything, just help me get in there."

"You can't go in. You don't believe."

"I—" Cass stopped herself, considered her words. The
wrong ones would make Gloria retreat even further. The
haze of broken memories and tangled thoughts around Gloria
seemed to condense and retreat when Cass was too direct,
when she brought up specifics. But specifics were what she
needed, a plan for gaining entry. "Did you believe?"

Gloria was silent for a moment. She touched her weathered fingertips to the chain link of the fence and let them
trail along the metal—surely Gloria wasn't the only resident
who walked off her next-day ills around this track.

"Two ways," she finally said. "If you're a believer, that's
one. It has to show, though. I was real and it showed. God
was with me then and it showed. Everyone could see it. You
don't have God on you, so that won't work."

Cass was surprised that the words stung. "Do you mean
that I..." She struggled to find the right words. "I don't seem
pious enough? I can be different, I can—"

Gloria was shaking her head. "God comes and goes but
he's always there, but they don't know that. You can't put

SOPHIE LITTLEFIELD

God on now—He'll come back when He's ready. But *they* don't know that."

"But how do I—what can I do to make them think I'm, you know, a believer?"

"You have to barter," Gloria said. "You can buy your way in but you have to ask the right one."

"The right one?"

"You have to ask the *right* one," Gloria repeated, enunciating with care, as though speaking to someone with limited powers of comprehension. Her breath, redolent with rot and withered hope, washed over Cass and it was all she could do not to turn away.

"Please, tell me who the right one is."

Now it was Gloria who wrapped her sunburned fingers around Cass's arm and drew her into the shade of a clump of creosote bushes growing from a ditch eroded into the edge of the path. Cass glanced around; no one took note of them. They were hidden from the interior of the Box by a series of clotheslines strung on poles, sheets and pillowcases and towels flapping in the breeze. Someone was singing on the other side, a tuneless, wandering melody, too distant for Cass to make out words. The scent of cotton drying in the sun reached her and she inhaled deeply, but she caught herself before she could close her eyes and let the smell take her back to Before.

"It'll cost you."

There was a shrewdness to Gloria now. No surprise; thirst could conjure thin moments of clarity. Cass remembered. No matter how far gone you got, you could always get your shit together enough to go to the all-night liquor store when you ran into the bottom of the bottle.

"How much?" she asked, thinking of the bike Smoke had traded, the things he'd bought for them, the merchants with their carnival booths of enticements. She hadn't wanted to take from him, to shift the balance in the strange and unwelcome ledger of their relationship, but what choice did she have? "I can pay."

"What can you give me?" Gloria's words were quick, eager, hungry.

"I don't know," Cass hedged. If she made it too easy, Gloria would tell her anything just to get the payoff quicker. "It depends on what you have to tell me."

"Let's get something now. Just a little." Gloria's voice went high and wheedling, and she twisted her lips into a smile that didn't mask her thirst.

"Soon," Cass said. "But we need to talk first."

"I can talk during, you know. I can talk and we can share. We could share, couldn't we?"

Her eagerness both repelled Cass and tore at her heart. It had been hard enough, Before, when she could drink her nights away in the solitude of her trailer. When she had a paycheck, no matter how paltry, to trade for the numbness. She'd never had to beg like this.

"How have you been getting by?" she asked Gloria softly.

Gloria blinked rapidly and glanced toward the far end of the Box, her fingertips going to her throat in a nervous, protective gesture. "I...do some things."

Cass suddenly understood. The blue tents—the groping in the dark and muffled cries of release. A hand job for a six-pack of warm beer. Ten minutes on your knees to buy a few hours of oblivion. And yet Gloria seemed to prefer life in the Box—drinking down the wages of cut-rate blow jobs, sleeping on a cot out in the elements, marking time with the level in the bottle—to life in the Order.

She'd come here thinking of the Convent as a place of

safety, of sanctuary. It was well guarded against the threats of Aftertime—Beaters as well as Rebuilders and raiders. But Gloria was clearly afraid of it, and she couldn't even tell Cass exactly what had become of Ruthie. Now, staring at the tall curved walls lit up with the yellow sun of midmorning, Cass wondered what waited for her.

"Let's just talk," Cass said gently. "And then we'll get you taken care of. I promise."

The sun was high in the sky by the time Gloria finished telling her what she knew, which guards on which shift traded with the outside, which took bribes. Gloria's words wandered and drifted and in the end Cass had no names to go by, just sketchy descriptions. Gloria said Cass should try in the late afternoon, which was the most coveted shift and hence the one that the most powerful guards in the Order— the crooked ones—kept for themselves. The Order's ranks had swelled and they were turning away far more would-be members than they accepted.

Even here, cunning trumped good intentions. Had it always been that way? Sometimes it seemed to Cass that the way it had been Before, the codes and habits of social order, were shifting and changing in her memory, like a dream she was forgetting. But all that mattered now was that the odds of buying her way in were better than talking her way in.

It wasn't much. But at least she could pay. It would have to do.

There was one last thing that Cass wanted, and Gloria knew someone who could take care of it. After Cass bought her a plastic soda bottle filled with cloudy liquor—the cheapest they had, signed for with Smoke's name—Gloria led Cass through the rows of tents on their way to the Box's only barber, sipping from the bottle along the whole way. Already she was more relaxed; the tremors in her fingers disappeared, and the deep grooves eased from the corners of her mouth and between her brows—almost making up for the vacancy in her watery eyes.

Near the end of the tents, where sleeping quarters gave way to a row of barter stands and shacks, a dusky-skinned man with a heavy, limping gait and chains looped from his belt stepped in front of them.

"Hey, Glor—i—a," he said drawing out the syllables of her name suggestively. "New batch come in this morning. Young ones, guess they went to DePaul community college, been living in a dorm there. Lost a couple on the trip... they're a mess. Better hope none of 'em decide to stay back here and cut into your business. They're smokin' hot, know what I mean?"

He pantomimed an obscene bump and grind, winking at Cass.

"Fuck you, Haskins," Gloria muttered, pushing him out of the way and stumbling past. "You'll be at my door by tonight begging for it."

"Just ignore him," Cass said, his laughter following them down the row.

"He'll be back," Gloria muttered, "Can't stay away."

But as they continued down the path it seemed to Cass that she walked with less certainty. Cass figured she understood: the biggest downside to making a living by selling off bits of your soul—what happened if one day they quit buying?

But by the time they reached the barber stand, Gloria seemed to have recovered, and when Cass tried to give her a hug she slipped away, her eyes already focused elsewhere. Cass watched her go, her long silver hair catching the sun despite its knots and snarls, and tried not to think about where she was headed.

A man tilted back in a deck chair under an awning constructed from a tarp, feet up on a stump, reading a paperback in the shade of a large straw hat. Elaborate vine tattoos snaked up both arms, disappearing into his t-shirt. He marked his place with a dollar bill and tipped his chair down. When he stood and took off his hat, Cass saw that his hair was shaved into an elaborate spiral pattern.

"At your service," he said with an exaggerated bow. "I'm Vinson. Can I do something for you today?"

"Yes. I...thought you could even it up."

She touched the jagged ends of her hair self-consciously. It was vanity, sheer vanity, and she felt her face color at the thought. She was doing this for Smoke, and that was not all right, so she forced him out of her mind and focused on her hair. It was her one pretty feature, according to her mother; at eighteen Cass had chopped it short and dyed it black, anything to further the wedge between her and Mim.

Growing her hair out had been a first step back, when she started to get better, when she started to believe in herself again. When she realized that to be good enough for Ruthie, she had to treat herself as though she was good enough. It had taken so long, so much hard work, to start to believe; and her hair had been a small daily reminder to take care of herself.

Now it was ugly again. But maybe there was a way to make it all right.

She looked over the table where the tools of Vinson's trade were laid out: a straight razor, scissors, combs, mirrors, a spray bottle of water. Small towels were folded and stacked. "I can pay, later. If that's okay. I—we—have credit."

"Ah," Vinson said. "You're the girl who came in with Smoke."

"You know him?"

"By reputation only, until last night. We had a drink to-gether."

Whiskey on his breath. The memory of their fevered cou-pling flooded Cass's mind, and she felt herself flush, her veins throbbing with the mad coursing of her blood. "Oh, he's, he's...around here somewhere."

"This one's on the house, then. For what he did, standing up to the Rebuilders. Times are only going to get harder. We'll need more like him."

"You think they'll come here?" Cass asked. "All this way?"

"They've already been here, make no mistake about that," Vinson said, pulling over a chair and motioning for her to sit. "Just the scouts so far, coming around to see what we've got before they send their little army in. Only I figure your pal Smoke might've given them something to think about."

He chuckled as he wrapped an old bedsheet around her, cape style, fastening it with a binder clip. He picked up the bottle and started spraying water on her hair, lifting it with his fingers. The cool mist felt good on her skin, and Cass relaxed a little.

"You mean, because he killed some of them."

Vinson snorted. "Not just anyone, either, angel. He took out Tapp—the guy who started that whole mess. Remember when they used to hunt Bin Laden all over the place Before? Well, it was like that—Tapp was the big leader, the figure-head, and your buddy Smoke blew his head off and left the body twitching like a stuck pig. And you can bet the guys he let go ran back to tell the story all over Colima."

Cass thought of Evangeline, her cruel eyes and ruthless smile. "They'll just keep coming, though."

"That's right. That's right. That crew's relentless. They ain't giving up, that's for sure." He picked up a well-tended, clean pair of shears. "So, this was a do-it-yourself job? No problem, I'm getting pretty good at cleaning those up."

Cass flinched with the first cut, but after that it went smoothly, as the shears found a rhythm. Vinson hummed, a tune familiar but also not, wandering up and down a minor scale. Cass closed her eyes and let drowsiness take her over. When she felt his hands in her hair, brushing out the stray cut pieces, she sighed with the pleasure of a moment of luxury.

"How about I throw in a little extra service? I don't exactly have customers lined up, and it's been a while since I got to try anything fun."

"What was it you used to do?" Cass asked, as he picked up a plastic tub of boxes and bottles that had been stowed beneath the table.

"Tattoos, mostly, and piercing. But don't worry, I'm trained for hair, too. Went to school and all, cut hair in a Supercuts before I got my shop."

Cass put her fingers to her hair. It was short and silky against her fingertips, longer in the back than near the front, where the new growth blended in. No one would know that she had pulled her own hair from her scalp, that a scant month or two ago she had been fevered and frantic. Touching her hair, Cass realized that for the first time she was able to swallow back the thought without it nearly killing her.

"Yes," she said softly. "Do it."

An hour later she smelled faintly of ammonia and her soft brown roots faded to white at the tips. Vinson waved away her promises to make sure he was paid. "I'll see Smoke tonight, I'll get him to buy me a drink and we'll call it square."

She didn't tell him that she'd be gone by then.

She searched for Smoke up and down the rows. A few

daytime drunks lay passed out here and there, but guards
rousted those in the neat paths and shuffled them off to the
area where Cass had found Gloria earlier. Cass figured that a
cot there was part of the deal for the most hardcore drinkers,
the ones who wouldn't spend money on a tent when it could
instead feed their addiction. Or—more likely—maybe even
these mean accommodations came with a price, and those
who couldn't pay were tossed out at night. She averted her
eyes from the bodies lying on the cots, limbs splayed over
the edges, and wondered what kind of man Dor must be to
send people back out to fend for themselves just because they
couldn't afford a cot.

She didn't find Smoke near the front, where a handful
of travelers were checking in with George, going through
the ritual of laying out their possessions on the table. She
searched the stalls, ignoring the vendors calling out offers
of underwear, socks, sweaters, grooming products, packaged
food. When she couldn't find Smoke anywhere in the camp
she steeled herself and ducked through a space in the rows to
where a makeshift bar gathered a variety of people standing
and sitting on plastic chairs. They nursed drinks from mugs
and plastic cups and smoked down expertly rolled joints. In
nooks created by blankets hung from poles, she saw people
shooting up or huddled over pipes. But still no Smoke.

The sun had begun to descend in the sky, and Cass was
starting to get nervous. Gloria had advised her to go before
the evening meal, while the deacons responsible for review-
ing candidates for the Order would still be assembled. Evenings were devoted to prayer and silence, as were mornings;
conversation was allowed only between the morning and
evening meals.

She considered asking around to see if anyone had seen

Smoke; so many people seemed to know about what he'd done, how he'd fought the Rebuilders. But the mortification of having been caught the night before stopped her. There was no way to know who had heard them and who hadn't.

Still, she had searched nearly everywhere...everywhere but the line of blue tents, and she stared at them for long moments, trying to decide. A few had their flaps tied back, flashes of a bare leg or braceleted wrists visible from the depths where women waited for customers, but most of the tents were closed, their occupants busy inside. Gloria was in one of them, Cass guessed, since she hadn't spotted her anywhere else. The thought pained her, and she wished she'd had something more to give Gloria, but she knew it wouldn't make any difference. Cass was not in a position to judge, and never would be again.

She turned away. There was only one other place she hadn't looked, a construction trailer mounted on blocks near the edge of the Box that backed up against the stadium. Its windows were shaded by miniblinds, and a guard sat in a chair out front. Cass had no doubt that this was where Dor kept his office. It was the only place left that she hadn't looked. She deliberated for only a moment before heading for the trailer—she could deliver the message from Sammi and make one last effort to find Smoke and then be on her way.

Up close she could see that the area around the trailer was tended even more meticulously than the rest of the encampment. Gravel had been raked into neat beds around three sides and edged with brick. In a neat row down the middle grew a row of coreopsis, young plants with only a few orange buds among the dark green leaves.

Cass looked closer, amazed. She hadn't seen coreopsis since the second strike, the one carried out on a rainy New

Year's day a few hours before the California dawn. The missiles had struck all across North America within moments of each other, and, remarkably, no reports of death had surfaced as the weapons struck deserts and plains and mountain gorges and broke apart, releasing their toxins. Some people said they smelled something bitter in the misty air of morning, but Cass didn't believe it; the poisons went to work with the brilliant efficiency that it had taken the world's scientists a decade to perfect, and by dusk of the first day of the new year, eighty percent of the plants that survived the first round of strikes began to wither and droop.

Coreopsis was a tough plant, weedy and fibrous, but that hadn't helped. A week into January it lay dead on the ground along with everything else. Yet here it was, like the tiny redwood seedlings they'd seen along the road, come back to life.

Electric cords snaked through the flower bed to a generator that hummed off to the side. In a canvas chair out front sat a boy too young to know how to use the semiautomatic rifle he held loosely across his lap. He watched Cass expressionlessly as she approached.

"Yeah?"

"I was wondering if I could see Dor," Cass said.

"Open hours at five o'clock."

Cass didn't point out the obvious, that she hadn't seen any clocks or watches in the compound, other than the one the young guard wore strapped to his wrist.

"I have a message from his daughter."

The boy narrowed his eyes, and his grip on the gun was suddenly not as casual. "He doesn't have a daughter."

"I say he does. Look, I'll wait out here while you ask him. I wouldn't risk it if I were you. Her name is Sammi."

The guard hesitated, glancing up the three metal steps to

the trailer's door. "Just a minute," he finally said. "Stay right there."

When he knocked sharply and entered the trailer, Cass exhaled a breath she hadn't realized she was holding. It took only a moment before the door was flung open and the guard came back out, followed by a man who stepped out onto the small platform at the top of the stairs. Cass squinted into the setting sun and took an involuntary step back.

Dor MacFall was not what she expected. He was a few inches over six feet tall and broad through the chest, his arms tanned dark and bulging with muscle in his plain navy t-shirt. His near-black hair was cut in a military-style brush cut, and Cass wondered briefly if Vinson was the one who cut it. Or, for that matter, if Vinson had done any of the ink that snaked up this man's arms. The design was clearly Aftertime, a twisted braid of kaysev leaves and stems done entirely in blue-black. Small silver hoops studded the cartilage of his ears, several on each side. He wore no other jewelry, no rings, not even a belt buckle—or, for that matter, a belt—in his canvas pants. His boots were well-worn leather, work boots suited for hard labor, and looking at him it was easy to believe he'd done more than his share.

Most alarming were his eyes. They would be called blue, Cass supposed, but the pigment was so pale that they looked almost like clouds. Unlike the Beaters, though, they were centered with large black irises. They were fringed by thick black lashes and would have been too pretty for a man if they weren't so frighteningly intense.

The other thing that Cass noticed about Dor was how close his shave was. Shaving in Aftertime had become an inexact science; even disposable blades were used over and over, sharpened by hand, imperfectly. A lot of men had adopted a technique of holding the blade away from their faces so as not to cut themselves and invite infection, so they were never free of stubble. She herself, only the day before, had cut herself with the dubious razor included in the tub of supplies Smoke had rented for their use, but Dor stood before her, glowering, his wide, firm jaw perfectly smooth with only the faintest shadow of beard.

His forehead, however, was crossed with a scar that stood out against the smooth planes of the rest of his face. It started at the hairline and cut across one eyebrow, ending at the top of his right cheekbone. A relatively recent wound, a couple of months old at most, still angry and raised. Maybe he'd gotten it fighting the Rebuilders, but as Cass stared into his cold eyes it seemed far more likely that Dor was a man who only looked out for himself.

"What do you want?" he growled, his strange eyes flickering.

"I have a message from Sammi."

"So I'm told. How do I know you're not lying?"

Cass blinked. "Why would I lie?"

"I don't know. Why would you? What are you selling?"

"I'm not selling anything."

His laugh was abrupt and contained not a bit of mirth. "Don't kid yourself. Everyone's selling something. Some people are just more honest about it. But I'll tell you what, you don't look much like a Girl Scout to me, know what I'm saying?"

Cass felt her skin grow hot as Dor's gaze traveled down her body; he didn't bother to mask his admiration.

"Look, do you want to hear the message or not?"

"I really doubt that—"

"She said to tell you she hasn't missed a night."

The change that came over Dor was complete and instant. He froze, but not before his entire body seemed to release its coiled, hostile energy and his crazy eyes lost their hardness. After a moment he lifted a hand to the back of his neck and left it there, a gesture of defeat as much as uncertainty.

"I don't know what that means," Cass added. "She just said to tell you she never forgets, and that she won't miss until she sees you again."

Dor stared at her for an uncomfortably long time, but Cass kept her shoulders squared, her chin lifted and stared back. It was the least she could do for Sammi.

Finally Dor dropped the hand from his neck and opened the door to the trailer. Cass thought he was going to leave her standing outside alone, but at the last second he turned.

"I think you'd better come inside."

31

IT TOOK A MOMENT FOR CASS'S EYES TO ADJUST
to the dim interior of the trailer. It was orderly and clean,
but jammed with shelves, a desk, several office chairs, and
an object that astonished Cass more than anything she'd
seen yet: an enormous flat-panel monitor with an open
spreadsheet.

She hadn't seen a computer in use since the Siege.

And there was Smoke, sitting in a straight-back chair
across from the desk, long legs splayed out in front of him,
arms folded across his chest. His eyebrows lifted slightly in
surprise, a slow smile warming his face.

"You know each other?" Dor said, not so much sitting as
crashing into his desk chair.

"This is the woman I'm traveling with, the one I told you
about."

"Then we've got a problem," Dor said. "One of you isn't
telling the truth."

"Nice hair," Smoke remarked, ignoring him.

Cass felt herself blush as she sat in the remaining chair, her knees brushing against Smoke's, and even that small contact rocked her in the hollow depths where sensation and desire twined together.

How was it possible that she could feel this way, as she prepared for her trip into the Convent, as she faced yet another round of unknown dangers? How could there be room for anything in her mind besides Ruthie, who was her waking thought and her evening prayer? And yet her body longed to touch Smoke again, and to touch him completely. She imagined sliding down onto the floor, onto her knees; she wanted to bury her face against his hard-muscled stomach, wanted him to run his hands over her shorn hair, to trace the outlines of her ears, to slip his fingers into her mouth. And then she wanted him to pull her up onto his lap, and she wanted to kiss him hard. The one taboo she could never break, she could never risk it, never take the chance that the disease lived in her saliva, that it waited and burned within her, longing for a host—none of that mattered as she thought about what it would be like. She wanted to taste his lips and tease them open with her tongue and she wanted him to meet her kiss with his own, demanding, unyielding, his hands in her hair, pressing her to him as he—

"We have a problem here," Dor repeated.

"Why would you say that?" Smoke said, though his gaze remained on Cass.

"You told me you came from Sacramento." Dor addressed Smoke, and while his tone was calm, there was a threat below the surface. Cass noticed that his scar looked even worse in the glow from the monitor. "She says she's talked to my daughter. My daughter's in Silva."

Smoke shrugged. "So what? You're an entrepreneur. In

these times, I'm sure that comes with risks. You have to… hedge your bets, right? So I said Sacramento…it's a small detail, unimportant to any business we might do. Where I come from doesn't matter. As you said yourself, anything I have to sell will be checked and authenticated before goods change hands."

Smoke had lied, then. Why? The answer came to her as he touched the small of her back, leaving his hand there, weighty and warm. A comforting touch.

He was protecting his own. The people of the school, they were his people. He'd said it himself: they were all he had. And while they had been strangers to him not long ago, if it made sense to defend anything at all Aftertime, he would defend them.

"Let's just say it goes to character." Dor focused his un-wavering gaze on Cass. "Tell me what you know about Sammi. All of it."

So she did, leaving out the details of her own arrival at the school. She told him that Sammi and her mother were healthy and had plenty to eat, that the school was well-guarded and stocked. She described the courtyard with its communal meals, the kids in the sunny room where Sammi and her friends led games and activities. She told him how Sammi had asked her to pass along her message, but didn't add that she recognized the hunger in Sammi's eyes for an absent father, the hurt and confusion. These things she kept to herself, because she knew how fiercely she guarded her own pain—and she would not betray Sammi that way.

Especially because Dor did not react while she talked. He listened dispassionately, jaw set, strange eyes heavy-lidded and inscrutable. When she was done, he nodded, once, and turned his attention to the keyboard in front of him. He tapped at a couple of keys.

"Thank you," he said.

"Well, what are you going to do?" Cass asked.

"Do?"

"About Sammi."

"You said she's doing well—as well as can be expected, under the circumstances, anyway."

"Yes, but she wants to see you," Cass said.

"What good would that do? The best way I can help her is by staying away."

"That's not—"

"Listen," Dor snapped. "Pardon my bluntness, but you don't know one fucking thing about what's best for her. If I go to Silva now, I leave this place unattended. My people are good—the best I can find—and they are well trained. But they need a leader. Now, Aftertime, more than ever. There's too much at stake, between the Rebuilders and the thieves and the damn zombies. There are people waiting and watching for a weakness and if you don't think they'll move in faster than you can turn around then you're deluding yourself. Not that I blame you. Denial's the best thing a lot of people have now, and you can look around this place and find proof of that at the bottom of every bottle, in every pill I sell, in the comfort tents. I don't judge. I provide. But I do defend what's mine."

His fury escalated as he talked, and he smacked his palm down flat on the desk for emphasis, making a row of pens jump and skitter.

Cass knew he was right. The community he'd built here was thriving, practically teeming with life, even if it was tainted and self-destructive. But it couldn't survive on its own energy alone; it needed a constant inflow of product and consumers, and someone to make sure the wheels of commerce kept turning.

"You could send supplies," Smoke said. He turned to Cass. "The road clearing we saw—he's got a hand in that."

"We play a minor part. Most of it's the Rebuilders."

"You work with them?" Cass demanded.

"Not with. But not against. I don't take sides," Dor said. "I'm neutral and I intend to stay that way."

"You're not neutral if you're supplying the resistance."

"That's Before thinking. It doesn't apply anymore."

"How can you say that? We're still human. We're never going to stop trying to build societies," Smoke answered. "As long as there's anyone left on this planet, people are going to be putting communities back together."

"And going to war over them."

Cass watched the interplay between the two men, as fascinated as she was repelled. An energy oscillated there, a sparking electric tension that seemed like it could erupt into violence at the slightest provocation. Two determined men, one passionate about justice, the other ruthless and cynical.

But she had her own quest to think about. Once she got Ruthie, she might have the luxury of arguing abstract points about the future of the planet. For now, she could only afford to be interested in how these two men could help her.

"I'm going into the Convent," she said to Dor. "I don't know if Smoke told you. I need some things. Personal stuff. And something I can trade."

Dor regarded her with renewed interest. "Why would you want to go in there? You don't strike me as a believer."

Cass shrugged, pretending a calm she didn't feel. She wasn't about to tell him about Ruthie; he seemed like a man who sought to know everyone else's trump card while keeping his own hand hidden. "I have my reasons."

"Fair enough." He let his gaze linger on her face. "It's

a waste of a damn fine woman, if you don't mind me saying."

"Maybe I like other women."

Dor laughed. "Won't make any difference if you do—they take vows of celibacy."

Cass raised an eyebrow—she doubted such a vow held much meaning. In a world where comforts were so desperately rare, it would be impossible to stop people from seeking out the few that remained.

"I don't plan to be there long enough to get that hard up," she said. "About those supplies…"

"I'll cover her, MacFall," Smoke said. His hand moved slightly lower on her back, his fingers dipping into the waistband of her pants. "Give her what she needs."

Dor considered, his scar creasing as he furrowed his brow with thought. "I can give her an escort, someone they'll trust. We can get the job done…provided you're willing to pay a premium."

"I think we've already established that I will."

The iciness in Smoke's voice highlighted the tension between the men and sent an unfamiliar thrill through Cass. There didn't seem to be a limit to the sacrifices Smoke was willing to make for her. Which was exactly what she needed, right? She'd do whatever it took—cheat, lie, steal from him if need be—to get to Ruthie.

Only, he was giving her everything she needed, without being asked. And that felt like standing at the edge of a cliff and being tempted to jump.

Cass forced the thought from her mind—there was nothing to be gained from questioning Smoke's generosity. Besides, this was a drama that held no place for her, a negotiation about far more than just her passage into the Convent.

"In that case," Dor said, pushing back from the desk and standing, "I believe our business here is done."

Cass and Smoke stood in the shade of a bent pepper tree. Before, it had been one of Cass's least favorite species, with its scabby bark and spiky, unadorned branches. Aftertime, it had endeared itself to her merely by surviving.

"I'll be out as soon as I can," Cass said. "As soon as I find Ruthie."

Smoke reached out a rough-callused hand and touched her face, drawing a line from her cheek down to her mouth, tracing the line of her lower lip. "I wish I could go with you."

Cass attempted a smile.

His eyes glinted with worry and frustration. "But I'll be here waiting. And if you don't come back soon..."

He didn't finish the thought. What could he promise, after all? The task ahead was up to Cass alone. Others had helped her prepare, but once she went inside, she was on her own.

"I *will* come back," she said softly.

Smoke stroked her mouth softly with his thumb and it was all she could do not to part her lips and to taste his work-rough skin.

"I want to kiss you," Smoke whispered, his face inches from hers, his voice rough and dangerous. "Let me kiss you."

"No." She shook her head, pushed his hand away, but he just pressed closer. She could feel his hot breath on her face. *"No."*

"I'm not afraid."

"I can't. I can't...I *won't* be responsible."

For poisoning him, for the chance—no matter how small—

that the disease lived within her, in her saliva, in her mouth and her throat, roiling and festering while she talked and breathed and swallowed. She would not take that chance. She would not let Smoke die because of her.

Like Bobby had. Like Ruthie almost had.

"I don't care—"

"*I* do." The anger in her voice took them both aback. Cass pulled away, and Smoke let her. They regarded each other in the golden light of late afternoon, a slight breeze carrying the scents of sage and wood smoke, the faint strains of someone's lazy guitar picking, and they might as well have been staring across a chasm a mile wide and deep.

"I care," Cass repeated, and then she ran, not looking back, straight for the way out of the Box and into the Convent and the next hard thing she must do.

She cared a great deal about not destroying anyone else.

But even worse, she cared about Smoke.

And that was even more dangerous.

32

THE SUN WAS SLIPPING TOWARD THE HORIZON
and the smell of food carried on the breeze when Cass made
her way to the front gate. Faye was playing chess with the
guard on duty, a young man with a dirty fedora pulled over
his eyes. He muttered something that passed for a greeting,
but barely looked up from the board.

"Everything you'll need is in here," Faye said, picking
up a pack from the barter counter and shaking the contents
out onto the table. A plastic water bottle—never opened, an
incredible rarity—rolled across the surface. There were socks
and underwear and kaysev cakes wrapped in cloth napkins.
There was a folded t-shirt and a packet of aspirin. "I can't
give you a weapon. If they found it, you'd be out on your
ass. Or worse."

Cass nodded, and Faye returned all the supplies to the
pack before handing it over.

"Back soon, Charles," Faye told the other guard as Cass

slid the straps over her shoulders. "Think hard before you make that next move, or I'll take you in three."

Cass figured that Faye was the best Dor had to offer. She reminded herself that Smoke was paying dearly for her escort to help negotiate entry. Dor was shrewd, but a part of Cass—the part that had promised a brave and tenderhearted girl that she would find her father—hoped there was more to it than that.

Hoped Dor cared whether she lived or died.

Faye didn't talk on the short walk to the stadium, and Cass didn't mind. She concentrated on the view, trying to fix every detail in her memory. The ruins of San Pedro seemed far less dangerous now that she was headed into the Convent. Behind them, the Box was lit up with strings of tiny lightbulbs like a city Christmas tree lot Before. The darkening hills were shrouded with purple nightfall, tree skeletons silhouetted in black. And the street they'd followed into town only yesterday, lined with wrecked and empty shops and apartments—it all seemed harmless now, a stage set of a town, the actors and stagehands due back from their break at any moment.

Cass had become a connoisseur of fear, had learned to sense its moods, its encroachment and retreat. Yesterday the fear had weighed upon her, slunk all around her, crushing and smothering and stealing her breath, a shape-shifter playing the unknown into a thousand different threats.

Today it was different. Today's fear was sharp and focused and came from within the stadium, beyond the curved windowless walls, and it was crafty and cruel, a foe that meant to outwit and inveigle. Cass made a small, low humming in her throat, gathering her anxiety into a single strand and twisting it out of the way.

She was so focused on her own fear that she didn't hear

the far-off wail for a moment, but it escalated sharply and pierced her consciousness.

"Sounds like they got one," Faye said, pausing to listen. Cass looked down the street that angled away from the stadium toward the center of town, following Faye's lead, and thought she saw a bobbing point of light.

"Got what?"

"A Beater. They've got this cart thing—it's like a dog-catcher van."

"You mean they catch them *alive?*"

"Yeah." Faye laughed softly. "C'mon, I told you they're fucking lunatics in there."

"Wait, so you're saying the Order..."

"They don't do it themselves. They pay Dor and he sends a team out. They've pretty much cleaned out the town but every once in a while you'll get a few that wander in. Usually they can only catch one and have to kill the rest."

Cass edged back a step, toward the stadium.

Other people had hunted the Beaters, back at the beginning. But when it became clear how hard it was to kill them, most people gave up. They were just so relentless. An ordinary human would stop if he took a bullet or a face full of acid or, in the case of the more resourceful citizens who didn't have access to anything else, a thrown hatchet or a rock flung from a sling.

But Beaters, when they came close to a potential victim, were almost unstoppable. They didn't seem to react to pain or injury unless it was mortal, and even in their death throes they would keep advancing. Everyone had a story of a Beater with a crushed skull or a severed limb spending its dying moment dragging itself toward its prey.

Too often it bit before it died.

"Isn't that...crazy?"

"They have gear." Faye shrugged. "Protective masks and all. Shit from the manufacturing plant. And if you know Dor, you know he believes in outgunning the enemy. They're armed from here to Sunday."

"But what do they do with them? I mean, the ones they catch?"

"That's their business," Faye said. "Some crazy ritual shit, is what I heard. Who cares? They pay out the ass."

Cass followed Faye across the street and along the broad sidewalk that circled the stadium, glancing back once, but the light had been extinguished and all was silent. When Faye stopped at a boarded-up entrance that looked like every other one and knocked on the nailed-down plywood, there was a click above their heads. Cass looked up to see a small window cut into the wall sliding open.

"Weapons?" a female voice demanded.

Faye slid her revolver from its holster. "Just the usual."

"Who's with you?"

"Wannabe. She's from Mariposa, showed up yesterday."

The story they'd come up with was that Cass had worked in a church-run child care center Before and missed the structure and leadership of the church, that she hoped to find a faith community from which she could help bring a set of guiding beliefs to Aftertime survivors. Cass had been skeptical that anyone would believe her, but Faye said most of the women being turned away didn't bother to disguise the fact that they were just looking for shelter.

"They want sheep, not opportunists. Act all pious and hungry for the light and whatever, convince them they can mold you, and you'll be fine."

"I can't believe anyone would sign up for something like that on purpose."

"Well, people are desperate to believe in something," Faye

said matter-of-factly. "You got a cult situation, it don't matter what they're selling. What people are buying is a chance to belong to something, for someone to tell them what to do so they don't have to think for themselves. Just like the fuckers who started this whole mess, trying to force their ideologies down other people's throats and getting everyone killed instead."

The plywood barrier slid open, its soundless, smooth glide hinting at well-oiled hardware and expert craftsmanship. It closed as soon as they stepped inside, and they found themselves in a small antechamber that still held the detritus of ball games played long ago, red-and-silver posters and pennants and a desk inscribed with the Miners' logo.

Two women waited, tensed and ready, in the small room. A short brunette with a strawberry birthmark on her cheek trained a gun on Cass, and a wiry young woman with crooked teeth regarded them from the raised platform that had allowed her to look out of the peephole. Both were dressed simply, in long-sleeved pink shirts and skirts that hung past their knees, their hair pulled back from their faces.

"Hey," Faye said by way of greeting. "Lorrie, Jennie, this is Cass."

"Take off your belts and packs," the guard with the gun ordered, ignoring the greeting. "Stand against the wall."

Cass followed Faye's lead, resisting the temptation to watch as the woman went through her things. While the dark-haired guard finished the pack check, the blonde frisked Cass quickly, mostly patting around her pockets and checking her shoes and bra, and Cass gritted her teeth to keep from reacting when she patted down her scarred back.

"Okay. You can relax. You'll get your things back later, after your interview."

"This what we asked for?" the first guard demanded as she hefted a small, paper-wrapped package that she'd taken from Faye's pack.

"Yes. Plus a little extra insurance."

"Yeah?"

"Yeah," Faye nodded. "Check it out after I leave, make sure it gets where it's going. The rest is for you, but I couldn't get the menthols. Just the Light 120's. Maybe next week."

The guard nodded and slipped the package into her skirt pocket. "I appreciate it."

"Likewise."

Cigarettes. In contrast to the drugs Dor moved inside the Box, the idea seemed almost quaint to Cass. It was ironic, how fiercely California had fought smokers Before, banning them from every square foot of public space. Now, something that could kill you over decades seemed like a good bet. Hell, maybe she ought to take up smoking herself now—odds were she'd be dead long before her lungs could fail her.

But no—there would be no cigarettes for Cass, nothing that would build a taste for her addictions. Nothing that would remind her of those feelings, of wanting more and more until wanting became needing. In the past, she'd let her addiction become the thing that mattered most, and she'd lost Ruthie as a result. No more. Even if she had only hours left to live, she didn't intend to spend any of them enslaved to anyone or anything.

She had made it this far. This much closer to finding Ruthie. And she wouldn't do anything to jeopardize their future together.

"Thank you for bringing me," she said to Faye, as sweetly as she could manage. "And God bless you."

The look the Order guards exchanged was laced with cynicism, but they said nothing.

Cass was pretending to look for answers. And they were pretending they had answers to give her.

Good. So far, everyone was playing their part.

33

BEYOND THE ANTEROOM WAS A BANK OF
elevators that no longer worked—and a stairwell that led
up five flights to a hallway that opened onto the skyboxes
on one side, and offices on the other. Cass was taken to an
office with a view out over the parking lot scattered with
wrecked and abandoned cars. The door clicked shut behind
her and the room was silent as a stone—soundproofed, she
guessed, so some pencil pusher could attend to the details of
running the place without distractions. There were book-
shelves, a couple of chairs, a corkboard that took up most of
one wall—a drab little room like in any anonymous office
building. The room where business was consolidated from
the sport spectacle of the rest of the stadium.

When Cass had come here as a girl, she'd been high on
the thrill of a stolen day with her dad. An adventure, just
the two of them—the first of many, he promised. She wasn't
about to believe *that;* her mom said Tom Haverford was

about as reliable as a busted clock, and he'd missed her birthday *and* Easter, off touring with the latest sure-thing band he'd hooked up with.

But at least there was this one perfect day: the snap of the tickets tearing, the shouts of the vendors cooking up sweet-smelling sausages. The heart-pounding first glimpse of the players in their tight white pants and red-and-silver shirts as they ran onto the field. Sitting close to your dad, his arm heavy around your shoulders, his high-five slap stinging your palm when Hugo Hawkins stole second. Wishing the game would never end.

Two lives later, Cass knew that baseball was a business just like everything else. Behind the handsome players and the green-green field and the cheering crowds were managers, bosses, arrangers of deliveries and collectors of profits, people who hired and fired and balanced budgets and greased palms and traded influence. Someone like that had worked in this office, and, because of that, the magic of that long-ago day never seemed more distant than it did now.

Finally the door opened and a woman in a pink skirt and blouse entered. She looked like she was somewhere in her thirties, with straight dark hair tucked primly behind her ears, but her wide smile was welcoming and generous. She extended both her hands and Cass let her enfold her own in a tight grasp.

"I'm Deacon Lily," she said softly. She had the kind of voice you leaned in to hear. "Welcome to the Order. You and I are going to have a nice chat and get to know each other, and then together we will decide if you are suited for life here among the Order. If the answer is yes, you will join the other neophytes. You will stay among them until we determine that you are ready to progress to acolyte status.

That may take weeks, or perhaps months. It depends on how quickly you learn and adjust to our ways."

"What if I'm...not suited?" Cass asked.

"Oh, let's not worry about that right now. Besides, you've already gotten Sister Lorrie's recommendation. She can be quite discerning, and generally when she sees potential in a seeker, there is a good reason."

Cass searched Lily's face for sarcasm but found none. "She was very...all-business," she said carefully.

Lily waved her hand, brushing the thought away. "The ones who interface with the outside, they have a hard job. Mother Cora says they have to steel themselves against the lure of the godless while keeping their hearts open to the possibility of grace, which is a very difficult calling. That is why only a few are called to be guards. Don't let her attitude put you off, because she is only protecting our sanctum from those who would seek to weaken us. Now you are inside, with us, and very soon you will start to see the beautiful truths that guide us."

Cass nodded and smiled as though Lily's words made sense, wondering if she really believed what she was saying.

Cass was intimately familiar with the many faces of denial, from the first whispers that allow you to shade the truth a complexion that suited you, to the most desperate and fantastic depths in which you traded your sanity for a version of reality that allowed you to continue to exist another day.

But contentment, even serenity, was not a state she associated with any place on the spectrum.

"Now, why don't you tell me what you've heard about the Order," Lily prompted, sitting in the chair behind the desk and taking a yellow pad and pen from a drawer.

"I heard this was a good place when you think you can't go on anymore," Cass said tremulously. Then she told the rest of her careful lie, one she had built from pieces of the truth. "I lived with my mother, when I was growing up. And…my stepfather."

Just saying the hated word caused a bit of the anguish that simmered deep inside to break off and lodge in her heart. She felt her face color with shame and grief, and blinked hard so she wouldn't cry.

This was why Cass had chosen this story; she knew she couldn't tell it without the pain coming to the surface. She wouldn't have to fool anyone—her desolation was real. And *real* was the thing she would trade to get inside, no matter what it cost her.

"Yes?" Lily said softly.

"My stepfather was not a good man," Cass continued, her voice quavering. "He was also…inappropriate. With me."

"I'm very, very sorry to hear that."

"Yes. He—" Cass broke off and Lily reached into the desk, coming up with a box of tissues—a practically new box of real tissues, which she slid across the desk. Cass gratefully took one and dabbed at her eyes. "I suppose you can guess. Anyway, I was estranged from them, but they lived in the same town as I did. After the Siege, I heard through friends that my mother had the fever."

"Oh, Cassandra…again, I am so sorry," Lily said, and for a moment Cass was drawn into her sympathy, tempted to tell her all about Mim, about her birdlike hands and diet of coffee and melba toast, her vanity about her size-six figure and the high heels she wore until the very end, even if she was just going to get the mail. About the padded bras she gave Cass for her eleventh birthday; about the way the bedroom door sounded when she slammed it shut the night Cass tried to tell her about what Byrn had done to her.

Instead she told the lies she had prepared.

"I loved my mother so much. When she was dying…and she was so hot, it was as though she was on fire from the inside. She couldn't bear to have anything touching her skin and so she lay on the floor, on the tile, and when I tried to give her water she just—she couldn't keep it down. And she was muttering all the time…she never slept, and I couldn't, I couldn't tell what she was saying and…"

Cass peeked out from her lowered lashes to see how her story was going over. In truth, she had taken the details from a woman she met in the library; Cass had listened while the woman told the story of her mother's death in her arms, how she'd held her until finally the unbearable heat left her wasted body. Cass's own mother had refused to see her, even when she was dying of the fever.

But Lily reached across the table and squeezed Cass's hand gently. "Right now, it is natural that you are hurting, that you are questioning God's decision to take your mother from you," she said. "But others have found comfort through a deeper understanding of His will and His ways. You can find that comfort in faith, too, Cassandra. Do you believe me?"

Cass fluttered her lashes. "I…don't know."

"So many of us have lost loved ones to the fever, to hunger, to senseless violence, to the Beaters. The loss is real, of course. But the anger it causes is not. You think you are angry at God for taking your mother, right?"

Cass nodded. She didn't say that she was no longer the person she used to be before Byrn came along. He changed her forever when he intercepted her on her way to the bathroom one night after she'd stayed up too late studying for a biology test. He'd traded her trust for a few cheap thrills, pretending that his hands on the thin fabric of her nightgown had been in her imagination, forcing her to scab over

her pain with self-doubt. Until it happened the next time.
And the time after that.

That person—the old Cass—truly was dead. And the new
Cass *was* angry. And no new-age faith-hawker was going
to take her rage away. But Cass took those thoughts and
carefully folded them, once, twice, until they fit back into
the place where she kept them hidden away. Their energy,
though, she summoned to feed this lie.

"What if I told you that you can learn to trade your anger
for forgiveness?" Lily asked. "For peace? For healing?"

"I don't understand."

"Yes. I know it's hard to accept at first." *Here it comes*,
Cass thought, *the hard sell*. "At first there were only a few of
us, women just like you, Cassandra. We were all hurting.
We had all lost someone. We found our way here, and we
prayed without ceasing. Faith was our only reward, but what
a glorious reward it was. Mother Cora founded the Order in
this place in the end days of the Siege, when all the nations
of the earth were at war with each other, and she prayed
until she was exhausted and then slept only long enough to
get up and do it again. Her first acolytes were women who
were also looking for answers through faith, and they began
to pray with her, and that allowed her to divide the work of
her prayer into shifts. Now—" Lily swept her hand in an arc
toward the interior of the stadium "—now there are dozens
of us praying at every moment of the day. And that's not
all."

The enthusiasm in her voice was too bright, too brittle.
The pitch was well-practiced, and Cass could understand
how easily a woman weakened by grief and fear could fall
for it, but underneath Lily's pious words, the pieces didn't fit
together. Cass focused on Lily's mouth, her bowed, pale lips.
"What else?"

"Tell me, Cassandra, is there room in your heart to forgive?"

"I—I don't know."

"There is a lesson in the Bible, one of my favorites—and also one of the simplest. In it, we learn that our Lord expects us to take the traveler into our home, the sinner to our bosom." She tapped her fingernails on the desk as she recited: *"I say to you, what you have done to one of these least ones, you have done to Me."*

Cass knew the passage well, from a long-ago game in church camp. The disinterested counselors made the girls form two lines, linking hands over their heads to form a tunnel through which they took turns running while everyone sang words like *I accept you as you are* and *There is no bridge we can't cross together.* Cass remembered the game because one of the older girls had tripped her, sticking out her foot as Cass ran through. Then she pretended to help her up, whispering, *God hates dirty skanks like you.*

The likelihood of God's affection for her was one of the subjects Cass took pains to avoid, but Lily seemed to be waiting for her to say something. "I know that one."

"Yes, yes, it's a beautiful lesson. But now I would like you to let your mind disconnect from what you have learned in the past," Lily encouraged. "Be open to what you will hear and see in the days to come. Be open to miracles—*true* miracles."

"What do you mean?"

"Close your eyes for a moment," Lily said. "You will do much more work in the days ahead, with teachers who are far more gifted than I. But I just want to share with you a glimpse of what lies ahead. The beauty of forgiveness, the glory of letting go of all that is hurting you—the hatred, the sorrow, the regret, the anger—most of all the anger, which is like a poison inside you—letting it all flow away. That is the work that we do here, in the Order."

Cass let her eyes drift shut. Despite herself, she felt herself responding to Lily's gentle voice, to the soothing rhythms of her words. She had a lovely voice; Cass wondered if she sang. Probably. All these religious types did, didn't they?

"That's it...now breathe with me. In...out. In...and hold...and now, very very slowly, breathe out for one, two, three...good, Cassandra. Very good. Let's do that again, together."

Cass let Lily lead her through the breathing exercise. She was really very good, much better than Elaine, who had tried something similar in the impromptu yoga group she started in the library. Better than the physical therapist who attended Cass's A.A. meetings from time to time and came over once or twice with gifts of tea and gingersnaps.

Cass had rejected the help offered by that woman, and Elaine, too. She'd always been aware of their agendas, their desire to lead her through their own personal programs. And Cass could not follow. She'd been made a rebel by all the years of trusting the wrong people, and she couldn't let go enough to trust Elaine, and while all the others in the library lay on their backs and stretched their arms over their heads and practiced the Three Kinds of Breathing with great zeal, Cass faked it and felt her sadness coil all the tighter in her chest.

But Lily was different. Lily's voice was gilded with hope and delight, and it was so tempting to think that such a thing might be possible for Cass, too, if she just followed along...if she let go of the torments that held her back...if she opened herself to forgiveness.

Of course it was all ridiculous, all part of the brainwashing, but would it really hurt anything if she played along, if she took this time to rest and relax? It had been such a hard journey, she had been on alert for so long, her body had been through so much.

"Just relax, Cassandra, lean back in the chair and let your hands rest loosely at your sides...that's right and now in again and hold..."

Cass breathed and she listened and she felt her mind loosen and settle like a bowl of batter that had been stirred. It was like sleeping except she could still hear Lily's soft words, like dreaming except the images in her mind were real things, memories of nice things. Ruthie, tucked under the bright quilt she found at a secondhand shop. A stray cat the neighbor took in, who grew sleek and fat—how Ruthie loved to pet that cat! Ruthie the day Cass took her back from Byrn, the dimples when Ruthie smiled and laughed and hugged her tightly around her neck.

Ruthie with the dandelions, the little yellow blossom under her chin.

The memory slanted in, surprising Cass. Dandelions...yes. There had been dandelions growing in the scorched lawn of the library. They had all been amazed the day the first one popped up, followed by another and another, pushing their tough stalks through the matted dead grass, defiant in the June sun, returning from exile. Cass had picked them and put them in jars and coffee mugs and still there were more, her own flower garden, and the morning after she brought Ruthie back, they went outside to see. The sun was up and it was safe and Bobby had dragged a PlaySkool plastic kitchen home with the raiding party the night before and they were setting it up in the courtyard. They'd seen a sandbox, shaped like a turtle, and they were planning to go back for it.

When you looked close at a dandelion you could almost believe the Siege had never happened. Hold it up to your face, inhale the sweet-bitter fragrance, watch clouds drift through the spiky leaves. Brush the soft petals against your face, and you were back Before, in the world you once knew.

Ruthie found a patch and squealed with delight. She began picking them, small hands tugging with determination, petals dropping to the ground, but no matter. *Pull up all the flowers—tomorrow there might be no flowers at all.*

Cass squatted next to Ruthie, her hands flat on the brick sidewalk. The bricks were cold against her palms, but the contrast with the morning sun beating hot against her back was delicious, and Cass closed her eyes and concentrated. With Ruthie back, she wouldn't feel so dead anymore. Maybe her senses would wake up again, maybe she would be able to taste and smell and hear the world around her again.

Cass concentrated on the sun on her back and the brick under her hands and listened to Ruthie's laughter and thought that later they might join the other families in the conference room that had been converted to a playroom, that the companionship that had eluded her so far might be possible now. Maybe she would take her turn reading to the children, playing hide-and-seek in the stacks, folding origami from paper torn from books. There would be conversation and laughter while the little ones napped. She would hold Bobby's hand when the dinner dishes were done and together they would tuck Ruthie in to sleep at night.

The thought was so tempting that at first Cass didn't realize that anything was wrong. The sounds didn't penetrate her mind, occupied as it was with happier places. And as for the reverberations under her hands, the thud of footsteps approaching—Cass had gotten sloppy. The caution she had honed so fine lay buried under joy of possibility, of having her baby back.

But then there was a frantic yell from the door, where the morning-shift guards had been standing and enjoying the sun.

Run—

They screamed at her but she had to get to Ruthie, Ruthie had wandered to the edge of the lawn, where the circular drive met the book drop, she had found a clump of yellow blooms, she was watching the Beaters with wide eyes, she didn't budge, she didn't know to be afraid, and Cass had to get her and she threw herself through the air running racing screaming but it was like slow motion like a movie she wasn't fast enough—

And somewhere in Cass's mind she knew this was only a memory *only* a memory and she tried to say "no" tried to push it back, stuff it down, cover it over, bury it deep deep down in her heart where it couldn't come out but there was Ruthie in the sun, there was Ruthie with her fistful of dandelions, her baby her precious—

And Cass screamed and screamed but no sound came out because she wasn't real anymore she was trapped on the inside with the memories and this time no one could help her as the terrible day came back with all its sharp sounds and flashing colors and settled into her senses and played across the wide wide screen of her mind and showed her how she had failed, failed, failed.

SHE WAS SCREAMING, THE PEOPLE AT THE DOOR were screaming, the Beaters were snorting and wailing—the world burst with sounds of rage and terror as she ran for Ruthie.

The cold brick and hot sun forgotten, she saw the Beaters stumble-run toward her down the street, over the curb, across the library lawn. Four of them or five; it was hard to tell as they crowded and pushed each other like hungry puppies, slapping and shoving and making their strange excited voracious sounds, and their greedy eyes locked onto Ruthie, who stood small and alone with the bunch of dandelions in her hand, breeze riffling a curl of hair around her chin.

Closer closer lungs tearing arms reaching Cass threw herself on top of her daughter, flung her small body into the dirt and pressed herself on top. Ruthie's heartbeat, rapid as a trapped rabbit's, fluttered against Cass's chest as she squeezed her eyes shut and tried to make herself big, enormous, wide enough to cover Ruthie so they'd never find her.

And then.

The way the earth beneath them trembled with the footfalls of the Beaters. The heavy thud of a boot tripping on her legs and then an infuriated scream as the Beater went down, falling on Cass's calves, hurting her with its weight. The smell—God, the smell, obscene in its bloom of foul rot.

A Beater's hand closed on her forearm and Cass jerked it away, seeing only the chewed fingers, the torn and missing nails, the crusted black blood and the oily pink of the most recent wounds on its wrist and forearm. The hand was grotesque, bone showing in a couple of places, a finger hanging loose and useless—but the grip was surprisingly strong and Cass could not free herself.

"Someone help! Get Ruthie!" she screamed. She couldn't see anyone, because the library was behind her, her only opportunity for escape a dozen yards away. And even then she knew there was no chance for her at all because the Beaters were upon her with their miscalibrated eyes and their lusting feverish mouths. Their hands scrabbled at her. She had expected ripping and tearing and pain but they closed their festering hands on her with singular purpose—they would not feed here, they would not take their first bite until they had her back in their nest.

Then they would lay her out on her stomach and kneel on her limbs while they feasted.

But Cass did not allow that thought to overtake her yet. She squeezed her eyes shut and kept screaming for the others to come for Ruthie and fought to make her body large, larger. She imagined that she was a great weight that would press down on her baby even while the Beaters tugged her and tried to rip apart her grip.

But she couldn't keep them away with her will. She felt her hold on Ruthie float away as they pulled her in four different directions. Panic made her stronger and she fought hard and Ruthie wriggled and cried out in fright and Cass's tears ran salty in her mouth. Cass opened her eyes and looked frantically for something, anything, that would help, and saw only the scattered yellow petals of the dandelions Ruthie had dropped, already curling in the sun in the dead grass.

And then—Bobby's shoes. How had she forgotten this? Bobby's shoes, an incongruously flashy pair of Nikes, silver appliquéd on black. Bobby favored army surplus but he'd loved these shoes, lifted from a routed and wrecked sporting goods shop, nothing he'd ever wear Before, but they appealed to his irrepressible sense of irony and he'd laced them with glittering silver shoelaces and teased Cass that they made him stronger and faster—an Aftertime superhero.

Bobby's Nikes were in front of her and Cass sucked air and screamed Ruthie's name one last time, *Take Ruthie, help Ruthie, let them have me* and she saw the shoes hesitate for only a second and then she knew that he knew she was right.

The Beater who held her forearm in his grip was suddenly torn away. Bobby kicked at it and went for the next one, but Cass felt herself being dragged by the pair that held her feet. Their voices crescendoed, a mad, incoherent cacophony chorded through with fury, and her body bumped along the ground, but Bobby had bought himself a few seconds.

The Beaters who were dragging her away let her fall to the ground at the edge of the lawn and then each seized a hand and a foot. She was lifted roughly, her spine scraping against the curb, and as the Beaters carried her away she craned her neck and saw Bobby with Ruthie in his arms, running to the door where others waited with blades ready, the Beaters in lurching, determined pursuit.

She watched helplessly as Bobby raced for the door and threw himself at the entrance, never letting go of Ruthie, who looked so small in his arms. Cass could not see her face, only her blue shoes and white socks and small fist still holding one wilted dandelion. Bobby's shoes flashed in the sun and then he was inside and Maynard, that was his name, the guard with the shaved head—Maynard's arm swung wide and one of the Beaters went down in a spray of arterial blood and the doors shut with a clang and Ruthie was gone and Ruthie was safe and inside the library and outside the doors were one bleeding Beater distracted by its own blood and one who pounded its body against the door as though it could bend the steel if it tried hard enough.

Ruthie was saved. Ruthie was saved. A prayer, a deal done—it took all the energy Cass had left and she stopped fighting. She lifted her voice to the God she long ago stopped daring to trust. *Hold her safe in Your arms. Love her for me.*

So that was done, and she closed her eyes and prayed for death and knew that instead she was headed for something far worse.

PAIN, AND A VOICE. PAIN ABOVE HER EYE, SHARP
as the jagged edge of awake—and a voice she knew.

"Cassandra, please, don't fight me, just let me—"

Cass rolled and her shin struck something hard and sharp.
The pain made her squeeze her eyes shut and she pressed
at her temples. She was lying on the floor, on carpet. The
air smelled like dust. She patted around her, found the legs
of furniture, opened her eyes and saw a frightened face, a
woman kneeling close, hair hanging in her face.

Sister Lily.

"Cassandra, you hit your head when you went down. I
just want to help you get back up to the chair. I've got some
cool water, I'd like you to take a drink now. The heat—"

"It wasn't the heat," Cass said. The words wobbled in
her mouth. She tasted blood and touched her lip with her
tongue. She'd bit her lip when she hit the table. "I was…
remembering."

She let Lily take her hand and help her up, a moment of dizziness passing when she settled back into the chair. The light outside seemed to have faded. Afternoon was passing by.

"That happens sometimes," Lily said. She poured from a pitcher and put a glass in Cass's hand, folded her fingers around it so it wouldn't slip from her grip.

Cass drank. Lily talked, Cass listened, she drank more. The water didn't go down easily; her throat felt tight, her gut uneasy. Ghosts of images skittered around her mind like trash on a windy day—Ruthie's eyes wide with wonder, the Beaters' grasping scabby hands, the silver swoosh on Bobby's Nikes. It was as though, now that it had been loosed, the past had slipped through the crack Lily made with her kind words and her breathing exercises and now the seal was broken for good.

"...a tight schedule, what with dinner..."

Their wretched hands closed on her shins, her arms. Sebaceous, oozing flesh touching hers, wiry tendons closed tight as she was lifted, Bobby clutching Ruthie tight and running, running, running away, never knowing she'd already been infected.

"...tour of our home, just a quick one..."

Had he watched as she was carried off, had he handed Ruthie to the others and looked down at his own torn skin and bitten flesh? Had his heart broken as he realized what he would become, as he did what must be done, chasing his own death down the path that once wound through agapanthus and lantana and birches along the river?

"Cassandra? Come on now, honey, let's get up."

Cass allowed Lily to help her gently from the chair. Lily was nice. And this was better; this would help her stop thinking, stop remembering.

"Let's get up," she echoed softly, her tongue feeling thick in her mouth.

"That's right. You're going to feel better soon. You probably need some food, something to settle your stomach. How long has it been since you had a good meal?"

She continued talking without waiting for an answer, ushering Cass out of her office and past the stairwell the guards used, down the empty corridor that wound around and around the stadium. Cass watched the concrete walls go by. When they entered the stands, blinking in the late-afternoon sun, she looked down onto the field and half expected to see the Miners there, warming up in the afternoon sun.

The fake turf was still verdant, and the field markings were still present in places. But in what had once been the outfield, an enclosure as big as a suburban ranch house had been erected, white tent fabric stretched to make a roof over walls built from two-by-fours and plywood and steel braces.

At the other end of the field, dozens of tables were lined up in neat rows along with a variety of chairs—folding chairs, plastic outdoor chairs, a few aluminum chairs from patio sets. Walls of wire shelving, the kind used for garage storage, had been joined to make a larder. Women in long-sleeved shirts and skirts that reached their ankles worked alone and in pairs, setting out dishes and stirring pots over cooking fires.

An entire long side of the field was lined with planters constructed from wood and filled with soil and, astonishingly, overflowing with a variety of plants. From far away, Cass couldn't tell what they all were, but brightly colored flowers tumbled from the planters under small trees and hardy-looking shrubs. And—could those be pole beans? And squash, or melons, their tendrilous vines overhanging the planters and trailing on the ground.

The Order was cultivating plants she hadn't seen since Before. Like the evergreen seedlings she and Smoke saw along the side of the road, these plants sprang from seeds and spores that had somehow survived the Siege.

Maybe the earth truly did want to be reborn.

Cass followed Lily down the stairs between the stands. Her legs still trembled, and she stepped slowly and carefully, afraid of falling again. Lily slowed her own pace to match, giving Cass an encouraging smile and touching her arm to steady her.

They passed small groups of women huddled together in the seats. "Praying," Lily explained. "There's not much else the stands are good for, other than exercise."

She pointed to an unenthusiastic queue trudging slowly up the steps a dozen yards away. The women wore drab beige and gray clothes. Their leader was dressed in pale lavender. When they reached the top they turned and started down again.

Before, Cass occasionally ended her weekend desert runs in the high school stadium, sprinting up and down the stands, enjoying the way her footfalls caused the metal benches to shudder and creak. It felt dangerous, and once when she fell she gashed her shin badly, but there was something irresistible about hurtling up and down the stands until the breath burned in her throat, until her heartbeat was so strong she could feel it in every part of her body, and when she finally collapsed, lying on one of the sun-warmed metal benches and staring up at the sky, she had the rare satisfaction of being utterly spent.

If it wasn't joy, it was as close as Cass ever got.

Once they were on the field, Lily led Cass toward the

tables. The turf felt nice under her feet, springy and re-
silient, and as they drew nearer, she could smell the food
being cooked and hear the conversation of the women. They
worked at wooden counters propped on metal legs, chopping
kaysev and what looked like new potatoes, sliding them into
pots of water that others carried to a hearth above a crackling
fire. Two women skinned a jackrabbit together, chatting as
they peeled the pelt away from the meat, their knives flashing in the sun. Cass looked away, but not before she'd seen
them lift the organs from the animal's body.

Food, she told herself, it was only food. And besides, this
meant that the rabbits had continued to multiply. Which
meant that the animals were finding their way back, Aftertime, too.

The realization brought an emotion that felt suspiciously
like hope, and Cass fought it, barely listening as Lily chatted
on about the meal being prepared. There was no place for
hope, not here, not yet. Not until she found Ruthie. Then—
maybe—she would allow herself to start believing in the
future again.

Cass tried to pretend interest in the things that Lily was
showing her, to focus on the water spigot that extended from
one of the dugouts. But she remembered how the players
looked that day, broad shoulders in the white jerseys piped
in silver, ornate red *M*s embroidered on the front. Where
they had lined up to bat, a pair of women dispensed water
to others who brought buckets and plastic bottles and large
reservoirs on wheeled carts. Lily explained how they had
tapped into the pipeline that ran from the Sierras all the way
to San Francisco, and Cass accepted a dipper of water, letting
it trail down her chin and into her neckline, cool against her
skin.

There was a laundry area where women stirred clothes

in huge vats of cloudy water. There were rows and rows of kaysev pods drying on cotton sheets in the sun. There were twisted electric cables snaking along the walls, connecting strings of lightbulbs to generators.

Lily led her back and forth along the vast field, showing Cass the inventions and activities and products of the Order, and though they passed the large tent-roofed enclosure several times, it was the one thing she never mentioned, even though a muffled grunting and snuffling came from behind the wooden walls.

When a bell clanged from the kitchen area, Lily made a tsking sound and put a hand to Cass's back, giving her a gentle push. "We'd best hurry," she said. "It won't do to be late to dinner on your first day, will it? And you'll feel so much better once you've eaten something."

Cass had grown accustomed to Lily's soft, soothing voice, and as they walked back toward the tables, it was lost in the sound of dozens of other conversations as women appeared from the entrances in the stands and swarmed the field. Fifty, a hundred, they kept coming, the old and the young, the tall and the short, the strong and the stooped. Most wore the bland shades of tan and gray and brown that Lily said signified they were acolytes, accepted into the congregation, but here and there was a woman in bright shades of pink and purple. The ordained, like Lily. The leaders, the teachers.

Lily led her to a long table near the edge of the gathering where twenty or so women were gathered, all of them dressed in white blouses and skirts.

"These are the neophytes," Lily said. "Like you. All of you are new. You will live together and study and pray together."

She guided Cass to an open seat near one end of the table, next to a young, pretty woman with wavy brown hair that fell in her eyes, and a solidly built blonde woman in her late forties.

"This is Cassandra," Lily announced as the women gathered at the table fell silent. Cass lowered herself to a straight-backed chair with a webbed-plastic seat and folded her hands on her lap. "She arrived today, and she's still a little weary from traveling. Please make her feel welcome."

Lily crouched down between Cass and the young woman on her left. "I just know you're going to do fine," she said softly in a tone that implied she wasn't entirely sure.

Cass wanted to reassure her, to thank her for her kindness, but her collapse in Lily's office had left her unfocused as well as drained of energy, and her head still throbbed with a spiking pain above her eye where she struck the table, and she managed only a weak smile.

"This is Monica. She's been here a week now. And Adele. You'll help Cass, won't you? Show her around...? Explain things?"

"Sure." The younger woman gave Cass a crooked smile. "Especially if it means I don't have to be the newbie anymore."

"I need to go to my table," Lily said, giving Cass a final pat on her shoulder. "It's almost time for prayer. I know you're still...finding your way, Cassandra. But just have faith and open your heart. Can you do that?"

Lily's smile was so encouraging, her touch so welcome, that Cass found herself nodding along. It wasn't so different from the third drink, or the fourth—the one that untethered her anxious mind from the dark place that was built of anxiety and worry and fear. When she used to drink, she pursued that moment when the lashings fell free and she drifted, when the numbness swirled in and the memories softened into vague shadows and it seemed possible that she might feel nothing at all, at least for a while.

She watched Lily go, weaving her way back between the tables filling up with women, and tried to hold on to the stillness. But when she turned back, all of the others at the table were watching her, and the momentary peace evaporated.

THE NEOPHYTES WERE YOUNG, SUNTANNED, wholesome girls and skinny, hollow-eyed beauties, nails chewed to the quick, their colored and highlighted hair giving way to several inches of natural-colored roots.

But there were a few older women, some her mother's age, and at least one who looked like she was pushing seventy. They fussed over the younger women, passing them dishes and refilling their water, chiding them to eat, to relax, to rest. Cass wondered how many of them had been separated from their own children, had lost them to disease or to the Beaters.

"Welcome, Cassandra," Adele said with a smile, lifting her glass in a toast. Monica clinked it with her own and winked. Before she could lift her own glass to the others, there was the squeal of feedback from a loudspeaker, and a tall, slender, silver-haired woman dressed in scarlet approached the platform. Silence fell quickly. The servers paused in their tasks, and heads were bowed and hands folded in supplication.

"That's Mother Cora," Monica whispered.

Mother Cora closed her eyes and tilted up her chin, smiling faintly. "Let us pray," she said, and the sound system picked up her well-modulated voice and carried it with surprising clarity through the stadium. All around her the women joined hands; Monica and Adele held hers and reached across the empty seats to the others. Mother Cora raised her hands slowly above her head in an elegant arc, inhaled deeply and began to speak, women's soft voices falling in with hers in a low susurration that filled the stadium and echoed back upon itself.

"Lord our Savior," her prayer began, "we, your Chosen, commend this and every day to Thee."

What followed was not so different from the prayers Cass remembered from her occasional forays into church, and she stopped paying attention to the words and instead sneaked glances at all the other women who were praying over clasped hands. She thought she would see at least a few others who, like her, were not able to lose themselves in prayer, who were not moved. Those who lacked faith, or who had been lost, or had turned away from God. Those whose suffering had changed them at the core, stealing pieces of the soul and leaving carved-out shadows in their place.

But as she searched the neat rows of women, they became indistinguishable from one another, their variations in shape and size and hair and skin color insignificant, forming a whole that was more than the sum of the individuals, pulsing with a life of its own. All the voices made one voice; all the clasped hands formed a chain that stretched from the old to the young, the weak to the strong. In that moment Cass felt the tug of the Order, the desire to lose herself, to become nothing more than another voice sharing in the prayer, if only she knew the words.

> *You have sent Your forsaken, that we may forgive*
> *You have sent Your tainted, that we may heal*
> *In Your glory we celebrate the body and the blood*
> *In Your name we consecrate ourselves to Your holy task*
> *Amen*

The echoes of *Amen* rebounded around the vast space, now nearly dark except for candles on the tables and a few strings of electric lights. Mother Cora descended the stairs and the spotlight shut off, and conversation picked up again.

"Hope you're not expecting much," Monica said, as servers placed steaming plates in front of each of them and poured water from pitchers.

"I'm not really hungry."

"Well that's good, since everything around here's pretty much inedible."

"Don't complain so much," Adele chided. "*You* didn't have to cook it."

"I'd rather be cooking than suffering through Purity lectures," Monica said. "Seriously, Cassandra, if you haven't sworn off sex already, listening to Sister Linda talk about your vessel of virtue will knock the urge right out of you."

"I'm—um, you can call me Cass." It was happening again, as it had at the communal bath at the school—the kindness of other women, the offer of friendship. But Cass didn't have the energy to engage.

"Don't mind Monica," Adele said. "She's got a good heart, she's just not used to following directions."

"I'm spoiled," Monica shrugged. "Only child, what can I say?"

"Monica's going to do great things here, if she doesn't get herself thrown out first," Adele said firmly.

"Adele's the only one who hasn't given up on me yet," Monica said. "I guess I'm the problem child around here."

"You just need to apply yourself a little," Adele said, and Cass saw a woman who needed a child to mother—a woman who once had children of her own to dote on, and was lost without them.

"Are there children here? Babies, little kids?"

She had to know. Just had to know if Ruthie had made it safely. She had failed her little girl, but Bobby had saved her, Elaine had nursed her, and someone else had brought her here. Cass had failed, but Ruthie had survived so much already. If she was being raised here, in the Order, that would be all right. As long as they were keeping her safe.

There was a pause, Adele's face draining of life and looking, suddenly, much older. When she spoke, her voice was soft and shredded as a tissue that had gone through the wash.

"The innocents have their own quarters. We don't see them much, after the baptisms."

"I've never seen any since I got here," Monica said, licking the back of a spoon. "And that's fine with me because I think it would freak me out. They don't let them talk. Can you imagine? My nieces and nephews never *stopped* talking."

"That's just for the ceremony," Adele murmured, but the energy had gone out of her words. "It's all symbolic, the way they prepare them. It's to make them all uniform so they're like blank slates, ready to accept the doctrine. Monica…I'm sure they let them just be kids, when they're in their own quarters."

"I wouldn't be so sure." Monica shrugged. "I'm just saying, it's pretty freaky that they—"

"You *don't know*," Adele snapped. "And it's best not to speculate. It's not your place."

Despite her sharp tone, Cass saw tears welling in her eyes. There was a silence, as Monica ducked her chin in regret. "I'm sorry, Adele," she said softly, covering the older woman's hand with hers.

Adele sighed and dabbed at her eyes with a napkin. "It's all right, sugar. But you don't need to worry about it. The children are being cared for so the rest of us can focus on our own spiritual growth. I mean, really, it's better, it's easier this way. Without the distractions."

Cass knew when someone was lying to herself—that was a skill every recovering addict had in spades—and Adele was working hard to believe she didn't want to be around children. Monica was part of that work, allowing Adele to mother someone while pretending she was indifferent to the youngest members of the Order.

Cass could do that, too. She could convince herself she didn't need to see Ruthie, to hold her, if only she knew that she was being cared for. Cass didn't deserve any more, not after she'd been so careless. She just needed to know her baby was safe.

"So this isn't too bad, right?" Adele asked, clearing her throat and forcing a smile. "I mean, for Aftertime."

"Yeah, sure," Cass said, though she'd barely touched her food, a stir-fry of kaysev leaves with a few grains of barley and herbs and bits of jackrabbit meat. "I'm just...I'm not that hungry. I guess all the excitement, and all—"

Monica rolled her eyes. "I know, more excitement than a person can stand. Deacon Lily gave you the grand tour, right? Only I bet they didn't show you any of the stuff they don't want you to see."

"Monica," Adele scolded her. "You've got to stop being so disrespectful. You're going to get us all in trouble again."

Monica managed an apologetic smile, showing a tiny gap between her front teeth. "I'm sorry, Adele. I really am. Only I don't understand why no one ever stands up to them."

"It's not *everyone*," Adele said, shaking her head in exasperation. "Honey, you need to understand that every organization has its bad apples. But you still have to show some respect."

"Cass, it was so ridiculous. No one has a sense of humor around here."

"What happened?"

"I forgot how this one prayer ended and I kind of made up my own verse in chapel. Mother Cora was *not* amused, and my ladies here all had to attend extra prayers because of me." Monica inclined her head toward the women at the other end of the table. "They're still kind of mad. That's why we're all alone at the bad girl end of the table."

"Well, honey, we missed tea," Adele said, patting her arm. "Can't get between the ladies and an afternoon snack, even if it is dandelion tea and rabbit salad sandwiches." She wrinkled her nose in distaste.

"You need to take it more seriously," a woman two seats down said. Cass hadn't realized she'd been listening. "Next time it's gonna be a reckoning. You've already had what, like three warnings?"

"Two," Monica mumbled.

"Okay, two," the woman said. "Third one's a reckoning."

"What's a reckoning?" Cass asked.

"Don't listen to them," Monica protested. "All I ever do is say what everyone is already thinking. There's no way they'd call a reckoning without more to pin on me than that."

"But what's—"

"Hush," the woman down the table hissed, as a deacon in deep lavender walked slowly past their table. Conversation died down until she was safely out of hearing range.

"Damn spy," Monica muttered. "Like to see where *that's* in the Bible. Especially when they're up there preaching faith, it would be nice if they had a little faith in—"

This time it was a different woman who interrupted. "Come on, Monica, can we please get through one single meal without you getting us in trouble?"

"Why're you even here if you're not a believer?" another added. All the other neophytes were turned toward them now.

"I *am* a believer," Monica protested hotly. "I'd put my faith up against anyone else's any day. I just don't believe in this crazy shit that masquerades as, as *real* faith."

But she kept quiet until the meal was finished and servers had cleared the dishes. Cass answered Adele's questions with a mixture of the truth—her job at the QikGo, her love of plants and landscaping—and lies and omissions. Lily had been right—the food helped, and by the time they filed out of the darkened stadium, their way lit only by the stars and the strings of tiny lights, her head had cleared, and the terrifying memories had receded back into the recesses of her mind.

37

BUT IN THE MORNING SHE AWOKE FROM THE dream of Ruthie again. Ruthie pressed beneath her, the snuffling wailing of the Beaters coming closer, her own screams ringing in her ears—she jerked awake in a twist of sheets sour with her own sweat, salt riming her eyelashes so that she knew she'd cried in her sleep.

For a moment she didn't remember where she was. The light in the neophyte dorm was ashy, filtered through burlap tacked along the top of the enclosure, which had been constructed from a length of the stadium's concrete corridor.

Only the neophytes were kept locked in. Lily, who had escorted her to the dorm after dinner, explained that once they became acolytes they would join the others, groups of women sharing quarters created from what had been restaurants and club rooms and offices and even—for the ordained—the skyboxes. They would be allowed to keep clothes and personal possessions—books, keepsakes, toiletries—in their rooms. But for now everything was common property.

"It builds a sense of community," Lily explained, showing her the shelves of towels and kaysev shoots carved into toothbrushes and the rough soap made from the oily center of kaysev beans. No doubt the manufacture of these supplies was part of what kept the convent humming with industry, but it served another purpose, too—preparing for the day when everything from Before ran out.

As the neophytes lined up for the two crude bathroom enclosures, acolytes brought buckets brimming with water and took away tubs heaped with dirty laundry before locking the doors for the night. To Cass's surprise they were allowed to wear whatever they wanted to sleep in, everything from Giants T-shirts to lacy nightgowns, but she had nothing but the clothes she was wearing.

She rubbed sleep from her eyes and looked around the empty room, surprised that she'd slept through the others' departure. Most of the beds were neatly made. Her bed was separate from the others, tucked into a corner. The newcomer bed, where Lily explained she would sleep for the first few transitional days. Next to it was a hardback chair and a small table on which a stapled set of pages rested. They were well-thumbed, the edges curling, and they looked as though they'd been typed on an old manual typewriter.

"You'll have two days to rest before you join the others for daily chores and study," Lily had said when she showed them to Cass. "Mother Cora likes for newcomers to spend time in reflection. And reading these."

There were hundreds of pages, single-spaced. "Who wrote all of this?"

"The founders. Mother Cora did a lot of it." Lily looked uncomfortable. "You can, you know, skim some of the parts.

You'll take your meals here until you're done. Just try to think of it as room service."

On the table next to the pages was a plate holding a thin, flat seeded kaysev cake and six almonds, and a tall glass of clear water. Cass put the glass to her lips and drank slowly, feeling the water wash down her throat, lukewarm but clean, the best she'd tasted Aftertime.

She ate her breakfast and washed herself as well as she could. After that, there was nothing left to do but pick up the pages.

WELCOME, SEEKER
DOCTRINE OF THE ORDER

Cass read the first page three times before giving up. The words refused to come together in her mind, the paragraphs swimming before her eyes.

Somewhere, not far away, the children of the Order were being cared for. Fed and clothed and sheltered and kept safe. That was more than Cass had ever accomplished. Much more than she'd managed already, and she'd only had Ruthie back in her care for a single day—a day in which she'd let her be bitten, infected, and nearly taken. A day that had caused her girl untold pain as she turned, then reverted, then healed in that small library room.

Cass tossed the pages on the table and lay back in her bed, pulling the sheet up over her head. Her breath fouled the air under the sheet, and she pulled her arms and legs in tight and made herself as compact as she could. She squeezed her eyes shut and wondered if, in here, her prayers might actually work.

The prayer she would say, if she allowed herself, was the old one, and for that reason Cass knew it was a bad idea.

It was the prayer from when she drank. On mornings like this, in beds not dissimilar, Cass breathed her own stink and reviled her own body and prayed only for God to let her forget—the things she had done, the things she had lost, the things she would do tonight. It was not a prayer of hope.

Someone would come, eventually. She had managed to sleep through the other neophytes washing and dressing and preparing for their day, but she would not be so lucky again. She would be expected to study, to eat, to make conversation. Cass had come here with hope and something even better—with thoughts of Ruthie dancing like diamonds in her mind, never far from her thoughts. But that was gone now. Yesterday, as Lily's kind voice stirred the silt from her memories, she had remembered.

And remembering stole her resolve. Cass wanted to be Ruthie's savior, but she was the one who had forsaken her.

She wanted to be Ruthie's everything, but she deserved nothing.

Cass pressed her face to the mattress and felt her tears hot against the cotton. She pressed harder, harder, until she couldn't breathe, and wished she could stay that way until the last of her life left her.

But her body was a traitor, and as she willed the air from her lungs and her mind went black at the edges, she knew that eventually it would seize deep drafts of air to sustain life, a gift she no longer wanted.

38

IN THE END, OF COURSE, SHE BREATHED. SHE
stared at the pages and ate the food an acolyte brought for
lunch, and slept and woke, and when the others came back
at the end of the day she listened to their talk and answered
when they spoke to her.

Monica offered her a gift, a single sleeping pill wrapped in
a page torn from a magazine printed back when there were
still celebrities to gossip about. Cass thanked her and turned
her down, but she wondered how many times she would say
no before she said yes.

"I don't understand any of this," she said instead, fanning
out the typed pages.

"Don't worry about it." Monica sat cross-legged on her
bed. She was wearing faded pajama pants printed with pen-
guins on skis, and a white tank top, and her hair was pulled
back from her face with a wide band. Her thin brown shoulders and the bangs that slipped out of the hair band made her

look like a teenager, though she'd told Cass she was twenty-two. "It's not like they test you on it or anything. It's just all of Mother Cora's crazy ideas."

"Did you read it all?"

Monica laughed. "*Nobody* reads the whole thing. Lily just tells Cora that you read it after a couple of days."

"Then what?"

"Then nothing, really. You get to be a neophyte. Big thrill."

"Monica...why are you here, if you don't believe any of it?"

"I didn't say I didn't believe *any* of it. I believe the basics. Know what I was doing, Before?"

"What?"

Monica glanced around the room. Some of the women were already in bed, others were reading by the light of the industrial fixtures mounted in the corners of the room. No one paid any attention. "I haven't told this to anyone but Adele, but I was going to go to divinity school. Down at Fuller. I wanted to be a minister. I mean not like right away but...someday. I was saving up."

Cass remembered herself at twenty-two. The account she started at the bank, where she was going to put away money for landscape design school. The single deposit she made—and the day not long after, when she took it out to buy a leather skirt.

"I'm sorry you didn't get to go," she said softly.

"Yeah. Well." Monica smiled and yawned. "Here I am, anyway. I like most of the people here. Even a lot of the or-dained aren't so bad. And three meals a day and a bed sure beats living on the outside. It's just—I don't like it when people think they have all the answers, you know? Especially when they make them up and then want to make you believe the same crazy things."

Early in the evening of the second day, there was a knock at the dormitory's single door. A key turned in the lock. Cass expected an acolyte bringing her dinner, but it was a gray-haired deacon in a ruby blouse.

She gave Cass a smile that didn't reach all the way to her eyes. "I'm Hannah. Sister Lily tells me that you have finished studying the Doctrine. Tonight you will join us for dinner, and afterward I will give you your new clothes. Congratulations, Cassandra."

Following Hannah down onto the field, Cass realized how little she had moved during the two days she'd spent confined to the dorm. Her legs felt tight, her heartbeat sluggish. It had been days since she'd ended her solo journey at the school, months since she ran flat-out through the Sierra foothills.

She needed to decide whether to make the effort to live, or let her ennui spread through her body until it atrophied and withered, but even the idea of making a decision sounded like too much effort. Already she wanted to return to her bed and just go back to sleep.

Hannah led her to the neophyte table, where Monica and Adele had saved her a seat near them. "I'll return for you later," she said. "There's something special planned after dinner, but I'll be back after that."

Monica waited until she was out of earshot. "Oh goody, maybe there's going to be fireworks. Or Jell-O shots."

Adele sighed. "You know darn well what it is, Monica. Come on, don't ruin it for everyone else."

Cass got through the meal as she had got through the past two days. She answered when spoken to, and forced herself to lift her fork to her lips until most of her meal was gone, all the while concentrating on keeping her mind as blank as she could. The night settled in as the servers cleared dishes and poured weak kaysev tea, and Mother Cora ascended the platform and took her place at the podium.

"Tonight we have something special to celebrate," she said. "There has been further progress with Sister Ivy. She is responding to our prayers!"

On cue, the doors to the enclosure at the other end of the field groaned open, and a large, wheeled cart rolled slowly onto the field, its top half a cage with a dark figure inside. In the rapidly descending night, Cass couldn't make out any of its features.

But the creature made a sound. At first it sounded like an engine turning over without success, an escalating whine that ended in clattering coughs before it started up again. Cass listened, goose bumps rising along her arms, knowing exactly what she was hearing: the call of a Beater, frustrated, hungry and lusting for flesh.

Sister Ivy.

39

"SISTERS—" MOTHER CORA'S VOICE RANG OUT like a pristine bell "—prepare to bless the fallen. We have prayed for Sister Ivy, and she is beginning to recover. Our faith is healing her!"

The cart rolled slowly toward the tables, stopping in the cleared space between the tables and the podium. The light from the strings of tiny bulbs did little to illuminate the Beater. It was wearing a long-sleeved shirt and a pair of loose pants, even shoes, and it pulled at the bars of the cart and its cries carried clearly through the stadium.

Cass remembered Faye saying that the Order paid Dor to capture Beaters. But she had never imagined this was their purpose: to pray over them, to...*heal* them? Unless this thing, too, was an outlier, like her...was that possible?

"Is it really getting better?" Cass whispered.

"Of course not," Monica whispered back. "Get real. They just drag them out here every so often and *say* they're getting better so everyone keeps praying. I mean, you think it's an accident they do this after dark?"

"Hush," Adele scolded. "Just leave Cass alone, Monica. You don't want to get her in trouble on her first night as a neophyte."

"Really? You're not going to tell her?" Monica demanded. "Just like no one told me? Come on, Adele, we talked about this, you said—"

"That was before you got in trouble twice," Adele hissed. "You don't have room for any more mistakes."

"Prepare for the blessing," Mother Cora commanded. Servers emerged from the pantries bearing trays with rows of tiny cups. In the flickering light from the larder, Cass saw that the cups bore ruby-red wine. They were barely bigger than a thimble, like dolls' cups.

"Not this," Monica muttered. "Not again, it's not right—"

"Shut *up*," the woman next to Adele whispered furiously. "I'm not taking punishment because of you anymore, Monica. Just buck up and get through it like the rest of us."

"If you hate it so much here, leave," another woman added, mouth pulled down in anger. "Mother Cora's healing them. All you're doing is getting in the way."

The servers spread out among the tables, setting a tiny cup in front of each woman. The moans of the Beater quieted, but it paced in its cage, shaking the bars. The effort of ignoring the sounds appeared to be too much for some of the women, who pressed their hands over their ears and squeezed their eyes shut.

When everyone had been served, the servers retreated with the last of the cups. Everyone watched Mother Cora expectantly. Her face bore the placidity of the devout, a serene smile tilting up the corners of her thin lips.

"Prepare to drink," she commanded, and the women

moved as one, lifting their cups as though for a toast. Cass held the tiny cup between a finger and thumb, surprised that it was chilled.

"And so we pray," Mother Cora continued, and the voices of hundreds of women filled the stadium. Cass glanced at Monica and saw that she alone did not join in, a look of disgust and anger on her face.

> *Dear Lord, it is our duty and salvation, always and everywhere to give You thanks for Your sacrifice.*
> *For our blood is Your blood, imbued with the healing spirit of life.*
> *In Your name we bless the fallen, in Your house we welcome them.*
> *By drinking we proclaim Your greatness and implore you to make us whole.*

"And so we drink," Mother Cora said.

Two hundred hands brought two hundred tiny cups to waiting lips, and Cass followed suit. But as the cold plastic touched her lips, Monica suddenly set her cup down hard on the table, splashing the wine.

"*Don't.*"

The single word carried on the still night. Hundreds of eyes turned their way. A guard posted at the edge of the tables turned, searching for the voice of dissent. Cass tossed back her wine in a single gulp, hoping to distract her, and it was on her lips to say something, anything, so she wouldn't notice the spreading red stain in front of Monica—

But the taste in her mouth was wrong, it was all wrong, it was metallic and harsh and familiar and unfamiliar. She felt her stomach heave and turned to spit on the ground but she caught sight of the deacon's angry expression and forced herself to swallow instead, swallowing down bile and the bitter filth she'd drunk.

Angry whispers erupted at their table.

"Monica, what did you—"

"All you had to—"

"This time you've—"

But it was too late. Guards were headed for their table; the first was already dragging Monica from her chair; Monica, who struggled, her expression both defiant and terrified. "Don't let them make you, Cass. It's their *blood*. The Beaters' blood. It isn't blessed, it isn't *anything*—"

Before Cass could absorb her words, the other guards reached Monica, yanking her arms behind her. She kicked at the table, crockery falling to the ground and shattering. Adele rose halfway out of her chair.

"Don't, Adele," Monica cried as she was dragged from the table. "Don't get in trouble for me. I'm fine. I'll be fine."

One of the guards hit her on the side of the head with something—a stick, a club, Cass couldn't tell in the dark—and Monica's words were abruptly cut off, her head lolling forward.

All around the table, women averted their eyes, refusing to watch as Monica was dragged away, toward one of the dugouts. Cora began to pray again and in a moment other voices joined in, until everyone was chanting and the servers began to spread out among the tables, collecting the cups.

Adele sank slowly down into her chair, her face pale in the flickering light. "Where are they taking her?" Cass whispered. "Is she going to be all right?"

Adele didn't answer. Her lips quivered, and she stared straight ahead, but in a moment her eyes drifted closed and she began to chant along softly with the others.

Near Cass was a glass with a few inches of tea left in it. She reached for it and drank deep, wished for another. She wanted to kneel in the dirt and push her fingers down her throat until she vomited up not just the blood but everything she'd eaten, not just tonight but since waking in the field. Every drop of water, every kaysev leaf, the food Smoke had shared in the school, the hoarded delicacies in the Box. She wanted to purge and purge until everything was gone, including her memories, not just of Ruthie but of Smoke and the way he'd touched her, of Monica's thin brown shoulders and ready smile, of the Beater in the cage and the tiny cups of blood.

The women gathered in this stadium had all drunk *blood*. Blood from a Beater, blood that ran through the veins of a being that was no longer human, no matter what they taught here in the Convent. Cass had seen the creatures feast; had seen the ravaged flesh of the Beater outside Lyle's house, jerking and twitching in death spasms as the last of its blood spilled into the earth.

But only Monica had protested, only Monica had rebelled, and she was immediately silenced. The ranks had closed behind her, as though she never existed. How long had it taken for the women to become inured to the horror, Cass wondered. How long until the liquid that passed their lips was no more evocative than communal wine?

How long until they *believed?*

Mother Cora let silence hang in the air at the conclusion of the prayer. In the cage, even the Beater was still, lying in a heap on the floor of the cart, one hand wrapped around the bars of the cage. Perhaps it had been drugged, so as to appear to be calmed by prayer. Slowly, Cora brought her elegant arms down to her sides, and then she smiled serenely out at the crowd. "This concludes our blessing. The Lord's grace be upon all of you, sisters, and good night."

Cass felt herself beginning to shake as the Beater cart was wheeled back into the enclosure and women began to rise from the tables, conversation starting up again as though nothing had happened.

"It's going to be all right." Adele leaned in close and whispered. "I'm going to tell them Monica didn't mean it, she wasn't feeling well. I'll tell them *I* told her not to drink. I'll tell them it was my fault. I don't have any warnings yet, I can afford one."

One of the other neophytes paused in front of Cass and gave her an unconvincing smile. "It's really hard at first. I mean...for all of us. But you'll get used to it. I promise."

"And even if that doesn't work, the worst they'll give her is solitary time," Adele continued, as though she hadn't heard. "Last time they put her in for a couple hours. If they're mad enough they might make her stay there overnight."

Before Cass could respond, she felt a hand on her arm and turned to see Sister Hannah. "Ready, Cassandra? We need to get you your new clothes before you go back to the dorm."

Cass touched Adele's shoulder as she followed Hannah away, but Adele seemed not to notice, her lips moving soundlessly as she calculated what she could trade for Monica's punishment.

Hannah led Cass to an office near Lily's and set her lantern on a desk, where it cast long shadows around the room. She opened a metal cabinet that contained a stack of folded white clothes, selected a skirt and shirt, and shook out the wrinkles before handing them to Cass.

When she reached for them, Hannah held on.

"As you know, neophytes dress only in white. You will receive a fresh change of clothes twice a week. I will take your old things." She let her gaze travel slowly down Cass's body. "What size are you...a four? Six?"

Cass tugged at the clothes, stiff from being line dried, and finally Hannah let go. "I'm not sure, anymore. Where can I change?" she asked as neutrally as she could, trying to keep the panic from her voice.

"Right here is fine."

"Isn't there... I thought—I mean, in the dorm, we use the changing rooms."

"It's all right. I'm ordained. Besides—" Hannah's smile turned predatory "—it's just us girls here, right?"

Cass swallowed hard. She stood and backed away from the chair, and skimmed off her pants, keeping her back to the wall. She folded them and set them on the chair, keeping her eyes lowered. She could feel Hannah's gaze on her, and the blood rushed to her face in both embarrassment and fear. She pulled on the white skirt; it was baggy on her despite the elasticized waist and came down past her knees.

Cass drew her shirt over her head, and then she was standing in front of Hannah in only her bra, the same plain white one the women had given her at the school.

"You act like you've never undressed in front of anyone before," Hannah murmured hoarsely and Cass hesitated in the middle of unbuttoning the folded blouse. Hannah was regarding her with frank appraisal, her gaze traveling across Cass's breasts, the expanse of smooth, taut skin of her torso, her hipbones visible above the sagging waistband of the skirt. "But I bet you have. A girl like you...I bet you have, plenty."

It wasn't the first time Cass had been the subject of a suggestive appraisal. It wasn't even the first time from a woman. But it was so unexpected, here in the Convent. Her heart thudded a panicked rhythm, terror of discovery making a metallic taste in her mouth. Her fingers remained frozen on the buttons of the white blouse.

"Turn around so I can see you," Hannah continued in a

silky tone. Her hand played at the V-neckline of her shirt. "*All* of you."

"I...I can't," Cass whispered, her lips numb with fear. She had to keep Hannah from seeing her back.

"Yes, you can," Hannah encouraged, but with an edge. "Because I say you can. And what I say goes in here."

And there it was, the relationship that Cass had been foolish enough not to consider. The powerful and the powerless. The hungry and the helpless. Why should it be any different here, where schemes masqueraded as faith, where trades made in the shadows fueled devotions pledged in the light?

How many bosses had tried something like this with Cass, grabbing her ass in the break room, asking her out for a drink to discuss a promotion or a raise? And how many times, Cass remembered, her face burning with shame as she twisted the fabric of the blouse in her hands—how many times had she simply gone along, because going along was easier than resisting?

"No," she said, frantically trying to figure out a plan. "I mean I...if you just let me get dressed I can...we can..."

A knock at the door silenced her. Hannah's eyes went wide and startled. "Get *dressed*," she hissed. "*Now.* You're not supposed to—"

But it was too late. There was the sound of a key turning in the lock and then the door swung open.

Mother Cora stood in the doorway holding a sheet of paper and a ring of keys. Her gaze took in the scene, and her eyes narrowed.

"Oh, Hannah, again?" She sighed heavily. "I thought after the last time—"

"It's not what it looks like. Not this time." Hannah's tone had turned from domineering to supplication. "I was only having her change in here because there was, there was someone using the common room—"

Mother Cora raised an eyebrow and frowned as Cass scrambled to jam her arms into the sleeves of the blouse, but it was buttoned shut. Frantically she worked at the buttons with shaking fingers.

"Here, dear," Mother Cora said, taking several steps into the room and reaching for the blouse. "Let me."

Cass backed away, and her foot struck something and she tripped. She tried to right herself but when her hand came down on the back of a chair it rolled, taking her with it, and she fell, hitting the trash can she'd stumbled over, and landed on her knees.

She scrambled to her feet, but it was too late.

"Oh good Lord," Mother Cora exclaimed. "Let me see you, child."

She put a hand on Cass's shoulder, her fingertips cool and her touch light. Cass flinched, but there was nowhere to go. "Hannah, do you *see?*"

Silence. Then, tentatively: "See *what?*"

"Don't be afraid," Mother Cora said. "You're the new girl, aren't you?"

Cass nodded.

Very gently, Cora took Cass's arm and turned her so that Hannah had an unobstructed view of her back.

Hannah gasped.

"She was attacked," Mother Cora said. "By the fallen. You were attacked, weren't you, dear? And yet here you are. You found your way here. The Lord brought you to us."

Cass said nothing. There was something chilling in the contrast between Mother Cora's soft, gentle voice and the sparking intensity in her eyes. Despite the kindness of her words, Cass now felt more afraid of her than she did of Hannah.

"You were *healed*. Weren't you."

Cass didn't dare speak.

"Healed through prayer?"

"I, um, don't know…" What answer would serve her best?

"Were others praying over you? When you were bitten? Did they save you?"

"I don't remember. I don't remember anything after I was attacked, until I…woke up."

Mother Cora put out a finger, and touched it to the edge of one of Cass's wounds. The touch felt strange and uncomfortable, but not painful. She traced the shape of the wound, the skimmed-over layers of healing skin sensitive to her touch.

"You woke up," Mother Cora repeated. "And were people praying, then?"

"I…" An idea occurred to her. "Yes." It was a reckless idea, but if it worked, maybe it would let her see Ruthie one more time. "I was in and out of consciousness for a while, and when I was awake, there were children praying over me. Young ones. They were saying… They were chanting something and then I slept and when I woke up again they were gone. And—and I was healed."

Cora sucked in her breath. *"Where?"* she demanded, excitement making her voice shrill. "Where did this happen? Where were the children?"

"Outside of town. In a field," Cass said, desperately hoping she wasn't making a terrible mistake. If this worked, she would get to see Ruthie. And then—*Dear God, I promise*—then she would leave the Convent, leave Ruthie in the hands of women who could at least keep her safe.

"She's lying," Hannah snapped. "Let me get Brenda, she'll get the truth out of her—"

"You'll do no such thing!" Mother Cora scolded. "Come here, Hannah. I want you to see this. Here. And here...the flesh is rebuilding itself."

She bent close to Cass's back. Cass stood very still. The women's scrutiny was a unique and burning mortification, but one she would endure.

"She could be contagious," Hannah protested.

"Nonsense. She's been prayed back to health, isn't it obvious? It's what I've said since the start. We just didn't know about the children. We didn't know it had to be children. It's as it says in Psalms—*Like arrows in the hand of a warrior are the children.*"

"She's making that up—she's—"

"Oh, dear Lord, this is a day I've been waiting for, a day I've prayed for." Mother Cora clasped her hands together and pressed them under her chin, beaming.

Cass looked from one woman to the other, their disparate expressions magnified by the shadows cast by the lantern light. Mother Cora's rapt excitement. Fear and disbelief on Hannah's face. Reluctantly, Hannah joined Mother Cora in examining the wounds. Cass tried to stay calm despite their proximity, barely breathing.

"I need to decide how best to share this news," Mother Cora mused. "There is so much to do. Oh, Cassandra, you are such a gift to us. A reward for our faith."

She turned to Hannah. "For tonight, I think it's best we keep her away from the others. I want to make the most of this. We'll convene later, and figure out what to do, but for now let's keep her in one of the reflection rooms. But make her comfortable. Do you understand me, Hannah? *Comfortable.*"

"Yes," Hannah said reluctantly, casting a malevolent glare at Cass.

"I'm sorry," Mother Cora said, taking Cass's hand in hers and squeezing it. "I don't want you to feel like a prisoner here—when you are so much more. Oh, Cassandra…you are going to bring such a great gift to all of us. Do you know what that is?"

Cass shook her head, afraid to speak, afraid to make the wrong guess.

"Faith," Mother Cora whispered, and that single word was like a coin tossed, its bright-burning and dark sides flashing in the air, and Cass knew that no matter which side the coin landed on, something terrible would follow.

ONCE MOTHER CORA LEFT, CASS FINISHED dressing. Hannah stared stonily out the window into the night, arms crossed, biting her lip in barely masked fury.

When Cass was ready, Hannah opened a desk drawer and took out a gun. "I know how to use this, so don't get any ideas," she said, slipping it into a pocket of her skirt.

They walked through the echoing corridor, now silent, nearly all the women having gone to their rooms for the night. They followed the corridor past the entrances onto the field and descended a ramp to the level below the field. They passed locker rooms and physical therapy facilities and, finally, a series of storage rooms and small offices.

"Here we are," Hannah said with fake cheer. "I'm sure Cora would like me to give you the honeymoon suite, seeing as how she thinks you're the second coming and all. But she never comes down here, so I wouldn't plan on submitting any complaints if you don't like the accommodations."

She stopped in front of a steel door.

"Don't worry," Hannah said. "It's perfectly adequate. At least, we don't hear many complaints."

She pulled the chain from her neck, a half-dozen keys jangling. But instead of opening the door she balled the keys in her fist and stepped closer to Cass. "Look. I don't know what happened to you, who made those marks on your back, and I'm sure it would be awfully convenient for everyone if you really were miraculously healed. But guess what—I don't believe you."

She leaned in so only inches separated them, her hot breath on Cass's face.

"I. Don't. Believe. You," she repeated, pausing for emphasis on each word. "I don't know what your angle is and I don't know how you figure you're going to work it. But there's no such thing as healing. Don't you think that if there was, we would have found it?"

"I don't know," Cass shrugged, trying to project indifference. "If all you're doing is standing around praying all day, I'm not sure you would have. From what I've seen—"

"What you've seen was a whole lot of shit," Hannah said, her face darkening with rage. "Which I guess we both know now. But you have no right to judge me. *No* right."

"I didn't—"

"Shut up," Hannah said, stabbing the bunch of keys into Cass's sternum, sending her stumbling backward. *"Shut up.* Unlike you, I came here because I'm a believer. And you know what I believe in? The future. I will do whatever I have to do to build the Order into something that works. A community. A *life.* Even if I have to put up with Cora's insane little Beater project."

"But what about me?" Cass demanded, figuring she had nothing to lose. "That part's true—I really was healed."

Hannah shook her head, lips pressed tight together in fury. "You don't have any proof. So you've got some marks on your back—that could have been anything. An accident. I don't know, some form of mumps or something you caught from your gutter-trash boyfriend. You didn't get better from prayer, you just…got better."

"That's ridiculous," Cass said. "You saw me. There's no way I could have done that to myself. I would have— *Anyone* would be dead from what happened to me. Unless something changed me. Unless I was healed."

But Hannah was shaking her head. "You could have had someone do that to you. And it's not as bad as it looks, as bad as Cora wants to think it is, it's just scratches and scabs, it's just—"

"Would you stake your life on that?" Cass demanded, her frustration making her belligerent. "If I bit you, would you be willing to bet that I wasn't infected then? What if I'm a carrier? What if—"

The blow surprised her, coming hard above her left ear, sharp enough to stun. Suddenly she was on the floor, warm blood dripping into her ear, her head ringing with pain. Hannah stood above her with her gun in hand; she'd slammed the butt into her skull.

"That's right, I wouldn't get too close to me if I was you," Cass grunted, pulling herself up off the floor. She was gratified to see Hannah edge backward. "Maybe you ought to start praying after all, for insurance."

"You think you're so smart. You think you can come here and…and suddenly you're the great hope. You're Cora's pet. Well, you might want to think again. I've got plans. I've got plans for you."

"Look, I never asked for any of this. All I wanted—"

"Save it. I don't really care what you want. It's about time

I start worrying more about what *I* want. After everything I've done, for the Order, for *her*..." Hannah shook her head with disgust. She sorted through the keys, then unlocked the door and shoved Cass inside. "Nothing's going to happen until morning anyway, so you'll have lots of time to think. Maybe you can come up with your own little theory so we can all get together and talk about *healing*."

Cass caught only a brief glimpse of her prison in the second before the door slammed shut, enough to know she was in an old weight room with a cot set up in the middle. She fumbled her way to the cot in the dark and lay down, wondering if Monica was locked up somewhere like this nearby. After what seemed like hours, she fell into a fitful sleep.

She woke to Hannah shining a flashlight in her eyes.

"So Cora's really going to do it. You're the princess, I guess."

Last night's fury was gone, replaced by a craftiness that was almost worse. As they walked back up the stairs to the main level, bright morning sun streamed through the walkway, and Cass smelled food cooking.

The women were gathered for the morning meal. Little had changed since the night before except for a wooden pole that now rose from the center of the platform up front, and a low table that held a tray covered with a white cloth. A drifting feather was lodged near the top of the pole; it quivered for a moment in the breeze and then broke free and floated away.

It was blue, a bluebird or blue jay feather, Cass didn't know. She had never bothered to learn anything about birds, and now whole species had been lost. Some sort of small, brown, undistinguished bird had survived and even flourished, and a flock of them chattered from the stands, watching and waiting to swoop down for crumbs.

The birds' chatter and the clink of cutlery vied with quiet conversation, but both fell silent as she and Hannah passed. As they neared the platform Cass noticed another feature: an iron ring, bolted to the wood floor. The pole was maybe four feet tall, with some sort of clamp attached slightly above knee level. Two metal plates opposed each other; they were padded with leather or vinyl and there was about a foot of space between them. Cass had no idea what the clamp's purpose was, but it looked ominous. She swallowed hard—what exactly was Cora planning?

Hannah directed Cass to a chair placed a few feet to the side of the platform. Two women, one in pale pink and the other in red, silently stepped away from a nearby table and arrayed themselves behind her. Cass guessed they were there in case she tried to bolt.

A murmur started in the back of the assembly and spread forward. Cass looked out over the crowd, shading her eyes from the sun, and saw two figures approaching from the field. Her heart quickened to see that one of them was Monica.

She looked exhausted, as though she hadn't slept at all. Her clothes were wrinkled and soiled. Her hair was tangled and knotted. A woman wearing a gray shirt and white pants—the only pants Cass had seen in the Convent other than the ones she wore when she arrived—and a long black braid down her back walked next to her, hand on her belt, where Cass was certain she had a weapon.

Monica passed directly in front of Cass without seeming to notice her. There were deep purple circles under her eyes, and she dragged her feet as she trudged to the platform.

Cass understood now why Hannah had been smug.

Whatever Cora had planned for Cass, there was also to be a public punishment—the reckoning they'd been talking about. But what were they going to do to Monica? The pole that loomed over the platform—was she to be tied to it, perhaps beaten? The things she'd done—challenging the doctrine, even refusing to drink the blood—did they really merit a public whipping?

Mother Cora appeared from the opening in the stands that led to her quarters, elegant in a wine-colored tunic and skirt. She said a few private words to the deacons gathered at the front table and gave Cass a warm smile as she passed.

The guard was binding Monica's hands behind her back, and Monica shivered, frightened and forlorn, in the morning chill.

Hannah followed Cora to the steps, bowing low before going to stand next to the guard behind the low table. Mother Cora regarded Monica with an expression that contained more sadness than anger, like a teacher whose favorite pupil had disappointed her.

"Sister Brenda, you may begin," she said into the microphone, and then she bowed her head and went unhurriedly back down the steps to her place at the head of the front table. The guard lifted the cloth and fussed with the contents of the tray while Hannah seized Monica by her dark hair and forced her to her knees, bending her head back forcefully so she could see what was coming, tears of pain streaming from her eyes.

Sister Brenda moved with studied grace, lining up objects Cass couldn't identify from a distance. When she was satisfied, she picked up a bowl and a sponge from the tray. She dipped the sponge into the bowl, drops of water sparkling in the morning sun.

She crouched in front of Monica and dabbed the sponge

almost tenderly at her face, then squeezed it so that rivulets of water ran down her neck. Monica sputtered and coughed, and Brenda returned the bowl and sponge to the table, and waited with her hands folded in front of her.

Hannah approached the podium, not looking at Monica as she spoke. "Sisters," her voice boomed through the speaker system, echoing off the far corners of the stadium. "We please our Lord with our works and our prayer, but we are weak. We are flawed. Each day we stumble on our journey and sometimes we fall. And then the Lord calls upon us to deliver what is due. Justice, my sisters—we are to serve as the hand of our Lord and return to each as she has done.

"We insult our Lord if we allow offenses against Him to stand. We must not invite the weakness to grow and gain a foothold. We must smite it with conviction. When we do as our Lord commands, the blemish is lifted, the penance is done and we welcome our sister back among us."

It was all double-talk, no mention of a specific crime, no chance for the accused to defend herself.

"Sisters!" Hannah's harsh voice rang out, as she pointed an accusing finger at Monica. "Here before you, our sister Monica awaits the cleansing of her sin!"

AFTER THAT THINGS MOVED QUICKLY.

Brenda picked up a long silver baton from the table and touched it to Monica's shoulder. When the girl jerked and fell backward, Hannah's grasp on her hair loosened, Cass realized the thing was an electric prod. The crowd gasped as Monica writhed and spasmed on the floor of the platform, her eyes rolling back in her head. Hannah picked her up under the arms and together she and Brenda wrestled her into place at the pole in the center of the platform. Hannah forced Monica's head between the padded clamps while Brenda spun a wing nut until it no longer turned freely, then twisted it manually until her prisoner shrieked in pain, held captive by the pressure.

She fought against the clamps, her face red and grotesquely distorted, lips pursed and cheeks bulging, squeezing up until her eyes almost disappeared.

"Sister Brenda, still the sinning mouth of our Sister Monica!"

A cry went up as Brenda selected objects from the table and bent to her task. In one hand was a long curved needle, a tail of black thread fluttering in the breeze.

As Brenda leaned in close, Monica made a keening sound and blood trickled from the clamp where it pinched tightly against her temples. The wail escalated to a scream as the needle pierced her flesh, but Brenda didn't flinch. She drew the thread slowly through Monica's lips, taking care not to let it tangle, and then she knotted off the ends.

As she poked at Monica's lower lip with the needle, starting the second stitch, Cass bolted out of her chair and made it almost to the steps. She was tackled from behind and went crashing to the ground. One of the women who had been posted behind her pinned Cass's arms and spoke into her ear.

"Bad idea," she said. Then she pulled up on Cass's arms, causing white flashes of pain. "Gonna be good?"

Cass nodded, gritting her teeth, as the woman eased up the pressure on her arms and led her back to her chair. The assembled crowd could not see the blade the woman held in her palm, but Cass could feel its cold sharp edge at her neck. If she made another attempt to break away, the blade could slice through her skin with ease. The guards were taking no chances—not even with her, Mother Cora's chosen one.

Brenda had made a couple more stitches. Tiny red dots of blood bloomed where the needle had gone into the skin— less than Cass would have expected. More shocking to see was the row of neat black X's sealing the outer corner of Monica's mouth. Saliva drooled from her dirty chin as she frantically moaned and struggled for air. Her breathing was becoming labored as one of her oxygen sources was slowly sealed shut, and the sound of her desperately trying to get enough air through her nose was as terrible as her cries of pain. Unless she calmed down, Monica was in danger of suffocation, of choking on her own vomit or her tongue.

Maybe that would be a kindness. The holes made by the needle were bound to become infected; there had been no sterilization of the skin—or for that matter, of the instruments.

The sharp, cold steel at Cass's neck kept her still even as the last stitches were tied off and Monica could only snort desperately for air, blood trickling down her grotesquely distorted chin.

Abruptly Brenda spun the wing nut counterclockwise. The clamps opened and Monica fell forward, out of the padded restraints. She would have hit the floor, but Hannah caught her and eased her into a seated position, bent awkwardly with one leg splayed out in front of her. Brenda took a key from her neck and worked at the manacle until Monica's other leg was freed, and then she moved the leg gently into place as though concerned only for Monica's comfort.

She stepped out of the way and her handiwork was on full display. Monica stared out into the crowd with pain-deadened eyes, her mouth a ragged row of angry black X's.

There was a swell of voices among the tables. Mother Cora took to the stage again and held up a hand for silence. She waited until the only sound was Monica's muffled whimpering.

"Sisters, the path of the chosen is not easy!" Mother Cora's imperious voice filled the stadium. "But you have taken up the yoke because you are *strong*. Because you are the ones who are called to act. Ours is a community of love, and the Lord never asks more than when he asks us to guide one of our own, because the guiding can be harsh. Today you saw the evidence of that."

Monica swayed as though she was about to faint, and Brenda stepped forward to steady her, but Cass wondered how many in attendance noticed. They were all focused on Mother Cora.

"Now, however, it is time for joyous news. Sister Cassandra," Mother Cora called with a regal outstretch of her arm. "Approach the altar."

Cass did so, knowing the guards would force her if necessary. Monica didn't appear to see her, though she passed a few feet away.

"Sisters, this is Cassandra, who has come to us on a mission from our Lord. He spoke to Sister Cassandra and commanded her to come here to us and make of herself a sacrifice. Our Lord promised Sister Cassandra that when she gives herself to the fallen, He will lift her up from their scourge. He will heal her fever and her wounds. He will make her whole again. With the power of our prayers she will join us in an exalted position as a full sister of the Order."

Suddenly, horrifyingly, Cass understood what Mother Cora meant to do: she intended to give Cass to the Beaters to be infected. The disease would take root and she would be shown to the others like an exhibit at a zoo, her flaming skin and pinpoint irises proof of the disease. She would shuffle and babble and slowly lose her awareness and for the second time she would start to pull out her hair and bite her own arms, and then at some point the disease—Mother Cora was counting on it—would reverse itself as it had the first time, and Cass would be the proof Mother Cora needed to further strengthen the faith of her congregation.

Mother Cora had run out of things to give them. Safety and sustenance might not always be enough—not when the women were forced to live under the rule of an unforgiving faith whose punishments were harsh and whose demands were draconian.

The Order could not succeed forever unless it delivered. One miracle after another was needed to keep the illusion alive. Shelter and safety had been miracles enough in the beginning. But that had been a long time ago now, and the women were hungry for more.

Cass was this woman's next miracle.

"And to witness Cassandra's sacrifice, we bring our most precious resource," Mother Cora continued, as a small commotion erupted at the back of the assembly. Cass scanned the field, looking for its source. "The next generation of the Order. The *children*."

Down the center aisle, between the tables, a girl of nine or ten made her way uncertainly. She wore a white dress that was too short for her lanky legs, and her freckled face was pink with anxiety. But most arresting of all was the fact that she had been shaved bald.

The hair and the dress, Gloria had said. *Scoured clean of this world.* Some religions demanded the hair be covered; the Order had taken it away entirely.

The first girl was followed by another, and another, each younger than the one before—and each one bald. All of them looked nervous and frightened, and they all wore white dresses. A child of six sniffled as though she was trying not to cry; another little girl wiped her eyes with her fists. The younger ones were accompanied by adults—their teachers, their tenders, women who looked as nervous as the charges.

As the smallest children came down the aisle, Cass searched frantically for Ruthie. Was it that one, with the pudgy arms, or there—but wasn't she too small? Wouldn't

Ruthie have grown taller by now? When the last of the children entered the aisle and walked toward the platform, Cass felt her heart seize with agony.

Where was Ruthie?

A loud rattling came from the direction of the enclosure at the other end of the field and the crowd turned to see the Beater cart emerge, being pulled by a guard whose face was covered by a white mask. Inside, the Beater howled, scrambling and stumbling as the cart rolled unevenly along.

And then, at the back of the crowd, one more figure hurried into view. It was a slender woman with a halo of frizzy brown hair—and a child in her arms. She was frantically smoothing the little girl's dress into place as she tried to catch up to the others. Cass leaned over the platform as far as she dared, craning to see. The child wore little black shoes buckled over white socks, and she pressed a fist against her mouth as she leaned against the woman's shoulder.

The same way Ruthie always had.

Ever since she was an infant, Ruthie had never sucked her thumb or a pacifier like other children, but she would press a fist to her mouth to comfort herself. How many times had Cass found her that way in her crib, sleeping sweetly with her hand curled against her sweet rosebud lips?

And there—even with her hair gone—Cass knew the shape of her baby's head. A thousand times she had run her hand over Ruthie's head. There were her long eyelashes, dark brown with sun-lightened tips. And there was the faintest reminder of the funny little fold in her pudgy forearm.

As the minder drew closer, the sleepy child yawned, and then she opened her eyes and looked directly at Cass, and in their bright emerald depths Cass saw her baby, her Ruthie, and knew that she had been wrong, so wrong—she would not leave here without her child—she would die before she ever let her go again.

Ruthie's bright green eyes widened, and she stiffened in the woman's arms. Then she started to thrash wildly, trying to get down, but the woman only held her tighter. Mother Cora's smile faltered as she watched the struggle. She covered the microphone and said something to one of the other women on the platform. The adults were guiding the children into a line across the platform, but they stepped aside to create a break in the row, and Ruthie's attendant hurried past and disappeared behind the others, out of sight. But Cass had seen and she was sure.

Mother Cora leaned back into the microphone. "I give you the future," she murmured, her voice amplified to fill the stadium. On cue, the children clasped each other's hands and lifted them into the air, and they looked like a chain of paper dolls, eerie and silent as stones.

Cass waited for them to pray, or sing, but they did neither. They stood still above the crowd, frightened and unmoving. *No, no, no talking,* Gloria had warned Cass. *You won't know her.* The women in the audience held their collective breath; they were waiting, too, both joy and grief reflected in their faces. Were they remembering other children, other times?

Mother Cora had bought Cass's lie, that it was children who had healed her. So Mother Cora had no choice but to bring them out now, when she was about to sacrifice Cass. As if reading her thoughts, Cora stepped forward and slipped a cool hand into Cass's and led her down the stairs to the Beater's cart. A few of the smaller children started to cry, but they were silent even as tears spilled on their cheeks. They had been trained—or threatened—effectively.

The Beater hung on to the wire sides of the cage, moaning softly and snorting its need and its longing. In daylight, it was clear that there had been no healing at all. It was as torn and scabbed and crazed as any Cass had ever seen, missing several teeth and most of its hair and chunks of its lips. Great patches of black and red filled in where skin had been torn away.

Cora avoided looking at the Beater as she handed Cass off to Hannah, who waited close to the cage's door. "Blessings on you, Cassandra," Cora said, before returning to the podium.

"Don't worry, it probably won't hurt any more than getting your mouth sewn shut," Hannah said quietly, so that only Cass could hear her. "And then you get that whole euphoria thing. That'll be fun, don't you think? Oh, you must be so excited."

The gloved and masked attendant who had wheeled out the cage was gone. The Beater had managed to jam an oozing and crusted hand through the bars. Strips of dead skin hung from its arm, and its scabbed lips were pulled back in a furious leer.

The women at the farthest tables scrambled to see what was happening near the stage, mounting chairs and tables to get an unobstructed view. The guards stationed at the periphery of the crowd moved closer.

Hannah seized Cass's arm. "Ready, Cassandra? I can guess what you must be thinking—this is gonna hurt like hell. And you know, I think you might be right."

She removed a key from the key chain around her neck. "You understand that I don't want to get too close, not being the Chosen One. You do the honors, Cassandra—open up, and shut the door behind you. And just so you know, Brenda's a hell of a shot."

Cass had only seconds left. She scanned the line of silent children one more time, searching for Ruthie.

I'm coming for you, she thought, and then she took the key from Hannah's hand.

42

BRENDA HAD SLIPPED ON A MASK AND GLOVES
and stepped up to the cage brandishing the shock baton
Monica had been stunned with. Stretching out strategically,
to be as far away as possible from the thing, she pushed the
baton through the bars and jammed it against the creature's
shoulder blades. It twitched and screamed and fell to the
floor, spasming in pain.

"Now," Hannah ordered. Cass fitted the key to the lock
with shaking fingers, trying not to look at the form shudder-
ing on the floor of the cart only a few feet away. "Get inside
or Brenda will shoot."

But there was one thing that Hannah couldn't know. In
the split second after Cass slid the key into the cage door's
padlock, she whispered Ruthie's name, and all the months
of longing and guilt and grief twisted into one fine strand
and pulled taut inside her. She opened the cage door, put one
foot inside, glanced at the wrecked abomination writhing on

the floor and then she did the one thing that even she would never have guessed she was capable of: she prayed, she called out to God and in one word asked His indulgence, asked for one more day one more hour one more minute with her daughter in her arms

please

and she seized Hannah's wrist and she pulled with everything she had and Hannah grunted and stumbled and she never saw it coming and she tripped and fell and there was Cass, Cass who had willed herself stronger than five women, Cass whose body had spurned and rejected disease, Cass who flung Hannah like a used and dirtied rag into the cage and then slammed the door shut and jammed the padlock back into place and flung the key in a spinning sparkling arc through the gilded sun of Aftertime until it disappeared far down the field, landing in a planter box of golden poppies the likes of which no one ever expected to see again.

The Beater was getting slowly to its hands and feet, foam and spit wetting its screaming mouth, as it crawled toward Hannah.

Cass turned away in time to see Brenda swinging the electric prod through the air toward her, but she dodged out of the way. Before she could recover her balance Cass slammed into her hard and Brenda fell, landing on the baton and screaming as it delivered its jolting energy into her body. Cass stomped on her jerking hand and she screamed harder.

Women shouted and guards fought their way through the crowd toward her, and Cass knew she had only seconds.

She scrambled up on stage, where the children had stopped singing and were clutching their caregivers and each other in fear. Monica leaned against the post, her eyes rolled up in her head, and Cass couldn't tell if she was even conscious, her mouth swelling into a grotesque clown's visage. A guard broke through the front of the crowd and Cass steeled herself for the shot but the woman stumbled and went down as the congregation surged around her, all the other women trying to get close enough to see the excitement. A few rows back, those pushing into the aisles surged over each other, trampling the ones who fell. There was a sound of a gunshot and one of the nearest acolytes fell to the ground, a red stain blooming on her shirt.

The children's caretakers were trying to herd them down the steps but the growing chaos slowed them down, the girls clutching each other in fear. And still none of them made a sound. Cass pushed through the line toward the back of the platform and there she was, the woman who'd carried Ruthie, crouched at the back edge, as though she was about to jump. It was at least a dozen feet down but she looked scared enough to do it—but where was Ruthie?

Cass fell to her knees beside the woman, grabbed her arm, shook her. *"Where is she?"* she demanded, but the woman fought her, scuttling sideways out of reach. "Where—"

The woman jumped, the sound of a bone breaking followed by screaming and she lay on her side, her leg bent unnaturally. A second woman jumped, narrowly missing the first, though she was luckier; she managed to get to her feet and staggered away, limping.

All through the stadium women panicked. Some crawled under tables. Some crowded the exits to the stands, pushing and shoving to get out. The platform's stairs were jammed with children, and Cass glimpsed a guard trying to find a shot at her between them. She glimpsed a hand clawing at the bars of the cage, but whether it was Hannah's or the Beater's, she was too far away to tell.

Cass crawled behind the line of children, their white dresses making a billowing wall. Two of the oldest girls picked up the younger ones to carry them to safety, and suddenly Cass saw Ruthie crouched down next to Monica, her small hand on Monica's ruined face as though trying to fix it.

Cass threw herself the last few feet and swept Ruthie into her arms. Monica stirred, her eyes rolling back in her head.

"Monica, you *have* to *move!*" Cass screamed, hooking her free hand under Monica's arm. Monica stumbled to her feet and nearly fell again. Cass wrapped an arm around her waist and dragged her toward the stairs. The last of the children, and the one or two adults who had not abandoned them in the melee, were descending the steps, leaving them alone and exposed, Monica stumbling against her as though she was drunk.

Cass scanned the exits, knowing that it would be next to impossible to get there in time, especially as she saw a guard edging around the Beater cage and another sprinting along the edge of the crowd toward her. Cass froze at the top of the stairs. The minute the children were out of the way, the guards would shoot, and she couldn't risk Ruthie's life—but she couldn't leave Monica behind, either.

The air cracked with gunfire and Monica slumped against her. Cass looked down to see a jagged hole in Monica's throat beginning to fill with blood and knew the impossible decision had been made for her.

She hitched Ruthie up tightly against her as Monica's body slumped at her feet. "I'm sorry," she whispered, bending to touch Monica's cheek, already clammy and lifeless. Then she ran to the back of the platform, hunched low, as the guards fired again and again. On the ground below, the injured woman was curled over her shattered leg, rocking with pain, but Cass didn't hesitate. She hit the ground at a tuck and rolled twice, shielding Ruthie as well as she could with her body. The turf scratched and burned her skin and she didn't care, and she came up running.

The move had bought her a mere second or two but she made the most of them, joining the crowds rushing for the edge of the field. Unlike the others, who fought to get to the safety of the corridors, Cass broke away at the last minute and slipped behind the planters lined up along the long side of the field. She pried Ruthie from her neck and pushed her through the bars separating the stands from the field, and then swung herself up, arms burning with the effort, and levered her body between the bars.

Ruthie's eyes shone with unspilled tears. She raised her arms to be picked up and Cass swung her up and ran, her feet pounding the metal benches as she zigzagged her way up the stands, eyes on the skyboxes, running as fast as she ever had, knowing no one could catch her now.

43

THROUGH THE SKYBOX, INTO THE STAIRWELL, down the stairs, careening off the walls rather than slowing to take the turns, and then she was in the anteroom. She didn't recognize either of the guards, who gaped at her and reached for their weapons as she burst into the room. The sounds from inside the stadium were muffled here, but she could make out voices and screaming and more gunshots.

"There's been an accident!" Cass panted, out of breath, her arms aching from carrying Ruthie. "The Beaters got out and it's chaos in there. You've got to let us out, let me get help."

"What happened?" the guard at the narrow window demanded. She pushed a pair of thick-lensed glasses up on her nose.

"A reckoning," Cass said. "It went all wrong. This child was hurt, and—"

"She doesn't look hurt." The other guard, a leathery-faced

woman wearing a thin lavender blouse with heavy black boots, hesitated with her hand on her holstered gun.

"A Beater got her. They shot it like four times. It went down but I think it bit her first. I need to get her some help, in the Box."

The guards exchanged a glance. The one wearing glasses backed away from Cass.

"What makes you think she's bit?" the other one demanded. "Is the skin broken?"

"You want to take that chance?" Cass demanded. "I saw it myself—it had its mouth on her. Listen to me, there's Beaters running around loose in there, you really want to stand around here chatting?"

No one said anything for a moment and Cass held her breath.

If they were true believers—if they shared Mother Cora's faith—they would never let Cass go. They'd just send Ruthie back to be prayed better. There was no reason for them to believe Cass, a stranger, not even a full-fledged member of the order.

The first guard backed up even farther. "Keep her away from me," she muttered.

"Just let us leave," Cass said, edging toward the door. "I'm going now. You can come with me if you want. You might want to think about what's going to happen if things get worse in there. Across the street, they can still lock that shit *out*."

She put her weight against the heavy latch, pushing it open, half expecting one of the guards to stop her. Ruthie's body was sweaty and hot against her, but she clung tenaciously. The door opened onto a brilliant morning. Cass staggered out onto the sidewalk and stood blinking in the sun. Seconds later she heard the sound of the door being bolted shut behind her.

"Cass!"

A man broke away from a small group of people gathered across the street and raced toward her.

Smoke.

He ran as though he didn't intend to stop, as though his life depended on it, depended on *her*—and then he stopped short, seeing that she held Ruthie in her arms. His hands hung useless at his sides. He looked from Cass to Ruthie and back again, eyes wide, breathing hard.

Ruthie clung tight; she still hadn't made a single sound. She pressed her tear-streaked face against Cass's neck, and though Cass had barely any feeling left in her arms, and her back burned from the strain, she gripped her precious child even tighter.

"This is my daughter. Ruthie."

"Ruthie," Smoke repeated, and her daughter's name on his lips was, to Cass's surprise, a sound she had always wanted to hear.

Hearing Smoke say her name, Ruthie twisted in Cass's arms and peeked out at him curiously, then leaned her head on Cass's chest and kept on looking at him, long-lashed eyes wide.

"She's…"

"Bald. I know," Cass said. "It'll grow back. They did it to all the kids, symbolized being scoured clean or something."

"I was going to say 'beautiful.' Those eyes…they're yours."

Cass shook her head. "That's just from being an outlier. The pigment doesn't fade, even after you recover."

"No, that's not what I meant. They're—" Smoke traced a shape in the air, a gently-tilted oval "—big, and turned up at the corners, just like yours. And she has your nose, your chin. Beautiful, like I said."

"Oh." Cass felt warmth creep up the back of her neck.

"What the hell is going on in there? It sounds like they've started a war—we were about to come in after you."

"It's…"

Moments from the past few days flashed through Cass's mind like pictures in the View-Master her daddy gave her when she was a little girl.

Her first glimpse of the field, greener than any real lawn ever was.

Mother Cora, arms lifted in prayer.

Monica's wrecked and bleeding mouth.

The girls, shaved and frightened, walking down the aisle like flower girls at a wedding.

The Beater screaming in excitement when Hannah fell into the cage.

Cass shook her head, unable to speak, her whole body starting to shake.

"Let me take her," Smoke said, and when he held out his arms, sun-gilded and strong, Ruthie regarded him for only a moment before she offered him one perfect small hand and allowed him to fold it in his own.

He lifted her gently and tucked her in the crook of one arm, and she reached for his face and touched it with her fingers. Ruthie was dirty and bald and her dress was torn and one of her shoes was missing and she was the most beautiful thing Cass had ever seen.

Cass's entire body ached, but when Smoke circled his free arm around her and drew her close, she went without hesitation, she breathed in the smell of him, salt and soap and worry, and when his lips found hers she kissed him thirstily.

She kissed him as though he was sustenance, as though he was life itself.

"We shouldn't," she whispered against his mouth, but he held her tighter and she pressed herself against him and kissed him again, deeper, harder, hungrier. Her body was exhausted and spent, but somewhere inside, the tiny part that refused to give up woke to his touch.

She had Ruthie. She had Smoke.

It was enough.

ACKNOWLEDGMENTS

The existence of this book is a testament to the tenacity and vision of two people: my agent, Barbara Poelle, who only accepts "no" when it suits her—and my editor Adam Wilson, who gets it and then some. In the moments when the story shines, it's because of them.

Thanks, too, to the entire Harlequin team, who made me feel welcome from day one.

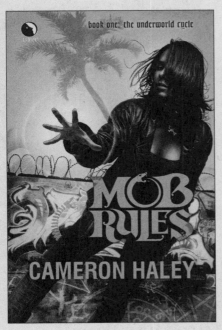

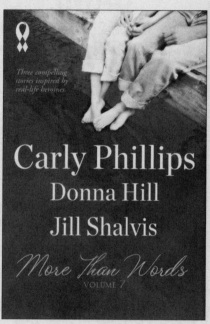

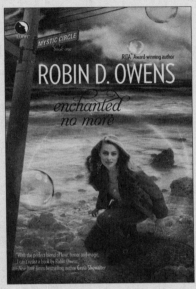

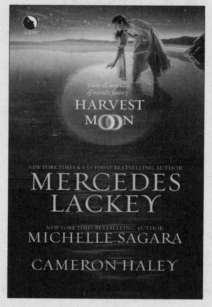

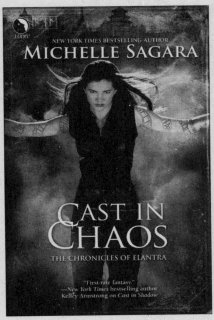

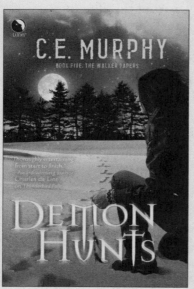